REBECCA SHAW

One Hot Country
Summer

Love in the
Country

Educated at a co-educational Quaker boarding school, Rebecca Shaw went on to qualify as a teacher of deaf children. After her marriage, she spent the ensuing years enjoying bringing up her family. The departure of the last of her four children to university has given her the time and opportunity to write. *The Village Green Affair* is the latest in the highly popular Tales from Turnham Malpas series.

Visit her website at www.rebeccashaw.co.uk.

By Rebecca Shaw

REBECCA SHAW

One Hot Country Summer

Love in the Country

One Hot Country Summer
First published in Great Britain by Orion in 2007

Love in the Country
First published in Great Britain by Orion in 2009

This omnibus edition published in 2011
by Orion Books Ltd
Orion House, 5 Upper St Martin's Lane
London WC2H 9EA

An Hachette UK Company

A CIP catalogue record for this book is available from the British Library.

ISBN 9781407234250

Printed and bound in Great Britain by Clays Ltd, St Ives plc

www.orionbooks.co.uk

One Hot Country
Summer

LIST OF CHARACTERS AT BARLEYBRIDGE VETERINARY HOSPITAL

Mungo Price	Orthopaedic Surgeon and Senior Partner
Colin Walker	Partner – large and small animal
Zoe Savage	Partner – large animal
Daniel Franklin Brown	Partner – large animal
Scott Spencer	large animal
Virginia Havelock	large animal
Valentine Dedic	small animal
Rhodri Hughes	small animal

NURSING STAFF
Sarah Cockroft (Sarah One)
Sarah MacMillan (Sarah Two)
Bunty Bird

RECEPTIONISTS
Joy Bastable (Practice Manager)
Lesley Jennings
Annette Smith

Miriam Price	Mungo's wife
Duncan Bastable	Joy's husband
Letty Walker	Colin's wife
Rose Franklin Brown	Dan's wife
Megan Jones	Rhodri's wife
Nina Dedic	Valentine's wife

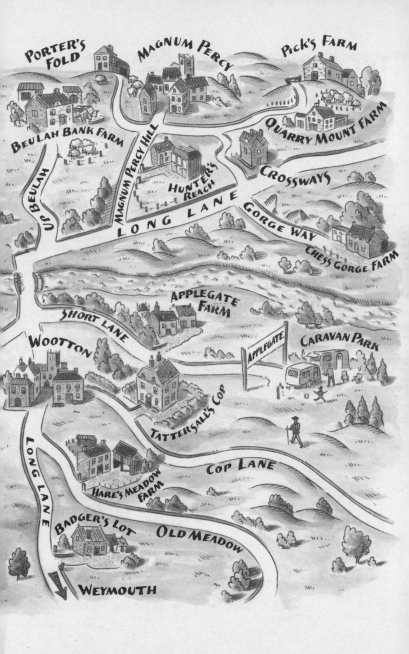

Chapter 1

Kate stepped out of her car, memories flooding back. How long was it since she'd last stood here? Three years, yes, three years since she'd first arrived at Barleybridge Veterinary Hospital as an accounts clerk to earn money while she re-took her A-level chemistry. Now here she was coming back as a veterinary student to 'see practice' for six whole weeks. Total, absolute bliss.

Someone opened a window and a waft of disinfectant blew across the car park. Kate welcomed it. This was what it was all about: the clean, sharp smell of disinfectant, of antiseptic, of anaesthetic . . . of dog, of cat, of rabbit, of . . . A car charged in from the main road and roared to a stop beside her own.

'Kate! Wonderful! I've so been looking forward to you coming.'

It was Joy the practice manager, a blonde bombshell of a person, full of vitality and bounce. She leapt out of her car and flung her arms around Kate.

'Just like old times! This is great. Come on, what are you waiting for? You're with Valentine this week. By the way, go carefully, he's persuaded Nina to come back to him, *again*, so Nadia is a thing of the past, though she lasted longer than most of his flings.'

The two of them went in through the back door and the first person they met was Valentine going through his post on his way to his consulting room. Nothing had changed, thought Kate. He was as handsome as ever and, if possible, even more attractive than she remembered.

His dark Eastern European eyes studied her from head to foot.

'Kate! You're mine all week. What a time we shall have. I become busier and busier, and you'll be a great help.'

'I look forward to learning a lot.'

'I have an idea you know more than enough already. You are so bright and very clever.'

Kate bowed her head in acknowledgement of his compliment. 'Let's hope I live up to your assessment!' She had to smile at him. He always left people feeling better about themselves and that couldn't be anything other than a good thing. She felt for his wife, though. Poor Nina. The times she'd left him never to come back and it had obviously happened yet again. He might be a great guy but it was time Nina called a halt to Valentine Dedic and his many short-term lovers.

Valentine handed her a new white coat, and as she put it on Kate could almost feel the authority it gave her. She slung her stethoscope around her neck and grinned at him. 'Do I look the part?'

'You certainly do, I shall have to watch my step. They'll be thinking I'm the student and you the vet!'

'I don't think so.'

'First client, Mrs Bookbinder. Chang for his annual boosters. You'll remember them, no doubt. Lovely client, devoted to her animals. She even has a graveyard in her garden where they all go when they die, headstones, the works. I suspect she'd like to call in the Vicar to do the honours at the service! Lovely woman, though.'

He opened the consulting room door, called out, 'Chang Bookbinder,' and, as Mrs Bookbinder sailed towards him, dragging a reluctant Chang along behind her, Valentine clicked his heels together saying, 'Good morning, Nerissa, you're looking on top of the world today.'

'Valentine! You utterly charming man.'

He closed the door behind her. 'This is Kate, my student for the week, I hope you won't mind her being present. She's very able and I'm sure will have a contribution to make to our consultation.'

2

'Of course I don't mind. I remember Kate. Now, Chang, less of the fuss and be a brave man for your mummy. Come along now. Right. I'll sit down and keep a low profile. That usually works, doesn't it, Valentine?'

She slid carefully down onto a chair and looked away from Chang so she didn't have eye contact, but even so, Chang rather obviously had taken exception to Valentine stroking him and trying to make friends.

'I'll prepare the booster and then, Kate, if you could lift him up onto the examination table, I'll do the business as quick as a flash.'

For a brief moment Chang's small fangs were bared and a slight growl could be heard rumbling in his chest. Though fully grown, he was small, even for a Shih Tzu, and Kate hadn't the slightest qualms about her ability to handle him.

When the injection was ready, at a nod from Valentine, Kate advanced on Chang and, speaking softly and sympathetically, she tucked a hand under his bottom and the other under his ribcage and began gently to lift him up onto the table. But she hadn't bargained for his hatred of veterinary treatment. One rapid, vigorous twist of his body and he'd left her grip, flown through the air and landed on the computer shelf, without getting all four feet firmly on. A back foot slipped off, the whole of him followed it, and poor Chang landed on the floor on his flank with an almighty thud.

There was a split second of complete silence and then Mrs Bookbinder shrieked, 'Oh, my God! Chang!'

Chang lay still, seemingly stunned by his fall. Kate went to pick him up but Valentine thundered, 'Leave him.' He swiftly plunged the syringe into the folds of flesh on Chang's neck and stood back.

Mrs Bookbinder was trembling from head to foot. 'Attacking him with the needle when he's in shock! How could you, Mr Dedic? He's too old for a fall like this, he could die. How could you, Mr Dedic?' Then she screamed, a long, piercing scream which echoed round the room. Nothing, but nothing, would stop her screaming.

Hearing her desperate screams, Chang decided to play sick and

3

poorly. He trembled a little, lifted his head and dropped it back down again, fluttered his little furry toes, looked as though he were about to rise and then dramatically fell back down again.

Mrs Bookbinder shrieked with horror. 'See! He is, he's dying! He is! Do something! Do something!'

Valentine took the lid off a plastic box and allowed the scent of the contents to escape. Kate caught the drift of chocolate and Chang's nose twitched slightly. Valentine then placed three chocolate drops on the floor, positioned so Chang had to get up to reach them. As though a miracle had brought him back from the jaws of death, he leapt to his feet, followed the trail of chocolate and gobbled them up. He stood there wagging his tail at Valentine and looking pleadingly for more, so Valentine, who couldn't resist Chang's soulful brown eyes, put a chocolate drop on the palm of his hand and bent down so Chang could reach it.

Full diplomatic relations having been restored, Valentine patted Chang on his head and said, 'There we are, Nerissa, everything taken care of. He should be on the stage.'

'Chang, you naughty boy! Come to Mummy who loves you.'

Chang, with a smug look, trotted across to her and allowed her to pick him up, and thrilled to her kisses and caresses with total abandonment.

'Thank you, Valentine. I shouldn't have screamed and carried on. I'm so sorry. I'm just relieved he's not hurt. I was very upset.'

'You'd had a shock, it's understandable. But don't make a habit of chocolate drops; he only got them because it was an emergency. We don't want him overweight, do we, now? Nothing worse than a Shih Tzu waddling along.'

'Of course not. Thanks for your help with Chang, Kate. He's not usually a naughty boy. Bye-bye, Valentine. By the way, did you get the pastrami I sent you when I was on holiday? It was very, very special, the best there is.'

'I did. I sent you an email to say thanks.'

'Ah! I can't always cope with my emails and sometimes I delete them by mistake. Taste good, did it?'

4

Valentine took her hand and squeezed it. 'Absolutely excellent, never tasted better.'

'Good, I'm glad. I thought you'd enjoy it. Only the best for my friends.' She stroked his bare arm, enjoying the manly froth of hair exposed by his short-sleeved jacket. 'Yes, well, I'd better go.'

After she'd left, Kate was tempted to tell him he was shameless where women were concerned but refrained. Instead she commented on his astuteness with Chang. 'I honestly thought he was badly injured, I felt terrible about it.'

'Well, he wasn't, although no thanks to you. You should have taken a better hold on him. Remember that next time.'

Stung by his abrupt criticism, but aware it was justified, Kate turned away to check on the next client. It was Miranda Costello with her rabbit, Lettice. Kate had a soft spot for Miranda.

Valentine grunted when he heard who was next. 'That damned rabbit of hers. Bites lumps out of everything, including me. Is it Lettice's teeth again?'

'It is. Miranda's nice, though, I've always liked her. Didn't know she had a rabbit.'

'Got her about two years or so ago. It's a vicious little beggar. Heigh-ho.'

Miranda got the same click of his heels and slight nod of his head as she marched in. 'Mr Dedic! Here we are again. And Kate! I didn't know you'd come back. Oh, how smart you look in your white coat. Are you qualified now, dear?'

'Hello, Mrs Costello. Lovely to see you again. No, I've got three more years to do yet.'

'I've said it before and I'll say it again, vets are better qualified than doctors. Anytime I'm ill, I shall be up on that examination table letting Valentine have a go.' Miranda giggled, then caught sight of Valentine's look of disapproval and wondered whether she should change to one of the other vets. She found Valentine rather unresponsive. 'It's her teeth again. Sorry.'

'Come along, Lettice, I'm all ready for you. No struggling now. It won't take a minute, if you're still.'

But Lettice hated the sharp explosive shock of her front teeth being snipped off. She braced herself, not understanding why it had to be done and not relating the ease of eating to the snipping of her teeth.

Kate found an old towel to wrap Lettice in to keep her claws from scratching either Valentine or herself. There must have been something about Kate which appealed to Lettice, because she allowed herself, without any resistance, to be wrapped and firmly held while Valentine tackled her overlong front teeth. In a trice Lettice was back in Miranda's carrying basket.

'Oh, Kate, you *must* be qualified. That's the best she's ever been, isn't it, Mr Dedic? The very best. Thank you, dear. Mind you're here next time. She's very special to me, is Lettice. I rescued her from my neighbours, you know. They bought her for their son and he didn't want her. She was emaciated and her coat all matted, terrible state, she was. They gave me the hutch, though, wasn't that kind? But she's not in it very much. I let her roam free, except at night, because of the foxes. She's such a beauty. I love this kind of tortoiseshell colouring she has. Very unusual, don't you think? I brush her every day, that's why she looks so good. The whole point is . . .'

Kate went to open the door, trying to edge Miranda out because she could see that Valentine was becoming exasperated. 'You've done a good job on her, she looks in excellent health now.'

'Oh, she is, Kate, she is. Thanks, Mr Dedic, see you again soon. Nice to see you, too, Kate.' Miranda went into reception to pay her bill.

Valentine did some magic on the computer so the staff would know how much to charge and said, 'That damned woman, she's nothing but a pain.'

'Miranda is lovely, so caring.'

'That menagerie she has is a disgrace. They're flea-ridden, allowed to run wild, and as for the mice, well . . .'

'How do you know she has mice?'

'Been there and seen them inside the house as well as out. I reckon she actually feeds the little beggars.'

'Feeds them? Help.'

'Exactly.'

'Even so, she's a nice person, even if she is a bit unconventional.'

'Ummm. Next one.'

By coffee-break Kate was glad for a pause, although she was there to learn and learn she would. It was vital to put every single minute to good use. She might not approve of Valentine's attitude towards some of his clients but that was nothing to do with her. Learning from his techniques was far more important, and client-handling was an equally important skill, which one didn't learn overnight.

The sugary coffee Joy handed to her was very welcome. If it hadn't been so hot she would have drunk it down in one big gulp. Then she heard the blast from the past which she had dreaded and her heart immediately pulsed with anticipation. Would he or wouldn't he be as attractive to her as he had been in the past? This was the moment to find out. Scott Spencer, coming in from visiting a farm, shouted, 'Coffee! Coffee! Where is it? The workers need sustenance. Thanks, Joy, timed that just right.'

He strode into the staffroom and stood sipping rapidly from his mug, the one he'd always used since he first came to the practice. God! Time had stood still then. The impact was just the same, just as vivid, just as hard to resist. But resist she would. She hadn't spent the last two years fighting off male veterinary students without learning a trick or two of self-preservation. Kate broke out into a sweat with the emotions hammering inside her. This . . . this she had not anticipated. She'd imagined she would be able to brush off her passion for him in a brief moment of firm self-control. It was appalling how powerfully her emotions were clamouring at her. Try she must to remain cool and self-possessed. 'Hello, Scott. How's things?'

Scott swung round to face her. A silence began as the others froze, awaiting their reaction to each other. 'Kate! Oh, my word. I'd forgotten you were starting today. How are you?' He advanced as though intending to greet her with a kiss, but Kate backed away and instead offered her hand to shake.

'I'm fine, thank you. You look well.'

'Married life, you know. Regular meals, moving house – keeps me fit.'

'Of course. I heard you were moving. Where to?'

'About two hundred yards from the Fox and Grapes. Very convenient! Brook Cottage, it's lovely, just what Zoe's been looking for. Nice garden with an orchard. Oscar will be in his element.'

'How is Oscar? He must be at school.'

'Just started and doing well.'

For some reason, which she couldn't have explained to herself if she'd tried for a year, Kate asked, 'Is it just Oscar still?'

'It is. Perhaps you'll be working with me one week. I'd like that. Be like old times.'

'I'll certainly be doing farm practice but I don't know who with yet.'

Valentine interrupted them. 'Ready?'

'Be seeing you, Kate. You know we're all going for a drink tonight? Fox and Grapes, half eight. You will come, won't you? I've just remembered it's supposed to be a welcome party for you.'

'I certainly will, of course. Eight-thirty. It'll be lovely meeting up with everyone again.'

Kate followed Valentine back to the consulting room on wobbly legs. Control. That was what she needed, control. She must not let anyone see how seriously she was affected by Scott. She flicked the appointments list on the screen but could only see Scott's smiling face: still that same tanned, healthy look, the thick blond hair, the lean, sexy body. And his eyes! Vivid blue. He was still stunningly attractive. But now he was married so he was definitely *verboten*. But she knew now, as clear as day, that she had made the most appalling mistake in coming back to the practice.

She heard Valentine speak to her, but had no idea what he said.

'I beg your pardon?'

'I said, who's next?'

'Sorry. New client, a Miss Eustace with a young Siamese for a general examination, to make sure it's sound.'

'It'll be a beauty, then. I've a lot of time for Siamese.'

'They're certainly very beautiful, but are they always sound? Too interbred perhaps?'

'Can be, I suppose. Same with any pedigree animal, though.'

Valentine went to welcome his new client. 'Miss Eustace.'

Miss Eustace, a bright, sleek woman of about thirty, with come-hither eyes and a great vibrancy about her, came in bubbling with excitement, her words falling over each other so eager was she. 'I picked her up yesterday from the breeder and I just want to be certain that she's OK. I love her already, though. I really do. If there is anything wrong with her I might have to put up with it, because I couldn't bear to part with her. What do you think?' Miss Eustace gently drew the kitten out of her spanking new carrier and stood her on the examination table.

She was spectacularly beautiful. Tippy-toed with good health, a milky coffee colour at her nose and tail, and a soft cream everywhere else. She rubbed herself against Valentine, purring and inviting admiration, her tail curling around Valentine's arm, as though she'd known him all her life.

'My word, Miss Eustace, I do believe you've got a cracker here. What have you called her?'

'I haven't chosen a name. Health-wise, how do you feel?'

The kitten submitted to an intimate examination without the slightest qualm. In fact, she revelled in it. Bold and confident were the words which sprang to mind.

'The breeder's seen to her initial injections, I assume?'

Miss Eustace nodded brightly.

'She appears to be in magnificent health. She'll give you many happy years of companionship. It's a privilege to have the opportunity of checking her out. I'll give you some kitten leaflets, about diet and general care, and my student will take your address, telephone number and the kitten's date of birth. She'll need regular boosters, of course; the details are all in this leaflet on the top. Good luck with her.'

Miss Eustace held out her hand to say goodbye and Valentine took it and held it for a little longer than necessary, but the smile he gave her, and the delight with which she reciprocated his *au revoir*, made Kate think they'd be meeting again before long, although it wouldn't be in his consulting room. After all, Valentine was in an excellent position for making contact again; all he needed would be on the screen in front of him.

The morning rushed along, with one client after another and so much for Kate to pick up. No doubt about it, Valentine was *busy*.

In the afternoon Valentine had three operations to do and then he was free. Not an arduous time for someone who was experienced and working every day, but for Kate, passionately determined to absorb all and every detail, it was exhausting and, at the end of the day, she fell in through the door of the flat feeling shattered and calling, 'Mia! Mia!'

Her stepmother rushed into the sitting room, flushed with working in their tiny kitchen on such a warm day, her hair tumbled and damp, her face glistening with sweat.

'Well?'

'Brilliant. Absolutely brilliant. I've loved it, but I'm starving.'

'You ate your lunch?'

'I did.' Kate didn't add that Scott had made a point of sitting next to her and paying her attention in such a way that she had become embarrassed. 'Every little bit.'

'Hungry?'

'Yes. I'm going out for a drink tonight with everybody. Half past eight at the Fox and Grapes.'

'Cold salmon salad with new potatoes? Mayonnaise? White wine left over from last night?'

Kate nodded. 'Have you had a good day in the shop?'

'The Gallery, my dear, the Gallery.'

They both giggled.

Kate drawled, 'So sorry, da-a-rling,' imitating the accent of the woman who employed Mia.

They giggled again.

'It won't be long.' Mia disappeared into the kitchen, wishing she'd dared to ask about Scott. That was the problem of going back to that practice. She'd doubted the wisdom of Kate returning, but Joy had rung up and asked for Kate to go. She'd been so keen it was hard for Kate to refuse. But Mia knew that Scott had broken Kate's heart, and however hard Kate tried she couldn't completely disguise the fact, certainly not from Mia. But then, Mia was exquisitely tuned in to Kate's emotions, as she had been ever since becoming her stepmother when Kate was a year old.

Mia called out from the kitchen, 'Your father would have been so delighted by today, he'd have wanted to hear about everything you've done.'

'I know he would. Just going to get washed.'

'Of course, after handling all those animals.'

Kate smiled to herself. Mia always worried about the germs she might pick up, but Kate rather felt that she was becoming immune to them.

Her hearty salad, followed by what Mia always called her 'meringue thingy', boosted Kate's reserves and she dashed away to her evening out revived and ready for meeting everyone.

The warm weather meant that every available window and door at the Fox was standing wide open, and the cheerful noise of dozens of people enjoying themselves flooded out into the car park. Kate had forgotten about the special conviviality peculiar to the Fox, it was very much unto itself and no other, and her spirits lifted as she stepped over the threshold, filled with pleasant anticipation.

She couldn't see her colleagues inside so she went into the back garden and found she was one of the last to arrive. To accommodate them all, two tables had been pushed together under the big beech trees to catch some of their shade. They were all there, happy, welcoming faces, and a positive flurry of kissing, hugging, back-slapping and chatter ensued. *He* was with Zoe, so too was Mungo with Miriam, and Joy with Duncan, who looked happier than Kate had ever known him, and too many others to note in one hurried glance.

Joy called out, 'Come and sit between Duncan and me, tell us all your news. There's such a crowd of us now, isn't there? And of course there's Virginia, too, whom you won't have met yet. She's out on a call. Don't know if she'll make it.'

Joy was always a fair-minded person but even she couldn't avoid pulling a disapproving face when she mentioned Virginia's name. But Duncan asked her what she would like to drink and Kate got carried away talking about college and what an exciting day she'd had, and they never got back to talking about Virginia again.

Mindful that she had to drive home, Kate monitored how much she was drinking and when Scott proposed getting the next round in, making notes on a piece of paper so he wouldn't forget who had ordered what, she asked for mineral water with ice and lemon.

Scott clapped a hand to his forehead and said, 'Water! On a night like this? Surely not.'

Zoe interrupted. 'Scott! Water she wants and water she gets.' She smiled and reached out to rub a streak of ink from his cheek where his pen had caught it. Kate caught sight of the love shining in Zoe's face, and Scott's almost embarrassed recognition of it. He flicked a glance at Kate to see if she'd noticed and when he saw she had, he looked quickly away.

The party got rowdier and rowdier, and when Mungo did an impression of a tutor he'd known at college and they'd laughed themselves helpless at him – even more so when Colin remembered him, too, and told a few spicy stories about the tutor's relationships with some of the women students – and the landlord apologetically asked them to cool it a little, they decided it was time they all went home.

Duncan took it upon himself to see Kate to her car. 'Now, Kate, my girl, keep well focused on your career. We're expecting great things from you. After all, you've the best of starts, haven't you, being at the Barleybridge Veterinary Hospital.' He nudged her to show he was joking. 'You don't want too many distractions, right?'

'Now who's going to distract me? They're all married.'

'That doesn't count for much nowadays.' He grinned, a charming, lopsided grin not often seen on Duncan's face.

'I must say, Duncan, if I may, that you appear much happier than when I saw you last.'

'I am much happier, thanks. Joy and I . . . well . . . we've come to a splendid understanding and we have the best years of our lives still to come.' He hesitated and looked up at the sky. 'I don't know why I'm telling you that. I do believe you must have the kind of face which makes people want to confide in you. Not a bad attribute for a vet. Goodnight, Kate. Sleep tight. So glad to have you back in the fold for a while, so to speak.'

When Kate got home she made herself a cup of green tea to calm her mind, and curled up on the sitting-room sofa to gaze out at the night sky. If she strained her eyes a little she could just see the practice building nestling by the foothills of Beulah Bank Top. Whatever she might have imagined about her feelings for Scott and how she'd definitely got them under control since the time he hopped back to Australia without so much as a backward glance, she knew tonight that control was the least apt word to describe her sensations. All those old emotions had come streaming back, and witnessing the love Zoe had for Scott had only heightened them, for she also knew what it was like to love the man. She must be the biggest fool under the sun.

Whatever, he was unattainable, completely and absolutely, so she might as well put him out of her mind. Put him out of her mind? That was a laugh. Who was she fooling? Only herself. She should never have given in to Joy's pleas to see practice with them. Never. But she had, and here she was in the throes of falling in love all over again. Damn and blast.

Mia came quietly in from her bedroom and stood in the dark beside her looking out, her hand resting on Kate's shoulder. 'It's turned chilly now, hasn't it, after such a hot day. They say it's going to be this hot for the rest of the summer. Hot you know.'

13

'Right.'

Mia stood silently for a while, looking out at the lights of Barleybridge, and then decided to ask, 'How was it, then, back with all your old fellow conspirators again? Who was there? Anyone I remember?'

'Graham's left, otherwise just the same. Joy, of course, with Duncan, who seems much, much happier than I've ever known him. Colin, but not Letty because of little John, and all the rest, Rhodri and Megan, of course. They're all wonderful. They made me feel so welcome and we had such a laugh. Even Mungo had us in stitches. They are such brilliant people to work with – caring, happy, devoted and such good fun, too. What more could one ask?'

'Nothing, I suppose. I'm glad for you, Kate, very glad. Just keep your mind on your goal. OK?'

Mia's hand squezed Kate's shoulder. 'Goodnight, my dearest girl.' She dropped a kiss on the top of her head and went off to bed. She'd not mentioned that Scott, but as Kate had deliberately avoided saying his name, did that mean he'd affected her just like he did before? Maybe he hadn't turned up, maybe, for once, he'd forgone a trip to the pub. After two years of never mentioning his name, had Kate succumbed again to his tremendous charm? No wonder if she did, he was gorgeous. Blast him. Mia wanted to boot him off the face of the earth. She, Mia Howard, would have something to say if she suspected for *one single minute* that Scott Spencer was making moves towards her Kate.

Chapter 2

Kate met Virginia the new vet the following morning. She was in collecting her visiting list and leaving a message for Mungo.

Joy said, 'Virginia, this is Kate, our student. Kate, this is Virginia.'

'Ah! Heard a lot about you. Accounts at one time, I think. White hope of the Barleybridge Veterinary Hospital, I understand? Eh?'

Kate didn't like the hint of a sneer in her voice but kept her temper and said as pleasantly as she could, 'Nice to meet you.'

Virginia had a strong, square face with a very positive chin. Dark-brown hair, cut very short, and large, grey eyes which appeared to criticize everything within their range. No make-up, not even a touch of lipstick, but a set of snow-white, perfectly even teeth, which would have done a Hollywood star credit.

'Mmm. I want Mungo to have this message the moment he comes in, Joy, it's important.'

'Well, he'll be down shortly, leave it with me.'

'It's important.'

'You said that. I'll give him it the moment I clap eyes on him. OK? By the way, Gavin from Lord Askew's sounded a bit anxious when he rang, so don't leave it too long.'

'Any idea?'

Joy raised an eyebrow at her abrupt question. 'No, none. I thought you would have known, seeing as you've been there a lot recently.'

'Have you a problem with that?'

'Me? Of course not. I'm a lay person. Who am I to question the

15

decisions of a qualified vet?' Joy had an innocent expression on her face which made Kate want to laugh.

Virginia picked up her keys 'That kind of sarcasm doesn't go down well with me. Be seeing you.'

So this was Virginia. Kate could understand why Joy had taken a dislike to her, which she had, there was no doubt about that. But they didn't have time to discuss it because Annette and the new reception girl, Lesley came in, closely followed by Scott.

Joy looked up. 'You two girls are late. I would have thought that sharing a flat would have meant that, between you, you could at least manage to get here on time. Fifteen minutes late. It won't do.'

'Sorry, Joy. There was a road accident and we got held up.'

'Next it'll be leaves on the line. You could have turned off and come the back way over the moor. It's longer but quicker than standing in a traffic queue. It's happening far too often just lately, it won't do.'

To take the pressure off Annette and Lesley, Scott murmured, 'Joy, light of my heart, I hope you're not cross with *me*.'

Joy beamed at him. 'You're a rogue, Scott Spencer. Don't you put your little boy look on for me. I'm too old to succumb to your charms. Here's your list. You're busy today, so get cracking.'

He winked at Kate. 'Can I take Kate with me?'

'You may not; she's with Valentine today.'

'Pity. Don't let that Omar Sharif lookalike steal your heart, Kate, because he's too fickle for words, is our Valentine.' As he noticed Kate's eyebrows raised he set off at speed, realizing how clumsy he'd been.

'I won't,' Kate called out as he disappeared. The lift of her eyebrows had been an attempt to disguise her feelings, but it hadn't worked because her heart was still thumping madly.

Joy said quietly, 'All right with him, is it? I thought last night—'

'I'm fine, thanks. Oh, here's Valentine.' Kate cut short any possibility of discussing Scott by following Valentine into his consulting room. She went straight to his computer and, switching on his list of clients for the day, said, 'Nice varied list today. First is

Mr Featherstonehough, with his cat. Remember his Rottweiler, Adolf. The fights he had with Mungo's Perkins – do you remember?'

'Of course. Right, let's start. Perkins is looking his age nowadays. I've a soft spot for him, you know. A great character.'

Kate glanced at him to see if he was serious. 'You sound as though you think he's about to give up the ghost.'

'Oh, he is. Don't say anything to Miriam and Mungo – although I'm sure they know it – but I do think old age is creeping up on him rather rapidly. Right.' Valentine went to the door and called, 'Chloe F.'

Mr Featherstonehough came in carrying his cat basket.

He was a gruff ex-police dog-handler, now owner of a cat whom he'd taken in after Adolf died and named after his dead wife.

'Mr Dedic, good morning to you. Good morning, Kate. It's my cat. I think I've come to ask you to put her to sleep.' There was a tremble in his usually clipped tones.

Valentine hated being told what to do and was a mite snappish. 'Now why should I be doing that?'

Mr Featherstonehough cleared his throat to disguise his emotions, which were clearly running high. 'There's something very wrong with her. Her behaviour's peculiar. She's startled by the slightest thing, she doesn't want to go out, when before she's been the terror of the neighbourhood's rats and mice, and sometimes she forgets herself and messes in the house, and that's not her. Most particular she's been all the time I've had her. And she's no fun any more, not like she's always been. I reckon there's something seriously wrong and I can't bear it.'

'Get her out of the basket and I'll have a look at her. Could be something quite simple.'

Handling her out of the basket as carefully as he could, Mr Featherstonehough gave Valentine a disbelieving look.

Kate observed Valentine's examination of Chloe, who appeared oblivious to him. His fingers were expertly pressing and manipulating her from head to toe, seeking an answer. Then he got a light to look closely into Chloe's eyes. He studied each eye for longer than Kate thought necessary but when she heard what he had to say she realized why.

Valentine put down the light and stood tickling Chloe behind her ears.

'I'm afraid . . . you see, I'm fairly sure, in fact, I *am* sure she has a tumour on the brain. I can't feel anything at all wrong with her otherwise, though we could do blood tests to check for various things, but to be honest, I'm sure the brain tumour is the problem, and it won't ever shrink. How old do we reckon she is?'

'Never really known. Always lively up until now. Behaved like a kitten since the day I took her in.' He lovingly stroked Chloe's head, but she gave no response. 'See that? Before she would always purr and rub herself against my hand. But there's nothing there now.'

'Looking at her teeth and such, I reckon she's about twelve or fourteen. Joints, a bit arthritic, getting, literally, long in the tooth and, well . . . by the look of it . . .'

'Is she in pain? I don't want that.'

'Not pain so much as lacking coordination and wondering what's gone wrong with her world.'

'Ah! Well, when I watch her in the garden and that, she keeps walking lopsided, kind of all off to one side—'

'She'll be badly confused, too.'

'I see. What about an operation?'

'It is my opinion that Chloe is far too old to withstand such a major operation. The cost would be prohibitive, and the outcome extremely doubtful. I can't honestly recommend that.' Valentine stood back from Chloe and studied her for a moment. Trying to soften the blow, he suggested, 'How about if you take her home for a day or two and see how you feel?'

'Won't help her to get better, will it? Just putting off the inevitable.'

'Well, yes, but it would give you time to confirm your suspicions, and time to adapt.'

Mr Featherstonehough contemplated Valentine's suggestion for a moment and then said, 'Right. I'm going to accept what you say, because I *know* things aren't right. I'll make her last few days really happy. Yes, I will.'

'Good chap. After all, she's had a good life with you, hasn't she? It would give you time to make a balanced judgement about her behaviour. OK?'

Mr Featherstonehough reached out to shake hands. Kate was stroking Chloe who sat patiently waiting. It always broke her heart when animals had to be put to sleep, even when she knew it was the kindest thing to do. She squeezed his hand in sympathy and almost caused him to break down, so she hastily withdrew her hand.

'Nice to see you again, Kate.'

'And you, Mr Featherstonehough.' She smiled as best she could.

'Come along then, Chloe, into your basket.' He gently lifted an unresisting Chloe back onto her blanket and shut the front

Valentine said quietly, 'Make another appointment when you feel ready.'

Mr Featherstonehough's smile was strained as he said, 'It won't be long, I can't stand her being so odd. I'll miss her, though.' He allowed his eyes to meet Valentine's.

'Of course you will, but you'll be doing the best thing for her. My day off is Friday this week if you would prefer me to see to her.'

'Thank you.' He went out, his military bearing at odds with his emotions, but he refused to allow himself to show weakness when in public. One mustn't, not under any circumstances. Tears had to be kept for his own fireside.

Kate, distressed about Chloe, blurted out, 'Oh, Valentine, were you sure? I mean . . . it's so awful for him.'

Valentine, shocked that she doubted his opinion, became angry. 'Sure? Was I sure? Of course I was. How would I give a diagnosis like that if I wasn't? What do you mean sure? Do you suppose I get off on putting animals to sleep?'

The angry, scornful tone of his voice humiliated Kate. 'I . . . I'm sorry. I didn't mean that, it's just—'

'I hate putting animals to sleep, but there's no room for sentimentality in veterinary work. If, to the best of your judgement, it has to be done then it has to be done and you move on. Don't ever question my decisions again. Right? Next?'

Kate, realizing she had made an error of the highest order, apologized profusely, but it didn't seem that Valentine was appeased by it.

She endeavoured for the rest of the day to keep a low profile and not anger Valentine any further. But it was difficult. His handling of clients couldn't be faulted and his veterinary decisions were, so far as she could tell, faultless, but somehow . . . somehow Kate didn't feel comfortable with him. There was always the feeling that, with only the slightest bit of encouragement on her part, he and she could be involved in an affair. A short blaze of emotion, after which Valentine would quickly become disenchanted, leaving her wounded and shattered. Then Scott's face came into her mind and she knew for certain that resisting Valentine would be far, far easier than resisting Scott . . . Kate decided to pull herself together. She had a plan for her life and it didn't involve an illicit affair with a married man. Both Duncan and Mia had warned her from getting involved with anyone, but what if she had already met the love of her life? What then?

On the Friday, Valentine's day off, Joy suggested Kate went out for the day visiting farms with Scott. Just one day, thought Joy, give Kate a chance to see how she felt about him, but she wouldn't make it a week. Definitely not. Not much could happen in a day, now could it?

'Remember your boots, Kate,' she said, 'and something in case it rains.'

'Rains? Haven't you noticed it's scorching at the moment? Be nice to get out, though. That'll be fine.' Kate nodded her agreement firmly. It would be good. Just one day with Scott all to herself. Then she remembered that feeling of someone having punched her in the solar plexus when he'd breezed in that first day.

She decided not to tell Mia about it being Scott she was shadowing that day. No, best not.

All the same, on Friday morning she couldn't contain her delight, and was enthusiastically away from the flat before Mia had set off for the Gallery.

Mia noticed, but didn't say anything. Kate was a level-headed girl and she had to trust her. But she worried all day, mainly because she herself knew how alluring Scott was. When Kate wasn't home by supper-time the worry mushroomed till it possessed her every thought.

But Kate hadn't even realized it was supper-time. She was hot and sweaty and definitely not worrying. They'd been visiting several of the farm clients whom Kate remembered from her days as an accounts clerk before college and they were all delighted to see her. A drink in the farmhouse kitchens was offered at almost every visit, which made Scott's day longer and longer, but neither of them cared. Kate was loving it. This was what being a vet was all about for her. Up hill, down dale, visiting, greeting, putting minds at rest, easing pain, connecting with clients, getting muddy and dirty, thirsty and hungry, above all, today, being with Scott, whom everyone liked and admired. Scott had looked at her just the once saying, 'Just like old times, isn't it?' They'd grinned at each other and the years felt to roll away and Kate had experienced the deep joy of Scott's company, as of old. The grin he'd given her convinced her he still had a corner of his being which belonged to her, and that was what she clung to throughout the long day.

However, Kate, though a valued friend, held no temptation for Scott any more. All traces of passion he might have had for her in earlier days had vanished on his marriage. Zoe was his lover, his wife, his beloved, the mother of his son, his comfort, his homemaker, his reassurance, his support all rolled into one.

He rang Zoe several times during the day, but always called her out of Kate's hearing. He just didn't want anyone to know that he, Scott Spencer, for so long the farmers' wives' and daughters' trophy, had fallen head over heels in love and was no longer a free spirit. But the more they thought they might still be in the running the better Scott liked it; then they were putty in his hands when it came to a cosy, life-saving mug of coffee and vast slices of homemade fruitcake in their kitchens after a long session saving lives on their farms, and he liked to keep it that way.

When he arrived home, Oscar was already in bed and Zoe was counting the minutes to his return.

'I'm home!'

'Sssh! Oscar's just gone off to sleep.'

'Oh! Good. Nice day?'

'Blow the nice day, give me a kiss.'

He ran his hands down her slender hips, relishing the shape of her bones, drew her closer still and kissed her with invigorating joy. They drew away from each other, both of them spooked by the instant passion they had aroused. Scott pulled her close again and smelt her hair. 'Lime and passion fruit?'

Zoe nodded.

'Gorgeous! Let's smell it again.'

He pressed her close to him again, burying his nose in her hair, sucking in a great breath of lime and groaned with desire. 'Dinner ready, is it?'

Zoe nodded again.

'Damn. Have to wait till later then.'

'I love you.'

'Zo! I love you.' He released her then followed her into the kitchen, loving the earnest manner with which she devoted herself to serving their meal. This was Zoe? The Zoe who'd despised the little-woman-at-home-slaving-over-a-hot-stove cliché? But here she was, offering him culinary delights he'd never imagined she possessed the skill to produce. But it was one of her ways of showing him how much she loved him; which she demonstrated every day of their lives. She presented him with a glorious rump steak cooked to perfection, with a helping of sauté potatoes and a huge, brightly coloured side salad.

'This is so tempting. Who'd have believed the Zoe of old could make such a meal as this?'

'The Zoe of old never had the time to cook like this. Now I can and I do it to make a real home for Oscar and for you, as I promised I would.'

'This is so tasty. I do appreciate what you do, believe me.'

'I only have to witness the speed with which you wolf it down to know that. So, how's the day been with Kate?'

'Absolutely excellent. She's going to make a very good vet. Everyone was so pleased to see her. She makes friends wherever she goes.'

'She's all right, is she?'

Scott looked up at her. 'All right? In what way?'

'Well, she held a torch for you, didn't she? Does she still?'

Scott chewed on a piece of steak, swallowed it and answered, 'I don't think it's really relevant now, is it? Not to me, anyhow.'

'I asked, and you promised to answer.'

'I never did.'

'You did, when we first married. That was one of our vows, absolute honesty, and you're evading giving me a straight answer.'

Scot put down his knife and fork and looked at her. 'Hmmm. I honestly don't know. She's playing her cards close to her chest.'

'I see.' Zoe knew all about Kate's shock when Scott had gone back to Australia so suddenly, remembered her struggle to behave normally despite her anguish. 'Well, keep it that way. It's the safest.'

'You don't need to tell me, you know that, Zo. She's just as attractive as ever. You know her kind of classical good looks, distinguished almost. Slimmer and better for it. Hard working, focused. She'll make a first-rate vet one day.'

'Had enough?'

Scott gave Zoe a wonderful, heart-stopping smile. 'Of dinner, yes, but not of you.'

'That's a good idea. I suppose we could have our pudding after . . .' Zoe stood up and Scott came round the table to stand beside her.

'We could, yes, I agree.' He began unzipping her skirt.

'Not downstairs, it's still light. Oscar might come down, you know how restless he is these hot nights.'

They climbed the narrow stairs squeezed side by side, his arm round her waist, his hand already enjoying her. This, he thought, was life as it should be lived.

Chapter 3

Nina was halfway through preparing Valentine's evening meal when he got home. He could tell by her back that her mood was not good. There were times when he wondered why on earth he put up with her. He sighed, kicked off his sandals and left them by the door. He'd spent his day off doing exactly what he liked. A few hours fishing on Chesil beach, an hour in the barber's waiting his turn for a head massage, a shave and a haircut, a long visit to the library, and then a drive along the coast to Lyme, where he sat in a café on the front, reading his paper, sipping an espresso, enjoying the cool breeze coming off the sea.

He never missed a day reading the paper, even if it was midnight before he got a chance to settle down with it. It gave him a window on the world, this strange world he lived in now, a world of good manners and laughter, of football and pubs, of feeling safe from terror, death and destruction, of political figures losing their jobs because of some trifling marital indiscretion. Where he came from that was the very least of their crimes, the very, very least.

He called out, 'Hi, I'm home,' but got no response. He didn't expect one, not with her back like that. It amazed him that her back could be so expressive. Tonight it was tense and hunched. Some nights it was lithe and supple, other nights provocative, intense. How anyone could be so changeable he couldn't understand.

After they'd eaten their meal in complete silence, Valentine knew it was a waste of time bothering to speak when Nina was in one of her moods. He cleared the dishes into the dishwasher, switched it on and waited for Nina's usual comment: 'That thing is useless. It's quicker to wash them by hand. One hour and five minutes it will take. Ridiculous.'

'But while it's working hard I am reading the paper, which is much more interesting than washing dishes.'

Nina shrugged. 'Met Virginia in the market today. She pretended she didn't know who I was, would you believe.'

'Peculiar woman, is Virginia. Unfeminine. Bad-tempered. Abrupt. Not the least bit attractive to neither man nor beast.'

'Good.'

'What do you mean?'

'Because then you won't be fancying her.'

'You're right there, for heaven's sakes. My God!'

'I met Hannah Wilson, too, the sister of Bernard, the one who used to be a nurse.'

'I know her, yes.'

'She complain to me about Virginia. She called to look at that llama Bernard keeps. Told him he'd no business keeping it, said problem was depression brought on by loneliness and that he ought to sell it to someone who has a herd. He was very upset. Hannah said she allowed him to have a bottle of Guinness he was so low. Virginia no business going round telling people that. It's a free world.'

'Trouble is, she was very probably right. She usually is. Damn bossy woman.'

'I'm not bossy.'

'No. Yes, you are in your own way.'

Nina sat upright, thrust her feet into her Indian slippers and asked what on earth he meant.

'Nothing really, just teasing. You're not bossy at all. In fact, just the opposite. If the phone goes I'll need to go out. I've a bitch to see to, she's close to whelping. Client says it looks as though it will be tonight.'

Nina grumbled. 'All your dogs seem to have difficult whelpings. It's your day off, someone else could go.'

'They are my clients and I promised. Why won't people listen to me when I say they shouldn't breed from their pets? It's not a matter for amateurs.'

'Please, Val, don't go out.'

'I must. It's my job. I could be late, just depends how it goes.'

Nina pouted, then poured him a whisky and tried to make him drink it. She knew he wouldn't, not when he very likely had to go out on call. But it was worth a try.

'Stop it, Nina. Please. I don't want it. You have it.'

She was still trying to persuade him to drink it when the phone began ringing. Valentine leapt to his feet. 'This must be it.'

Nina watched him answer it. He gave the caller his utmost attention. Nodding his head, asking the appropriate questions, agreeing to come. 'Of course, sounds imminent to me. I'll leave immediately.' He put down the receiver. 'That's it. Any minute. Got to go.'

Nina waited for his kiss, he always kissed her before he left. And he did, one of his lovely kisses full of promise, which was the very closest she was able to allow him to be to her.

The door banged shut and the noise echoed through the empty house. Basically, thought Nina, she should treat him better than she did. He deserved it.

The 'bitch' in question was the sleek blonde with the come-hither eyes, namely Eleanor Eustace. She smiled sweetly as she watched Valentine cross the bar lounge of the George, the best hotel in Barleybridge. Nothing but the tops for Eleanor.

He saw her because she stood out from the rest of the comfortable punters in the bar, with her glossy, well-groomed hair and slender figure. Her gleaming, sun-tanned legs were crossed, her shapely knees emphasizing her sexiness. As he threaded his way between the tables Valentine flicked his eyes from one side to the other, checking if he recognized any one. He didn't particularly want a scandal. One sighting and the news would be back at the practice by morning. That kind of complication he most certainly didn't need.

'Valentine! Glad you could come.'

'I couldn't wait. How are you? Feeling on top of the world by the looks of it.' He reached across the table between them, took hold of her hand and raised it to his lips.

His gesture excited her. 'You charmer, you.'

'Good manners, that's all. How's the nameless kitten?'

'Nameless no longer. She's called Choo. C-h-o-o.'

'Choo?'

'Couldn't think of anything suitable so I plumped for Choo. Which she does – chew, I mean, all too spectacularly.'

Valentine nodded. 'Choo. Sounds quite good. Is she well?'

'She most certainly is. Come to think of it, I mustn't be long. She gets upset if I leave her, starts attacking the furniture.'

'I'm sure you'll find a way of stopping that. Too costly.'

'You're right there. She got up on a lamp table I have and scratched the lampshade to pieces. My flat's going to be wrecked. But,' Eleanor shrugged, 'I can't help it, can I?'

'I am always amazed by the way pet-lovers tolerate their belongings being shredded. I looked inside a car once because the dog in it was barking and was appalled by the state of the upholstery; there wasn't a single seat or armrest which hadn't been ripped open. Really, it's not on, Eleanor.'

'I'm called Ellie by my friends. Do you have animals?'

'No. Nina has asthma, we can't.'

'That's the first time you've mentioned your wife. What's she like?'

Valentine hesitated. It never did any good in a new relationship to tear the wife to pieces. For some incomprehensible reason, it seemed to him, women promptly put up a united front and the man was diminished by it. 'We've kind of lost touch; she has her job, I have mine. You know how it goes.'

'Children?'

'None, and I don't hanker after any, either.'

'What does she do, then?'

Valentine had to think quickly. Tell her the truth that Nina did nothing at all and she'd think he'd made an almighty boob. After all, his wife's status reflected on his ability to attract an exciting woman. Tell fibs and he'd be embroiled in questions.

'Government Secret Service,' he said. 'Can't talk about it. Very hush-hush.'

Ellie's deep-green eyes lit up. 'Hell! How exciting. Is she foreign like you?'

'She is.'

'So it's a question of using her language skills, then.'

Valentine nodded. 'And you? What do you do?'

There was a significant pause before Ellie answered. 'I don't need to work. I have private income from a childless aunt, so I gave up work two years ago. Now I just enjoy myself – shopping, going to the health club, eating with friends, going up to London. I'd like to do all that with you . . . if that's possible.' She reached across and stroked his hand, smiling temptingly.

Valentine tried to cool her blatant wooing of him. 'I've never met anyone with a private income before. Not having to work! That's amazing. Absolutely amazing. Ever?'

'Ever. So I'm free all day. Every day. You must get days off sometimes.' She smiled sweetly at him and Valentine found himself warming to her.

'Of course I do. Saturday or Sunday and always a day in the week.'

'You're a stunning man. Very sexy.'

'Me?' He managed to look as if this was the first he'd heard of it.

'Didn't you realize. You modest fellow, you. Of course you are. And a vet, too. That's very appealing in itself.' She sipped her drink, eyes admiring him above the rim of her glass. 'You haven't got a drink. Here, I'll buy it for you. What do you want? I know, we'll both have a cocktail.'

Valentine tried to resist the cocktail idea but she pressed the point vigorously. 'Don't tell me you're one of those men who hate the little woman taking the initiative? Please. What century are you in?'

Ellie tripped away to the bar on her very high-heeled sandals, her very short skirt leaving almost nothing to the imagination. Valentine was swept away by her. She was so *willing*. Falling over herself to get him into bed. Well, she wouldn't be disappointed, that was for sure. He'd never had a complaint.

Halfway through her cocktail she confessed she'd paid for a room at the George for the two of them.

Valentine was unnerved by the net that was closing around him. Usually he set the pace and he wasn't too sure he liked being ambushed like this.

Ellie eyed him cautiously. Surely he wasn't going to get all stuffy and remember he was a married man, not when she was revved up to go. 'Come on. We'll finish our cocktails and then up the wooden stairs! I shan't be a disappointment, believe me.'

The wicked smile she gave him almost made him decide to visit the boys' room and then quietly disappear out through the back exit, which he had done once before when he was being wooed against his will. But suddenly he fancied her. She was very irresistible. In fact, totally and completely irresistible. He got to his feet and held out his hand. 'What are we waiting for?'

Ellie gulped down the rest of her cocktail, grabbed his hand and set off at a goodly pace for the stairs.

He arrived home to Nina at two o'clock in the morning. Before going into their bedroom he showered, put his underclothes, shirt and trousers in the linen basket and rolled into bed gently to cause the least disruption he could. But Nina, half-asleep and waiting for his return, had heard his key in the lock.

She snuggled up to him and said, 'How many?'

'How many?' Wondering what on earth she was talking about.

'Puppies, you idiot.'

'Oh! Right. Six, plus one I couldn't revive. So it would have been seven. But the puppies are robust and the mother very pleased with herself. So is the client, very pleased. She was thrilled by my expertise.'

In the dark he smirked at his duplicity. Then he thought about Ellie and wished to God he'd not let her charm him into her bed.

30

He just knew she was trouble with a capital T, but the danger thrilled him. He slipped an arm around Nina and thought about Ellie's body compared to Nina's. They were a world apart. The one eager, well practised and innovative, the other, this one laid in his arms right now, afraid, anxious and unresponsive. And no wonder, considering what she'd been through.

When he thought about her experiences in her teens he cringed with horror. All that fear and desolation at the loss of her entire family and her appalling vulnerability when she faced the world completely alone. She had lived with terror for months and months. Dear God. Poor Nina. He tightened his hold on her, kissed her cheek, straightened her nightie for her, sought hopefully for some response from her, imagined he felt a slight stirring, only to find her screaming at his touch.

'Hush, hush,' he murmured. 'There. There. Hush. Not wanting anything, nothing at all. It's your choice, as always. That's our understanding, isn't it?' He dug into his bedside drawer, found the tissues and wiped her eyes.

Her sobs slowed and she clung to him for strength.

'Cup of tea, eh?'

Nina nodded. 'Oh, yes, please.'

While he waited for the kettle to boil he heard the shower running. Valentine shook his head in despair. Still cleansing herself and yet he'd barely touched her. He couldn't justify his betrayal of his marriage vows when he went with women like Ellie, because he'd known when he married Nina that married life would not be glorious between them, not for a long time, but surely, surely the time might come soon when it could be glorious and rewarding for the two of them? The kettle whistled its readiness and Valentine filled the teapot and went back upstairs.

Nina was back in bed, damp and sorrowful. 'I'm so sorry. I do try.'

'I know you do. Here, drink your tea.'

They sat up side by side drinking, both silent and contemplative. It was Nina who spoke first.

31

'You see, Val, I wish I could come to you . . . all new and fresh. No one longs for that more than me. But it just not possible.'

'Look. Stop worrying about it. That only makes matters worse. You should dwell on the fact that I love you, very much, and I'm still here waiting, aren't I? Sex between you and me would be *loving*, not brutal and savage. *That* is what you need to concentrate on, not what happened in the past. Love and gentleness, you know.'

Nina put down her cup and saucer and slithered down under the sheet. 'I dream about it, yes, dream about it, and I try, but straight away that hideous terror comes back and I fail you.'

'Never mind, never mind, go back to sleep.' He didn't dare touch her again, not even in sympathy.

Ellie came back into his mind. She really was a cracker of a woman. An absolute cracker. One of the best, but it couldn't be the George next time, too risky. And he wouldn't call her immediately. He'd leave it for a week perhaps, or ten days even. He mustn't appear eager.

But he saw her again at his Saturday clinic. Choo was limping badly and Ellie was so distressed she couldn't even hold her for Valentine to examine, so Kate had to step in to help.

'Kate! Don't squeeze her, you're stopping her breathing.'

'Sorry. That better?'

Valentine carefully examined Choo, pressing gently on her tender paw, searching for the problem. Poor Choo mewed angrily and twisted and turned to escape her torturer.

'Right here, look, between these two pads, see it? A really deep cut and there's pus there, too. Must have stepped on glass or something.' He looked up, too absorbed in his professional work to properly acknowledge the woman in whose arms he'd laid only two nights ago. 'How long has she been limping like this, Miss Eustace?'

Stung by his apparent coldness, Ellie answered, 'Yesterday morning. I'd been playing with her in the garden and when we went back in the house I realized she wasn't walking right. Is it serious?'

'No. But she's in considerable pain, and it could turn nasty. Hold on, Kate, I'm going to examine her again. It may need a stitch.' Valentine poked about between the tiny pads of Choo's paw to decide just how deep the cut was. Little Choo gave a shuddering cry, and Ellie burst into tears. 'A stitch I'm afraid. Yes, definitely. It's gone very deep and won't heal without help.'

Ellie, when she saw the blood and the needle and the thread, clutched hold of Valentine's arm. 'Oh, my God! Will she come through it?'

Valentine, entrenched in veterinary mode, answered sharply, 'Of course. I'm giving her some antibiotic as there's a mite of infection there.'

Little Choo's spirits flickered back to life now she'd been stitched and the immediate pain was over with. That was until her antibiotic injection, which frightened her all over again. When she was handed back to Ellie, she cheered up.

'Please, Miss Eustace, she must *not* go out in the garden for a few days, no matter how tempted you are by the warm weather. I want this wound keeping as clean as possible. In the house but not outside, right? If she begins limping again bring her straight back. Otherwise there's no need to make a return visit.'

Ellie looked up at him, her eyes glowing with admiration. 'Are you sure I don't need to come, just to make certain?'

'Absolutely. A dab with some antiseptic on a piece of cotton wool or with a cotton bud might be helpful, but don't let it soak. I want it keeping dry. There we are, Choo, off you go. What a brave kitty you are.'

Ellie put her back in her carrier, gushing thank-yous to Valentine for his skill. Kate went to type the details in the computer. Valentine had placed a mirror above the computer – no doubt so he could take a surreptitious check of his appearance while entering data – and through the mirror Kate saw Ellie give Valentine a kiss right on his lips.

'Thank you so much, Mr Dedic. I'm sorry I was such a softie.' Her face stayed close to his as she whispered something to him.

'No need to apologize, you were worried.' He nodded.

She nodded too, picked up the carrier with Choo inside it and went off, thanking Valentine again as she went. But Kate, turning away from the computer screen, saw the wink she gave him and Valentine saw she had and looked away. So, Kate thought, I'm right, then. They are seeing each other.

That night Kate asked Mia what she thought about the situation. 'You see, I know Nina and I know how badly disturbed she is, and how often she's had to tolerate Valentine having affairs, and here he is having another one, and I *know* he is, and Nina's only been back with him for a matter of weeks.'

'Look, Kate, it never does to interfere between married people. All that it does is cause trouble and you'll be left in the middle, being loathed by both sides. It just doesn't do.'

'But—'

'Believe me. I know I'm right.'

'I feel so sorry for her. She has no friends, no one to turn to.'

'Her having no friends is not your fault. You've lots of friends but that's because you put effort in, like you must with friends, keeping contact and things. She's got to do the same.'

'He's a . . . well, I don't know what he is actually, because as a vet he's so thoughtful and so talented, and yet as a person I despise him.'

Mia finished the last of her cider, put her glass down and wagged her finger at Kate. 'Just watch *you* don't get involved with him. He's lethal, take my word for it.'

Kate had to laugh. 'Oh, Mia! You're so right. How is it you see so clearly about things? I always get so involved I can't see straight at all.'

'Age. That's what it is. Experience. I used to work in an art shop where the manager thought he was God's gift to women. God's gift! Huh! Why, I can't imagine. He was weedy, chinless and slimy, with a kind of piping voice that was very irritating.

Absolutely ghastly. Always ready to pat your hand or squeeze your shoulder, and if you passed something to him he would hold your fingers for longer than necessary. Then one day he patted my bottom and I slapped his face. After that my life at work was hell.' Mia shuddered. 'It crossed my mind to pay him back by telling his wife what he'd done. She was at least a head taller than him, big busted, big bottomed, with a voice like an army sergeant major. The idea of the two of them ever . . . well, anyway, you know what I mean. But I bet if I'd told her what he'd done to me she'd have defended him to the very last and claimed I was lying, and it would have been me with the broken jaw not him.'

'Hmmm. Trouble is, Valentine is so attractive.'

'I know. I've met him. He is. Blast him. He's got everything.'

There was a hint of longing in Mia's voice that made Kate say tentatively, 'Since Dad died . . . I wouldn't mind, you know, if ever you found someone . . . I'd be delighted for you. I'm not meaning you need my permission, that's not what I'm saying, I just don't want you to consider my feelings. You won't, will you?'

'Find someone? I might. I may meet the love of my life . . .'

That phrase, 'love of my life', echoed in Kate's mind, the very phrase she'd used when thinking of Scott.

'. . . then again I might not. If I do I would take the plunge. Can't afford to look happiness in the face and reject it. Living a life of regret ever after never does.' As an afterthought she added firmly, 'But not till you've qualified.'

Kate felt mean and small in the face of such sacrifice. 'Look Mia—'

Mia held up her hand to stop her speaking. 'I mean it.'

'*Please*, listen. He may walk into the Gallery tomorrow. If he does, and you really want him, don't, whatever you do, wait till I've qualified, I couldn't bear it.'

Mia smiled. She stood, picked up her glass and Kate's, and headed towards the kitchen. She hesitated, then turned back to say, 'Thank you for saying what you did about not needing your permission. You never know, Monday might be the first day of the rest of my life. You're a dear girl. Very dear.' She grinned and winked, then disappeared.

Chapter 4

They'd grown accustomed to bright hot days and sweltering nights when sleep was almost impossible, and the following Monday morning promised to be exactly the same as it had been ever since Kate came back. A hot summer they'd been promised and a hot summer they were getting.

Joy's first job that day was opening every available window. They'd had mosquito netting fitted to each window that not only allowed the fresh air in, or as fresh as was possible considering the temperature, but kept the bugs out and the animals in. She glanced at the thermometer and saw it was already registering 80°F, 'Already! Hell's bells!'

Scott came in through the back door. 'I heard that,' he shouted.

'It's eighty degrees! If it's that now, what's it going to be by lunch-time?'

'This is normal where I come from. In fact, quite cool. Ask Mungo for air conditioning. The animals would love it, and so would the clients. But let me be there when you ask, then I can witness Mungo having one of his fabled explosions.' He laughed and she joined in.

'You're not being fair. The expenses of running a practice like this, with everything of the highest quality, including the staff, is enormous. I don't wonder he explodes about money.'

'Oh, yes? The partners are making money like there's no tomorrow. I know – I'm married to one.'

'OK. OK. Now, how is Scott this morning?'

'Full of life, thanks. And you?'

'Very happy. Duncan is thoroughly enjoying his job, working

as he does now in an office full of like-minded people, which makes life wonderful, so I'm happy, too.'

'Good! Give me my list.'

While he studied it, Joy watched him, thinking that marriage had mellowed him. 'Your day with Kate went all right?'

'Absolutely fine, thanks. Everyone loved seeing her again; she's very popular.'

'She is.' There was a cautionary note in Joy's voice which made Scott look at her. 'You're not . . . ?'

'No, to whatever it is you're asking. Hadn't you noticed I'm a married man?' He pulled out from his open-necked shirt a heavy gold chain; threaded onto it was his gold wedding ring. 'I can't wear it when I'm working, so I put it on this chain of Zoe's. OK? Never worn jewellery before but I do now.' Scott fingered the ring a moment before replacing it inside the neck of his shirt.

'Well, yes. You are. I just wondered.'

'Wonder no more. Right. I'm off. I'll have her for a week, if you want. Anytime she prefers farm practice.'

'I know. She's with Virginia this week.'

'God help her, then. Bye.'

Virginia had picked Kate up from the flat so there was no need to call in at the practice. She never popped in to collect her list, considering it a social requirement that had nothing at all to do with her work. She could bring up her list of calls on her laptop and get on with the job. She also loathed having a student. Always had done. Student equalled spy, and she hated that. Virginia considered herself an excellent vet, and Kate presented a challenge because she seemed more entrenched in the practice than herself. Knew more about everyone, including the clients, and, above all, was well liked, which Virginia had to admit she wasn't. Tolerated perhaps, but not well liked, and certainly not loved, like Scott and Colin and Mungo and Rhodri and, of course, Valentine.

'I'm sorry, I didn't catch what you said.'

Kate repeated her question. 'Where are we going first? I haven't seen the list as you picked me up.'

'It's not necessary for all this face-to-face first thing. Best get on with the work. We're going first to see Bernard Wilson's llama.'

'Oh! Right. Old Gert. She's a lovely old body.'

'No, she isn't a "lovely old body". She's a sad, depressed, lonely old thing, greatly in need of companionship. I wish he'd give her to someone who has llamas, then at least she'd be with her own kind.'

'You have a point there. But Bernard Wilson loves her.'

The gearbox growled as Virginia tussled with the car, wishing she had an automatic. 'Loves her! What's that got to do with anything? The needs of the animal come first.'

'Of course, but—'

'But nothing. She's old anyway. Bernard probably wants me to put her down. Best thing, too.'

Kate burst into protest. 'Put her down? Old Gert? Whatever for?'

Virginia snorted with derision at Kate's indignation. 'I'm telling you, if Gert could think, which she can't, that's exactly what she'd want. Poor old Gert indeed.'

Knowing she was committing a cardinal sin by comparing one vet with another, Kate couldn't stop herself from saying, 'Scott wouldn't say that, nor would Dan. They'd solve it somehow.'

'How?'

'Well, I haven't really thought about it. Llamas are hard to come by, so maybe a companion of some other kind would be a good idea.'

Virginia pulled into Bernard Wilson's yard, and the peaceful morning, filled with hot sun and the countryside shimmering in the heat, was shattered by the barking of Bernard's beagles. They now occupied state-of-the-art kennels, a vast improvement on the condition they were in when Rhodri and Dan first came upon them. A litter of puppies rushed to the fence enclosing their play area, happily trying to bark and look angry.

Kate smiled and, poking her finger through the wire, chucked them under their chins, getting her finger thoroughly slobbered over. The row of seven eager puppies, with their bright eyes and wagging tails, made a joyous picture.

'Aren't they lovely? He's doing really well with them now, and getting quite a name as a reliable breeder. Mia told me he has a waiting list for puppies, which is excellent news.'

'Who's Mia?' Virginia asked without a scrap of interest in her voice.

Kate stood up. 'She's my stepmother and I couldn't have a better. She's great.'

'Mmm.' Virginia called out in her huge voice, 'Bernard! Bernard! We're here. Where's Gert?'

But it was Bernard's sister Hannah who appeared in the doorway of the farm kitchen. 'Bernard's gone to the market. There's only me.' She was big and jovial and welcoming and made everyone she met smile.

Not Virginia, though. 'Come to see Gert. How is she?'

'Still limping. She's still in the stable. Thought it best, as she's a devil to catch when she knows it's the vet. Come to think of it, she's a devil to catch any old time.'

She led them to the last stable in the row. At one time they were dilapidated and ready for tumbling down, but the arrival of Hannah had brought about massive improvements to the farm buildings as well as the house, and now they were almost fit for a human being as well as animals.

'Here we are. Hello, Gert. Look who's come to see you.'

Gert stood aloof, staring at the group in the doorway with a haughty look.

'You know Kate?'

Hannah turned to smile at her. 'I know Kate, yes. I hear you're doing excellently at college, Kate.'

Kate smiled. 'I try.'

'Well, then, you can give us an opinion, can't she, Virginia?'

Taken by surprise Virginia said, 'Of course. Let's hear what you have to say, Kate.' She leaned against the stable door, arms folded, waiting for this much-admired person to make a fool of herself.

'Which foot is it, Hannah?'

40

'Right front.'

Kate hadn't the slightest knowledge of the anatomy of a llama, but common sense told her they didn't limp for fun nor to draw attention to themselves.

'Could I see Gert take a few steps?'

She was wearing a bright-red halter and Hannah took her matching lead down from the stable wall, hooked it on and led her out into the cobbled yard.

She was certainly limping. It appeared her front right foot was almost too tender to put any weight on. Kate stopped her and, talking gently to her, lifted her bad foot up so she could examine it.

She examined all four of her feet and then said, after taking a deep breath, 'It's my opinion, for what it's worth, that she needs her nails trimming. Simple as that, especially that right front foot.'

Kate had seen hate come into someone's eyes and be instantly subdued, but never with such venom as in Virginia's just then. Her eyes widened, her mouth opened and shut, and then, swallowing as discreetly as possible, she said, 'In that case, go get my clippers from the car.' She didn't move a muscle. Not one.

Kate said, 'Do you think I'm right, then?'

'We'll see.'

For one dreadful moment Kate thought she might insist that she do the job; it was a skill she hadn't yet mastered. However, Virginia took the clippers from her when she held them out for her to take. While Kate held the lead, she hefted Gert's foot up and started work. Deep in the middle of her right foot she also found a sturdy piece of gravel that must have been hurting her in addition to the problems caused by her long nails.

Mercifully, Hannah didn't even attempt to catch Kate's eye, for which she was grateful. Virginia did a wonderful job of trimming and almost before they knew it the job was done and Kate was asked to give Gert a short walk round to see the improvement. She was a little tentative at first but soon plucked up her courage when she found it didn't hurt any more.

41

Hannah was grinning with delight and relief. 'There we are, Gert, your Bernard will be glad to see you walking like that. No reason is there, Virginia, why she shouldn't go out in the field now?'

'No reason at all, Hannah. I caught it before there was a chance of any infection setting in caused by rubbing.'

'Thank you very much for sorting her out. Bernard's been getting quite worried about her.'

'All in a day's work. Be seeing you. Invoice at the end of the month.'

Kate noticed she always said that as her indication she was leaving.

'Right.' Hannah stood for a moment and watched Kate and Virginia walking away.

Before they reached the car, Bernard's old van rumbled cautiously into the yard. It was, in fact, part van and part animal transporter, created with more enthusiasm than skill by Bernard himself. The back of the van had been doubled in height, making a very unstable and thoroughly illegal vehicle, but one to which Bernard was deeply attached.

He jumped out, sweating and crumpled, shouting, 'I've got her a pal.'

Hannah shouted back, 'A pal? What is it?'

A very wide plank of wood, strengthened by Bernard in times past, was propped carefully to the back of the van, thus making a sloping exit for whatever animal was inside. Bernard latched it with tremendous care to the back, knotting and re-knotting the ropes to make sure it wouldn't move.

'Daisy! Come on, then, Daisy!' Bernard opened the back of the van and they saw him take hold of a rope. Gradually, and with great care, something emerged. It was a llama, a young, very pretty llama, with huge, appealing liquid brown eyes, startled and afraid by emerging into the bright sunlight and new surroundings. He walked her towards them.

Kate had to say something. 'Bernard, where did you get her from? It's a she, I hope.'

'She is. Some stupid bas—' He glanced at Virginia and said, 'Sorry, some stupid fool brought her to the market, hoping he'd find a buyer. I knew he wouldn't and I also knew old Gert needed a friend, so I pretended to be indifferent and I've got her for a song.'

Hannah snorted her disbelief. 'I bet! Well, anyway, she looks pretty enough, and only young. Let's see how Gert takes to her.'

She was so young that she tried getting milk from Gert's udder, who seemed to recognize what a baby she was and didn't protest. 'My God! She is so young. You fool.' Hannah said to her brother.

Bernard muttered, 'Don't you fret, old Gert'll get to like her.'

And old Gert did. She nuzzled Daisy, and the two of them took an instant shine to each other.

'See! What did I say?'

'I'll tell you what I say: it'll be Bernard who'll be up feeding the poor thing, morning, noon and night, and not Hannah. I've too much to do. At least the stable's big enough for them both. We'll leave them in there today.' She turned to speak to Virginia, who'd remained silent ever since Daisy had shown herself. 'What do you feed young llamas on? Do you know?'

'I do not. I wonder how she came to be away from her mother so young? I'll get someone at the practice to ring the zoo. They'll know what to feed her. They'll ring you back, OK? I'm glad you've got her, Bernard, she's just what Gert needs. Though it might be difficult to keep little Daisy alive. I'll just have a quick look at her. Stethoscope, Kate.'

Virginia examined her and found her fit and well. 'She's in good shape, but milk is of the essence at the moment. Don't want her to dehydrate, nor fall by the wayside from lack of nourishment. I'll ring the practice right now.'

While Virginia made her call, the other three made a fuss of Daisy and Gert, and then, rather reluctantly, decided to put them both in the stable to allow them to bond.

Curious, Kate asked, 'Bernard why the names Gert and Daisy?'

'An old music hall act my mother loved, and Gert seemed to suit her when we first got her. Now we've got both of 'em, I thought, what else? It's got to be Gert and Daisy, see. Leave the top door open.'

Virginia switched off her mobile. 'They'll be in touch shortly. The zoo will ring you direct, so I suggest you get paper and pen ready and make notes. It's vital to get it right. Must go.'

Kate picked up the stethoscope and the clippers and headed for the car. She turned round to wave as they reached it and Hannah, while Virginia was getting in, gave Kate the thumbs-up. They both smiled.

Virginia viciously flung the car into gear and drove off with wheels spinning furiously and dust flying. 'The arrival of Daisy has not made me forget what you did to me in there, humiliating me like that. I was looking for joint pain, never thought about feet needing trimming. I don't know why. But you managed it, didn't you? Mmm? Showing me up.'

'I didn't intend to but at the time, Gert, not your ego nor my ego for that matter, was uppermost. Just one of those things. I went for the simplest solution and it worked.'

The rushing sound of Virginia's breath being forced through her narrowed nostrils was not pleasant. 'If I'm going to spend the whole of this week being shot down by a year three student I shall not be very nice to know. So just watch your step.'

Kate casting caution to the four winds, answered back. 'So if I come up with a solution I've to let you make an even bigger fool of yourself by letting you make a mistake? Not that I know better than you – after all, I've not had enough experience to be able to do that time after time – *but* I can't allow an animal to suffer, can I?'

An emergency stop brought the car to a halt and almost sent Kate through the windscreen. 'Are you saying that I am in the habit of making major mistakes?'

Kate spread her hands on her knees, palms up. 'Of course not. I just happened to strike lucky, that's all. It was a simple matter of

44

you overlooking the obvious, anyone could have done it and I'm sorry if I upset you. In future I shall ask for a conference, shall I?'

'I only confer with a qualified vet, OK? Let that be an end to it.'

She shoved the car into gear and they roared away with Kate feeling battered and Virginia cursing the day Joy asked her to take Kate with her for a week. Then she remembered that smart little pub on the top road before Lord Askew's and the thought of it went a long way to soothing her temper. 'I need coffee.'

'There's a nice café down by the King George Bridge.'

'I mean real coffee, well served and worth the effort. We'll call in the White Hart. My treat.'

'Oh! Right, thanks. I've heard of it but I've never been in there.'

The car lurched round the turn-off to it and Kate rather thought she might be lucky to survive the week in one piece. She'd always thought Scott's driving was hazardous but in comparison to Virginia's, it was like being driven by one's great-aunt. She thought of Scott and wondered whom he would be visiting today. Might be an idea to ask Joy to give her a week with him, she was sure she would. The prospect made her pulse race and she longed for it to be Scott taking her to the White Hart, where they could indulge themselves with veterinary talk and coffee. For a brief moment she pictured his slender hands and his hair, which had responded so quickly to the strong sun, developing blond streaks that only enhanced his good looks. A half-smile crossed her lips. God! She'd have to stop this.

Virginia flung out of the car and hurried across to the open door of the pub. Up here the wind was blowing slightly, taking the edge off the intense heat. Kate gazed up at the vivid blue sky and saw a hawk hovering high in the sky, so she waited for it to swoop . . . and it did, hurtling to the ground like a rocket. It paused only for a moment on the ground and then was up and away with its prey tightly gripped.

Virginia was already seated and giving her order when she got inside. 'Caffe latte for two, please. That all right, Kate?'

Kate nodded. 'This is very nice. It's just right, isn't it?' She looked round the delightful lounge area and found it very appealing. The huge open fireplace was stacked with logs ready for the winter, its stone exterior covered with genuine warming pans and real horse brasses; nothing masquerading as antique. The plush carpet and comfortable chairs were so tasteful, and the old hunting cartoons on the walls well worth studying.

Virginia showed pleasure in the fact that Kate appreciated the place just as she did. 'It is, isn't it? I found it quite by chance a month or so ago. In winter that log fire will be fantastic. I like this kind of thing, much better than modern chrome and plastic. Genuine and old and graceful. How they make it pay, I do not know. They have five bedrooms upstairs, they showed me round the first time I came, which are gorgeous. Just gorgeous. Not what you'd expect when you see the building from the outside. Perfect for a clandestine affair.' She laughed but her pleasure didn't reach her eyes.

As it happened, Virginia was sitting with her back to the small reception desk and the staircase so she didn't see two people coming down the stairs. But Kate did. And she froze. Valentine with Eleanor Eustace. They both looked very pleased with themselves.

She pretended to sniff to give herself an excuse to bend down and bury her head in her bag searching for a tissue. What if they'd seen her? Though she guessed they hadn't, they'd been far too absorbed in each other. She'd been right after all, then, and now she was a real live witness to it. What should she do?

To keep Virginia's attention so she wouldn't see the two of them leaving via the front door, Kate told her a story about Scott, who was once flattened against a cowshed wall by a bull. By the end of it the two of them were laughing hilariously, which revealed a different side to Virginia. Kate determined to make more of an effort with her. But the thought occurred to her as they left that she was now an accomplice in this illicit affair of Valentine's because she'd just protected his secret. Damn it!

She had the idea that Virginia would enjoy Lord Askew's,

would feel she was in her own kind of class. Kate dabbed her face
with a tissue to get rid of the sweat, brushed her hair, now so long
it was down by her shoulder blades, and followed Virginia, but
only after she'd sprayed herself with some perfume called Very
Irresistible that Mia had bought her last Christmas.

Lord Askew was waiting. It had been two years since Kate had last
seen him and he was still a mountain of a man who desperately
needed to lose weight. His face fell when he saw it was Virginia
who'd come to attend one of his precious horses. But it lit up
again when he saw Kate.

'My dear Kate. What a long time since I saw you last. How are
you? Not qualified yet, I guess.' He pumped her hand up and
down enthusiastically, patted her shoulder, and then put his arm
round her and whispered, 'Pity you're not qualified and then I'd
have two vets for the price of one.' And His Lordship roared with
laughter at his own joke. Then recollecting how much this visit
was going to cost him, and not attempting to hide his
disappointment, he said grumpily to Virginia, 'I was expecting
Dan or Scott, why are they not available?'

Virginia worked hard to control her temper. 'Dan's on holiday
and Scott has a full list of calls today. I am well experienced with
horses.'

'Maybe, but they've got instinct, too, and I don't know which
is more important. However, I'm very concerned about Galaxy.
He's precious to my daughter and he's doing brilliantly, right at his
peak. She wants – well, I do, too – only the very best for him.
Come and see.'

Virginia followed him meekly into Galaxy's luxurious stable.
Both she and Kate saw immediately that this horse was in distress.
Occasionally he snorted and stamped his feet, moving restlessly
with anxiety and fear, and sweating copiously. He was a splendid
piece of horseflesh; even someone unaccustomed to appraising
horses could see that. With his magnificent head and wonderful
physique, Kate could see how very valuable Galaxy was, not just
money-wise but emotionally, too. You didn't spend hours and

hours training such a horse without becoming deeply attached to him. Kate felt nothing but pity for Galaxy as he waited, trembling, to be examined, and she fervently hoped Virginia would make the correct diagnosis.

Chapter 5

On the Tuesday Virginia called again at the flat to pick Kate up. It was hotter than ever and Kate had the distinct feeling that she'd walked into a sauna when she went out onto the pavement.

'My God! It's hotter than ever, and it's so early.'

Virginia didn't answer.

'Not in a mood for speaking? Well, it is hot.'

'I don't have moods, and you'd do well to remember that.'

'Sorry. I thought everyone had a mood some time in their lives.'

'Well, I'm the exception. Right?'

Kate mentally shrugged her shoulders. Obviously it wasn't the day for casual conversation. Oh, well. 'First call? Can I take a look?'

'Feel free.'

Kate scanned the list. 'Oh, help. Lord Askew's again. Galaxy.'

'No other. I've tried antibiotics as a precaution – obviously they haven't worked. I can't stand him still being in pain.'

'Should we ring Scott? Ask him what he thinks?'

Virginia turned to Kate and gave her a twisted, angry smile. 'Has it never occurred to you that I might be able to manage equally as well as a bloke?'

'Well, apparently you can't. If things are going well Lord Askew never asks for a return visit. He thinks we charge more than enough for the first visit.'

'Do you have any idea how annoying you are?'

'I didn't know I was.'

49

'Everlastingly reminding me of my mistakes. It's a very annoying habit.'

'Sorry.'

'Just keep your mouth shut, especially when we're at Lord Askew's. Right?'

'Of course. I shan't say a word.'

And she didn't because Galaxy was showing no improvement, and Lord Askew had summoned his daughter, Lady Mary, from Wiltshire to see what she thought. Virginia greeted her with excessive enthusiasm and received a broadside from Lady Mary.

'I haven't driven here this morning for social chit-chat. You saw this horse yesterday, gave him antibiotics and there is absolutely no improvement whatsoever. A child could see that, so what are you going to do about it?' It must have been her superior tone of voice and her upper-class accent which made her attack feel all the more intense.

Virginia was boiling by the time Lady Mary had finished speaking and she replied in kind. 'An imbecile knows that antibiotics take time to work. One day is by no means sufficient to decide whether or not they have been effective, Lady Mary.'

She held out her hand to Kate and, without a word passing between them, the stethoscope was handed to Virginia. She gave Galaxy another intensive examination. There was a deathly hush in the stable yard. Leaning over the half-door were Lord Askew and his head groom Gavin, and inside with Kate and Virginia were Lady Mary and one of her brothers.

It was the brother who spoke first. 'Well, what do you think the problem is today?' It was the sarcasm in his voice which irritated Kate and Virginia, and Kate almost spoke, then clamped her mouth shut, recollecting her promise before they arrived. Virginia had no such inhibitions.

'He has a temperature still, which is a little surprising, but I don't honestly think he is any worse. We'll give him a couple more days on the antibiotics and . . . let's see, today is Tuesday so I'll come back tomorrow unless there's any worsening of the situation, in which case give us a call.'

Virginia handed the stethoscope to Kate and made to leave.

Lord Askew said, 'Invoice at the end of the month.' His clever imitation of Virginia's voice left no one in doubt who he was mocking. He opened the stable door to let her through and as she passed him he said, 'If all this goes desperately wrong I'll have Mungo Price hung out to dry, right?'

The threat didn't appear to rattle Virginia at all. In fact, she seemed even more positive that she was doing the right thing. 'That won't be at all necessary. Good morning to you all.' She bit back her usual parting shot about the invoice and she and Kate headed for the car.

Kate turned to wave goodbye and was faced by three grim, unresponsive faces. Her wave died a death before she'd done it. A deep feeling of dread stirred inside her and she wondered if Virginia really was working on the right lines, but daren't say anything which might put her expertise in doubt. After all, the Askews lived and breathed horses, and Virginia didn't cover much of the equine work of the practice. But with Dan being away . . .

Virginia drove out of the stable yard with dust and gravel flying off her spinning wheels. They just missed the left-hand stone pillar as they left, and Kate opened her window to help cool her down, but Virginia wasn't having it.

'I have the air conditioning on, close the window.'

'I don't want to interfere, but—'

'If you want to live don't say it. I know what I'm doing. What I can't stand is the arrogance of that lot.'

Tentatively, Kate reminded her that the Askews were obsessive about their horses and maybe did have something to contribute.

'There you go again, belittling me. Hell! Where is it we're going next?'

'The Parsons at Applegate Farm.'

'Damn! It's the other way, isn't it? I've missed the turning.' She swung round in the road and roared off again, making Kate feel sick.

When they arrived at Applegate she stood in the lane, glad to be out in the air, and took several deep breaths to calm her queasy stomach. Past experience made her get her boots out from the back.

Virginia snapped, 'No need for boots, surely?'

'Haven't you been here before?'

'As it happens, I haven't.'

'Well, unless there's been some dramatic changes we'll need them.'

'Oh! Right. Their bull OK to handle?'

'Haven't seen it since I went to college, but I do know that Phil is its best friend and he'll be able to handle it.'

'Mmm. Well, if that's the case we might be OK.'

Kate heard a hint of a tremor in Virginia's voice. 'He'll be tied up. Don't worry.'

'Who said I was worrying? My God, who's that?'

'Phil's wife Blossom.'

'She looks like the local tart.'

Blossom was wearing pale lemon shorts and a matching tank-top with the thinnest of shoestring shoulder straps. Her hair was tied up by a narrow length of diamante-encrusted yellow ribbon which sparkled in the bright sun, and she was in what she called her 'full warpaint', the blue eyeshadow having been applied even more boldly than usual.

'Hi there. I think we haven't met. I'm Blossom Parsons. Why, it's Kate! How are you?' Kate was treated to a great hug and lots of kissing, but Virginia got a straightforward handshake.

'Blossom, this is Virginia Havelock.'

'How do you do? I'm sorry Phil isn't here this morning – he's got another hospital appointment. We've called you for our bull, Star. Gashed himself quite badly letting off steam in the field. Phil thinks some stitching might be needed. He's hardly slept all night for worrying. I just wish he were here but it couldn't be helped.'

Star was standing disconsolately in his stall and scarcely noticed the three of them entering his kingdom. There were two strong ropes tied from his nose ring to two big no-nonsense rings in the stone wall of the stall, so he had no freedom to move or toss his head.

'Phil tied him up before he went. Takes no risks after what happened to Scott and Hamish.'

'Kate told me,' Virginia said, inwardly gasping at the beauty of him. She had expected, from the state of the farm yard, that it would be a poor specimen of a bull. To be greeted by such magnificence was beyond belief. 'He is fantastic. I can't believe it. Just fantastic. What a splendid animal.' She reached over the wall and patted his richly coloured flank. 'Now, young man, where have you hurt yourself?'

Blossom answered on Star's behalf. 'On his other side, down his back leg. It's about six inches long but very deep, and it bled a lot. There's like a flap of skin, sort of hanging.' Blossom blanched at the thought and grabbed the top of the gate to steady herself. 'You wouldn't think I'd been a nurse, would you? But when it's one of the animals . . . Star's very touchy about it. I don't think we've brought you out on a fool's errand.'

'Mrs Parsons—'

'Everyone calls me Blossom.'

'Blossom, then. It's such a pleasure to see such a wonderful beast, it's worth coming to see him even if he doesn't need stitches.' Very slowly, talking to him all the time, Virginia climbed over the gate and went to his head. Running her hands over him, caressing him, soothing him, she ducked under the ropes and made her way down the other side of him, slowly, slowly, with no sudden movements, and examined the cut.

'Kate,' she whispered softly, 'moving slowly till you're out of the byre, go to the car and get my bag of stuff. Blossom, it needs stitches quite definitely. I'm going to give him a mild sedative to calm him and a local anaesthetic.'

Blossom looked appalled. 'He's never needed a sedative before. Phil'll have a fit. He's always so easy to handle.'

'For Phil maybe, but not when I'm going to stitch him. It's a jagged tear, it'll take time and we don't want to leave scars if we can help it. He's young and beautiful, aren't you, Star?'

Kate soon returned with Virginia's enormous 'bag of stuff'. Star could just see Kate out of the corner of his eye and gave her a baleful look. She was almighty glad he was within his stall and doubly tied up. She gave Virginia ten out of ten for courage.

'Kate, don't climb in. It's best if I work alone. Hand me the stuff when I ask for it.'

Silence filled the byre while Virginia injected and cleansed and stitched, moving steadily and soothingly so as not to antagonize Star. When she'd finished she cleared up and moved cautiously to get out of the stall. A final pat and a little chat and she was out.

Kate breathed an audible sigh of relief. 'That was brilliant.'

Blossom reached out to stroke Star. 'What a good boy you've been, what a good boy.'

At that moment in came Phil. Kate was surprised to find he'd dispensed with the balaclava he normally wore, and though he looked odd to her, it was interesting to see his face and his eyes for the first time. The scarring the flames had caused which he'd always kept hidden under his balaclava, had obviously been sufficiently reduced to make him feel comfortable for people to see it. One of his eyes had an eyelid which the plastic surgeon had made look almost normal but not quite, and he still had red scarring down his cheek on one side, so he wasn't perfect but at the same time very acceptable.

'Hello, Phil. It's Kate. Remember me?'

'Yes. How's Star?' Phil turned abruptly to look at Virginia. He didn't bother with introductions; he was too concerned about his beloved bull.

'I've given him a sedative and a local anaesthetic, stitched him up and, all being well, he's going to be fine. He should stay in here—'

'But he goes out in the field every day. He loves it, gets rid of his energy. You should see him when he gallops about, you can't take your eyes off him.'

'Maybe, but I don't want him galloping about and possibly disturbing my stitches. We don't want him scarred, do we? Not when he's such a fine animal.'

Phil climbed over the gate and went to undo Star's ropes,

examined the stitching and then put his arms round Star's neck, muttering sweet nothings into his ear.

Phil's casual handling of Star amazed Virginia and she watched, fascinated. Reluctantly moving away, she said, 'Right then, we'll leave you. If you have any worries, ring the practice and leave me a message, OK? Invoice at the end of the month.'

Kate picked up Virginia's bag and the two of them went back to the car.

'I see what you mean, Kate, about the yard. Is it always as mucky as that?'

'Oh, yes. Dan managed to persuade Phil to clean and distemper the cow byres in the interests of hygiene, but the yard never improves. He's too busy talking to his animals and giving them treats. He only farms because he loves it, not to make money.' As they got back into the car, Kate said confidentially, 'I have heard, though I don't know for definite, that he owns the Applegate Caravan Park and that's why he can indulge himself.'

'Strange couple. Very strange. Right, back to the practice and we'll have lunch en famille, so to speak.'

'Oh, right. You don't usually.'

'Well, we will today. Do you have a problem with that?'

Kate glanced at Virginia's profile and realized she was worried. She guessed it was Galaxy that was causing her concern.

By the time they got back, Colin, Joy and Valentine were in the staffroom munching their lunches. A new delicatessen had opened up just down the road and, from the packaging, Kate knew that's where they'd bought their food.

'I think I'll try the new place, too. Shall I get something for you, Virginia?'

'I've got my own, thanks.' Out of her bag she brought a small pack of sandwiches, spread a rather smart linen napkin out on her knee and began to eat.

'Good morning?' asked Joy.

Virginia looked up. 'Yes, thanks. Busy, you know, as always. Met Blossom Parsons for the first time. Odd pair, aren't they?'

'Yes, but we love 'em.' They all nodded at Joy's assessment of them. 'Great friends of the practice, those two. He's so much better since his operations. Smartened himself up no end.'

Kate agreed. 'I'd heard but I was still surprised when I saw him. His face isn't perfect, but they've done a brilliant job.'

Rather too casually, Virginia enquired if Scott was coming in for lunch.

Colin replied that he did sometimes but then sometimes he went home to Zoe instead. 'Besotted, he is. Absolutely besotted. Never thought that Barleybridge would lose its very own Romeo, but that's just what's happened.'

Kate abruptly snapped, 'I'll go and get my sandwich. Won't be long.'

'There'll be a queue by now.' But Joy was too late with her advice, for the door had already closed on Kate's heels.

If Colin – unobservant, wrapped-up-in-himself Colin – had observed that Scott was besotted, then it must be true, Kate thought. Oh, hell. What absolute hell. She wanted to spit and swear and weep and gnash her teeth. This was a fate worse than death itself. She slammed open the door of the delicatessen and went to inspect the serried ranks of sandwiches. She chose the least attractive, cheapest pack of egg and cress to serve as a hairshirt. It was all she deserved. Falling for Scott all over again when he'd married for love and not because of Oscar! She was a fool. Damn and blast. It served her right. What she'd imagined as a marriage of convenience had in fact been a love match, but then she had had a warning when she'd seen the expression on Zoe's face when she'd smiled at Scott, and she'd not heeded it. She slapped her money down on the counter, spotted some particularly gooey cream cakes standing invitingly beside the cash desk and hurriedly snatched one to add to her bill.

Back in the staffroom, Scott had joined the lunch party. Joy had made coffee for everyone and they were happily chatting together as they always did; comparing notes, laughing, joking, talking about holidays and wondering how Dan and Rose were getting on with their three little babies in a gite in Northern France.

'How they'll manage with a six-month-old, an eighteen-month-old and one not quite three, I do not know. Rather them than me,' Joy stated emphatically.

But Kate ate silently. There was the love of her life sitting not more than five feet away from her, chortling about some comment of Colin's and thankfully oblivious to her pain. Her heart was so appallingly stressed by Colin's remark she found she'd nothing to say about anything. Indeed, she might never smile again, ever.

Not even when Scott caught her eye and smiled at her could she reciprocate with even the briefest of smiles. Damn him. Just damn him. The thought of a whole afternoon with dear Virginia felt like crucifixion on a grand scale. When her food had gone down and she'd drunk her coffee and begun to sweat with the closeness of the room and the general heat of the day, she couldn't take the pressure any longer. Standing up she said, 'It's too hot. I'll sit out on the old bench for a bit,' and plunged outside, glad to escape them all.

The sun was beating down. Even the seat itself was hot and she shuffled about trying to find a cooler spot on the wooden planks. There wasn't one, so she had to suffer, but the cool breeze coming down from the hills did help to calm her.

The back door opened and out came Colin. Surprisingly, he joined her on the seat. Looking up at the hills across from the car park, he said to no one in particular, 'It's true what I said about . . . you know . . . Scott. He has fallen madly in love and so has Zoe. It's not just Oscar which has brought them together. Best to steel yourself. You know, forget him. Your career's more important. You're too fine a person deliberately to break up a marriage, I'm quite sure about that. So do a complete about-turn, OK?' He stood up, still without looking at her, and walked away to his car.

As he disappeared out onto the main road, Scott emerged. 'Virginia said to say she's just coming. Keep out of this business about Galaxy. It's a hot potato, right?'

Kate shaded her eyes to look up at him and replied, 'I know. I'm really worried. There's something she's not seeing, I'm sure, and it's such a valuable horse.'

'It could blow up in her face. I'm concerned too.'

'Hadn't you better do something about it yourself? I'm not saying anything – I get my head bitten off if I do, and it's not my place to speak up, being a student – but you can.'

Scott patted her shoulder. 'I shall. You keep out of it, that's a good girl. Must go.'

Kate watched him dash away to his Land Rover. The heat didn't affect him in the slightest; in fact, he seemed to flourish in it, and she wished she did. Heat exhaustion was beginning to drain all her resolve and determination and, what was worse, making her say things which, in usual British summer temperatures, she would never dream of uttering. Blast Colin for his comments about Scott. She supposed it was for her own good, because he really cared. Well, thanks Colin, she thought, don't mention it again. You've made your point.

The door burst open and Virginia appeared. 'Feeling better?'

'Yes, thanks. Ready for off?'

'I am.'

As the afternoon progressed, the heat ground Kate down into a shadow of herself. Anything Virginia said she agreed to without a murmur of dissent and by six o'clock she longed for home and a shower and . . . well, time to think about Scott.

'This is our last call and I've no car to get home in. Is it possible you'll be going past my flat?' she said at the end of the day.

Virginia squealed into the yard at Tad Porter's, pulled up with brakes still squealing, and said, 'Am I such an ogre that you have to *ask* if I'll take you home? Naturally I will.'

'Sorry, sorry, shouldn't have said it. I just can't face going home on the bus, it's so hot.'

'I don't understand the impression people have of me. I know I'm abrupt but I am well-meaning. You can rely on me to take you home.'

She sprang out of the car and marched across to the farmhouse door. Connie came at her knock and declared Tad was in the rear cowshed, out the back, with her sick house cow. 'Put her in the back 'cos it's cooler there. And would you take him this drink before he passes out? Hand–milked, she is. I think it's mastitis but I keep her that clean I can't understand why she gets it.'

Virginia nodded to Connie, who went back inside out of the heat. One thing about old stone houses, they did keep cool on days like this.

The rear cowshed was a goodly walk from the farmhouse and they were glad to enter and feel the chill air on their skin. Tad was crouched on an upturned bucket smoking his pipe, patiently waiting for them.

'You've come.' He stood up, touching the peak of his cap.

Virginia greeted him with, 'Hello, Mr Porter,'

He peered at her through the gloom. 'Hello. I 'aven't 'ad the pleasure before. Why, Kate, didn't know you'd qualified. What a nice surprise. So you're . . . ?' He stared up at Virginia, his narrow, hollow-cheeked face looking even more gaunt than normal in the shade of the cowshed.

'I'm Virginia Havelock, the new farm vet at the practice. Come to see your sick house cow.'

Tad offered his hand in welcome. 'She's precious, is this one, Connie's favourite. Bluebell's the name. 'Ave a look. I've tried everything before we called you. Not much money in sheep at the moment. I think I'll 'ave to diversify, like old Bernard Wilson.' A slow grin spread across his face. 'Making a packet out of 'is dogs, is the chap. So don't find something expensive wrong with 'er, cause I can't afford your sort of bills. Sorry and all that. If there's not much hope and you decide to put her down to save me money, we'll tell Connie it was all too late. Not let on, eh?'

For some reason, even though Tad wasn't in her social bracket, which counted for a lot in Virginia's book, she'd taken a liking to Tad's honesty, so she patted his arm and smiled. 'We'll see. Ah! Here comes Connie.'

Tad swung round guiltily, thinking Virginia was teasing him but she wasn't. Connie came in to observe, carrying two bottles. From her apron pocket she took two plastic cups and handed them with the bottles to Virginia and Kate. She wiped the sweat from her face on the corner of her apron and said, 'Sorry. Just occurred to me you'll be thirsty, too. Homemade lemonade. Fresh today. Well, what do you think's wrong with my Bluebell?'

Kate drank and drank from her bottle, leaving the consultation entirely in Virginia's hands. Wow! That felt better. By the time she'd surfaced from her dehydration Virginia was saying, 'It is mastitis, her left quarter's in quite a bad way. Stitch in time, Tad, you know. Would have been better if you got help sooner. However, we'll try.'

After they'd treated Bluebell, Virginia undid her bottle top, poured some lemonade into her plastic cup and drank it down almost feverishly.

Connie watched her with satisfaction. 'I was right, you did need it. Take the rest with you. Now, will this mean another call?'

Virginia looked from one to the other, and eventually said, 'Kate, write down my mobile number. If there's no improvement – though I've packed her full of drugs and there should be – ring me on this number and I'll fit a visit in, but mum's the word.' She placed her index finger to her lips and grinned.

Tad protested. 'Don't want to do nowt illegal, like.'

'Like I said, mum's the word.'

She didn't say, 'Invoice at the end of the month', as she usually did, simply drank another cup of lemonade and asked Kate to pick up her bag before they went back up the field.

Before they got to the car Kate braved Virginia's wrath and said, 'Mungo'll explode when he knows what you've said. His favourite saying is, "We're not a charity."'

'He won't explode if he never knows. So mind you don't tell him, right? It's my decision.' She awarded Kate a grimace full of venom and Kate wished it were Saturday, when she'd finish shadowing Virginia. But it wasn't.

What made her say what she said next she would never know, she blamed it on the oppressive heat: 'Still, at least it proves you're human.'

About to start up the engine Virginia took her hand off the ignition key and, staring out of the window, said, 'That is just about the bitchiest thing anyone has ever said to me.'

'Well, you do exhibit a very hard exterior most of the time.'

'That's me. That's who I am, tough, unapproachable, but good at my job, OK? The clients can't have it every way – sweet and kind *and* clever at the job.'

Kate thought of Dan and decided to say how she always felt about him. 'Well, Dan is. He's very forceful, knows his own mind – speaks his own mind, come to that – but is always diplomatic and very kind. So far as equine work is concerned, he saved Galaxy's career with astute observation when he wasn't even at Lord Askew's to look at him; he'd gone to see a cow. That's how clever he is. So one can combine the two.'

'Can one indeed? Kindly leave my emotional life to me. It's obvious you're a little upstart, but seeing as we have to tolerate each other until Saturday we'll make up and be friends again. Right?'

They'd been heading towards the flat for about five minutes when Virginia asked right out of the blue, 'When is Dan back?'

'Next Monday.' After a pause Kate added, 'But Scott has lots of instinct and even Lord Askew acknowledges he knows what he's doing.'

She got no reply to her suggestion.

Chapter 6

Joy asked Mungo about air conditioning Wednesday lunch-time when, trying hard to be reasonable, the heat was really getting to her. She deliberately spoke up about it when other members of the staff were present, including Colin, Scott, Lesley and Annette.

Mungo had just put his head round the staffroom door to leave a message for Virginia, so he was in a hurry and not in the best of moods for new ideas.

'What about air conditioning?' Joy asked in a belligerent tone. 'It would benefit the animals and certainly help the staff. We're working under very difficult conditions in this heat.' She wiped her forehead with a tissue to emphasize her point.

The rest of Mungo exploded into the room. 'Air conditioning? What the blazes gave you that idea?'

'Surprise, surprise! The weather, believe it or not.'

'Open a few windows.'

'We've done that and we still can't breathe. The animals are feeling it, too.'

'Change in the weather at the weekend, colder and rain. Then we shan't need it.'

Scott decided to stir things with a big spoon. 'We're making money. Why can't we have it and make people's working lives that much more comfortable? Think about coming in—'

'This is the end of the matter. I've said the weather's changing, we'll be OK soon. Another few days. You'll see.'

Joy couldn't believe his intransigence. 'That's not the point. With all this global warming stuff, we're going to be getting hotter and hotter summers. The intensive care room has air conditioning. Couldn't we just extend it?' Joy got the bit between her teeth and followed that up with hands on hips and a toss of her head. 'All right for you. It doesn't seem to matter how hot it gets, you don't suffer, but the rest of us do. And the clients are complaining.'

'Joy!' Mungo thundered. 'No air conditioning. Right? I don't want to hear another word.' He left the room, slamming the door behind him.

'He might shut his ears to it but they *are* complaining. This isn't the last he's heard of it. Believe me.'

Colin said diplomatically, for he hated rows, 'Waiting time for small animals isn't all that long, is it now? Twenty minutes at the most.'

'Well, you can keep out of it, Colin. You don't have the soaring temperatures to contend with in your air-conditioned car. Lucky for some.'

Scott couldn't resist saying, 'I did tell you he wouldn't like it.'

'I sometimes think he's *driven* by accumulating money. That's all he judges things by.'

It was Scott who came up with the idea of getting Miriam on side. 'She knows just how to handle him. He's not aware she does, but she does.'

Joy thought about his idea for a moment and agreed he had hit the nail on the head. 'You have very few brilliant ideas, Scott, but that is one of them. Full marks. I'll go up to the flat right now and talk to her about it.'

Colin, who was just leaving the staffroom, whispered, 'I wouldn't, if I were you, he's dashing up there right now.' They listened for his footsteps on the stairs.

'He is. Blast it. I'll go later. I'll get us air conditioning if I have to resign over it.'

Scott got to his feet. 'Must be off. The last time you did that you came back to us. He might not take you back twice.'

'His Achilles heel is being unable to manage without me.' She smiled smugly. 'He'll have me back.'

Slyly Scott muttered, 'That Lesley is shaping up very nicely. She's exceedingly efficient, far too bright for a receptionist. I wonder what size shoes she takes?'

'I don't know. What do you mean?'

Scott suggested she might take exactly the same size as Joy.

Joy rolled up her morning newspaper, which happened to be handy since she'd been reading it during her lunch-hour, and chased Scott out into the corridor.

He nimbly avoided her blows and fled for the back door. 'Be seeing you!' he shouted as he left.

He had to smile at Joy's defeat. He'd warned her that the answer would be no, but she hadn't heeded him. It always surprised him that Mungo was, ninety-five per cent of the time, polite, considerate, urbane, helpful, sympathetic and could charm an angry, disappointed client quicker than anyone he knew, but the other five per cent could be the very devil.

This afternoon Scott was doing something he knew he shouldn't: interfering. Seriously interfering. Virginia had consulted him about Galaxy, which had cost her a great deal of emotional turmoil as she wasn't the kind of person who thought other people were cleverer than she herself. He'd been amused by her approach – subtle but also desperate.

'It's not that I'm flummoxed in any way by my diagnosis, that is sound, but even I understand Lord Askew is a valued client with a lot of social clout, so we need to tread very carefully, because the practice can't afford to lose him. But . . .'

'Yes?' Scott had said.

'I would appreciate another opinion. If Dan was here—'

'But he won't be for another week.'

'Exactly.'

'Shall I sneak in a visit without saying anything to anyone?' He'd tapped the side of his nose with his forefinger.

Her relief was all too evident. 'I would appreciate that. Not a word, though. Right?'

So here he was wandering off to Lord Askew's unofficially.

Quite by chance, he knew that the whole of the Askew tribe

were away at a family wedding, though he hadn't let on to Virginia, so he'd only have Gavin to witness his visit.

Galaxy was standing in his stable, head hanging down and looking very unwell.

'Don't like the look of this, Gavin.'

'Neither do I.'

'A nasty infection. Show me the antibiotic Virginia has given you.' When he read the dose he concluded that it wasn't large enough for a horse this size, though he didn't say so to Gavin: he had to watch professional etiquette.

Then he began a minute examination of Galaxy from his nose to his tail. He palpated every inch until he came to a place on his flank where Galaxy flinched and tossed his head when he pressed it. Scott tried again and the same thing happened. He continued his sensitive searching for any further tender places but found none. He went back to the tender spot and pressed again. This time a very small amount of pus came away. It was very little to be causing Galaxy to have such a temperature and to be in such pain.

'Thanks, Gavin. Be in touch.'

Scott roared away to his next call, speeding along to catch up. Inside he was steaming. Virginia had missed something of tremendous importance, which wasn't actually visible from the outside but inside was clearly causing havoc. If they weren't careful, blood poisoning would be next – if it hadn't already taken hold – and then Galaxy could be a goner.

Scott almost jerked with the shock of it all. The implications were enormous. A horse of Galaxy's standing would be worth hundreds of thousands of pounds and where would that leave the practice? The insurance might not even cover it. The small print would more than likely not allow a pay-out when veterinary expertise was at fault. As if he wasn't sweating enough with the heat, he was now sweating with panic.

He pulled up in a lay-by and dug out his mobile. 'Virginia? It's Scott. Right flank, small hole, very tender, pus coming out. Not noticed it?'

He didn't get a reply.

'Hello. Can you hear me?'

A small voice made its way to Scott. 'Yes. I can hear you.'

'Whatever you have to do today, go immediately and double the dose. Really clout it with a massive injection, too. Find the place and see if the pus is getting worse. I haven't said anything to Gavin nor anyone else, but do it immediately.'

'I've another visit to do and then—'

'Never mind what you have to do first, do this. I insist.'

Despite the seriousness of Scott's news, Virginia was instantly on the attack. 'Don't you start telling me what to do.'

'Shut up and listen to me. You asked me and I'm telling you. It is serious. An insignificant hole like that shouldn't be causing him so much angst. Obviously there is much, much more going on inside. Temperature, pain, it's clearly something monumental. Either you go instantly or I shall be compelled to tell Mungo. And I mean it.'

'You wouldn't dare.'

'I would. Are you going?'

Resigned to her fate, though clearly not wanting to face up to it, Virginia agreed to go. 'All right. I will.'

'Pronto. I'll ring again in an hour. Whereabouts are you?'

'Declan Tattersall's.'

'Right. Just *go*.'

Scott decided lunch at home would give him a chance to keep out of everyone's way and not let the cat out of the bag by mistake.

Zoe was playing cricket in the garden with Oscar and his friend Piers. They made a lovely picture. Zoe was batting, Oscar bowling and Piers fielding. Oscar the poor little chap, was red-faced and sweating, but enjoying himself immensely.

'Out, Mummy!'

'Oh no!' Zoe saw Scott coming in through the gate. 'Darling! How nice. I wasn't expecting you. Lunch?'

Scott nodded. She kissed him, and he kissed her back with enthusiasm.

'Enjoying yourself?'

'I am. Boys, shall I make you a picnic for the garden?'

The two of them nodded their agreement and carried on playing on their own.

'That Piers is such a nice boy. Do you know, he's only five but has a two-year-old sister and another on the way. I don't know how she copes.'

Scott looped his arm around her waist and the two of them went into the kitchen.

Zoe loved her big new kitchen. It was so much bigger than the one in their old cottage and she revelled in it. She laid their lunch on the kitchen table and Scott took lunch out for the boys.

'Here we are. Piers, this is yours, with cheese and not ham, seeing as you're vegetarian, and this one with apple juice is yours, Oscar.'

He went back in, filled with desire for Zoe but knowing they couldn't. 'What are you doing this afternoon?'

'Not what you fancy! I'm taking the boys swimming and then Piers is going home. They do play so well together. It's a pleasure having him here.'

'He's a nice boy.'

'By the way, we've missed out again. I'm not pregnant.'

Scott reached across the table and stroked her hand. 'I'm so sorry. Next time, perhaps.'

'That's what we keep saying, but it never happens. I know I've asked this before and now I'm asking again: we must do something serious about it. You and me. Together.'

'I thought that was what we were doing.' He gave her a lopsided grin but Zoe wasn't in the mood for laughing about the matter.

'Two years we've been trying and heavens above, we've not exactly been celibate all this time, have we?'

'You can say that again. No, we haven't.'

'I imagined I'd start a baby straight away considering only one time produced Oscar, but oh no. Please will you go with me for advice? Only advice.' She smiled pleadingly at him, hoping that perhaps this time he would give in for her sake.

Scott pushed his unfinished lunch away. 'There's nothing wrong with me. I know that for a fact.'

'How do you know?'

'There just isn't. We're not that kind of people, the Spencers aren't.'

'You can't exactly say that your mum and dad were prolific. Just you and your sister, eleven years apart.'

'That was choice, that was.'

'That's not what your dad said to me when he was over.'

Scott flared up. 'Have you been discussing our lack of offspring with my dad?'

'Only because he asked me why we hadn't produced another grandchild for him. That's all. I can't understand why you're so touchy about it. There's scores of people who have to consult infertility experts and we're no—'

To bring an end to a conversation he did not want to continue, Scott leapt up from the table and, as he went out of the dining room, he said without turning to look at her, 'I am absolutely adamant: I am *not* going to a clinic for advice. It'll happen all in good time. There's nothing wrong with me, and I don't expect there's anything wrong with you. That's my last word.'

Zoe shrugged her shoulders, pushed aside her dinner plate and began the leftover plum pie. She couldn't see what could possibly be the reason for their lack of success in conceiving, which she desperately wanted for Oscar's sake as much as their own. Biologically her time would be starting to run out and she felt there was an urgency about the matter. Blast Scott. But as she said that a smile spread across her face. God, how she loved him; even more now than when they married. He was such a joy to be with, and he'd proved to be far better husband material than she'd ever dreamt of.

Her mother had said all marriages were a gamble, which they were, some more than others, but both she and her mother had gambled and won because her mother was happier than she had ever been and had positively glowed with happiness all the time she and Ivan had been married. As she spat out the last stone in her plum pie, Zoe vowed not to mention the clinic ever again, because Scott obviously had a typical male attitude to his own potency, and she wasn't prepared to hurt his feelings any more. What she would do, though, was to attend a clinic on her own to make sure *she* wasn't at fault.

The distress her idea had caused Scott was still there the following morning, despite them making up again before they slept that same night. He was tetchy as soon as he opened his eyes, and the only thing on which he really focused his mind was Galaxy.

He gave Virginia a call as soon as he got into his Land Rover.

'Hello, Ginny. What's the situation, then? Have you been again this morning?'

'I'm about one mile away. Last night I changed the antibiotics and increased the dose, gave him an injection too, like you suggested, to see if that does the trick. Thanks for going yesterday. By the way, the name's Virginia.'

'Ouch! Sorry. Ginny suits you, though. The matter is very serious, you know. You could lose him.'

There was a short silence and then he heard a long, hissing sound like the drawing-in of breath, and Virginia saying cautiously, 'Are you . . . do you mean that?'

'Absolutely. I think Mungo should know.'

'If I tell him . . . no, no, not Mungo.'

'I think when you get there today Galaxy'll be worse and the poison, whatever it is, will be going right through his system. You should have acted more seriously much earlier.'

'At first I didn't see the puncture mark that you spotted. Neither did Gavin. Are you blaming me for all this?'

'If the cap fits wear it, but don't expect me to haul you out of the fire, because I shan't. If he doesn't improve today then . . . .' Scott maliciously made the sound of someone having their throat cut. 'The practice will be in very deep water and only Virginia to blame.'

He heard the phone go dead and sat staring out of the windscreen, wondering if he would have spotted the problem at first. He didn't like the woman – she wasn't feminine enough for his taste – but he didn't want to contribute to her downfall . . . On the other hand, he had been to see Galaxy and kept it to himself, which, strictly speaking, put him in the wrong.

An hour later he rang her again. No reply. Then he sent her a text message and still no reply. Half an hour later he rang again.

'It's me. Scott. Well?'

'He's worse. I've been instructed to get a second opinion. But they won't have you. Got to be someone outside our practice, His Lordship says. Won't have it any other way. God! He means business.'

He could hear how panic-stricken this tough nut of a woman was. 'Then you have to tell Mungo. Straight away. This is urgent. Believe me. I'm not telling him, 'cos I know nothing about it, do I?'

Her phone went dead again so Scott switched off. Quarter of a million pounds compensation? And then some. What Scott hated the most was that magnificent horse, with so much achievement still ahead of him, dying. The poison must be insidiously creeping into every one of his organs. God! What a mess. If she hadn't found that puncture hole at the beginning, what on earth did she think she was treating in the first place?

Just as Virginia finished speaking to Scott, her phone rang again, and when she saw who was calling her she broke out in a sweat.

'Good morning, Mungo.'

'Just had Lord Askew on the phone, Virginia. Meet me there in half an hour. If you get there first don't go in, wait for me before you speak to anyone at all. Neither Gavin nor Lady Mary nor Lord Askew.'

The phone went dead, leaving Virginia hollow inside. None of her in-built powerful resources were there to be drawn on. She'd made a terrible mistake and she couldn't see a way out of it. How on earth had she missed that puncture on his flank? More attention to detail and less trying to impress might have been the answer. Oh, damn. She was close to tears, but determined not to cry in front of Kate. Stern resolution was more appropriate.

She called in at the public lavatories in the centre of Barleybridge, splashed water on her face, dug out an old lipstick from the bottom of her bag, combed her hair, did her well-tried trick of winking at herself in the mirror to boost her ego, but found it didn't work and left despondently for Lord Askew's.

Having deliberately dallied her way through Barleybridge in the hope that Mungo would be there before her, she arrived flustered and afraid. She didn't drive through the archway but braked outside in the park. Kate tactfully said she would wait in the car. Virginia went into the stable yard, to find Mungo in close consultation with Gavin. From the tone of their conversation it sounded as though he'd already examined Galaxy.

Mungo looked up. That normally handsome, good-looking face was grim. Virginia's heart sank, then sank even further when she saw both Lady Mary and Lord Askew coming out of Galaxy's stable.

She braced herself and marched towards them with a spring in her step. 'Good morning, everyone. Fine day.'

Mungo was the only one who answered her. 'We've got a second opinion arriving any minute now – Giles Standen-Briggs. Have you heard of him?'

'No. I haven't.'

Mungo pulled a face. 'You soon will have. Well-known equine vet, highly respected, used to be Lord Askew's vet until Dan Brown put in an appearance.'

There came the throaty roar of a very superior car and into the yard swept Giles Standen-Briggs.

Lord Askew went forward to greet Giles. They shook hands vigorously and Mungo and Virginia could hear him thanking Giles profusely for agreeing to come, even though they'd had an ignominious parting of the ways the last time they'd met.

'Don't need to introduce you to Mungo Price. But this is Virginia Haverlack—'

Virginia interrupted. 'Havelock, actually.'

Lord Askew swung round on her and shouted, 'It doesn't matter what the hell you're called. The misdiagnosis remains the same and Lady Mary is more than likely witnessing the demise of a horse of great value, both financially and . . .' He broke off, too full of emotion to control his voice, and, after a pause, added, 'She's losing a great friend. Come along, Giles.'

Out of professional respect, Mungo and Virginia stood just outside the stable door while Giles examined Galaxy. Almost immediately he found the puncture in his right flank. Since yesterday it had begun to swell and more pus was coming out, but still nothing like enough to make him as ill as he was.

Giles went over him with the stethoscope. Not a word was spoken by anyone until finally he came out of the stable and indicated with his head that he'd like a consultation with Mungo.

Four pairs of eyes watched covertly while they talked together, standing several paces away from the group. After about five minutes they came across to declare their decision.

Mungo had a lot of animosity towards Giles Standen-Briggs, partly because of incidents in the past and partly because the man irritated him with his overdone style and arrogance, but this time he had to concede that he was right.

Giles stated quite certainly, and with a great deal of veterinary expertise, which frankly went over the heads of the laymen receiving the news, that nothing could be done. 'His internal organs are already invaded by whatever it is has entered his body, especially his spleen, and I am afraid no amount of drugs will alter that. It is all too far gone. Had he received better treatment earlier there might have been a chance. I'm sorry to have to say that the very best action we can take as far as Galaxy is concerned is to have him destroyed. He's in pain and it will only get worse. If you respect him, then that is what Mr Price and I recommend.'

He laid a comforting hand on Lady Mary's arm but she thrust it off. 'Oh, I see. Brilliant equine brain but nothing more to advise other than killing him. I won't accept it.' She stamped her way round and round and round in circles until she broke down and wept. Mungo offered her a shoulder to cry on and cry she did.

Lord Askew boiled with fury. His face purple with rage and disappointment, he vaguely patted his daughter's shoulder, raised his fist to within inches of Giles's nose – the vet hastily stepped back – and then thrust his face so close to Mungo's that he could see the hairs in Lord Askew's nostrils. 'I'll have you for this. Every last penny. It's all your fault for employing vets who don't know their job. She,' his arm shot out, his index finger shaking, in the direction of Virginia, 'caused all this. She never spotted the problem. Delay. Delay. Delay. Tinkering about with paltry treatments. Now what happens? He's to be shot. A beautiful creature like him, in his p-p-prime, ending up as fodder for a pack of hounds.' Lord Askew turned away, overcome with emotion. To no one in particular he said quietly, 'I can't stay to watch. Get it over with, the sooner the better.' He strode away, shoulders hunched.

Lady Mary emerged from the comfort of Mungo's arms to say, 'Are you absolutely sure that he can't be saved?'

Mungo nodded sympathetically.

'I'll stay. Just give me a few minutes and then . . .'

No one had looked at Virginia since Giles had begun his examination. She was standing outside on the cobbles, leaning against the stable wall, ashen-faced and waiting for the hatchet to fall. She'd done some stupid things in her time, and had been asked to leave her previous practice though they kindly allowed her to make it look as if it was her decision to leave to go to another job rather than being sacked. That was a sad blow, but the cause was the same as this – just not paying enough attention to the job, blithely skating through each call instead of focusing meticulously on the job in hand. Well, this time it was her demise good and proper.

All Mungo said as they left the stable yard was, 'See you back at the practice when you've finished your calls. I don't know what to do with you.' He then turned on his heel, got in his car and drove away without a backward glance.

Virginia went back to her car, which, fortunately, she'd parked well out of the view of everyone, seeing as Kate was sitting in there waiting for her.

At the sight of her face, Kate leapt out of the car. 'Virginia!' As she spoke, the sound of a shot rang out and Kate knew the answer. 'Oh, no. Oh, no.'

Virginia was more distressed than Kate had ever seen her and, for the first time, Kate touched her, by putting her arm round her shoulder.

'I-I-I don't know what to do. Mungo is so icy cold I can't bear it. I've to finish my calls and then see him back at the practice. Hell, Kate. I've been a fool. Impetuous almost, not like me really.'

'Let's get on with the calls, right?'

'I don't know if I feel well enough. How can I behave normally with this hanging over me? Tomorrow I could be clearing out the flat and not only homeless but jobless, too. I just can't cope.'

'Be brave. Do the calls and I'll wait until you've seen Mungo. You can spend the night at our flat if you don't mind the put-up in my bedroom. See how you feel? Eh?'

Virginia nodded and, after about five minutes, pulled herself together, thanked Kate for the offer of some company for the night, then switched on the ignition. 'Where is it we're going next? I bet Mungo's already telling everyone back at the practice.'

But Mungo had gone straight up to their flat to find Miriam. She had just got back from taking Perkins for his midday walk. One glance at his face told her the worst had happened. 'Oh, no. Not Galaxy. They've had to put him to sleep, haven't they?'

''Fraid so. It was unbearable. I didn't stay. Just let Giles do it.'

Scandalized, Miriam said, 'You don't mean he got Giles for a second opinion?'

Mungo nodded. 'It felt to be a real kick in the teeth.'

'I don't believe it, not when he knows the animosity between the two of you. To say nothing of his instant dismissal when His Lordship asked Dan to take over from Giles. What brass-necked cheek the man has.'

'She'll have to go, won't she?'

Miriam slotted her hand into the crook of Mungo's arm, intending to suggest otherwise, but Mungo spoke first.

'The stupid woman. How can I have any faith in her after this? Told me she'd ridden since childhood, done a lot of equine work at college, knew the job inside out and, being short-handed with Dan away, I told Joy she could cover. Worst decision I ever made. God, what a mess. I don't think we're covered for veterinary mistakes. Which this is. A monumental mistake, actually.'

Mungo flung away from Miriam and slumped down full-length onto the sofa, kicking off his shoes as he did so.

'Whisky?'

'At this hour?' He half shook his head and then changed his mind. 'Yes, please. I'll have to suck mints before my clinic. But hell, I need it.'

Miriam poured his whisky neat, made it not quite but almost a double, and handed it to him. She squeezed herself onto the sofa at the end nearest his feet, and massaged them while she waited. Gradually what colour Mungo had in his face came back and, by the time he'd drunk to the bottom of the glass, he looked more like himself.

Miriam, seeing the improvement in him, decided to offer advice. 'It seems to me that if Virginia goes immediately that will be tantamount to admitting she was in the wrong and it wouldn't look good to the insurance people, would it? You might not have any confidence in her but for the time being it might be as well if it *looks* as though you have.'

Mungo laid his head against the cushions and closed his eyes, but not for long because Perkins nudged his knee with his nose. When that didn't draw his attention, Perkins laid his head on Mungo's knee and gazed at him with loving eyes. Mungo opened one eye. 'All right. Yes. I know you're worried. So am I, only more so.' He reached out and stroked Perkins' head and Miriam waited.

'He's a great dog, isn't he? He always knows. Don't you, old chap. Eh?'

Miriam smiled. 'Did you hear what I said about Virginia?'

'I did. Sound common sense and I think I'll do just what you say. Let her stay on under a cloud, but to the outside world I shall demonstrate my confidence in her . . . well, what small amount of confidence I have. Even if I get the insurance money to cover Askew's claims there'll always be that niggle there – what has she done, or rather not done today? What will she do tomorrow?'

'The sad part is, my darling, poor Lady Mary losing that superb horse. I saw him jumping once at the Agricultural Show when he first started, he was just fantastic even then. So proud and she rode him like they were one being. Wonderful to see.' Miriam traced Mungo's profile with her finger, from his hairline right down his throat to the hollow where it joined his collar-bone. She kissed his mouth and remembered how very much she loved him. 'We'll get through this, you'll see. We have had worse to face before, haven't we?' Perkins shuffled his chin about on Mungo's knee, demanding his share of attention.

'You do know we are talking hundreds of thousands of pounds.'

Miriam almost jumped with the shock. 'My God! Surely not.'

'Oh, yes! That's what he's worth, and knowing Lord A, he'll be asking for the maximum.'

'I'd no idea. But if the insurance don't pay out we shall be finished.'

Mungo looked at his watch, disengaged Perkins' head, patted him and then stood up. 'My first client is due. Got to go. I don't relish it. What a mess we're in. Where are my mints? Blast that Virginia. Damn and blast her.'

Chapter 7

Had he known how devastated Virginia was perhaps Mungo would have been more sympathetic. He'd spoken to her at the end of their working day and left her feeling like a wrung-out dishcloth. Not because of his temper, or because he'd bad-mouthed her, but because of his disappointment in her as a vet.

'How could you have missed such a thing?'

'You didn't see how small the hole was—'

'I did.'

'Oh! Right, I didn't know you'd examined him. However, I missed that hole and quite simply did not realize just how significant it had become.'

Mungo tapped his index finger on his desk as he told her what he wanted her to do. 'I want a minute-by-minute detailed report on everything that happened and everything that was said each time you visited. Times. Dates. What you did. At what stage you changed the prescription. Everything. I need paperwork, you see, for the insurance company. Been bad enough if it had been a guinea pig but a world-famous horse? Please. It throws appalling doubt on your competence. Not just doubt, but grave doubt. What the blazes did you think it was when you first went?' Mungo held up a hand to stop her explaining. 'No, don't. Tell me in your report. I shall want it . . . let me see . . . it's Thursday. I shall want it by nine a.m. on Monday morning. Not one minute late.'

'Right, so be it. Nine a.m., Monday morning. Full report. I'm deeply, deeply sorry.'

Mungo ignored her apology. 'Don't speak about it to anyone at all. No one. Not the stable lad, the head lad, nor a farmer nor his wife, nor anyone anywhere at all, especially not to anyone who owns horses. *It is a closed book.* The rumours that will be flying round this very minute . . . well, I can't bear to think, and we've got to protect the practice, first and foremost. So it's lips clamped tight shut. The last thing I want to say is this: one more incident and it could be the end of your career. I shan't let you do what you did at your last practice, where you were allowed to leave graciously and given time to find another job.' He looked up at her and saw the momentary shock on her face which she quickly disguised. 'You didn't know I knew did you? The veterinary world is small, Virginia, remember that. Cancel any plans for your weekend. Get to it.' He got out a big brand-new file from a cupboard, wrote in large letters the word 'Galaxy' on it and put it in prime position on a shelf to await the first of many papers to be filed in there, the first one at nine o'clock on Monday.

Mia's caring manner and the kindliness with which she fed her, housed her and the considerate way she made sure the put-up was organized went a long way to salving Virginia's wounds. But with the bedroom light out, and the curtains so heavy they kept out the light from the night sky, her whole world tumbled about her ears with terrible suddenness. With Kate sleeping only feet away she tried hard to hold back the tears but in minutes they came rolling down her cheeks.

'Sorry. Forgot to use the bathroom.' She crept out and gave way to her tears sitting on the lavatory in the tiny bathroom. She couldn't go back into the bedroom until she knew for certain she'd stopped weeping.

Kate knew she was crying because she'd heard the smothered snuffles before Virginia had got out of bed. It was monumental what she'd done, and Kate wished to goodness that when she was with her at Lord Askew's that time she'd mentioned her unease. But she hadn't and this was the consequence of not speaking up. If only.

Before she knew where she was Kate was in tears, too. That

beautiful horse. Lord Askew's anger. Lady Mary's colossal distress. If only she, Kate Howard, had spoken up. Well, another time when she felt uneasy she would. Kate turned over and looked at her clock. Virginia had been in the bathroom for almost twenty minutes. She flung back the sheet and went to knock on the bathroom door.

'Virginia. It's Kate. Come out. Come on. Let's talk.'

But there was no reply

'OK, I'm going to get us a whisky each. It'll help us sleep. We'll sit on the bed and talk. You come out while I get the whisky. OK?'

She heard a muffled voice say, 'OK.'

They sat on their beds for almost an hour, sipping their whisky and talking over the whole problem. Kate wound up their conversation by saying that crying solved nothing, it was true she'd not noticed what was right under her nose, and all she could do now was brace her shoulders, ride the storm and do as Mungo asked. After all, he hadn't sacked her, had he? Which they'd all expected, and who wouldn't?

Horrified, Virginia blurted out, 'You mean, they all know back at the practice, even the lay staff?'

Kate nodded and continued her mini-lecture. Mungo hadn't lost his temper. He hadn't gone berserk, which she'd expected he would. In fact, he'd been quite calm and controlled, hadn't he? He'd have been justified in sacking her on the spot but here she still was with a job. And remember: *'Time and the hour run through the roughest day.'* So they should go to sleep.

Kate didn't know how much good she had done but Virginia did put down her glass, nodded her agreement, swung her legs back into bed and turned her back to Kate.

They both slept until the alarm rang.

There were not many calls for Virginia the next day, it almost seemed as though the whole of Barleybridge had decided to ostracize her. By lunch-time Joy said, 'Go home. If there's a call I'll ring you. Give you a chance to get on with that report.

Mungo's going to Lord Askew's to smooth things over as soon as he's finished operating. Well, that's what he intends. Don't take it to heart, Virginia, it could have happened to Dan or Scott or Colin, they're just as vulnerable as the next man . . . or woman. Don't forget that.'

Virginia gave Joy a wry smile. 'I doubt it.'

Joy couldn't resist saying, 'Well, frankly, I doubt it, too. They don't worry about giving a good impression, so they concentrate on the job in hand and do it well.' She looked at Virginia with both eyebrows raised and a sardonic look on her face.

All Virginia wanted was for the floor to open up so she could disappear for ever.

Kate stayed around at the practice, helping here and there, taking a turn on the reception desk, though Joy said it wasn't quite right her doing that, but Kate didn't mind keeping busy.

Scott had also had a slow day and came in about four o'clock because he'd no more visits to make and fancied some company. Zoe had collected Oscar from school and was taking him to see her mother in Weymouth, then leaving him there for the night while she went to a hen party of a school friend of hers. 'Just a chance for Joan to see him for a while,' he said to Kate now. 'And Ivan, for that matter. He's very fond of Oscar is Ivan. He hasn't any grandchildren, you see.'

'That'll be nice for them. Is Joan enjoying being married?'

'Is she? She is. Best day's work she's done in years marrying that man. She's so much easier to get on with. I say, Kate, would you like a meal out? I don't like the idea of cooking when I go home. Cooking for one has never been one of my hobbies.'

'I remember your bachelor days, I don't think there was an eating establishment anywhere in Barleybridge that you hadn't tried at least once.' She grinned at him and some of their old camaraderie returned, so she agreed to have a meal with him. No harm in that.

'We had some good fun trying them out, didn't we?'

'We did.'

They went early, as there didn't seem much point in hanging around with nothing to do.

'I bet as soon as we begin eating I'll have a call.'

'Fingers crossed it won't happen. Valentine and Rhodri have been slack today, too; just one of those coincidences.'

'Kate, how did you get on with Valentine?'

'Fine, thanks. Although he's so full of his fascination for women. God's gift, you know. First chance he gets he's in there.'

'He didn't try anything with you, did he?' Scott studied her intently over the rim of his wine glass.

She didn't answer until he put his glass down. Her fingers played with the stem of her own glass and then she said, 'No, he didn't. Valentine has other fish to fry.' Kate didn't look Scott straight in the eye when she said that and Scott sensed a story behind her reticence.

'So . . . ?'

'You know something, don't you?'

Scott looked innocent. 'Me? No.'

Under the table Kate playfully kicked his foot. 'You can't fool me. You do. Come on let it all spill out.'

Scott had to grin. 'OK. Zoe and I saw him with an expensive-looking bit of goods one night in the cinema. They weren't in the least bit interested in the film.'

'Are you sure it wasn't Nina? They are back together again.'

'No, it wasn't Nina. That poor woman – I don't know how she copes.'

'Neither do I. I reckon one day there could be a murder.'

'Who would be murdering who?'

Kate picked up her knife and fork and attacked her food with vigour. 'I think it would be Nina murdering Val. She'd be such an attractive-looking person with only the minimum of effort, and she obviously adores him or she wouldn't come back time and again, and that's worth something, being loved. But Val can get anyone to love him . . . except me.'

'Ooooh! You obviously know who he's seeing.'

'Sorry, Scott, I can't tell. It would cause trouble at the practice so I'm honour-bound.'

'I don't know why you should be, but OK. I say, what about the cinema tonight? Would you come?'

Kate strove to keep her feelings under control and made it look as though she was concentrating on eating. Should she? Shouldn't she? Dare she? Her heart bounded and to her horror, she flushed bright red, so she kept her head down and didn't reply.

'I take it that's a no.'

She longed to go with him. 'I might. I might not.'

Scott bent his head to peer at her face, but she kept it down, hoping he wouldn't see her blushing.

'I think that's rather sweet, you blushing. Not many girls do that nowadays.' Out of the blue he filled their silence by taking hold of her hand and saying very considerately, 'You know, I am really and truly married for life. I'm not on the pull, all that's changed. You do understand that, don't you? It's Zo and me, me and Zo for always. That's how it is. So we'd just be friends going together, if that's what you're worried about.'

Kate's throat had tightened up and she could barely speak. She understood he was declaring that there was nothing between them any more. Totally zilch. She knew that, but he'd said it and that made it certain. Definite. Positive. Unchangeable. An area never to be visited again. The stark truth, which she'd been avoiding, was out there in the open. The temptation to burst into tears came over her. Then she found she'd said, 'OK. Let's.'

Scott grinned. 'We're both adults. No harm done.'

'I'll ring Mia, otherwise she'll worry.'

'Of course. How is she? Still painting?'

'That is the one question which is bound to anger her. She hates it if people ask her that. They're only being interested, but it sounds to her as though she's a clever child being patronizingly patted on the head for being clever.'

'Oops! Sorry. I didn't mean it like that.'

'I know. She's doing awfully well. Almost wondering about giving up working at the Gallery to concentrate on her commissions, but then she remembers hers is the only salary coming in at the moment so she keeps going. Her miniatures are very sensitively done.'

'Pudding?'

For once Kate shook her head. 'Too full. This hot weather is putting me off eating, thanks all the same. We'll share the bill.'

'We won't. When you're earning big money I'll let you share, not till then. Virginia's in a great big hole, isn't she?'

Kate picked up her bag. 'Thanks for this. I did intend to pay my share.'

'Of course you did. What do you think? About Virginia?'

'I felt uneasy, like I told you, but I just wasn't expert enough to intervene.'

'I went to see him,'

'You didn't? I didn't know that.'

'Only Gavin knew, the family were all away at a wedding. She's scared to hell, is our Ginny. She was very grateful to me for going, but didn't like the pressure I put on her. I said outright that she could lose him. Got everything?'

He might be firmly married but he still couldn't resist teasing the waitress and making her laugh, just like the old Scott always did. Kate glanced down at his hands as he sorted out his credit card and saw he wasn't wearing a wedding ring, but then he wouldn't, being a vet, it would only get in the way when he was working. But the fact served to make him more available to women who didn't know him, though, come to think of it, was a wedding ring a bar to flirtation and fun nowadays? No, it wasn't. Kate set forth to the cinema more cheerfully than she could have imagined possible in the circumstances, and went to bed that night her mind filled with Scott: his handsome, tanned face; his strong, sensitive hands; the smell of his aftershave, which regularly lingered about him all of the day; that love of life glowing in his vivid blue eyes; and, above all, the thrill which ran through her if ever they made contact.

*

Saturday was Kate's last day shadowing Virginia, for which Kate was grateful. It hadn't been too difficult on Friday because they'd had so few calls to make but she couldn't expect it would be the same today. She sensed that at every farm they went to, the owners would be agog with the gossip about her, and no doubt the story would have been embellished a thousand times over, because they all loved to hear of a downfall of any kind, especially if it involved Lord Askew seriously biting the dust.

Virginia called for Kate as usual, but her face was sullen.

'Yes? What's happened?'

'What do you mean what's happened? Only what can be expected – I had three calls cancelled last night. They wanted Scott or Colin. Damn and blast that Lord Askew.'

'Ah. Sorry. What are we going to do?'

'There's two calls to do and then that's it. Finito. I shan't even have earned my salary today. That can't go on.'

'Well, we shall have to do those two calls absolutely to the best of our ability. Charming, helpful, considerate, on the ball—'

'You sound like one of those business consultants who declare they can put your business into profit after one lecture. For God's sake, shut up.'

They'd gone about a mile towards Hunter's Reach when Virginia, without warning, pulled over to the side of the road and switched off the engine. Her hands were trembling, her lower jaw was juddering and her face was drawn and ashen.

'Virginia?'

But she didn't reply.

'Virginia! What's the matter?'

'I-I-I . . .' By now her fingers were locked tightly together and the trembling had completely taken over her body.

'I'm nipping into this café and getting you a cup of tea. Stay right there.'

They were parked on a double yellow line but that was the least of Kate's worries. She explained her problem in the café, asked could they sell her a cup of tea to take away, her friend had been taken ill in the car and . . .

They did and Kate went outside and tried to hand it to Virginia, who couldn't take hold of it because she was shaking so much. She'd have to get help. She rang the practice and found herself talking to Miriam. 'Miriam? Kate here, I don't know what to do. We're in a bit of a mess. You know I'm shadowing Virginia? Well, Virginia's got two calls to make this morning and she's pulled in and can't drive any further. She can't speak at all. I'm terribly worried about her. What do you suggest? I've got her a cup of tea but she can't take hold of it because she's trembling so much.'

'Oh, hell. This contretemps with Galaxy's brought this on, I expect. You've got a problem. Well, you can't sit there all morning. Can you drive her back here? Joy will sort out her calls, and if necessary we'll take her to hospital.'

'I've never driven this car. Will Mungo mind?'

'No, of course not. Come back here. Pronto. How far away are you?'

'We've just turned up Magnum Percy Hill.'

'That's not far. Drive carefully. See you in a few minutes.'

It was a nightmare journey, the traffic was gridlocked. Kate wasn't used to the car, and moving Virginia into the passenger seat had taken all her strength, because she couldn't seem to respond to any request, no matter how simple. While they waited at the traffic lights Kate glanced at her and thought: she's frozen, that's what it is, frozen by stress, everything's stopped functioning.

Miriam was waiting on the bench by the back door and leapt to her feet when Kate pulled up. Between the two of them they got Virginia out of the car and in through the back door.

'We'll take her up to the flat. Do you think we can manage her up the stairs?'

'We'll have to. It's the best place, quiet, you know. We don't want half of Barleybridge knowing what's going on.'

'True. Come along, Virginia my dear, up the stairs. One leg and then the other. Now, make an effort, please.' Miriam heaved from below and Kate pulled from above, and eventually they arrived at the top of the stairs. The kitchen was the nearest so they went in there with her and sat her on a chair.

'Rest your elbows on the table, that's it. Now I'm going to raid Mungo's brandy. Hot milk and brandy. Is that OK?'

Virginia's response, the first real one they'd witnessed, was to nod her head. Kate collapsed in a chair, exhausted by the heat and her exertions.

'The doctor should see her, don't you think, Miriam?'

'Get a clean tea towel, second drawer down, and wet it to make a cold compress for her forehead. It'll cool her down. Open the big window, too, get some air blowing in on her.' Miriam gently shook Virginia's shoulder. 'Now, Virginia, are you there? Here's the brandy, drink it steadily.' She whispered softly to Kate, 'We'll wait to see if she comes round. Seeing the doctor would make it official and could ruin everything for her.' Miriam stood behind her and held the compress to her forehead.

They each had a glass of chilled water from Miriam's fancy fridge and awaited results. The cool air blowing in through the big open window was refreshing, and Kate began to feel so much better after her fright. There was something about Miriam's kitchen which was specially warm and inviting. Was it the lovely window looking straight out towards Beulah Bank Top, or the pretty curtains now blowing in the breeze? It could have been the lovely mellow, earthy colour of the tiles, or perhaps just the sweetness and charm of the kitchen's owner.

By the time Virginia had finished her glass of Miriam's medicine, she was beginning to thaw. Her rigid limbs began to slacken, and her brain, having completely seized up, now appeared to be functioning again. She didn't know where she was, but there were Miriam and Kate both beside her smiling encouragingly.

'You're in my kitchen, you know, in the flat above the practice. Feeling better now, my dear?'

'Yes, thank you. Funny thing is, I don't remember driving here.'

'I think you froze with fright. Well, stress perhaps. Don't worry, you're quite safe now.'

Virginia began to get to her feet. 'I've two calls to make. I must go. They'll be wondering where I am.'

Miriam pressed her hands down on Virginia's shoulders. 'You're going nowhere at the moment. Colin is doing your calls so that's attended to and you can relax a while longer. It's my coffee time. How about it?'

'I wonder you can bear to speak to me after what I've done, or rather not done. I'm so sorry about it, so very sorry. I don't know what to do.'

'Neither do we. But first things first – we need that detailed report.'

'I'm halfway through it. I stayed up almost all night working on it. I know it's got to be absolutely accurate if we'll have solicitors picking holes in it. To say nothing of the insurance people.' She buried her head in her hands and groaned.

Miriam put the wet tea towel down in the sink and sat at the end of the table nearest to Virginia, so she could hold her hand. 'See here, my girl, you are in very difficult circumstances, I know that, but with Colin away on holiday for the next two weeks, you will need to work. Dan's back, thank goodness, so it won't be too bad, but work you must. Just remember that. Whatever they say, whatever stories are flying about, your job still has to be done. In any case, you'll be better being thoroughly occupied than sitting at home brooding.'

Virginia looked at Miriam for the first time. 'Has Lord Askew made any moves yet?'

'No.'

'So we don't know how he's taken it.'

'Don't fool yourself. He's taken it very badly and so has Lady Mary. She's a damn bossy woman is Mary, and I haven't much time for her, but right now she has all my sympathy. She adored that horse, he was her life.' Seeing Virginia beginning to freeze again, Miriam changed tack. 'The plus side is that Mungo is on your side . . . and all of us, too,' she wasn't too sure about that but said it just the same, 'so you've lots of support.'

Kate ventured to say, 'It was a very small hole.'

Virginia turned to face her and bitingly remarked, 'Thanks for that wonderful piece of comfort, Kate. Thank you very much indeed, that's really softened the blow.'

'I didn't mean it like that, I only meant it could have happened to—'

'But it didn't, did it? It happened to *me*.'

It must be the brandy talking, thought Miriam, though it did sound as though recovery was taking place. 'How about if you go home and get on with that report Mungo wants? Make sure it's accurate, completely accurate, every single line.'

Virginia stood up. 'Yes, I'd better go. Thanks for everything. You too, Kate.'

Both Kate and Miriam waited for her footsteps to fade and were just about to discuss what had happened when they heard Virginia's footsteps coming back up the stairs.

'Car keys?'

'In the ignition.'

When she'd left a second time Miriam said. 'Better tell Joy what's going on. Mungo's got appointments all morning so I can't disturb him.'

Kate said, 'I'll go see what Joy wants me to do. Mungo appears to be taking it all very calmly – I'm surprised.'

'He's not at all calm actually. It could be the end of us, you know, as a practice. Financially, you see, because Lord Askew'll claim, no doubt about that, and rightly so. There'll be a post-mortem, of course.'

Kate went off to find Joy, feeling as though she were walking through treacle.

Chapter 8

Joy decided that Kate could shadow Valentine for the rest of the day, which she was quite willing to do. Anything was better than doing nothing, and she did still want to use every single minute at the practice to the best advantage.

She went out with a question for Joy partway through one of Valentine's consultations. Having sorted the problem, she headed back to his consultation room when someone called out, 'Kate! Kate!' There was an urgency about the voice and it was one she didn't immediately recognize.

She turned to see who it was. 'Why, hello, Nina. How nice! Long time no see. How's things?'

But Nina wasn't up for pleasant conversation this particular morning, she was angry. 'I've come to see you.'

'Oh! Right.'

'Is it you sleeping with my husband? Have you no scruples? There's a name for women who steal other people's husbands.'

Kate was stunned. 'Me? What do you mean?'

Silence fell at the waiting room end of reception. This was the kind of thing people enjoyed; some intimate snippet about the staff, and intimate appeared to be the right word in the circumstances. Any discussions of their animal's prowess or illnesses were forgotten. Lesley, who was on the computer making out a receipt for a client, pressed the delete key by mistake, said damn; the waiting clients froze and Joy catapulted herself out from the back.

With arms out wide Joy called out, 'Nina!' She hugged her and kissed her on both cheeks as though she hadn't heard a word of what had been said. 'How lovely to see you! What a nice surprise. Come in my office and tell me what you've been up to of late.'

But Nina thrust her aside. 'It's Kate I've come to see.'

'Well, that's difficult because she's shadowing Valentine today.'

That hadn't been the most sensible remark to make. All it did was inflame Nina even more.

'Is she indeed? Well, now, that's coincidence.'

Nina stepped closer to Kate, who'd been hoping to slide away into a consulting room – and it didn't matter much whose room it was. Nina brought her arm back and smacked Kate right across her face not once but twice. 'I'm not going to stand back and let this go on. This time I'm taking initiative. Me, Nina Dedic. I thought better of you than this, Kate. You're not his usual run of women, they're more often tarts who think it exciting to have the danger consorting with a man like Val. He's mine. You understand he's mine and this has all got to stop. I say stop, do you hear me?' She looked ready to beat Kate up.

Kate opened her mouth to deny any such thing but Joy beat her to it. 'My office, right now, and you, Kate. Nina. I insist. Not out here, please.' She grasped Nina's arm and almost dragged her into the back corridor.

Kate meekly followed, her mind buzzing with the horror of knowing exactly who was seeing Valentine. Question was, did she tell all?

Joy nodded to Kate to close the door behind her and then spoke in a low and firm voice to Nina. 'Now, see here, I have known Kate for a number of years and I have never, ever known her tell lies. So if I ask her if this is true, what it is you accuse her of, then we both will believe it if she says no. Because I will know she's speaking the truth. Right?'

Nina looked stubborn and uncooperative and wouldn't look at Kate or Joy.

'Now, Kate, are you going out with Val? Yes or no?'

'No. I am not. I work with him but I do not go out socializing with him.'

'There,' said Joy triumphantly, 'there, now that's the truth.

Kate has said no. So there's no more to be said. And never again are you to come here and accuse a member of my staff of any such thing.' She softened her tone of voice. 'Now, a cup of tea in the staffroom and you and I will talk it over together, just by ourselves.'

She gave Kate a nod of dismissal and Kate crept out, glad to be free. Should she tell Nina about Eleanor Eustace? On the other hand, it might all be over by now and she'd do worse harm by mentioning it; Valentine had a habit of swift romances and then even swifter changes of heart.

The first words Valentine said when she re-entered his consulting room were, 'I thought I heard Nina's voice.'

'Yes, she's popped in.'

He was treating a cat that had waved its tail too close to its owner's new log fire and scorched its tail. He continued to discuss future care with its owner in between quizzing Kate. 'It needs keeping dry. Best use the cat tray again for a couple of days. Don't want it getting it wet or muddy outside. It should heal OK with no problems. On the other hand, if it still looks angry in a couple of days . . . What did you say she wants?'

'I didn't. She's just popped in, like I said.'

'. . . so come back after two days and we'll take another look.' He glanced at Kate. 'I'd better go have a word.'

Kate shook her head. 'She's with Joy drinking tea.'

'Ah! So, take care. See you in a day or two. Did she appear angry? She sounded it.'

'Yes.'

'Right. Don't worry, it's nothing too serious; you shouldn't need to come back. Good morning.'

The client said, 'I'm not sure what you've said. Do I come back in two days or do I come back only if it isn't getting any better? I don't know what you're saying to me and what you're saying to Kate.'

'Sorry.' Valentine was obviously in a daze. Nina coming in had thoroughly upset him. 'Come back in two days. Please.'

Valentine completed the details on the computer once the

client had left and swore quietly under his breath. 'Go out and see if Nina's gone for me, please.'

Kate wanted to protest but decided not; it would just complicate matters and that she didn't want. But she only needed to put her head out of the door to know that Nina was still on the premises, shouting and carrying on as only Nina could. The tea hadn't been effective, then. 'She's still here.'

All of a sudden, there was a flurry in the back corridor and out burst Nina, heading straight for Valentine. He retreated into his room, his arms held wide . . . and she launched herself into them sobbing. Kate quickly pulled the door closed and left them to it.

The waiting clients strained to hear but the door was solid and they couldn't catch a word. Thwarted, they turned to Kate for enlightenment.

'Have you been going out with him, then?'

Kate emphatically shook her head.

'I wouldn't blame her if she did.'

'Neither would I!'

'Between him and Scott I don't know which to choose.'

'I wouldn't worry too much, I don't think you'll get a choice.'

'What cheek! I can always imagine, though, can't I?'

Kate escaped to the staffroom, and began sorting out the coffee mugs and getting the kettle on. In the end it was none of her business what Valentine got up to in his spare time. But she hated knowing about Eleanor Eustace and keeping quiet about her. Poor Nina, she deserved better than this. She'd ask Mia tonight.

The door to the staffroom burst open and in came Valentine with Nina. She came straight up to Kate and apologized for her behaviour. 'I'm so sorry. Please, please accept my apology. Of course I was wrong. Val told me so, and Joy did too, and I'm sorry. It was unforgivable, absolutely unforgivable. You're not that kind of person.'

Kate hugged her as much from guilt as a willingness to accept her apology. Kate was taller than Nina and, as they hugged, Kate could see Valentine watching her closely. The sod, thought Kate. The total, complete and utter . . .

She didn't get any further because Valentine asked her for coffee for the two of them. 'Nina has it black. I have it black with sugar. I'll take mine back and get on with my client list, if you'll look after Nina for me.'

'Of course.'

Kate could have crawled away under any convenient stone. She didn't want to have to talk to Nina. What could one say?

'Kate, I was sure it was you. He is seeing someone, I know it for a fact. I found a receipt in his trouser pocket for meal I did not have with him in the White Hart. Where is it? Do you know it?'

'Yes. Up on the moors near Beulah Bank Top. I think.'

'I know I am a fool, but I love him so very much, I can forgive him anything.' Her eyes filled with tears.

'He is very attractive. I'm sure it's mostly the women who do the pursuing. Perhaps it's not always his fault. But he certainly isn't being pursued by *me*.'

'I know that now. I realize. Kate! Can I ask! Do you know who is?'

Kate's heart fell to her feet, but she was saved from the horror of lying to Nina by Mungo calling for coffee. He always had his in his consulting room and never with the staff, but this morning, thank heavens, that was what he wanted to do. She could have jumped up and kissed him. Instead she jumped up and made his coffee just how he liked it, strong, with milk, and two heaped spoonfuls of sugar (which Miriam was not to be told about).

'Excellent. Thanks. Good morning, Nina. How are you?'

Nina swallowed hard and tried to sound bright and happy. 'Very well, thank you, Mungo.'

He reached forward and kissed her cheeks continental-style, and gripped her hand in welcome. 'Working?'

'No, not yet.'

'In that case . . . I tell you what, your coming is very fortuitous. Go and see Joy before you leave. We've a reception vacancy coming up. It would suit you. You've just the right personality, warm and welcoming, and you've computer skills. I'm sure

93

Valentine would be delighted to have you here. We certainly would.'

Nina shook her head very positively. 'He wouldn't.'

'Of course he would. If I speak to him about it, how about that? He wouldn't refuse me. It would be great for you. Among friends, eh?' Then he added hastily to cover his back, 'Of course, it would be one month's trial to see how we like you and you like us. Eh? What about it? I think I've been inspired in coming up with this idea. I'll go and ask him right now.' Before Nina could stop him, he'd gone to find Valentine.

'He won't agree. I know he won't.'

Kate felt to be between a rock and a hard place. 'Mungo is very persuasive.'

Mungo slipped in to speak with Valentine between clients. 'Brief word. I've suggested Nina comes to work here on a month's trial. We'll need someone in reception now Lesley's leaving, and Nina quite fancies it. What do you think?'

Valentine appeared to implode. His cheeks bulged with anger and he went rigid with temper at the realization of what Mungo's suggestion would mean to him. 'How dare you suggest such a thing! My private life is none of your business. I will not agree.'

'I don't think you're in any position to disagree if I insist.'

'You can't insist if I say no.'

'You can't say no.'

'I can't say no? Of course I can. I may not be a partner but I have some rights.'

'You've no rights, at ... this ... moment. I'll say one sentence,' he paused to sip his coffee and then held up a finger, 'and you will agree.'

Valentine raised his eyebrows disbelievingly.

'Two nights ago, the White Hart, with a sizzling blonde. I never knew it was a knocking shop. High class, I'll give you that.'

Valentine broke out in a heavy sweat. No one will see us here, it's too isolated, Eleanor had said. Much better than the George, she'd said. He knew she meant trouble right at the start and still he'd acquiesced to her pursuit of him. Would he never learn?

Mungo grinned wickedly. 'She starts in reception, on Monday, otherwise I shall reveal all to her. It's up to you.'

Valentine didn't want Nina to know. He could be unfaithful to her so long as she didn't *actually* know, only suspected. He'd smoothed things over this morning with her but it had been hard. There was no alternative. Damn Mungo Price. Damn him. It must mean Miriam knew, too, and that he did not like, Miriam knowing the worst side of him. Blast. Mungo was certainly the sharpest knife in the drawer this morning. 'Very well. Damn you.'

Mungo grinned devilishly. 'One up to me. You're a sod, Valentine. A complete sod. I don't know why I'm not telling her anyway. But I'm not. I think her having a job is more important to her and her stability. At least she can keep an eye on you in shop hours.' He shut the door rather more sharply than was needful.

As he passed the staffroom he put his arm round the door and gave Joy the thumbs-up. Joy grinned at him and went to offer Nina the job. One month's trial starting on Monday. Excellent. That solved the problem. New staff were scarce on the ground at the moment. The icing on the cake would have been actually hearing Mungo telling Valentine that he knew about his amours. As if Val hadn't had enough this morning with Nina's outburst and then finding out that the world and his wife now knew about his latest conquest. Joy wondered who she was. She could have laughed except she was so angry for Nina's sake.

Kate arrived back at the flat to find that Mia was late home, so she started on the meal for the two of them. As she chopped and sliced and got the wok going, Kate became aware of just how emotionally strung-up she was. It had been the day of days. First, all the distress of Virginia's mini-breakdown, then the appalling moment when Nina had accused her of being one of Valentine's conquests in front of the waiting room full of clients, then being left in charge of Nina and *then* having to shadow Valentine for the rest of the day and finding him in a steaming temper. When he accused her of suggesting to Mungo that Nina worked on reception, it was the final straw.

'I did no such thing,' she'd said. 'I was there when he proposed it, but I did not suggest it to him, it was all his own idea. Mungo came in the staffroom for his coffee,' she'd paused when she remembered how odd that had seemed, 'and suggested it himself, so it was nothing to do with me. Right? OK? It was entirely Mungo's idea.'

Valentine had backed off, but it didn't soothe his bad temper. What Kate dreaded was him getting angry with a client, because she wouldn't know what on earth to do. At least her week with Virginia was over and she'd soon be shadowing – yes, believe it or not – Scott, without *asking* Joy, too. She was ecstatic. A whole week with Scott. Her mind whirled with excitement. Imagine seeing the love of her life every day for a week. She dwelt on his looks, his voice, his charisma. Then her concentration deserted her, the knife slipped and she cut her finger. By the time she'd found the First Aid box Mia was home.

'Kate! That looks nasty. Here, let me help. Sorry I'm late. There we are – oh! It's bleeding through the plaster. I'll wash my hands and I'll finish dinner. I don't fancy blood on my chicken stirfry even if it is yours! Wrap a tissue round it to catch the blood and press on it.'

The first question Mia asked when they sat down to eat was, 'Had a good day?'

It took all of half an hour for Kate to reveal everything that had happened. By the time she'd finished Mia was shattered. 'Kate, what a day! No wonder you're exhausted.'

'Well, yes, I am.'

'In the long run you shouldn't say a word. You didn't lie to Nina, you simply didn't tell all the truth and, for her sake, that's perhaps as well. Seems to me, Valentine is perfectly capable of acting in his own best interests. Though Mungo might question you as to why you never said when it all came up.'

'And if I do tell?'

96

'Seeing as she's going to work there and you'll have left in another four weeks, my advice is to keep mum. Best avoid conflict.'

'I just wish I'd been in the room when Mungo told Valentine about Nina. She's so glad for the job and she's just right for it. Kindly and warm, she is. Mungo was like a dog with two tails all day.'

Mungo talked to Miriam about his *coup de grâce* that evening.

'So, do you think I did the right thing?' he asked. 'I'm convinced I did. I don't know why we've never thought of employing Nina before. She's ideal. Like part of the family, you know.'

Miriam replied, barely able to hold back her laughter, 'You are living very dangerously. One day your chickens could all come home to roost and there'll be a conflagration downstairs with Barleybridge-wide repercussions.'

Then Miriam did laugh till tears rolled down her cheeks. Between bursts of laughter she managed to say in short blasts, 'He deserves it. He is just so . . . blatantly unfaithful. I feel very sorry for Nina. I really do.'

'It's all right then with you, if he keeps his affairs under wraps?'

'Well, no, I didn't mean that, but he does deserve all he gets.'

Mungo watched her put her tissue away. 'His woman looked well off, didn't she? Very smart clothes and obviously panting for the chap.'

'Mungo! Is there any wonder? He is gorgeous. I guess sometimes they go after *him* and not the other way round and he finds it hard to refuse. It must be very flattering having women running after him. Hard to resist if you're sexy like he is. He can even charm Mrs Bookbinder.'

'Wow! I don't know who is worse – him or Scott.'

'Oh! Scott's altogether different now he's married Zoe. He's fallen for her in a big way.'

'How do you know all this? I never notice.'

'That's what's so beautiful about you, Mungo, you're such an innocent, you don't see what's going on right under your nose. Have you got Galaxy's post–mortem report back yet?'

'No. Not that it will make much difference. Whatever caused it we shall still be to blame. I just wish I'd never agreed that Virginia could cover for Dan. But I did. When he comes back on Monday there'll be hell to pay.'

Chapter 9

Virginia was at the practice at 8 a.m. sharp on the Monday delivering her report to Mungo. She was anxious to be prompt, and had set the alarm for six-thirty to make sure she was there on time. She placed the file neatly on his desk right where he couldn't possibly miss seeing it. At the back of her mind she wondered if she should have altered that paragraph halfway down the fifth page, and turned back to pick up the file again and check it. No! She wouldn't. It was fine as it was. She'd stand by what she'd written.

Virginia turned to find Dan coming in looking for Mungo.

'Oh! Too early for him, am I? How's things, Virginia?' Dan noticed her cast a swift look at the file on the desk. 'What's this? Something going on I ought to know about? New idea you're floating, eh?' His craggy face creased with smiles, he waited for her reply.

Mungo walked in before Virginia answered. He looked grim but found sufficient bonhomie to ask Dan about his holidays and if the children were all well. To Virginia he said, 'You've brought it, then? Absolutely true? Accurate? I's dotted? T's crossed?'

Virginia, her confidence at a very low ebb because of the hours of sleep she'd deprived herself of in order to do a first-class job on her report, almost strangled herself trying to appear nonchalant in front of Dan. Her throat so constricted she couldn't speak, she nodded instead.

Mungo couldn't let the moment go. 'While you have been away, Dan, I'm afraid Lord Askew's Galaxy has had to be . . . well . . . shot. Virginia knows about it, don't you?'

99

Momentarily Virginia found her voice. 'Yes. We don't know the whys and wherefores . . . yet. Not till the post-mortem.'

'Dead? But he's only what, eleven or twelve? Surely not?'

Mungo waited for Virginia to reply, but saw her throat straining to speak although nothing would come. 'We don't know. It's all very mysterious. Poor thing, right at the height of his career. Lady Mary is devastated.'

Dan was devastated, too. He'd once saved Galaxy with an intuitive diagnosis and had been the Askews' favourite vet ever since. Now this! Beyond belief.

He looked fiercely at Virginia. 'Well, I want an explanation. Please.'

'I – I haven't one. Well, I have . . . he must have rolled sometime and punctured his right flank . . . on a rusty nail or some such; no one noticed and an infection got in. They delayed calling us out so the infection was well progressed before I even got there.'

Dan breathed deeply to get control of himself and said, 'I'm going to see the Askews. It's the least I can do.'

Mungo began to boil over, stabbing the air with an irate finger. 'You'll do no such thing. No such thing. We stay away from there until I've got things sorted.'

'I am going.' Dan turned on his heel and left the office.

Mungo couldn't allow this to happen. He raced out down the back corridor and out into the car park. Dan was already revving up. Mungo leapt for his driver's door and flung it open. 'Do you hear me? I *cannot* afford for someone to go up there. It'll look like guilt, as though we're worried.'

'Well, aren't we? Worried? Though I see she's still in your employ, even though she lost you a top-rank valuable client like Lord Askew. I can't believe it of you. Take your hand off my door this instant. What a start to my first week back.'

Dan revved up again and Mungo sprung away from the door, allowing Dan to leave, not that he had much option. The man had gone completely mad.

Back inside and breathing heavily, Mungo thought: He's right, what *am* I doing still employing her? Then he remembered Colin and Letty and little John had already left for their holidays. Well, reluctantly he had to agree Miriam was right, they needed Virginia for these next two weeks. And if he sacked her it *would* look as though he thought her guilty of neglect, which she was of course, but no, he couldn't sack her, not for a while yet.

Dan seethed with anger and disappointment all the way to Lord Askew's and arrived full of temper but managed to get it under control just in time. He wanted to arrive contrite and full of sorrow: furious anger would achieve nothing.

He went straight to the stables to find Gavin standing in Galaxy's now empty stable.

Dan removed his hat and stood silently looking around. Galaxy's strong personality still felt to be there, and it shook him. His anger faded and all he felt was sorrow. Galaxy's energy, his confidence, his spark were gone for ever.

'Sorry about . . . you know. Came as a real blow to me when I got back today.'

Gavin nodded. 'This'll always be his stable. I loved 'im.'

'Not surprising, he was a splendid animal.' Dan paused for a moment and then asked, 'Any of the family about?'

'Having breakfast. Tread carefully. The girl's heartbroken.'

'The girl?'

'Lady Mary. Taken it very badly.'

'Ah! Right, that's understandable. Be seeing you, Gavin.'

When Lord Askew was told that Dan was waiting to speak to him he asked to have him shown into the breakfast room. Two of his sons and Lady Mary were eating with their father. Dan apologized for interrupting their breakfast.

'Not at all, not at all. Charters! A drink for Mr Brown. Tea? Coffee? Pull up a chair.'

'Coffee, please.'

Dan, eager to say what he'd come to say, immediately came out with it. 'I am appalled at what has happened. I've come straight round. Couldn't do any other. Will you please accept my deepest regrets?' He looked at each of them in turn but received no reply. This forced him to continue speaking. 'It would be foolhardy of me to say, "If only I'd been here." I don't know what else I could have done, not having examined him nor read the post-mortem report. But even so, *I am very sorry*. That's what I've come to say.' Dan thanked Charters for his coffee and took a sip.

Finally it was Lady Mary who answered him. 'Sorry! Sorry? That word hardly—'

'Nevertheless, it's sincerely meant.'

She put down her piece of toast and said, 'Neglect. That's what it was.'

'The practice genuinely does feel very deeply about the situation, Lady Mary.' Dan didn't feel he should apologize outright because that would mean taking all the blame, which he wasn't prepared to do, just in case.

She snorted her disagreement. 'Not the practice. Him!' She had her butter knife in her hand at that moment and she stabbed the air with it in her father's direction. 'I was away with Constellation and had left him in charge. He refused Gavin permission to send for a vet. Four days he waited, knowing, *knowing*, that things were looking serious, then he finally gave in.'

Dan raised an eyebrow at Lord Askew.

The silence which filled the room lay heavy on Lord Askew. Finally he said, 'If I let Gavin call in the vet every time he asked I'd be bankrupt.'

'Father! Gavin knows what he's doing. You're a skinflint. A miser. A Scrooge.'

Dan felt sorry for His Lordship; he was obviously devastated by Lady Mary's attack. Lord Askew's hands dropped from the table onto his lap and he sat there shaking his head slowly from side to side.

One of her brothers spoke up on his father's behalf. 'Steady, sis. Pa doesn't deserve this. He's right, he already forks out all the money for your horses and it's an expensive hobby, as you well know—'

'Hobby!' Mary got to her feet. 'How dare you? Hobby indeed.

Hobby!' Her face flushed darkly and Dan could see her father in her.

Lord Askew said, 'Now, Mary my dear, now, now. I don't regret one penny of what I pay, but one has to keep a sense of proportion about it. I haven't a bottomless pit of money, much as I should like to have.'

Mary dropped back into her chair. 'Sorry. Sorry. But it's true all the same, you waited too long.' She turned to Dan. 'But the fact also remains that . . . that . . . *Virginia* person failed in her job. The woman is a stupid fool, or careless, or thoughtless, or all three. If she'd acted more vigorously, given him a much bigger dose of medication, then perhaps we might have had a chance.'

'That we shall never know. The infection which got into that puncture hole was vicious, and it got a hold immediately. Maybe it had already got a greater grip on his vital organs than anyone could possibly have expected. The PM will tell us more. Meanwhile, nothing and no one benefits from all this arguing. He's gone and time spent regretting his death is wasted time. Constellation is your prime objective now, and, as we all know, he is exceptionally promising and already winning or being placed. That's what you have to concentrate on, Mary, because the combination of his eagerness and your brilliance is a sure recipe for success.' Dan leaned across, lightly touched her hand and smiled, the whole of his face lighting up with his compassion for her loss.

Mary gripped his hand and thanked him, then reached across and kissed his cheek. 'Thank you. Of course you're right. I'd almost been persuaded to go back to using that Giles Standen-Briggs because I was so wild with what had happened, but I shan't. You're ten times better than him, and I've told Father so, but he won't listen, he's adamant he wants to use Giles.'

'Right.' Dan hid his deep concern behind a poker face.

Mary and her brother left His Lordship and Dan alone.

Dan finished his coffee before he spoke. 'She's right. We don't want to be coming out to every little problem – believe me, we're too busy for that. Gavin can deal with the small things but when it's a valuable horse or any animal in actual *pain*, and he was obviously in pain, then we want to be called out. Any time of the day or night, OK? That is if we are to be your vets in the future.'

Lord Askew, without looking at him, nodded his assent. 'Can't bear for her to be distressed. Terribly foolish thing I did, ignoring it. Our only girl, you know, love her to bits, as they say. I'd lose all this,' he waved a hand at the paintings on the walls and the gleaming antique furniture, 'all of this, so not a hair of her head would be harmed. The boys can stand on their own two feet with no help from me, but Mary, . . . ah, well.' He sat more upright and finally looked at Dan. 'I'll wait for the post-mortem before I make a definite decision. I won't forget that woman's lack of professional skill, and it's Mungo's fault for employing her. Has he sacked her?'

Dan got to his feet. 'No. I've a long list of calls to make, so I'll be on my way. Thank you for the coffee.'

'Good morning to you.'

Dan left him sitting at the breakfast table, deep in thought.

He got back in his Land Rover and whooped all the way down the drive. He may not have got a definite 'yes' but it was certainly something very like it.

Kate was as yet unaware of all this confrontation.

She'd got up a good half hour before her usual time, ready for her first day shadowing Scott, and had come in for some disapproval from Mia.

'You do know what you're doing, Kate, don't you?'

'Of course I do. I know he's married, and very happily, but I can't help but be enthusiastic, not after the week I've had with Virginia. He's a very skilful vet and I'll learn a lot.'

'That's not what I'm worried about. You know full well what I mean.'

Kate paused for a moment in the middle of hunting in the hall cupboard for her boots, which she'd only put in there on Saturday evening. She straightened up and, facing Mia, said very firmly, 'Yes. I do know what I'm doing and no, nothing untoward will happen, believe me. He's already told me how committed he is to Zoe and I wouldn't have it otherwise.'

'So what's the excitement all about, then? You're lit up like a Catherine Wheel.'

'I'm not.' But she was and she knew she was. It felt like the first day of the rest of her life. At the same time she knew she was behaving like an idiot teenager, all bright-eyed and adoring. But she couldn't help herself.

'I only say what I do because I don't want you hurt all over again. It was so painful before, and don't say it wasn't because it was. I love you, Kate, more than anyone or anything, and you stepping head-first into the same situation is more than I can take.' Mia began searching for a handkerchief in her pockets.

'There's no need for that, crying and such. I've grown up, I know what I'm doing. In any case, he's head over heels in love with Zoe, and he's told me he isn't on the pull with anyone at all. So, don't worry.' She heaved her boots out of the cupboard and gave Mia a kiss, on both cheeks for good measure 'God! I'm so hot after digging about in there, I could do with another shower. No time, though. Have a good day, Mia, and don't worry if I'm late, Scott's always late. Bye!'

While waiting at the traffic lights she dug in her bag, got out a bottle of her favourite perfume and sprayed herself lavishly. It made her cough and then, during the coughing fit, the lights changed, so she had to set off still coughing, as the cars behind her were already tooting their anger.

As she swung into the car park, Scott was getting out of his Land Rover. He was in khaki shorts, a khaki short-sleeved shirt with pockets and epaulettes, his broad-brimmed Aussie hat, three-quarter socks and heavy mountain boots. He waved enthusiastically to her and headed inside, holding open the back door for her to precede him.

'Morning! My, you're looking great this morning. Had a good weekend?'

'Yes, thanks. And you?'

'On call. Four, that's all, so it wasn't too bad. Just got to get my list.'

Scott, being Scott, saw Nina and greeted her with delight. She got one of his big hugs and several kisses. 'Am I glad to see you. You'll perk up the reception area like no one else. Good luck with it.'

Nina was embarrassed. 'I'm nervous, I do know that.'

Scott decided to boost her confidence. 'You? Nervous? With all these friends around you? My God! Nervous? Just listen to the woman.' He kissed her again for good measure, picked up his list, read through it swiftly, hooked his arm through Kate's and together they went down the corridor and out into the boiling heat.

Scott leapt into the driver's seat. 'She needs boosting, doesn't she? It must be so humiliating for her, him going round like a tom cat.'

'Scott! Be honest, you used to be like that, didn't you, in your bachelor days?'

'Exactly.' He shoved the Land Rover into gear and they roared away towards Phil Parsons'. 'I was in my bachelor days then, but not now. I'm a one-woman man, and loving it.'

'Good, I'm glad.' Kate meant it, – well, almost. She'd said it to convince herself she had all her hormones in check, but after one glance at his profile and the quick flash of his eyes as he turned his head to question why she was looking at him, she knew for certain she was very wrong. He still overwhelmed her common sense. She clenched her hands tightly and looked straight ahead, wondering why on earth Joy had given her a whole week of this hellish challenge without even asking her if she wanted it.

'Nina must be very forgiving, mustn't she?'

Scott studied the crossroads where the road to Wootton Causeway, Short Lane and Long Lane met. Two lorries and a farm tractor, three cars and the courtesy bus from the caravan park passed before he could turn. 'Gets busier round here. Yes, she must be forgiving – and very much in love with him.'

At Applegate Farm Kate changed into her boots and followed Scott into Phil's filthy farm yard.

'Phil! Phil?'

He emerged, the new Phil transformed by his progressing cosmetic surgery, waving cheerily. 'Another beautiful morning. Isn't it stunning?'

'It is, Phil. It is. I don't need to introduce my student, do I?'

'Of course not. Good morning, Kate, you certainly brighten my morning.'

Scott got down to business. 'Pygmy goats? That right?'

Phil nodded. 'One of 'em seems to have got something nasty – she's listless and eating well, but losing weight. I'm frightened of the others catching it. Come and have a look.'

The two of them followed Phil to his pygmy goat enclosure. They were all happily skipping about, especially the new babies born in the spring, who were scampering about, chasing each other or chasing nothing at all, pestering their mothers for milk and enjoying life to the full. One couldn't help but admire their enthusiasm.

'Which one, then?'

Phil reached over the fence and scooped up the one nearest to him. 'As it happens, it's this one, Pearl. I'm doing well, you know, selling my goats. Forty pounds each these are going for when they're ready, and I've customers queuing up for 'em.'

He and Kate watched Scott examine Pearl. She was white with deep black patches on her flanks and a black blob all over her nose, which somehow gave her a very sweet, comical expression.

Phil relished Scott's evident appreciation of his goats. 'Ruby and Sapphire and Garnet appear to be OK, in the best of health as you might say, but not Pearl.'

'Who chooses their names?' Kate asked.

'Who do you think? Blossom, of course. She's not here at the moment. She's taken Hamish for an interview at the Agricultural College, hoping to get him a place. He won't be accepted 'cos he's no school qualifications, but she insists, so they've gone for the interview. She's that proud of him. Well?'

Scott straightened up and looked Phil in the eye, knowing there'd be trouble. 'Well, Phil, you know I'm a straight talker, don't you? Listlessness and eating well, but losing weight? I've a suspicion it's Johne's disease. It's common in all ruminants, but I have to confirm it with a blood test.'

The colour drained from Phil's face. 'You mean stick a needle in and take blood out?'

'Brace yourself, Phil. Yes. Kate, get the equipment from the car, please.'

'But what *is* this disease you think she's got?'

Scott explained. 'It's passed on down the generations. Sometimes it manifests itself or it passes on to the other goats. Pearl will develop antibodies to it and they'll be detected in the blood test. But sometimes they have Johne's disease, there are no signs in the blood test but the symptoms are still there. A further blood test will find antibodies and then we know for sure. She'll go steadily downhill and will inevitably die. Slowly.'

'Ahhh! Look. Do we need to make sure? Can we just leave it? What does it mean?'

'If I'm right, it would mean that a responsible breeder wouldn't breed from her again, because of the chance of passing it on. As a precaution, though I don't promise it will work because it could already have been passed on to the others, she should be isolated. I'm adamant about that.'

Phil gripped the edge of the fence for support and stood contemplating his situation. 'Isolated? *Isolated*? But it might not be what you said, it could be something else.'

'Of course it could, but we have to find out. Not natural to be eating well *and* losing weight, is it? And I can't think of anything other than Johne's disease at the moment. A sample bottle and a syringe, Kate, please.' Kate handed them to him and Phil resigned himself to what felt to him to be a dramatic episode in his life. 'I-I-I can't hold her. Will you, Kate?'

'Of course. Just look the other way. It's for the best.'

'Is it?' Phil turned his back on them, his knuckles going whiter and whiter because he was clutching the fence so tightly. 'Is it over?'

'It is.' Kate hid the sample in her trouser pocket. 'You can turn round now.'

Just then they heard the rumble of the Parsons' van.

'Don't tell Blossom till we know proper,' Phil said. 'Nor Hamish, come to that.'

Blossom emerged from the van and, for a split second, they weren't entirely sure it was she, because she was wearing a black business suit with a pale turquoise silk shirt. Her hair, which she'd had coloured light-brown, thus disguising her usual peroxide blonde, was coiled in a French pleat and her make-up was ultra-discreet. Hamish was wearing a smart summer suit in beige linen with a shirt and colourful tie.

Neither Scott nor Kate could quite believe their eyes.

Kate, trying hard to disguise how gobsmacked she was, said, 'My, you look good the pair of you. How you've got on? Phil said you'd gone to the College.'

Hamish didn't wait for Blossom to answer on his behalf. 'They're sending a letter to let us know. Next week, they say.'

Blossom said, 'He's done really well. Spoken up for himself and answered their questions properly, no hesitation.'

'Them questions was easy. Animal husbandry and finding out how committed I am. That was all. It was a doddle.'

Kate nodded her approval. 'Well done. You'll just have to wait and see now, won't you?'

Blossom patted Hamish's arm. 'Go in and get this expensive suit off, right?' When he was out of earshot she added, 'Doesn't he look good in that suit? Wish there was a wedding to go to, to get some use out of it.' Kate noticed that it looked as though an idea had occurred to her, and wondered if Blossom was thinking of making her and Phil legal. Blossom continued, 'The College staff had a word with me and said they were impressed by him and would give him serious consideration. A whole year, he'd be there. Every day. I hope it works out.'

Scott said, 'And so do I. I'll be off then, Phil.' He winked at

Phil out of sight of Blossom, but he saw she sensed Phil's apprehension and, to divert her attention away from goats, he said, 'I haven't seen my little namesake this morning. She usually comes out to greet me.'

Though he didn't know it, it was the worst thing he could have said. Blossom's face crumpled and she only just managed to mutter, 'She's gone missing,' before she broke into weeping. Kate put her arm around her and gave her a squeeze, and Scott could have cut his tongue out. Appalled at what he'd done, and feeling bad about his little namesake, Scott asked, 'Gone missing? My favourite cat? How long?'

Phil said, 'Fourteen days ago.'

Blossom emerged from her handkerchief long enough to say, 'It's fifteen now.'

Scott remembered the very anecdote to boost her hopes. 'Oh! Fifteen days? Well, there's still hope. I know someone who lost their cat and, after a year, when they'd finally given up hoping it would ever come back, they adopted a replacement from a cat sanctuary and the *very next day* their own cat came back. The original one gave the new one a real pasting, thus sorting out the pecking order, and then they settled down to a happy life together. So you never know.'

Blossom brightened considerably at this piece of news and reached up to give Scott a kiss. 'Thank you for that. Thank you.'

'Well, we'll be away. Good morning to you both, and best of luck with Hamish and College. I hope it turns out all right.'

When they'd got back into Scott's Land Rover Kate had to ask. 'Was that true? About the cat?'

'Absolutely. I reckon their own cat had gone to live in a house not far away and had been keeping an eye on its original home, saw to its horror they'd got another cat and decided to return. It is true, honest. But I'm upset about Little Scott. She was a gem.'

'According to you, it may not be the end of her.'

'Then again it might. On our way to Chess Gorge Farm we'll take this sample into the practice and have coffee. Find out the latest news. Right?'

'You're turning into a gossip.'

'What else can you expect when I live in a cottage with roses round the door and I have Zoe's mum for a mother-in-law?' He turned to grin at her, and saw her feelings about him spread right across her face. He cringed inside at the responsibility he felt, so quickly looked away and drove through Barleybridge, kicking himself for problems that were a direct result of his philandering in the past. Damn and blast.

Kate noticed how quickly he'd looked away and felt acutely embarrassed, so when they walked in to the practice she went straight to the ladies' to splash her face with cold water to cool down her cheeks. How old was she? Twenty-two and still blushing. Time she got a life.

In the staffroom Joy was making an early coffee. 'I might have known you'd be in the moment I put the kettle on. You have an uncanny ability for that, Scott, did you know?'

'I've only come in to hear the latest gossip. That true, Kate?'

'It is.'

Scott persisted. 'So, is there anything of interest, Joy?'

'Well, if a full-scale row between Mungo and Dan is news, then that's it.'

'About Galaxy?'

'Yes. It finished with Dan racing out to his car with Mungo in hot pursuit telling him not under any circumstances to go to Lord Askew's and Dan saying he was going, it was the least he could do. So he did. But we haven't heard any more.'

'Wow! Post-mortem results not in yet?'

'No. Virginia's in a strop over it, too. And Valentine is like a volcano about to erupt because of Nina being here, but she's made a very good start, so,' she beamed at the two of them, 'I'm glad to have two people who are patently getting on well; it makes a change. Well, what's happened to the two of you this morning?'

Scott, still stinging over his discovery about the state of Kate's emotions, said, 'Very little actually. Except Little Scott, my namesake at the Parsons', has been missing for fifteen days.'

'Oh! That's a pity. She was a dear little cat. Blossom will be shattered.'

'She is. So am I. What chance of me finding an identical one and pretending someone brought Little Scott into the practice?'

Joy looked sceptically at him. 'Honestly! Fat chance. You're getting sentimental in your old age.'

'It's marriage, it's rounded off all my corners. Which reminds me.' He dug out his mobile and, saying, 'Excuse me,' wandered out to phone Zoe.

Joy looked at Kate and said, 'All right?'

'Fine, thanks. Yes, fine.' But she spoiled the whole effect by flushing again.

As gently as she could, Joy suggested she would be willing to change Kate to shadowing someone else if she wished.

'Oh, no. I'm absolutely fine. Got over the teenage crush stage.' I'm getting good at lying, I am, thought Kate.

'Well, that's all right, then.'

Scott came back in. 'Right. Lesley's just taken a call from Hare's Meadow Farm. Cow having a problem delivering a calf. Sounds nasty. So we'll call there first. Ready?'

Kate sprang to her feet and set off after him. Joy watched them leave and wondered. Kate might say she'd got over her teenage crush, but judging by her face she had not. Ah, well. Worse things happened at sea. But still she worried, because Kate had become the daughter she'd never had and if Scott kicked over the traces with her, she'd personally throttle him. Then she remembered how much in love Zoe and he were and felt reassured.

It wasn't often they got a call for Hare's Meadow Farm, which was not far from the Parsons' farm. Benny and Laura Taylor were very self-contained and got on with the business of farming by flogging themselves day in day out with a devotion some farmers would do well to emulate. Absolute cleanliness, well-tended fields, superb quality beef cattle, and an ability to avoid the expense of calling in a vet taken to a fine art. Therefore, Scott knew it must be serious.

There were three designated parking spaces in the farm yard, one occupied by a tiny Smart car, the second by a gleaming scarlet utility truck and the third vacant. Scott parked in the third space and the two of them got out. It was the first time Kate had been there, and she looked around as she dragged her boots on. Cheery boxes of geraniums filled every window sill, the farm cat sat in the sun washing her face by the farmhouse door with a litter of kittens playing about her, four splendid pedigree hens clucked their way along the cobbles and out of the cowshed on the far side came Benny.

So this was him. Benny, was the star poker player in the area. To play poker with Benny you had to have wads of money in your back pocket and a brain like a scalpel. Regular poker parties were held at their house, and a place at their card table was greatly prized. He was extremely tall, with a shock of black hair which seemed to stand on end, as though he'd been plugged into the mains all night. His hands appeared too large and awkward to be able to manipulate a pack of cards with finesse, and his boots, well, they were very large and gleamed with polish. But most impressive was his face. Being a big man he had a big face, and it looked as though lumps of stone had been used in its construction. But when he smiled, as he was doing right then, the whole world appeared to light up.

Kate's hand was engulfed, Scott appeared to be of only normal height in comparison, and Benny said, 'It's urgent. Calf's stuck half out. Can't move it and we'll be losing it soon. By the breadth of its forehead it's a bull calf. Come and do your best.'

He led the way to a huge barn where he wintered his cattle in the very worst of the weather. Kate nearly fell back in horror. Something she had never seen before was happening right there in front of her. Hell's bells! This was ghastly. The mother was standing calmly, loosely roped to a ring in the wall of the barn, her rear facing them as they walked in. Half in and half out of its mother's body was a rich dark-red and white calf, its head and front legs dangling out. Alive, that was obvious, but in desperate straits.

'When did this start?' Scott asked, stripping off to put his calving gown on.

'During the night. He got as far as this first thing and I can't get it any further. Is there a chance?'

'Caught by its hips. Big calf, too big for her. First calving?'

Benny nodded. 'I've been with her half the night, but my hands are too big to get at it.'

'The mother's still straining hard, but I'm going to slow that down, otherwise I shan't be able to move it with all that muscle squeezing so fiercely. She must be tough to be still straining after all this time. Cows never cease to amaze me.'

Scott gave the cow the injection and stood back to wait for the straining to lessen, his hand on her flank. Kate couldn't resist stroking the calf's head. Its predicament horrified her. She looked into its beautiful great dark eyes but they gazed back blankly.

'Scott?'

'Yes?'

'Will you—'

Scott abruptly interrupted her. 'Ah! That's better. Put your hand here where mine is. Feel it? The tension lessening. Now we can do something.'

He went to satisfy himself that pulling it out was not possible. The mother mooed her objections and no wonder, the calf was stuck very tight. Experience told him it would mean the ropes and considerable heaving, but first he tried turning the calf to make it fit the shape of the birth canal more closely than it was at the moment. He embraced the calf in a full hug, his arms encircling it right where it emerged from its mother. Then Kate saw his arm muscles bulge as he attempted to rotate it a little, but that didn't work. So he tried again with a different grip. Still his idea didn't work, so Scott braced himself to rotate the calf the other way. It only needed a centimetre or two of movement but the calf was too tightly jammed. Benny's face was contorted with anxiety, Kate was full of admiration for Scott, but he was too intensely occupied to notice. The third time, when his strength was beginning to run out and it looked as though all hope was gone, he moved the calf literally a matter of a couple of centimetres and somehow it looked to occupy the space more comfortably. Scott stood back, a look of satisfaction flooding his face. He was sweating with the exertion but much happier. 'Right, you little trouble-maker. Ropes, Kate, please. Benny, help me pull.'

He skilfully knotted the ropes to both the calf's front legs, saying to Benny, 'Steady pulls, both together when I say the word. No jerking, just slow, steady pulling. Take a good grip. Right. Go!'

It seemed to take an age before there was any improvement in the position of the calf, but then it began to happen and suddenly, with a great sploosh, the calf landed on the straw. Alive! For a newborn calf he was huge.

'You were right, Benny, a big bull calf it is. My! He's a beauty! Look, Kate. Isn't he fantastic?'

'He is. He's magnificent.'

She helped Scott to clean him up and clear his mouth, and despite the exhaustion of his birth in no time he was trying to stand up and his mother was taking notice of him, all pain apparently forgotten.

While Scott was checking that the mother's reproductive areas were in good nick, Kate looked at Benny and was embarrassed to see tears running down his cheeks. 'Isn't birth a miracle?' she said.

Benny choked on his tears and grunted, 'Always is. A miracle. A real miracle. Thank you, Scott. You got it just right. Wash up in the outside john and come in for a drink. You need it. I'll tell Laura.' He pulled his mobile from his pocket and rang his wife.

What better place was there to be than in a barn, on a hot sunny day with the smell of newborn calf, of straw, of human endeavour, filling the air? Kate was enthralled and convinced, if she needed convincing, that being a vet was the best occupation in all the world.

After they'd both washed in the outside lavatory, they followed Benny into the house. The Taylors' kitchen was immaculate and shining, the very latest in stainless-steel luxury. Laura had laid out a variety of drinks on the immense kitchen table. She must have been almost six feet tall and glamorous with it. Kate envied her style; she was less a farmer's wife, more a supermodel on holiday.

Scott eagerly glugged down his glass of cold water and said, 'He's a beautiful calf, Mrs Taylor, well worth the effort.'

'Good. I'll go out and see him in a minute. Can't bear to see the pain. Neither can Benny, but he manages better than me.'

They stood chatting for a while and then Scott said, 'More calls, got to go. Keep an eye on the mother, Benny, she's had a hard time. Be seeing you.'

When they got into the Land Rover, Scott turned to Kate and said, 'Your face! When you saw the calf, I thought you were going to faint on me. I'm proud of you, we'll make a vet of you yet.' He spontaneously reached across, smiling from ear to ear, and kissed her. Kate returned his kiss with vigour, for he'd kissed her lips and not her cheek as she'd expected, and then she almost died of embarrassment. What must he think of her? Scott looked deeply into her eyes and then looked away. 'Sorry. Mistake. Shouldn't have done that. Let's go.'

But the atmosphere was intense between them and Kate blamed herself. All he'd done was give her a peck of a kiss, and she'd responded by going into overdrive. It left her feeling furious with herself. Scott revved the engine and away they hurtled. Kate felt desolate with love for him, but a small voice at the very back of her mind asked, 'Or is it lust?'

Chapter 10

The following day Galaxy's post-mortem results came. Dan happened to be in the staffroom reading his morning post when Mungo shouted to no one in particular, 'Is Dan around?'

He went to see why Mungo was shouting for him. 'Yes! Here I am.'

Mungo flung the papers across his desk. 'Here's your answer. The post-mortem results.'

Dan studied every single line of the conclusions before he spoke. 'My God! Bloody hell! He hadn't a chance. It must have been well advanced before we were called in. Whatever Virginia had done she couldn't have saved him.'

Mungo shook his head. 'Don't know about that. If she'd done a blood test first there might have been a chance, but when you study how much antibiotic she prescribed it was like feeding an elephant a jelly baby. Too little, far too late.'

'Look, Mungo, can I go tell them? They've forbidden Virginia to set foot on the estate ever, so she can't go.'

'OK. If you're not too busy go today, the sooner the better. Take this photocopy of it, not the original; I want that. It's damned bad news. Do your best, his account is a large slice of our client list and we can't afford to lose anyone at all at the moment. – let alone what will happen if he claims?' He raised a finger in salutation, which Dan took as 'just go and let me get on' and left the office, bumping into Scott as he set off for the back door.

'You'll be interested in this. It's the post-mortem result.'

Scott skimmed through the report. 'Crikey! Would you believe that. His spleen totally shot to pieces . . . so that hole on his flank was significant, then. Well, I never. I did say to Ginny there was something very odd about it all. But they'd have known things were going seriously wrong before they got us in. Lord Askew knocks hell out of Gavin if he thinks he's called us in when there's no need, so in a way he's only got himself to blame. Are you going to see them?'

'Yes, right now.'

'Well, remind them of that fact. If we'd got there earlier, if we'd had a chance, we might have saved him.'

'On the other hand, he probably would never have regained his superb condition again.'

Scott shrugged. 'You could be right. Good luck, though, it's not an easy task.'

As Dan was leaving, he said with a smile, 'Does she like you calling her Ginny?'

Scott grinned. 'No, but I do, just to annoy her. Have you seen Kate this morning?'

'No.'

Kate was on her way, but running late because she'd had a bad night and felt completely rotten as a result. It was that kiss which had caused the problem. OK, you did kiss people nowadays without giving it a second thought, even complete strangers sometimes. What she loathed about herself was kissing him in return, and not just a peck of a kiss but a clinging one. She blushed just thinking about it, and even more when the driver behind her tooted because the lights had changed to green.

Well, today was another day and she'd made a resolve around three a.m. that morning that it was the end of her thinking of Scott as someone she loved. She definitely didn't. He belonged to Zoe and that was that. Kate pulled into the practice car park and there was Scott, his driver's door open, standing waiting for her.

She parked her car, picked up her belongings from the passenger seat, locked it up and dashed across to him. 'So sorry I'm late. I couldn't gear myself up this morning. Are we busy today?'

'Medium. Get in.' He sensed her discomfort and guessed what caused it. He'd have to be careful how he treated her. Keep it cool. No more kissing, though he could well do with some TLC, as he and Zoe had had the row to beat all rows last night.

They'd woken up Oscar, who had dissolved into horrendous tears and couldn't be pacified. It made Scott feel a heel and Zoe even angrier with him. This morning they still weren't reconciled and Scott felt desolate. All because he refused to go to a clinic to see why Zoe hadn't conceived. After all, a thoroughly all-male Aussie like him didn't do that kind of thing.

How to prove he *was* a potent virile Aussie? He couldn't, unless he went for tests, which he wasn't going to do. But . . .

'Scott, your list says Hunter's Reach first.'

'Does it? I'm going completely the wrong way, then. Sorry.' He swung the car round at the first wide stretch of the road and headed back to Hunter's Reach. Fact remained, he refused to go to a clinic to prove anything at all. It must be Zoe at fault. Yes, that was it. It would be Zoe, so *she* could go and get tested. Then they'd be OK. He brooded on the estrangement, the very first of their marriage, all the way to Hunter's Reach. He'd be damned if he'd rush home tonight in a big hurry; she deserved to be let stew for a while.

He swung into the gateway to Hunter's Reach, parked and pulled on the brake. It was the home of two people who, as far as Scott was concerned, merely played at being farmers. They purported to be sisters but Scott had grave doubts about that. They were so unalike: one with a dusky skin and black hair, the other fair with mousy hair and prominent teeth. But they steadfastly declared themselves as the two Misses Butler, Verity and Felicity. I should cocoa, thought Scott. It would be one of their dratted donkeys taken ill again. They were old and a complete liability health-wise.

But it wasn't. They'd brought him out just to give their cats booster injections. As both of them were perfectly capable of driving and each had their own vehicle, he failed to see what made them demand a home visit. But he said nothing to them of his opinions.

'Good morning. Beautiful hot day, isn't it? Boosters for Maud and Myrtle, I think you said.' He looked at them standing there in what they thought of as countrywear, several shades of brown and khaki with Timberland boots (which never seemed to get dirty, unlike his own) looking pleasant and welcoming.

'Scott, how lovely of you to come. Just the man we want to see.'

'You've met Kate? She's my veterinary student for the week.'

'No. How exciting. Going to be a vet. Excellent. If you're anywhere near as good as Scott, you'll do all right. We've never caught him on the back foot, not once. Nobody better. Come along in.'

Their praise boosted Scott's low spirits but he still felt angry that they thought his valuable time, which could have been spent more profitably, was being used on such an unspectacular job. Boosters belonged in the consulting room not to a farm vet call. Still . . .

The house appeared to have been furnished from a catalogue, a superior one but definitely a catalogue. It was contemporary, bold, simplistic, and not the least comfortable. Scott mentally shrugged his shoulders. What the hell? At least his Zoe knew a thing or two about interior decoration, she'd done a magnificent . . . Then he remembered he was angry with her and concentrated instead on the boosters.

Verity and Felicity – or, as they gigglingly preferred to be called, Vitty and Flip – disappeared into the kitchen and re-emerged carrying their cats.

'Kate!' Kate stepped forward. 'Hold Myrtle, please.' He pressed the needle briskly into the fleshy part of Myrtle's neck, then did the same for Maud. Discarding the syringes into a box he kept for the purpose, he said, 'That's that. See you again sometime,' and quickly made for the door, but Flip caught him by his coat-tails, as it were.

'We did just wonder if you would take a peep, just a peep, at one of our donkeys. It won't take a minute. Just for your opinion.'

Scott knew this was going to happen. They did it every time. Got the vet out to attend to a case and then rapidly popped in another request, hoping it would slip through the net and wouldn't be charged for.

'OK. Come along, Kate. You like donkeys, don't you?'

'Well . . . er . . . yes, I do.'

They were taken out to the field at the back of the house where the five donkeys lived during the day. 'See the light-grey one? Is he limping?'

Scott laid the question at Kate's door and hoped she knew how to play it. 'Well, Kate, can you give us a *diagnosis*?' She heard the emphasis on the word and knew what was expected.

'Yes, he is. Right rear. Definitely limping.'

'Nothing too serious, though?'

'Can't tell without an examination.' Kate put her hand on the gate catch as though preparing to go into the field.

Hastily Flip protested. 'Please don't worry. It's enough for you to confirm our worries. We'll take care of him.'

'I think in the interests of your animals he should be looked at. Professionally. Just in case. Don't you, Scott?'

'Oh, yes. She's good with donkeys, is our Kate.' He watched her marching across the field and admired the purpose in her step and the swing of her hips in her pale linen trousers and short matching shirt. She was turning into a stunner, was Kate. The swing of her hair as she walked was very sexy.

Kate crossed the field, attempting to look far more confident than she felt. The light grey donkey was too idle to make a fuss and run away from her so she was able to lift all four of its feet and examine them closely without the breathless exercise of trying to catch him first. What he needed was his hooves trimming, but not seriously. Perhaps in the next month.

'Hooves trimming. Right rear worse than the others.'

Scott claimed, 'I'm afraid I shall have to charge for that diagnosis.'

Flip had no inhibitions about the matter. 'Charge? But you've done nothing.'

'We were asked to do the cats' boosters and the donkey comes

121

extra. I can do it now, if you like, but my student says it's not urgent. Just as you like.'

'Oh! It can wait, then. He's not limping that badly. We're not paying just for a *look*.'

'Sorry. I won't be caught with this trick again. Call us out for the real reason next time, not some trumped-up thing. Myrtle and Maud should have been brought in for their boosters. Come on, Kate. Thanks for your diagnosis. Well done.'

'But she's only a student. We thought it might be serious, that's only why we asked.'

'I know she's a student but a very exceptional one. She'll be right.'

'We'll change vets. That's the best thing.'

'To Standen-Briggs? He'll charge twice as much as we do. But good luck.'

He stormed out of Hunter's Reach complaining furiously. 'They do it every time. I knew they would. Well, that's that. For what business they bring our way we may as well be rid of them.'

'You are in a bad mood today.'

'I am. Do me a favour? Have something to eat with me when we finish? I'm in need of TLC.'

'No, thanks.' She longed to say yes. Longed to. But she mustn't, although it would be interesting to learn what had made him so bolshie today.

'Why not?'

'Because.'

'Because nothing. Come, please.' He looked at her with his little boy in need of spoiling look and she just could not miss the chance. Refuse him? When he was upset? Certainly not.

'All right, then.'

'Excellent! My choice of venue.'

'Not too smart, I'm not dressed for somewhere posh.'

Scott smiled.

'OK. Somewhere quiet, then.'

'Fine by me. Let's press on.'

Quite by chance they saw Dan approaching them when they

were driving on to their next call. They both pulled up and wound down their windows.

'Hi, Dan,' said Scott. 'What's the news at the Askews'? I'm assuming that's where you're coming from.'

Dan pretended to pull his forelock. 'I kowtowed. I couldn't see any other way. If Rose had been there she'd have been in hysterics.'

'Ooops! That doesn't sound like our Dan!'

'It isn't, it definitely isn't, but what can one do? He'd already confirmed that he did encourage Gavin and Chris to wait as long as possible before incurring the cost of a vet for Galaxy, but I wanted to be absolutely sure he understood our position.'

In fact, he'd been quite wrong to feel optimistic after he'd called the day he got back from holiday. Lord Askew had not been won over, as he'd thought, and had since become more intransigent than ever, blaming Virginia from start to finish and taking no culpability for his tardy decision.

But when Dan had asked him today whom he'd intended having as his vet now, Lord Askew had been stumped. 'I . . . I . . . I've still to decide.'

'Standen-Briggs?'

Lord Askew had opened his mouth to answer but didn't reply.

'It's difficult, isn't it? You know you have two excellent equine vets at the Barleybridge practice.' Dan had leaned back against the stable wall, arms folded, waiting. He hadn't dared let a smile flit across his face, but it had been difficult not to.

Lord Askew had walked out of the stable and stood out in the glaring sun. 'No Virginia. Not for any of our animals. Right? Scott or you.'

'Done!' The two of them had shaken hands vigorously and then Lord Askew had marched away towards the house.

Dan said to Scott now with a note of triumph in his voice, 'At least he's decided to stay with us. You know Ginny must take a lot of the blame, though. She ought to have known that the antibiotic she prescribed was minuscule compared to what he should have had.'

Kate muttered, 'It was. Even I guessed that.'

Scott pushed on with the most important question as far as the practice was concerned. 'So have we *all* been allowed back into the holy of holies?'

'You and I, that's all. By the way, I saw Gavin as I was leaving. He looks ghastly. Really ill. He's taken it very badly. Feels to blame, I expect. Must go. Done far too much genuflecting this morning. I need to get on with my calls.'

Scott thumped the steering wheel with his fist. 'Brilliant. It calls for a celebration tonight.' He drove off at speed, from time to time chortling with delight.

Kate remembered Virginia's mini-breakdown. 'I'm sorry for Virginia. She's been devastated by it all. She's certain she'll be getting the sack. What about the insurance? Is the practice going to suffer?'

'The Veterinary Defence Society will step in. They'll squeal a bit, but that's what they're there for.' Scott turned to look at her. 'It will be a salutary lesson for Ginny Havelock. Far too uppity. Let's ask Valentine and Nina to come with us tonight, shall we? Make Nina feel as though she belongs to the family, so to speak? What do you say?'

'Oh, absolutely, what a good idea. Shall we give Nina a ring right now?'

'Do that.'

So Kate did ring and Nina was delighted and said yes they'd come. 'We'll meet up at the practice, shall we? Val should be finished by six.'

'Fine, that's lovely. Glad you're free to come.' Kate replaced Scott's mobile and wished the last few minutes hadn't taken place. It wasn't fair. Just when she was full of joy thinking about being in a twosome with Scott, suddenly it had become a foursome. Damn. Just damn.

Kate was horrified when she realised where Scott was heading for their evening out. Oh, no, not the White Hart, please not. But it was, and Valentine followed them into the car park. What must he be thinking right now? She could tell they'd had a row about going out this evening because Nina was far too cheery and Valentine far too miserable for it to be otherwise. So even as they rolled into the car park at the White Hart, she guessed the row would not be over.

Scott leapt out shouting, 'I've booked a table,' and strode in, full of pleasure at the prospect. 'Have you been here before, Kate?'

'Only for a coffee with Virginia. She likes it because it's "select".'

Scott looked over his shoulder. 'Come on, Val, hurry up. We'll have a drink before we sit down, shall we? Look at the menu while we do. Looks a nice place. Benny recommended it. What do you think, Kate?'

Nina hastened after them. 'Val's just gone to the men's room, Scott.'

'What's his favourite drink, Nina?'

'He's drinking vodka and tonic at the moment.'

'Right. Kate, Nina?'

They'd settled themselves at a table in the window which gave them a lovely view of the surrounding countryside. The hills rising in front of them, the brilliant blue, cloudless sky above with birds soaring high, mere pinpoints in the heavens, what could be more pleasurable on a wonderful summer night like this? Eventually Valentine joined them, just as Nina was pointing out a buzzard hovering, being mobbed by rooks.

Scott looked at his angry face and said, 'Something not pleasing you, Val? Don't you like it here?'

'Of course I like it. Just got a bit of a problem which I can't solve, that's all.'

Nina reached across and stroked his knee. 'Can I help?'

'No.'

'Oh, right. Here's your vodka and tonic. Cheer up. We're here to enjoy ourselves.'

Valentine grunted a reply, which none of them could understand.

The other three chatted away, discussing gossip at the practice, life in general, and especially the marvellous summer they were enjoying.

'I can't remember a summer like it since I came to England. It's the best ever,' Nina said.

Scott enquired if she was enjoying working in reception.

'Best thing I did agreeing to do it. It so rewarding and I'm really getting on top of how to deal with clients. Joy says she'll soon be able to retire.' Nina giggled. 'I don't think.'

'Why not? I think it's doing you good.'

Nina, squeezed into a corner closest to Scott, answered his compliment by kissing his cheek and linking her arm in his. 'I've only been there a week and I feel so much better about myself, don't I, Val?'

Kate, for whatever reason, began to feel uneasy. Nina's friendliness was somehow not getting the right response from Val. To divert attention from Nina's psychological improvement, which obviously was pleasing Val not at all, Kate suggested they got menus to look at and she leapt to her feet to get them from a pile on the bar counter.

On her way back to their table she looked at Valentine and noticed his eyes were filled with apprehension, and flitted back and forth, as though searching for someone. Then his eyes swivelled to Scott and the venom in them shocked Kate. What on earth had Scott done to deserve that look?

However, it was all explained when, to her horror, she saw Eleanor Eustace walk in. She was dressed as though she'd been sailing, in brief white shorts and a minuscule navy and white top. Her gloriously tanned skin was gleaming with moisturiser, a navy and white scarf partially covered her blonde hair and she wore a pair of beaded flip-flops on her feet. She looked stunning. Kate froze. Eleanor glanced round the reception area and briefly her eyes skimmed past Valentine. Now Kate knew why Valentine was so twitchy and had been to use his mobile in the men's room. He must have planned to meet her here and Nina accepting Scott's invitation had completely ruined his plans.

Valentine ignored Eleanor, put an arm round Nina's shoulders and smiled intimately at her.

Nina's smile was full of relief. 'Oh! You're feeling better, then. All you needed was to relax and have a drink. Now. What shall we choose from the menu?' She snuggled comfortably into the crook of his arm and the two of them studied the menu together.

Kate chose steak, Scott chose steak, Nina and Valentine chose sea bass. Then Scott caught a glimpse of Eleanor and said, 'Wow! She's a cracker. I wonder who *she's* waiting for?'

For someone like Eleanor, who was clearly greedy for admiration, Kate was surprised she didn't look up when she heard Scott's 'wow' – he certainly said it loud enough for her to hear. Valentine looked like a man about to be burned at the stake. Tense, nervous and edgy, he was paying deliberate attention to Nina to let Eleanor know he was not available.

Kate feared she might come across, but she didn't. And then she saw the reason why. She was waiting not for Valentine but for someone else. A tall man, well over six feet, approached her. Well-cut navy shorts, expensive scarlet T-shirt, navy slip-ons, a strong profile with fine blond hair brushed back from his face without a parting. A handsome older man, and very attractive.

He took her arm and kissed her. She hooked one of her gleaming bare legs around his. Kate couldn't resist a peek at Valentine's face. He was livid with anger at Eleanor's flagrant taunting of him. She must have got his text message and arranged a meeting with another of her amours.

Kate got to her feet 'I'm starving, let's eat.' Walking into the dining room didn't mean having to pass close to the two of them, much to her relief.

Throughout the meal, Valentine was almost speechless, Nina couldn't stop talking, and Kate felt as though she'd swallowed a gobstopper and it had wedged in her throat. Scott couldn't understand what had happened to the evening.

The painful meal was eventually over and they thankfully wandered back into the big reception area for coffee. Eleanor and her escort had disappeared and Kate was hit by the idea that they'd gone up to one of the bedrooms, because they definitely hadn't gone into the dining room – she would have seen them – and if they came down while . . . which of course they did, with Eleanor hanging on her boyfriend's arm, looking glittery and exuding sex appeal. Valentine was seated facing the staircase.

His hands were clenched tightly, resting on the table close to his coffee cup. Nina offered him more coffee from the pot and his hand jerked so much when he picked up his cup and saucer in response to her saying, 'More coffee, Val?' that his knuckles thrust against the coffee pot and it flew out of her grip, the coffee spewing all over the table before the pot fell onto the carpet.

Nina looked as though she'd been hit. She sprang to her feet to prevent all the coffee running down the front of her, and Scott grabbed a paper napkin and tried to mop her up. Kate rescued the coffee pot from the floor and Valentine did absolutely nothing; nothing at all. He was like a man in a hypnotic trance. Scott, having had enough of battling against the awkwardness which had descended on an evening he'd organized with such enthusiasm, declared himself ready for bed, and sorry but . . .

Valentine eagerly agreed, put his arm through Nina's to encourage her to leave quickly, and Kate followed, feeling sticky and uncomfortable from the evening's events. She slipped thankfully into Scott's Land Rover and, waving madly to Nina, they swept away with alacrity.

'Well,' said Scott, 'perhaps you could tell me why the evening was such a disaster? It shouldn't have been but it was.'

Kate stared out of the window. She owed Scott an explanation at the very least, but could he be trusted not to divulge Val's secret?

'Valentine was a bloody pain the whole time, when he's usually fun to be with, Nina was like a cat on hot bricks and, as for you, you looked as though you'd eaten a lemon just before you came out.'

'I did not. Well, perhaps I did, but not really. Can you keep a secret? Really keep a secret?'

Scott sensed some very special gossip was about to be revealed and he readily promised his discretion. 'Scout's honour. Honest. My lips are sealed.'

'Up until tonight Valentine has been seeing that girl in the bar. The one you said "Wow" about, and I think he'd made an arrangement to meet her there, not knowing that was where you'd planned for us to go. If you remember, Nina accepted without consulting Valentine.'

'Hell. No wonder he looked so sour at me. It's a wonder I wasn't struck dead. Does Nina know, do you think?'

'She knows he's up to something, but *who* it is, no, she doesn't. She originally thought it was *me*. No way. I thought Eleanor—'

'You know her name!'

'She's a client of ours. You didn't know, of course. I thought she intended coming over and speaking to him, but no, she's too clever for that, she hit him where it really hurt—his ego. What I hate is Nina being so pleased with whatever scrap of attention he pays her.'

Scott looked ahead at the road and after a moment said, 'The sod. The absolute sod. Still, he must have had a terrible shock when that fellow walked in. He got his just reward there, didn't he?' Then he started laughing, and laughed so much he couldn't see the road, so he had to pull in to the side and turn off the engine.

Kate had never seen him laugh so much for so long. 'It's not that funny. In fact it's very sad . . . for Nina, you know. She's just back with him and he's at it again. Will nothing stop the man?'

Scott began laughing all over again. 'His face! What a damn shock he must have had. Serves him right.'

Kate wasn't laughing, and Scott wanted her to, so he tried tickling her ribs but that didn't work, she wriggled away from him and then he caught her eye, and before they knew it they were kissing.

Suddenly, and all too soon as far as Kate was concerned, Scott drew back and apologized. 'I'm terribly sorry, Kate. I got carried away by the moment. Please forgive me, it won't happen again.' He sat back in his seat sober and embarrassed.

When Valentine got in to his car, ready to drive home after what had been the most disastrous evening of his life, Nina spoke up.

'Valentine, I'm not a fool. You were expecting to meet someone in that bar, weren't you, and I spoiled your plan by accepting Scott's invitation.'

'That is ridiculous. Whatever makes you think that?'

Nina was looking out of the window. 'You were so angry when I said I'd accepted Scott's invitation, I couldn't understand it. But now I do.'

Valentine, already violently disturbed by Ellie's betrayal, exploded. 'You've come up with some mad ideas about me in the past but tonight is the maddest yet. Completely and absolutely, ridiculously mad. In fact, it could be classed as evil. Evil, do you hear? Evil.' He breathed in through narrowed nostrils, but instead of Nina being beaten into pulp by his outburst and his heavy breathing, she simply laughed.

'Where did you meet her?'

Valentine didn't reply.

'I said, where did you meet, whoever she is?' Nina said that loudly and angrily, her fists looking ready to beat him, resting as they were on her thighs, clenched, prepared for action. 'Answer me! Answer me!' Such was her temper she struck her thighs with her fist as she spoke.

Valentine had no idea how to deal with this new Nina. Eventually he muttered, 'You're quite wrong, you know, quite wrong. It's all going on in here, it's simply not true.' He tapped his temple and glared at her, deeply concerned that she had become so perceptive; this wasn't what he wanted at all.

'Drive me home right now.'

'When I'm good and ready.'

'No. Right now, Val. I insist. You ruined our evening, and I was so looking forward to it. I can't forgive you for that.'

Valentine did as she asked, finding himself unable to cope with this empowered Nina who'd suddenly emerged. If getting a job did this for her after only two days the sooner she left the better.

Damn and blast Ellie. Playing with him like she did this evening. He'd guessed she would be trouble and he was right. No way was he seeing her again, but then he remembered her eagerness, her inventiveness, the slinky temptress in her.

Chapter 11

Nina was on the reception desk by 7.30 a.m. the next morning, sorting lists, answering calls for appointments, smiling though she didn't feel like smiling, not when she and Valentine had slept in separate bedrooms and he'd left without eating breakfast. Not that he ate much in the morning; strong black coffee with plenty of sugar and a couple of croissants with peach preserve was all he ever had. The phone rang and she answered; 'Barleybridge Veterinary Hospital, Nina speaking. How may I help?'

The main doors, including the inner glass ones, were fastened wide open to let in as much air as possible before any animals arrived, so she had no warning that a client was already arriving. When she eventually looked up and saw the woman from the bar last night rushing in with a small cat wrapped in a blanket, coincidence was the word which sprang to mind. It was an amazing coincidence. Nina quickly noted the message the caller wished to leave and then, seeing the woman's extreme distress, she rushed round the end of the reception desk asking, 'Oh, my goodness! Are you all right?'

Breathless with distress, Eleanor said, 'It's my cat, Choo. She's eaten something she shouldn't and she's terribly ill. It's Val I need to see, he deals with her. Is he in today?'

'He is.'

Poor Choo vomited and writhed and howled with pain.

'Ooops! Oh, not again. She's been ill since early this morning, and I realized it was getting serious. Has she been poisoned, do you think?'

'I'm not qualified to say. Go to Mr Dedic's consulting room.

Here we are.' Nina opened the door and found Valentine, seemingly in the depths of despair, seated in a chair at his computer, his mind apparently a blank. When he saw Ellie he leapt to his feet. She handed him Choo and burst into tears. Valentine laid the kitten on the examination table and Ellie, seeing his hands free, flew into his arms and sobbed, 'Val, Val! Is she going to die? Tell me! Tell me!' She smothered him with hysterical kisses. Valentine tried to thrust her away saying, 'Let me look at her. Please!'

But she clung to him, sobbing and calling out, 'Val, make her better, please. I know you can.'

In a flash Nina knew that she was actually the woman he'd intended meeting last night at the White Hart. Before she could say anything Valentine asked her to take this hysterical woman into the waiting room, to sit her down and get her a glass of water, while he examined Choo.

Walking like an automaton, Nina did as she was asked. She led the woman out and sat her down on a chair. Her throat was so constricted and dry she could barely speak. 'I'll get the glass of water for you. Stay right there.'

Blinded by the horror of the situation she found herself in, Nina bumped into Joy, who was just arriving. 'Whoops! Sorry, Nina! Why, my dear, what is the matter?'

Nina gestured towards the waiting room and Joy went to see. All she saw was a dishevelled woman, seated, head bent, weeping. Joy put her arm round her shoulders. 'Come, come, my dear, it can't be that bad.' After all these years Joy had a good line in comforting clients in distress. Nina came back with the glass of water and thrust it into Ellie's hand, by which time Valentine had appeared in the waiting room.

'She's been vomiting at home? That's why you've brought her in? Mmm? No diarrhoea?'

Ellie nodded, not looking up. 'No diarrhoea.'

'She's very ill and dehydrated. We'll have to keep her in and see how she goes. Put her on a drip. Any idea what might have caused it?'

Ellie shook her head and didn't look up.

'Right. Well, there's nothing you can do for her sitting here, so I suggest you go home and ring us about lunch-time for a progress report, or we'll ring you if there are . . . any further developments. Try not to worry. She'll have the best of treatment, believe me.'

Ellie reached out, took hold of his hand and pressed her lips to it fervently. 'I know. I know. If anyone can make her better, you can. Thank you.' Valentine tried to snatch his hand away but she stroked it three or four times before she let it go.

Joy was mystified by this performance, wondering what on earth must Nina be feeling.

Nina was crushed by the horror of what she was witnessing. So this woman *was* definitely the very one he was seeing. She'd thought the woman Valentine had intended to meet hadn't come last night, but she had and had humiliated him in a way which Val would find not only mortifying but very undeserved. Out of the blue she found it very amusing and began laughing, wildly and out of control.

Even more mystified, Joy went to take control on reception as the clients were already arriving for their early appointments. Lesley began her working day by clearing up Choo's vomit and, when Joy had a moment, she rushed Nina into the staffroom and thrust a glass of water in her hand. 'Sit there till I come back. I need an explanation.'

Sarah Cockcroft, unaware of the sensation in the waiting room, attended to Choo as Valentine had instructed. She was chatting to Choo to put her at her ease, cheerfully putting her in a cage in the intensive care room and sorting out her drip when Joy walked in.

'Sarah, do you know anything about this?'

'About Choo Eustace? She's—'

'No, about her owner and Val?'

'Nothing at all. He's not been . . . has he . . . not again.'

'Well, there's gratitude and there's gratitude. But kissing the vet's hand. Please!' She raised her eyes to the heavens and clapped her hand to her forehead, then walked out to find Nina.

Joy knew it wasn't the moment for laughing, but when Nina

told her what had happened the previous night at the White Hart she had the gravest difficulty in keeping a straight face. 'Oh, dear. However, the show must go on, Nina, and I want you back on that desk as soon as. I know I sound hard but it's a fact of life. You know what he's like, he's your husband, *you'll* have it to deal with. But being kind and understanding? Well, no, I don't think so. I'm glad you laughed about it, that's the kind of treatment that might do a lot of good.' She patted Nina's shoulder and said, 'Be tough and stand tall. You've put up with enough.'

The news about the incident in the waiting room flew round all members of the practice far quicker than it took to tell, even as far as the farm vets scattered around the outskirts of Barleybridge.

Scott and Kate were having a very quiet time meandering along to three appointments and wondering how to fill the rest of the day. After their third call, Scott rang in to say he was off to Applegate Farm to give the Parsons news about their goat Pearl, and heard from Lesley about the events that morning. Kate, listening to his end of the conversation, was bursting to hear what had happened but at first there was no chance of her finding out because he couldn't stop laughing.

'Oh, God! I ache with laughing!' Then he began howling with laughter all over again.

Tugging at his sleeve, Kate demanded to be told.

So he did and they both laughed. Scott finished the story by saying, 'When is that man going to learn his lesson? I wouldn't mind but Nina's a lovely person – fragrant, sweet, non-confrontational, fragile almost, pleasant. She's too nice to be messed with.'

'Come on. Let's go to Phil's. They might offer us a coffee.'

When they got to Applegate Farm, Phil and Blossom were far too fraught to be serving coffee. They'd heard mewing first thing that morning and Blossom was convinced it was Little Scott, but they couldn't locate where she was.

As Scott and Kate arrived, they were moving a stack of logs standing against the wall of the house. Blossom, distraught, was haphazardly pulling the logs away but at the same time making it even more difficult to reach the wall, where it seemed they thought Little Scott might be imprisoned.

So Scott took charge. He organized Kate to move the logs shuffled away by Blossom to a spot further away, then got Phil systematically to shift the logs one by one, hand them to Scott himself, who then put them where Kate could get at them to stack elsewhere. As they got closer the mewing got louder, weak but still there.

'How's she got behind these logs?' Scott wanted to know. 'They're so tightly packed.'

'Keep going. How can she be alive after seventeen days? It's impossible.' Phil muttered, sweat pouring off him with effort and anxiety. 'Blossom, calm down! We won't make any progress at all if you keep throwing logs about. Just steady down.'

But Blossom couldn't, she was hysterical.

Scott said, 'Blossom, go and get us all drinks of water, would you? Please, I'm gasping.' She responded immediately to his request, because caring for people was her great motivation. Before she went she whispered to Scott, 'Will she live?'

'Believe me, if she does it'll be a miracle, but if she's anything like her Uncle Scott she will.' He squeezed her arm and she hurried off, returning in a moment with the glasses of water. Scott drank his right down to the bottom. 'I tell you what, Blossom, Little Scott will need water when we get her out.'

'Of course she will.' Blossom dashed away again into the house, glad to be making a contribution.

They'd reached the last four and also the biggest of the logs, far too large for Kate to be able to move them, and the mewing had grown louder and more agitated. Phil speeded up his log-moving. 'It must be an old air grate we know nothing about. Oh, God! Look! There she is!'

From behind the small squares of the old air grate they could see Little Scott's dear pink nose and two amber eyes, now set deep in her skull. Phil tried getting the grating off with his fingers but it was ancient and well fastened in. 'Here, Scott, give me a hand.'

'We need something to force it off. How about a big strong

screwdriver and a hammer; get the end of the screwdriver into the cement and then hammer it off.' He knelt down and talked to Little Scott. 'Sweetheart, hold on, we're nearly there. Come on, sweetie, who's a brave girl, then.' He poked a finger through one of the squares but little Scott was so stuck fast she couldn't even reach to touch it with her nose.

Scott's compassion for Little Scott moved Kate to tears. This tough Aussie had a heart of gold. She treasured that fact, and wished for the impossible.

Phil came back with the biggest screwdriver Kate had ever seen, and the real rescue began. He stripped off a layer of pullover, then, as he began work, a second layer was removed, then off came his T-shirt so finally he was down to his vest. 'These bloody old places are built to last and not bloody half,' he said.

But the air grate eventually came half away and that was just enough for him to get his hand through and gently pull little Scott out. She'd been confined in a very narrow space and came out with her legs clamped tight under her body and unable to move a muscle. Phil laid her on the concrete, expecting her to stand up, wobbly maybe but able to stand, but she couldn't and rolled helplessly over on to her side, still with her legs tightly tucked beneath her.

Blossom screamed. Hamish, who'd been keeping the pygmy goats company and had just arrived on the scene, went a ghastly green colour, and Phil had tears running down his cheeks.

Scott ran his hands over Little Scott, feeling every joint, caressing her hips, feeling her flanks, looking into her eyes and he felt loaded with pain. He couldn't believe she had a hope in hell of surviving. But try he must.

'Water!'

Blossom held the water bowl for her to lap, but Scott knew she hadn't the strength, so he put his finger into the water and, lifting her lips, rubbed round her mouth, her teeth, her gums. They were dry, bone-dry, so he did it two or three times, gently and thoroughly. Despite the hot weather she was shudderingly cold to the touch, which was a bad sign. Scott decided she needed a bath first. A warm bath might help to loosen her limbs, but most of all because she was covered in urine and excrement, which had made her fur matted, almost solid, and didn't allow him to massage her limbs. 'Let's take her inside out of the sun. She needs a warm bath to clean her up. Warm some water and put sugar in it and a drop of brandy – it'll help warm her through.'

He laid Little Scott in the kitchen sink and supported her with one hand while he swished the warm water over her, softening the dried matted fur, which gradually began to loosen so she looked more like herself. Blossom offered her hairdryer, and Kate held her while Scott dripped the mixture he'd thought up, tiny drop by tiny drop into her mouth, but it ran out of the corners. Scott felt her throat to see if she was trying to swallow, and suddenly detected a slight movement, so he persisted, and gradually her automatic swallowing mechanism began working very slightly. 'There's hope! She's getting it down. Just a little.'

Blossom clasped her trembling hands under her chin, desperately hoping. Phil was sitting in his rocking chair, rocking frantically. Hamish was still a strange greeny-white. As for Kate, she was filled with longing for Scott to bring the cat round. Seventeen days trapped like that, without food. She must have had some water, like condensation to lick at or something, to have survived so long. The stressful part was seeing the immobility of her legs. And she was so thin. So very thin. It wasn't necessary to touch her to *feel* her bones; you could see them sticking out. Every single one. Hips, legs, ribs, even her skull were all prominent.

'Kate, it's her circulation. We need to get it going. You work on the right side, I'll work on the left. Smooth, firm movements, steadily, not jerky nor quick, with a small amount of pressure, or we could cause her pain.'

The two of them worked with extreme gentleness, and as they did so Scott administered his magic mixture. Slowly but surely, there came a slight movement in her limbs, measured in millimetres that was true, but it was *movement*. A tremulous sigh of relief was heard from everyone gathered round Little Scott, and the feeling that they might be successful warmed their hearts.

Blossom made a snatch lunch of ham, bread rolls, carrot cake, fruit and very cold juice. While they ate it they left Little Scott to rest, lying on a blanket in her old familiar basket by the fireplace.

Scott declared, 'We're not out of the woods yet by a long way, but there is hope, which I didn't have when we got her out. I told you she would be tough with me for an uncle.' He beamed from ear to ear, thrilled to bits that it looked as though Scott might survive.

Blossom got up, marched across to him and kissed him full on the mouth. 'You're brilliant. Great. Thank you so much. We shall be for ever indebted to you, Scott.'

'My instructions are to—'

Phil jumped up from his chair and left it rocking back and forth, back and forth. 'You're not leaving? You can't. She's not right yet.'

'Honestly, any minute now my mobile will go . . .' Just as he said it his phone rang 'Joy! No, I've not been missing. No, we are not having an alcoholic lunch somewhere. I've been rescuing Little Scott. You know she was missing? Well, we've found her . . . yes, I'd finished my calls.'

Blossom snatched the phone from him and shouted, 'Joy, it's Blossom. We think we've saved her life. Scott's been his usual brilliant self, but he needs to stay a little longer just to keep an eye on her. Things are touch and go still, you see . . . yes, well. What? That seems a bit harsh . . . OK then, we'll pay for his time. Right. Here, Scott, she wants to speak to you.'

She handed the phone back and watched his face as he listened to Joy. Scott knew that Joy must have asked for his return to the practice and he had to agree with it when Phil and Blossom were overhearing. He put down his phone and continued eating without saying a word.

Blossom knelt down beside Little Scott's basket and stroked her all over.

Scott said softly, 'That's just what she needs. Gentle movement all over her body but especially her legs; it'll stimulate her circulation. Firm but comforting, if you get me. Feed her Scott's magic mixture every hour till bedtime. If she starts to refuse it, give me a ring. Her legs should be getting more relaxed. It'll be a slow process but, fingers crossed, she'll be OK. I don't think she'll manage to walk today but don't worry. Ring anytime. I don't mind. Better go. The boss has spoken. Sorry.'

Kate and Scott said their *au revoirs* and were just leaving when Kate reminded Scott the reason for them coming today. 'Oh! Right. I forgot. Pearl. She has shown up with the antibodies to Johne's disease, rather sadly. She's still getting some quality of life so I don't suggest putting her to sleep yet. You'll know when the time comes. Very sorry. So as far as breeding from the others, I hesitate to suggest it, but in my opinion you should have a clean sweep of them all and get new stock which have been tested regularly for it. Then you know you're making a fresh beginning with nothing on your conscience.'

Phil and Blossom were so overcome with anxiety about Little Scott that the news didn't appear to penetrate their minds properly – that Scott meant to put all the goats to sleep – so he was able to leave without suffering their usual devastated reaction to their animals having to be put down.

Hurrying back to the practice, they spotted Virginia coming towards them in the opposite direction. Scott slowed down at the widest part of the road to have a chat.

He called out, 'Hello, Ginny. Haven't seen you for days. How's things?'

Virginia grimaced at his familiarity in calling her Ginny, but didn't reprimand him for once. 'I'm fine, thanks. Apparently the Veterinary Defence Society is going to pay Lord Askew out, but take into account he was partially responsible by delaying asking for our help, so that clears the practice from any financial responsibility. I feel much better about the whole thing.'

'Mmmm. I see. I understand Dan did a monumental job on His Lordship – all the cards on the table type of conversation – which made Lord Askew more accepting of the situation. So he needs a big thank you from you. It should never have happened anyway.'

'OK, OK. I didn't pull up just to have a lecture from you. Anyone would think you were the senior partner, and I've already had enough from him.'

'Well, Ginny, I am about to become a partner, if everything goes to plan, so then I shall be able to say how I feel and mean it. Sorry, but there you are. Don't want to be nasty but the practice and its reputation mean everything to me. Bye!'

He roared off back into Barleybridge steaming with temper. 'She thinks because the money side has been sorted that makes everything all right. Well, it hasn't. People have long memories. She's a thoughtless bitch, is Ginny, I've no time for her.'

'She looked more cheerful, I thought. She had a mini-breakdown over it, you know.'

'Did she indeed. Oh, dear. How sad.'

Kate had to say it. 'You never make mistakes, then?'

Scott was silent for a while as he negotiated the horrendous roundabout near the hospital. Once clear he admitted to – well, almost admitted to – a mistake when he worked at home in Australia. 'But I realized what I'd done and rectified it in time.'

'Is it true what you said to her, that you're going to be a partner?'

Scott nodded. 'Not finalized but almost. I'm taking over Zoe's partnership.'

Kate looked hard at Scott. 'I never thought she'd do that. Is she expecting, then? Is that it?'

The long silence which followed her question puzzled her. Scott was always upfront about things and she'd expected an immediate answer.

'No, and don't mention it again, if you don't mind.'

They swung into the practice car park. Scott switched off the engine, got out of the car and stalked in by the back door.

Kate evaded getting into the argument with Joy by going to have a word with Nina, who was on duty that day.

'Hello, Nina. How's things?'

Though she'd only been in the job a matter of days, Nina had blossomed. Almost gone was the shy, diffident Nina; she'd been replaced by a jollier, confident person, still nervous but smiling and, well, proud.

'I'm well, thanks. I am loving this job so much, you've no idea. I should have been doing this years ago.'

Kate leaned across and patted her hand. 'Good, I'm glad.' She cleared her throat. 'What's happened about little Choo?'

'Much recovered and going home later today, no need to keep her in. Must have been something nasty she picked up. Val's given her something which has put it right.' Nina sighed. 'I do realize who the owner is. Although I didn't know *you* knew who she was. I must apologize for thinking, even for one minute, that you were his latest.' She sighed again. 'She's so . . . so . . . glamorous, isn't she?'

'Your figure is just as gorgeous,' said Kate sincerely, 'your skin equally as good, your eyes are an intense velvet brown, which is very sexy, and you tan beautifully. *I* just go lobster-red. What's the difference between the two of you?'

Nina didn't answer immediately but when she saw Scott coming into reception she hastily remarked, 'But she's got *oomph*!'

'Oomph?' Kate had to laugh. 'She has, but so could you! New make-up, new hairstyle, new wardrobe. Just flaunt yourself.'

'Flaunt? What is flaunt?'

Scott interrupted them. 'There's nothing more for us today, Kate, unless an emergency comes in. If it does, I'll do it by myself. So Joy says you can go home.'

He strode out, intent on disappearing fast, leaving Kate to explain to Nina what flaunting meant.

Chapter 12

Scott felt he'd had rather a rough day, what with finding Little Scott in such a bad way, his flare-up with Virginia, which he could have phrased rather more sensitively if he'd thought about it, which he hadn't, and Kate thinking that perhaps Zoe might be pregnant. She most certainly wasn't, and she wished she was and so did he, and now she was becoming obsessed by not being pregnant. He fully understood what she meant when she said her biological clock would be running out and, when he gave it some quiet thought, he knew she was absolutely right. He'd love to have a houseful of children. In fact, they'd bought a four-bedroomed cottage with that very objective in mind.

He gave the accelerator some extra welly to get up the steep hill to the house and on gaining the level ground he slowed down to have a think. It was strange that they didn't conceive, and it certainly was not from lack of opportunity. In fact, he had only to see Zoe and he'd begin feeling randy. She was just so perfectly splendid in bed. She satisfied his every need, and he hers she said.

She was in the garden, tying up an old climbing rose to the new trellis he'd fixed up for her. Oscar was helping her, wearing his sun hat and a pair of shorts, smears of sun cream across his shoulders. God! He looked marvellous. He was such a bright, courageous little boy. Typical Spencer. For a moment he regretted that he hadn't known him from the moment he was born. From his photos he knew he hadn't been one of those red wrinkly babies you see sometimes. He'd been fair-skinned and blond from the start. Yes. He definitely wanted more of the same. Right.

143

'Zo! I'm home.'

'So I see. You're early.'

'Not much work at the moment. You know how it goes.'

'I do.'

Scott crossed the grass and embraced her, delighted to have her wholesomeness in his grasp.

She kissed him energetically and then said, 'Steady, Rover. Down, boy!'

'And you, Master Oscar, give your daddy a kiss.'

Oscar ran to him with his arms outstretched, hoping to be swung up into Scott's arms to be an aeroplane, and he was; Scott spun and spun until Oscar was dizzy.

Zoe shouted, 'He'll be ill! Do stop, darling.'

'Daddy! Daddy! Again. Again!'

'No, Mummy says you'll be ill. This looks good, Zo, and you've made a good job of tying the twine, son. It'll look great when it gets established in its new spot. I need a cup of tea. Want one? Oscar, you too?'

Oscar nodded. This new Aussie man went into the kitchen and began to make cups of tea. He looked out of the window at the apple tree and wished there was a pram under the shade of it with Spencer Two asleep in it. Maybe he'd have to go to this damned fertility place and get sorted, but then he remembered he'd decided it was more than likely Zoe's problem and not his, so he changed his mind.

They sat under the apple tree, drinking their tea and eating Scott's favourite fig biscuits while Oscar played on a small trampoline they'd bought him when they first moved in. Out of the blue Zoe said, 'By the way, I went to the clinic.'

That sinking feeling Scott got whenever the damned place was mentioned surfaced again. 'And . . . your results?'

'I've got the all-clear. No blocked tubes or anything. Ovaries OK. Womb OK.' Zoe said nothing more, drawing no conclusions, thus leaving a silence for him to fill.

'I see.' Peeved at being excluded from her decision, he grumbled, 'You should have said you were going.'

'Why? Would you have come with me?'

Scott couldn't look her straight in the face. 'Well, no, I don't think so.'

'No one needs to know.'

'If I went, you could bet your bottom dollar I'd meet someone who knew me. Couldn't very well say, "I've come about my dodgy leg", could I?'

'Just trying to think who you might meet. Rhodri? No, he's firing on all cylinders, with another one on the way. Certainly not Dan, not with his tribe. Nor Colin, who seems to have got the hang of things after all these years. No, I think you'd be pretty safe.' Zoe pursed her lips and nodded confidently.

'Umm . . . '

'Are you going?'

'Is there a waiting list?'

'A bit of a one.'

'I'm just not willing to go.'

'Even though it's my dearest wish?'

'Even though it's your dearest wish. I can't bring myself to do it. It's like putting yourself in a position of failure, and just think, you might get that mindset and never recover. I might even become impotent just thinking about it.'

'You? Impotent?' Zoe began to laugh, she laughed and laughed, choked on a sip of tea she took to stop herself laughing and then had Scott thumping her on the back to help her recover. When she finally pulled herself round he kissed the nape of her neck, enjoyed it so much he kissed her again in exactly the same place and knew how much he loved her and persuaded himself in that moment that he'd go to the clinic, but not tell her of his change of heart. Going secretly, he could perhaps just manage it.

Kate had never mentioned to Mia that she and Scott had kissed and how he'd apologized. The memory of it set all her insides tingling with passion, and struggle as she might to squash all those kinds of feelings, she burst into flames when he touched her by chance. When he had kissed her she shot clean out of control.

But Mia was more perceptive than Kate had imagined, and was praying for the week with Scott to be over. When she saw the glow in Kate's eyes as she walked in that night her heart plummeted.

'Hi! Had a good day?'

Kate explained about Little Scott and how they were desperately hoping she'd pull round, that Scott seemed to have done all the right things and how frightened Phil and Blossom had been.

'Good thing he was around, then.' The hint of annoyance in Mia's voice put Kate on the alert.

'I've got my feelings under control about Scott. I do wish you'd stop warning me about him.'

'All I said was it was a good thing he was around. That's all.'

'It's the way you say it. I'm OK, honestly. He's just another colleague.'

'Kate! You are fooling yourself. I'm sorry, but you are.' Mia turned away and left her standing in front of the huge living-room window staring out at Barleybridge town. She had to admit Mia was right. Scott was demonstrative with his feelings, she knew that. He embraced everyone and thought nothing of it, so perhaps she was no different; just another female in need of a hug. As soon as she admitted that to herself she felt as though she were standing under a powerful cold shower, the icy chill of the water washing over her and bringing her to her senses. The cold invaded every single centimetre of her, and when it reached her heart she shuddered. She honestly felt she would never be warm again, yet the suffocating heat of the day had grown more intense the later it got. It was now six o'clock and the sun was still blazing in the sky. Even the trees were motionless, right to their topmost leaves, and here she was shaking with cold.

There simply wasn't any point in hankering after Scott. Nothing would come of it and if he did make overtures to her, her conscience couldn't allow her to be enticed because she couldn't do anything to harm Oscar. He'd been without a father for the first two years of his life and now he had one she wasn't going to be responsible for making him lose him all over again.

Thank you, Dad, she thought, for bequeathing me a powerful conscience, thanks very much. But Scott wasn't going to make real overtures to her, never. She had to accept that.

Kate picked up her sandals from where she'd abandoned them when she walked in and called to Mia, 'Just having a shower.'

'OK. We'll eat a bit later tonight. It's so hot, I don't feel like eating yet.'

'Neither do I.' In fact, I might never eat again, she thought. This could be terminal.

She stood far longer under the shower than she usually did, keeping the temperature at tepid to slow her erratic heart. She'd been a fool allowing Scott to take over her heart and mind like this again. After all, he'd run away from her that time and gone back to Australia. If that didn't show how fickle he was . . . She was renowned at college for her common sense and here she was going into meltdown over a man. Help! She didn't care if she was forty before she found the right marriage partner. She'd wait and wait.

'Mia!' she called when she emerged from the bathroom. 'The new *Pride and Prejudice* is on at the Plaza tonight. Shall we treat ourselves? Go watch it and then have a meal in my favourite Italian?'

Mia's spirits soared. 'I'd like that.' Just like it used to be. Hallelujah! 'I'll go just as I am. I'll pay for the meal.'

'I'll pay for the seats. Come on. Your car or mine?'

'Mine. Hurry up.'

They flung themselves out of the flat, drove hell for leather into Barleybridge, parked in the cinema multi-storey and raced for the ticket machine. They got into their seats two minutes before the film began.

Mia sank back gratefully into her seat. 'Thank heavens for air conditioning. This is wonderful.'

When it came to Darcy on the verge of weeping over Lizzie it was Kate's undoing. She struggled to hold back her tears, glanced at Mia and saw she was dry-eyed – well, almost – and followed her example. After all, it was only a film. But it was so touching.

Kate came out of the cinema revitalized by having her mind taken over by the drama she'd watched and feeling freer than she had done for some time.

The cinema was part of a shopping complex and to return to the car was a marathon of stairs and corridors. Initially they got to floor five when they should have been on floor three and at the wrong end of floor three when they came out from the staircase a second time.

Mia grumbled, 'This is ridiculous. No one would think we were grown women able to read. Oh, look, there's Valentine. And is that Nina?' She waved furiously. 'Hi, Valentine. Hello!'

Kate, waiting to get into Mia's car, looked up and saw him.

He was just locking his car and standing beside him was Eleanor Eustace – dressed more for the beach than the cinema. Kate waved vaguely – Valentine returning an equally vague greeting – and rapidly seated herself in the car, waiting for Mia to start up. But Mia liked to compose herself before she drove off and required time to sort her mirrors, settle her skirt, sort the gearbox as though she'd never driven before, re-set her rear-view mirror, put her driving shoes on, as she hated driving in sandals, by which time Valentine and Eleanor were passing Mia's car, hand in hand.

'I didn't realize Nina was so glamorous. She looks stunning.'

They glided away down the ramp and out into the sunshine.

'Why haven't you answered me?'

'Because I can't believe what I saw. That *was* Valentine, like you said, but it wasn't Nina he was with. It was his latest bit on the side, Ellie. Hand in hand, even when they knew I'd seen them. Well, that's that. I'm going to confront him. Sorry, I know you said I shouldn't interfere, but I shall. Tomorrow. To his face. He might have all the charm and the good looks and the sex appeal but—'

Mia gasped. 'You mustn't, you really mustn't.'

'But I shall, and I shan't do it quietly, either.'

So she did just that. At lunch-time, when she and Scott, having another slow day, had returned for a quiet lunch in the staffroom. Joy was there, too. Valentine came in clutching his packet of sandwiches and fruit, and found his fruit juice which he kept stored in the fridge.

In a pleasant, conversational tone, Kate asked Valentine, 'What did you think to *Pride and Prejudice*, then, Valentine? I thought it was excellent, a wonderful adaptation.'

Before he could answer, Joy burst in with, 'Did Nina like it? She said she wanted to go.'

'He didn't go with Nina, did you, Val? Oh, no.' Kate smiled sweetly at him, and was so set on exposing him for the betrayer he was that she didn't notice Nina had come in to eat her lunch with Valentine.

Valentine froze. He didn't know Nina had come in, either, because he was sitting with his back to the door. 'My private life is nothing to do with you.' He took another bite of his sandwich and avoided catching anyone's eye.

'It is when you flaunt your bit on the side right in front of me.'

Joy, horrified, said, 'Kate! Take care.'

'Well, he did. He walked past . . .' Kate realized there was something terribly wrong and paused.

The next thing she heard was Nina's voice. 'Who were you with, Val? It certainly wasn't me.'

If Kate could have died at that moment she would have, gladly. Mia had warned her.

Nina didn't dissolve into tears but stood her ground. 'Well, I'm waiting.'

Valentine continued chewing his food, so Nina asked Kate.

This was the last thing Kate wanted, but she couldn't think how she could avoid answering. Eventually she said, 'It's none of my business. Val should tell you.'

Nina went to stand in front of Valentine and when he still didn't answer her question she kicked his foot. 'Well?'

Valentine stood up. 'I do not wish to discuss my private life in public. Bring your lunch and we'll talk in my consulting room.' Without looking to see if she was following, he stalked out, so Nina went out, too, leaving a ghastly silence behind her.

*

Valentine slammed his door shut after Nina and said, 'It was very much against my wishes that you came to work here but Mungo insisted and I can see it is doing you good, but it doesn't mean you can supervise my private life. You never have done and that's how I want it to stay.'

'Your private life! I didn't think married people had a *private* life other than the life they spend with person they marry.'

'Well, Nina, I need one. We're not married in the way most people mean by marriage and I . . . well . . . I need . . .' He shrugged.

Valentine knew full well that would put an end to her questions. It always did and it always would. This time was no exception. Nina began to tremble and in a moment was in his arms. He hugged her, smoothed her hair, dried her tears, told her he loved her, but she did understand, didn't she? 'Mmm?'

Nina nodded. 'But for everyone to *see*.'

'I'm sorry about that, I didn't intend for Kate to see. Not to hurt you.'

'But it does hurt me. She's a tart, is that Eleanor Eustace, and you can't see it.'

'Oh, I can, but . . . she's, she's got such a hold on me. If I refuse to meet her she does things to upset me, like at the White Hart that night. I don't want you hurt but . . .' He released her and went to look out of the window, wondering if he'd resolved matters satisfactorily. He gave her time to make up her mind . . . he was in a fix, there was no doubt about it.

Women like Eleanor were not his sort, but something about her excited him and he couldn't resist her. If he'd had any sense he would have refused to see her again after she humiliated him in the bar that night, but there she was the next day with her sick cat. What lingered in his mind was a slight suspicion that she'd given Choo something nasty to make her sick on purpose, as an excuse to see him again and heal the rift between them. For that alone he should refuse to see her again, but then he wasn't certain about it, it could have been coincidence. Which led him back to remembering her naked and demanding, running her hand tantalizingly up his spine . . . but it was Nina's hand he now felt on his back, Nina urging him to turn away from the window, Nina's arms around him, hugging him.

'I'm so sorry, Val. One day, one day, I will. I do love you, and I'm always grateful you were willing to marry me and bring me here. I know you love me.' She squeezed him tighter. 'And it will happen one day, you and I.'

Nina kissed his cheek and went to lean against the examination table the better to admire him. He was male beauty at its superb best, and exuded sex appeal like no other. The improvement needed to be in herself; not to make herself into an expensive-looking tart like Eleanor, but to change herself from *within*. Then, maybe, she'd beat the deep-down horror she had of Valentine making love to her. This was what war had done to her, what that attack in the depths of the night had done, twisted her so the very thought of it, even as an act of love, revolted her. Perhaps then she'd get what she'd wanted since the first day she'd met him: love and devotion.

Nina trembled at the thought. 'See you later. I'm going shopping when I finish. I may be late.'

In her head she kissed him and left. But kissing him inside her head was not enough. Damn that Eleanor. Damn and blast her.

The ghastly silence they'd left behind in the staffroom was eventually broken by Virginia coming in for a brief chat. She stood in the doorway wondering why Scott, Joy and Kate were so silent. In fact, surprisingly for her, she sensed the atmosphere was teetering on the edge of electric. 'Have I missed something?'

Joy cleared her throat. 'No, not really. Well, yes. Kate put her big foot in it by asking Valentine if he'd enjoyed *Pride and Prejudice* last night at the cinema.'

'What's wrong with that? Perfectly civil question.'

'He wasn't there with Nina.'

'Oh! That tart of his, Ellie, as she prefers to be called. She's so free with her favours that—'

'You know her?'

'Surprise, surprise! I got invited to a party the other night and she was there, quizzing me about Val. Embarrassing. I've left some samples on your desk, Joy. I should have done the tests yesterday, so it's urgent. Sorry.'

Joy followed Virginia out to ask her if she would have Kate shadowing her again for the following week.

Virginia was about to say she preferred not to, but changed her mind. 'That's fine. Yes, OK. She keeps me on my toes.'

She shot out to get on with her calls and left Joy wondering if she'd done the right thing.

'Kate! A word, in my office,' she said and settled in her chair. When Kate arrived she said straight away, 'I'm putting you with Virginia next week.'

'Oh! Right.'

'Don't sound too enthusiastic about it.'

'Well, we had a rough week. Just hope it's better this time.'

'It will be. I have noticed she's softening a little.'

'Oh, good. Does she know I'm with her.'

'Yes, and didn't hesitate when I asked her. By the way another time when you know some gossip about a member of staff, could you keep it to yourself? It's none of your business and I only interfere when it's affecting the practice. OK.'

Kate apologized. 'Sorry, but he's getting absolutely blatant about it. He knew I'd seen him, yet he walked past the car holding hands with her. He just seemed as if he didn't care, and I feel so hurt for Nina. She's such a lovely person, he doesn't deserve her.'

'Leave it, Kate, please. It's none of our business, and you're a student not a member of staff. So forget it.'

'Sorry. I shall not say another word about them.'

But she was distinctly put out about the whole situation and said so to Scott as they set off for their afternoon calls.

'Well, Joy's right,' he said. 'It is nothing to do with you or me. If he cares so little about his marriage then so what? That's up to him.'

'But it's turned me into a liar. I knew but I couldn't say anything, and that's not nice.'

'Kate, forget it. You didn't make him go out with her.'

'No, but I know he called her using the details on the practice computer.'

'Hush up. I'm calling at Applegate Farm to see Little Scott before we go to Tattersall's Cop. They rang me, asked me to go when I had a chance.'

'Good. She's OK, is she?'

'So they say.'

They zoomed into the turning for Phil and Blossom's. Pulled up, got their boots on – though the hot summer had made their farm yard much drier, they did it out of habit – and marched across to find someone. Neither Blossom nor Phil nor Hamish were anywhere to be seen about the farm, so Scott knocked on the farmhouse door and opened it calling out, 'Hello! We're here.'

All three of them were in the kitchen dozing in chairs, and the reason was evident. A large empty champagne bottle and three empty champagne flutes stood on the table.

Phil's rocking chair moved slightly and a fuzzy voice said, 'Hello! Who's that?'

'It's Scott and Kate. Phil, what's all this about?'

Blossom woke and then Hamish. They stretched and yawned and endeavoured to pull themselves together.

'Well?' asked Scott. 'Champagne for lunch?'

Phil stood up leaving his chair loudly rocking back and forth. He pointed at Hamish. 'It's all his fault. He's gone and got in at the College. So we're celebrating.'

'We've arrived too late to join in, then?'

'No!' Blossom shouted. She got up, tipping poor Little Scott on to the floor. 'Sorry, Little Scott. Sorry. No, there's another small bottle for two in the fridge, you can have that. Two more flutes, Hamish, please. Come on, you've got guests!'

Kate said, 'Well done, Hamish. Well done.' She patted him on the back, as he leaned down to get their glasses from a bottom cupboard.

Hamish grinned at her. 'I've got to do well in the first term or it's curtains.'

'Then it's all up to you.'

Hamish popped the cork on the bottle and expertly poured two glasses for them. 'It is. But I'll make it work. I will, I'm determined, and it's thanks to Blossom and Phil for taking me in and not letting the Social know where I was. Best thing I ever did coming here and staying put.' He smiled at Blossom and she smiled back, glowing with pleasure at his success.

'So is this really why you asked us to come?'

'No, we wanted you to see Little Scott.' From the drawer in the kitchen table Blossom got out an old cotton reel tied to a length of string. 'This is her favourite toy. Watch.'

She dangled it above Little Scott's head, enticing her to jump for it. The cat swept up into the air, caught the reel between her two front paws and swung on it for a moment before she fell down to the floor.

'How's that, then? Athletic, she is. Everything firing on all cylinders. She can jump up on to the top of fences, balance along them, run up the field with me, everything – just like she's always done. I'm thrilled to bits.' She continued enticing Little Scott with the cotton reel, running round the kitchen table with the cat in hot pursuit.

Very quietly Phil said, 'She doesn't leave Blossom's side since . . . you know what. We don't talk about it in front of her, don't want to upset her, but that's the truth. Wherever Blossom goes, so does Little Scott.' He wiped away a tear from his eye. 'Thanks for all you did. Without you we could have lost her.'

'I'm just sorry Joy insisted on charging you for what I did.'

Blossom, quite out of breath and sitting down again in her chair, whispered, 'She only charged for the blood test for Pearl, and nothing for you saving Little Scott's life. Generous, that.'

Somewhat relieved at the outcome Scott drank the last of his champagne and said, 'Must go. So pleased she's doing so well after

'. . . you know what. Such a stroke of luck finding her. How did she get in that air vent, by the way?'

'It was a hole in the airing cupboard. She used to like to go in there, even on hot days, and we didn't know it was there. But we've blocked it up with a brick now so she can't fall down the air vent and get stuck again. Although she doesn't go in there any more, not since . . . you know.' He reached across and stroked her head, and they all had a sentimental moment.

'Got to go,' Scott said again eventually. 'Glad about College, Hamish. Bye!'

Kate, the moment she got back into the car, said, 'Isn't it ridiculous? You and I know she doesn't understand what they say, but you have to fall in with their thinking, haven't you, or you cause offence.'

'Something like that. But please note, she doesn't go in the airing cupboard any more, so she's wise enough for that.'

Disdainfully Kate suggested, 'That's probably because they remember to keep the door shut.'

'Oh, you matter-of-fact person you!'

For a moment, they stared into each other's eyes: Kate thinking how she loved the proportions of his face, so perfect, so appealing, and Scott thinking how tempting she was.

Chapter 13

After a weekend spent alternately trying to keep cool by swimming in the outdoor pool at the Leisure Centre each day, and then attempting to develop a good tan by sunbathing in the communal gardens belonging to the flat, Kate went back to the practice less eagerly than she had done the previous Monday. Working with Virginia again simply did not appeal. But see it through she must with as much goodwill as she could muster.

Virginia picked her up at eight o'clock precisely and they roared off to visit Bridge End Farm. They were new clients and Kate briefly checked Virginia's top-of-the-shop map book on the way.

To make conversation she said, 'Ever visited Bridge Farm?'

'That's where we're going, isn't it?'

'No, we're going to Bridge *End* Farm, which is not the same although they are neighbours. The owners of Bridge Farm have six sons, not one of them married. Shall we go there by mistake on purpose?' Kate giggled and waited for her reaction.

Virginia laughed. 'We're not that desperate, are we? Farmers' sons? I don't think so.'

'They're all fine figures of men. Very tall, well made and handsome. I don't think there's a girl in Barleybridge whom they haven't taken out at some stage. They're very good marriage material!'

Virginia, distracted by a foul, all-pervading smell which hit them as they turned in through the farm gate, didn't reply. 'My God! What on earth is that?'

Kate checked their call list. 'Just says "guinea pigs" down here.'

*

Accustomed as they both were to Phil Parsons' farm and its filth and dilapidation, neither of them could believe such utter devastation. Stables, cowsheds with holes in their roofs, one where the outside wall was in imminent danger of falling down, doors missing, piles of rubbish everywhere, and that terrible overpowering stink.

'What do they do here? Farm what, I ask?'

Knowing how outspoken Virginia could be, Kate dreaded the owner making an appearance, and braced herself.

The house door slowly opened and a frail, little old lady emerged, her spine so bent her face was permanently looking at the ground. She made a big effort to look at them, but didn't quite succeed.

'Two girls. I hadn't expected that,' she said. 'What are things coming to? I'm glad. I wish my sister and I could have done something worthwhile.' Her voice was surprisingly strong, with educated undertones.

'Now, Miss Patterson, what can we do for you?' This was Virginia speaking in such a tender voice Kate couldn't recognize her tone.

'It's the guinea pigs. We've tried so hard, but Louisa can't do the work any more and things have got . . . quite out of hand. We don't know who to turn to. We can't pay you, but something has to be done.'

The break in her voice was almost more than Kate could stand, so she took hold of her arm saying, 'We'll see what we can do. You lead the way.'

The mixture of emotion on Virginia's face was hard to define. That phrase of hers, 'invoice at the end of the month', had no place here because there was no way it would get paid.

Defiantly their client replied, 'We bred guinea pigs for the science laboratory, but we've lost the contract and now we've nothing to feed them on. I know people disagree, but if I had a child who was ill, and experimenting on guinea pigs meant a medicine that might save their life, well, what would one do? Say no thanks? I don't think so.'

It occurred to Kate the sisters had nothing to feed themselves on, either, for the arm she was holding was all bone.

Miss Patterson led them to the first of the buildings and they went inside. Through the gloom they could see row upon row of hutches stacked four high, right from one end to the other. Kate stayed supporting Miss Patterson while Virginia inspected the cages – every single one, all four layers – slowly and methodically. She was squatting down looking into one of the lower ones when Kate heard her grunt with displeasure. Or was it disgust? She came back to report.

Miss Patterson was trembling as Virginia approached her. 'Veterinary, there's another lot in the next building, but not quite as many as here. You can see, can't you, we don't know which way to turn. I wouldn't trouble you if it hadn't felt so cruel of us. We're just beaten into the ground with the whole thing.'

Virginia tut-tutted, cleared her throat and, with a voice full of understanding, said, 'Well, now, Miss Patterson, you are in a sorry state. I've got a thermos of coffee in my car. Would you share it with us while I have a think?'

'Oh, yes. Come inside. I called you because you're the first one in the Yellow Pages – you know B for Barleybridge – and because once, long ago, I met Mungo Price at a party and thought he was perfectly beautiful, such a lovely, compassionate man.'

'He still is.'

In the kitchen Kate sat her down on a chair, and went to find clean mugs. The kitchen shelves, cupboards and worktops were immaculate, and when she opened a cupboard looking for cups she found that the inside was immaculate because it contained only two tins of baked beans and one of Spam. The next cupboard contained a charming old china tea set, which made Kate deeply upset; such elegance amidst such poverty. Whyever hadn't they sold it to help their finances?

'Here we are, I've found the cups and saucers.'

Virginia was silent, trying to decide what on earth to do. If she reported it, they'd probably be prosecuted for cruelty and neglect. If she didn't, it left the practice having all the sorting-out to do all for nothing. At a guess, half the guinea pigs were already dead and the condition of the living ones was scarcely any better than dead. Empty water bowls and no food in sight told its own story. 'Is your sister not joining us?'

'We're twins, you know. I'll go and get her. I'm Emily and she's Louisa. Louisa, my dear, can you come?' She struggled out of the kitchen and while she was out Kate whispered, 'Well?'

'It's horrifying. I've never seen anything so bad.' Virginia shook her head in desperation.

They poured the coffee out and waited for Louisa to appear. When she did it was like seeing a mirror image, for her spine was also curved though not quite so badly as Emily's.

'You won't be angry, will you?' she said. 'We've done our best. But we can't do it any more. Thirty years we've been in this business, not that we wanted to be, but circumstances   after our father died . . .' Louisa sat herself painfully down in the nearest chair. 'This smells good. Thank you.'

She set about drinking her coffee as though her life depended on it. Starving, thought Kate, definitely starving to death.

Virginia broke the silence. 'I shall be back early this afternoon with a solution. Things obviously can't go on as they are with the guinea pigs, and I think facing the fact that *you* can't go on as *you* are would be a good idea, too. This is a good property, which . . . no. Let me have a think.'

She stood up. 'Before we go, Kate and I will see that the guinea pigs have water at least. Rest assured we shall be back. Where is your outside water tap? Will you show me?'

She refused to allow Kate to look into the cages, so Kate carried the water from the outside tap in buckets and it was Virginia who opened each hutch and filled the water supply.

When they left Virginia was grim-faced. 'You say nearby Bridge Farm has six grown-up sons?'

Kate nodded.

'Are they the sort who would help?'

'Not sure, but their dad rules them with an iron hand. He'd insist, I think.'

'Good, then that's where we're going. This minute.'

'Come to think of it, their mother rules them with a velvet glove, but it's just as effective.'

Virginia parked in the lane outside Bridge Farm and wandered round the corner into the yard.

A man was sitting on a chair in the shade. A massive pint pot stood on the cobbles beside his chair and he was sinking his teeth into a slice of fruitcake. A piece broke off, which he deftly caught and put on his plate.

Kate introduced them. 'Gideon, this is Virginia, a new vet at the practice. Virginia, this is Gideon Bridges. I think he's son number two, or is it three?'

Gideon put his plate down on the cobbles beside his pint pot and got up to shake hands. 'Good morning. Have we sent for you?'

'Good morning. No, we've come on an urgent mercy mission. Is your dad about?'

'He is. Dad!' Gideon bellowed in a huge voice and his father appeared in the house doorway. Virginia saw that Gideon took after him, red-haired and tall, with similar facial features.

'You're wanting me?'

'Well, I'm wanting to borrow a couple of your sons.'

A wicked grin appeared on Mr Bridges's face. 'Are you indeed? Must say, you're very outspoken, no beating about the bush. Well, they're well set up and very capable. What exactly are you wanting them for?'

Gideon blushed.

Virginia explained the situation. She finished by saying the Misses Patterson were at the very end of their tether. 'Losing their contract means they've very little income, so neither they nor their guinea pigs are getting fed, that's why so many of them have already died. And to my mind the two of *them* will be next.'

Mr Bridges bellowed, 'Ben, come here! Now!'

To Virginia's eyes, the man who appeared looked just like Gideon. Ben nodded an acknowledgement of her and then turned to his dad.

'See here, Ben, the veterinary needs help over at the Misses Patterson. Them guinea pigs they've got are dying from lack of food and she needs someone to take the matter in hand. Take the trailer, all the guinea pig food we have, and some matches to set fire to all the dead ones. A bale of hay and some of those carrots that we got from the market last week should help. Take Gideon and do what the veterinary says. Right. I'll come over with your lunch about twelve.' He turned away and went back inside the house, having apparently said all he needed to say. Which he had, and for which Virginia was very grateful.

Within minutes they were going back over to Bridge End Farm. Kate was despatched to keep Louisa and Emily inside the house while the grim task of clearing up the guinea pigs' hutches was undertaken by Ben and Gideon. For grown men they were remarkably obedient to their dad and, what was more, eager to assist.

First Virginia opened every single hutch one by one and lifted out the dead, closing the doors if there were any still alive. If none had survived, she left the door wide open and Gideon came along with big plastic bin bags, cleared out the foul-smelling hay, cleaned the hutches with a big scrubbing brush and hot water from the kitchen tap and the disinfectant they'd brought with them, again leaving the door open so they knew which ones were all right to use for the survivors.

'Bring out your dead! Bring out your dead!' called Ben, who was picking up the dead ones and placing them in a wheelbarrow. 'Just like the Black Death, this is. God! It's terrible. We'd no idea. It stinks in here.'

It took the best part of two hours, the end result being a massive pile of dead guinea pigs, waiting to be disposed of, and clean, well-scrubbed cages with the survivors in with fresh bedding and enjoying their first good meal in weeks. A litter born only that morning was comfortably housed and now had some hope of surviving. But it occurred to Virginia that homes had to be found for them all and her heart sank at the prospect.

'I've counted. We've got one hundred and twenty-three

guinea pigs plus four new babies born today. That's all that's left out of over three hundred. Can you believe it? I'm appalled.'

They were scrubbing their hands under the outside tap when Mr Bridges appeared. He was carrying several plastic carriers. 'Brought food for all of you, including Louisa and Emily.'

Virginia was delighted. 'Thank you very much indeed. Thank Mrs Bridges for me, please, she's so kind. We do need it.'

Mr Bridges took Virginia to one side. 'We'd no idea things were as bad as this. They don't mix, you know. Live like hermits. My wife's damned upset that all this was going on and we'd no idea. So sorry about it.'

'Not your fault. I have to go and finish my calls. I'm going to leave your boys to burn all the dead ones. I'll be back tonight when I've finished to see what we're going to do. I've no answers springing to mind as yet.'

Mr Bridges shouted across to Ben, 'Siphon some petrol out of my tank and throw it over them guinea pigs. It'll make it quicker.'

As Virginia and Kate left the farm, Kate enquired why she hadn't been allowed to help. 'I'm pretty tough, you know, I could have helped. Instead I spent, what, two hours talking to two old ladies, one of whom, namely Louisa, is a dear sweet old thing but definitely not entirely with it.'

'Because it was gruesome and I thought it one step too far for a student vet. Believe me, it was appalling, I can't describe . . . the most I can say is it was appalling.'

'I see. I can't imagine what those guinea pigs must have gone through. Trapped in there, unable to escape and slowly dying.' Kate shuddered.

'Exactly.'

'Question is, what is to be done about them all?'

'I've no idea. They're not even attractive guinea pigs. Just very ordinary. Putting down the ones which were too far gone and clearing out the dead is the least of the problem. Damn and blast.'

'The other problem is the two sisters. They are starving to death like the guinea pigs. The farm buildings, including the house, are well past their sell-by date, and they don't have the money to do them up. They ought to sell and use the money to buy a flat in a sheltered housing thingy.'

Virginia paused at the lights and said in a kind of this-is-a throwaway-statement-and-I'm-just-making-conversation way, 'Those Bridges boys.'

'Mmm?'

'How does a farm that size support them all? Why haven't they left and got their independence?'

'Don't ask me. You didn't see the best of them, that's Gab the eldest. There isn't a girl in Barleybridge who wouldn't give her eye teeth to marry him. As for the others, they're all up to something. They'll buy and sell anything for cash. They have a pedigree flock of chickens, pedigree rabbits, ponies . . . They also specialize in breeding and training border collies, too. All sorts of bits and pieces, legal and otherwise. Ducking and diving, you know the sort of thing. But they are all so good-natured. Josh, another of the sons, works for Megan Hughes at Beulah Bank Farm, you know.'

'I see.'

'Mrs Bridges is a dear. She feeds them like kings. A mug of her morning coffee, half a pint of it with cream and rum, sets you up for the week. In fact, I think they don't leave home because they can't find anyone who can cook as well as their mother.'

'What? Nowadays? You're kidding me.'

'I'm not.'

'Kate, I think we'll call in at the practice on our way and speak to Mungo about what we've done. Just clear the lines a little, perhaps. Mmm?'

'That might be a very good idea. Bet you five pounds he'll say, "We're not a charity, you know."'

'Ah, he won't, he'll be too mad. Well, all right then, you're on!'

Mungo was sitting in his office contemplating the world in all its weird and wonderful aspects. One thing was for certain: the practice was doing enormously well. Never better. The staff, both vets and lay staff, were all pulling together with great enthusiasm and he decided that in many ways life had never been better. The only fly in the ointment was Valentine Dedic with his love affairs, but the clients adored him and no wonder, professionally he couldn't be bettered, but his private life . . . Through the window he saw Virginia getting out of her car. Now she could be another problem. They'd regained Lord Askew's confidence — all down to Dan, of course — but it had been a close-run thing. Funny woman, the more you knew her the less close you became. She was self-absorbed, withdrawn, over-confident and not really very good at what Miriam called her 'people skills'. She waved to him through the window, and he waved back. The less he had to do with her the better.

But then there she was, standing in his office doorway saying, 'Good morning. Oh! It's really good afternoon, isn't it? I've lost count of time. Can I come in for a word?'

'Yes. I've twenty minutes before my next client. You, too, Kate, come in.' He looked directly at Virginia. 'You've a problem.'

'Not so much a problem . . . well, yes, it is a problem. We were called to Bridge End Farm by the Misses Patterson this morning, mainly because they cannot cope with all their guinea pigs any longer.'

'Guinea pigs? What's the problem with a few guinea pigs, for heaven's sake.'

'Well, it's not a few, is it, Kate?'

Kate shook her head.

'*Now* it's one hundred and twenty-three, plus four babies born while we were there.'

Mungo's eyes went wide with surprise. 'What the blazes have they got so many for? Didn't they realize about the birds and the bees?'

Virginia tut-tutted at his levity. 'No, they made a living from breeding them for science laboratories. Now the labs don't want them any more, so their contract's been cancelled and the Pattersons can no longer cope. Firstly because they've no money to buy feed for them, secondly because they're too old and fragile

164

to do the work involved, and thirdly because, well, because they are totally outfaced.'

'You said, "*now* one hundred and twenty-three". What does that mean?'

'Well,' Virginia drew in a great big breath to steady her nerves, 'I had to put down loads of them, and dozens of them were already dead. Over two hundred had to be disposed of. I feel faint at the thought of all that cruelty, but the Miss Pattersons aren't to blame. They're too ill and too fragile to look after them. Circumstances overwhelmed them. I can't report it to anyone, like the RSPCA, or the two of them will be prosecuted.'

'So you've spent what, two, three hours attending to all this? Valuable time when you could have been earning money. I've your salary to pay every month and you've not earned a penny towards it this morning. We're not a charity, you know.'

Kate couldn't help herself, she began to laugh. She tried to smother it but the tension of the morning came pouring out of her and the laughter wouldn't stop. Mungo, who held her in much higher esteem than he held Virginia, frowned at her and then saw the funny side of what he'd said, and he too began to laugh.

Miriam, who was coming down from the flat on her way to go shopping in Barleybridge, was drawn into Mungo's office by the laughter.

Virginia, usually almost totally devoid of a sense of humour, and forgetting her bet with Kate, couldn't for the life of her understand what they were laughing at. 'I don't know what's so funny about it. It's very serious and I don't know what to do.'

Miriam said, 'What's all this about?'

When she heard, Miriam didn't find it funny, either. 'I understand Emily and Louisa were left almost destitute when their father died. He'd spent all the money he had on gambling and drink, re-mortgaged and all they had left when he'd gone was no career, no money and money owing on the farm. They've struggled for years. They must be ancient now.'

Kate said, 'They are. They've been quite well off at some stage, they're genteel ladies through and through, but they've no idea about anything. The guinea pigs need thinking of, too.'

Mungo studied the pair of them and eventually asked Miriam if she had anything to say.

'Off the cuff, no. But what about feeding all those guinea pigs? Today, every day, right now?'

'We got the help of two of the Bridges boys temporarily,' Virginia said, 'but we can't expect them to find the feed and do all that work for very long. They were very helpful, weren't they, Kate?'

'They were.'

Miriam said, 'Are the sisters looking in good health?'

It was Kate who answered her. 'No, they're starving, like the guinea pigs, and Louisa's lost her marbles, too.'

'Remember that chap you met who was doing exactly what the Pattersons are doing and reckoned he was making a mint? Who was that, Mungo?'

'Heavens above, that was years ago. I'll have to think. Sounds like my client is arriving. Got to go. See you later.' He went out to greet his next client and they all heard him welcoming them, and admired his charm and compassion, but Virginia still had no answer.

Kate broke the silence. 'I'll come with you tonight and help feed them all.'

'Thanks, but the Bridges boys offered, although I would be glad of your help in the morning before we start our rounds.'

'Gladly.'

Unable to relax until she'd made sure the guinea pigs were all right, Virginia went back to the Pattersons that evening on her own. She drove with the windows down instead of the air conditioning because it felt fresher to do so. Was this long summer never going to end? In the past she'd enjoyed hot weather but this had gone on for what seemed an eternity without even the relief of a massive storm to cool things down. As she swung into Bridge

End Farm gateway she spotted an ancient saloon parked close to the stables where the guinea pigs were housed.

At that moment another of the Bridges' boys came striding out into the yard. Dangling from his hand were two dead guinea pigs. She knew he was one of them because of his looks. He was tall, well built, with thick auburn hair and dark eyes just like Ben and Gideon, but he was taller then they were and more prepossessing. She didn't think his father would have quite the same control over him as he had over the others.

She got out of the car and held out her hand. 'I'm Virginia Havelock, farm vet at Barleybridge Veterinary Hospital. It was me who did the dirty deed this morning. It was a dreadful job. Come to check on the guinea pigs. I was expecting Gideon or Ben.'

He gripped her hand so tightly she wondered if she'd ever have the use of it again. She managed to release it as he told her he was Gabriel, always known as Gab.

'It's very nice to meet you. I've nearly finished. Some lot of guinea pigs they've got. Unfortunately,' he hoisted the two dead ones for her to see, 'another two have died. Ben and Gideon remembered it was their first rugby practice of the season tonight, so I volunteered to come instead. Just sorry we didn't know what was going on here. Bad, that.'

Virginia was only half listening because she was studying the man. She was curious about the scar which ran from his temple and disappeared into his thick hair, his dark brooding eyes fascinated her, and she liked his height. Being almost six feet tall herself, she appreciated a tall man. Mentally she shook herself and endeavoured to speak normally. 'Our biggest concern is what the blazes we'll do with the guinea pigs. There's so many of them and they're not even attractive-looking. No one will want one for a pet.'

'I can't help on that score. In any case, they need building up. They're all far too skinny; you can see their ribs.'

'I know. Will you thank your mother for lunch today? It really was most kind.'

Gab looked to be making a decision and, having made it, he

coughed a couple of times before saying, 'Mother forgot it was rugby practice tonight and she's made too much supper. Like to join us? You could thank her yourself, then.'

'I could. Well . . . er . . . won't I be intruding?'

'No, she'll be delighted.'

Still she hesitated. She gazed far away into the distance and then, finally, agreed. 'Thank you, then. I will.'

She explained she'd go see the Misses Patterson before she left. 'Just to reassure them.'

Gab watched her march purposefully across the farm yard. Bit abrupt in her manner, she was, but he sensed something rather vulnerable about her . . . something needy. One thing was for certain, he decided: she needed a man and he could fit the bill very nicely, because he was sick of the empty-headed tarts in Barleybridge who were only after his body. He needed someone more substantial, with a brain and ambition and a zest for life. His thoughts turned to Megan Hughes and that tender place she'd left behind in his heart. Briefly he yearned for her and was stung with jealousy that Rhodri Hughes had won her and not him. Now he was approaching thirty-five, perhaps he and Virginia could very satisfactorily make a go of it. She just needed defrosting a bit. Well, quite a bit. He was still smiling at the thought of defrosting her as she walked back to her car. He raised a hand in greeting and she smiled.

Chapter 14

Nina had taken a big step that very day. In her lunch-hour she had an appointment at the hairdresser's in the precinct to have her hair cut. To anyone other than Nina it would be a small step, but to her it was symbolic of her transition from the past into her future. She'd had very long hair since she was a small child. Her mother had cherished it and spent hours grooming it, shampooing it, cutting it to encourage more growth, buying ribbons and combs and clips to decorate it, and though Nina wanted it cut, because she hated the weight of it impeding her at every turn, her request was always refused.

But her long hair had been used to hold her down when she was attacked after her family had been killed. So what had been the pride of her mother's life became an instrument of her torture.

However, as the long lengths of her black-as-night hair fell to the floor in the hairdresser's, Nina became horrified at what she was doing.

'Stop! Stop!'

The hairdresser put down her scissors. 'I did say it was too much to do all at once. It's still down between your shoulder blades. Look.' She held up the mirror so Nina could see the length of hair still left.

The hairdresser was right; it was too much all at once. Nina looked down at the floor, saw her beautiful, shining black hair laid there and her resolve began to crumble. She shouldn't have decided to have it cut very short. No, she should not. Then Nina thought about Val, of her need for him and his for her, and how she was trying to leave the past behind her. This was her big gesture, a new beginning.

'Go ahead,' she said. 'Short, like I showed you in picture. Right now, before I change my mind. Please. I insist.'

Another quarter of an hour and all her long, gleaming black hair lay on the marble floor. Looking in the mirror, she could see the tips of her ears and a fringe across her forehead. Her hair, no longer dragged down by its own weight, was springy, as though it might have a bit of curl once it had got used to the idea. It felt strange. How odd that she could flick her head from right to left and feel no weight at all.

'You could sell this, I'm sure,' the hairdresser said, holding up a length of her hair.

Should she keep some of it for old time's sake? No. That would be clinging to a time she must forget.

Nina said, 'That's wonderful. Thin it out a bit, please, and make a bigger fringe. I'll tuck the hair at the sides behind my ears.'

'Central parting?'

Nina nodded.

It was Valentine's day off so he didn't know about Nina's decision to cut her hair. He'd been sailing off Weymouth with a friend from his university days, he'd said, and arrived home about eight. He'd rung her to let her know he was on his way home and Nina, because she felt so very different, was convinced he would be able to tell what she'd done by the tone of her voice, but once she put the receiver down, common sense told her that of course he couldn't.

When Valentine walked in he shouted from the front door, 'Wonderful day, fantastic sailing, I'm going for a shower, won't be ten minutes. Your day OK?'

'Fine, thanks. We've been busy.'

He ran upstairs, not bothering to go into the kitchen, and, while showering, he recalled his day. The hot, burning sun and the brisk breeze which made the day just bearable had deepened his tan. Ellie had worn another of her 'sailing outfits', close-fitting, leaving nothing to the imagination. Gleaming and tanned, she added a powerful element of fun, and his male pride was boosted by the admiring glances she drew from men on the other boats.

In ten minutes, as he'd promised, he walked into the kitchen.

Nina, busy laying the table, didn't look up. If she had she would have seen the horror on his face.

'What the hell have you done?'

Nina smiled. 'You can see what I've done. Had my hair cut. I should have done it years ago. I feel as though I've been liberated, it makes me feel so free. I love it. Don't you?'

She turned to smile at him and saw his horrified expression.

'My God! Nina. You should never have done it. I should have been consulted.'

'It's my hair.'

'I know it is, but I'm your husband and I needed to know.'

'I thought I'd surprise you. Do you like?' Nina twirled round to give him the full effect.

'It's not you any more. You're someone else and I . . . just don't like it.'

'Well, it will take me a long time to grow it again, and I'm not.'

'Aren't you worried that I'm disappointed?'

'No, not at all. I'm still Nina, your wife, I haven't changed.'

'But you have. I'm very grieved about it.'

'If you had spent as much time as I have grieving about *you* then you would have something complain about. I've wept hours of bitter tears over you and your . . . women, so I don't see why I should worry about me and my hair not pleasing you.' Nina turned on her heel and went back to the cooker, steadfastly determined not to apologize for giving him such a shock.

She could feel Val burning up behind her and wasn't surprised by his angry grabbing of her arm and turning her to face him. 'That's another thing, I don't want you working any longer at the practice. Give in your notice, whatever, say you don't enjoy it, anything, but stop working there. I won't allow it.'

'I won't give up, Val. That job is saving my life. It's not a

171

super-important job, but I love it. The money is immaterial when we have your salary coming in every month, but I am doing it. So—'

'Nina! What's come over you? I insist. I've said you've to leave.'

Quietly – so Valentine almost couldn't hear – Nina said, 'So I won't meet that woman, is that it? Eleanor Eustace? She's not good enough for you, Val. She's a tart, and not really up to your standards.'

Furious that Nina had intuitively arrived at the same conclusion he had the first time he'd been with Eleanor, Valentine clenched his fists and shouted, 'Who I go out with is no business of yours, do you hear me? None of your business.'

'How can it not be? You are my husband.'

Seething with temper, Valentine said the first thing that sprang into his head. 'Husband? Me? I don't think so. In name but nothing else. Is there any wonder I go elsewhere?'

Nina, aware this was the first time either of them had spoken so freely about his life outside their marriage, plunged in with another intuitive piece of ammunition. 'Like you did today? Mmm? A college colleague? I knew when you said it you were lying. You never ever see anyone from university, ever. It was just another cover-up.' Nina viciously added, 'I just hope she was seasick.' She turned away to finish serving their supper, her hands shaking and the broccoli jumping anywhere but where she wanted it to go.

Valentine snarled, 'And if it was Eleanor, do you blame me?' Knowing he would hurt her beyond anything he'd said before, he added disdainfully, 'With you for a wife?'

Nina picked up the dinner plate intended for Valentine and flung it at him with all her might. His hands went out to stop it hitting his forehead but instead they tipped it so the food fell all the way down the front of him, then the plate fell to the floor and smashed.

He didn't speak.

She didn't offer to help clean him up.

He grabbed his napkin from the table and began wiping himself down.

She calmly took her plate to the table, set it down, spread her napkin across her knee and began eating. With satisfaction she noted her hands were as steady as rock, and her heart wasn't beating furiously as she might have expected.

He stood looking down at her from the opposite side of the table, emotion after emotion flooding his face. For once Nina had made him speechless. Suddenly she was strong and she'd never been strong before, not since he'd known her. This was a whole new Nina, not the beaten-into-the-ground Nina, the scared, the inadequate, terrified, inept, out-of-control Nina, and he didn't know what to do with her. So he turned on his heel and ran up the stairs two at a time to rid himself of the evidence of her newborn strength.

Valentine dumped his clothes in the linen basket, dressed again and returned to the kitchen. A day's sailing had given him a huge appetite. 'My dinner? Is there anything left for me?'

'There's bit of everything but not much fish.' By this time she'd almost finished her plateful. She sat for a while to give him time to sort out his own dinner. Old habits almost got her to her feet to make as decent a plate of food as she could from the remnants, but she changed her mind. He was a grown man and perfectly capable, as he proved the times when she'd left him for good (and then come back because she couldn't live without him).

He solemnly and silently ate the leftovers. It wasn't nearly enough but it would have to do. 'I'll fill up on cheese and biscuits. Are there any?'

Nina nodded but did nothing to assist him. So he fumbled around in the cupboards and the fridge and finally got himself set up, but not as elegantly as Nina would have done it. She went to get a slice of cheesecake for herself. Valentine watched her eat it. A slice of that would just round his meal off quite beautifully. He went to get it himself.

By the time they'd finished eating, the heat of the day was gone, and Nina decided to take her coffee into the garden. She tossed her head to remind herself about her beautiful new hairstyle, poured a cup of rich dark coffee from the cafetière and wandered off to her favourite seat in the gazebo, now covered densely with honeysuckle and providing shade. She'd once thought about hanging herself from the oak tree which dominated the very end of the garden in the early dark days of their marriage. Why hadn't she? Because of this man coming out into the garden this very moment carrying a mug, this man who had made her his wife to get her to safety in England. She owed him such a lot. She loved him so very much.

He sat beside her, not speaking. They must have sat for twenty minutes in silence as the sun began to go down. Valentine broke the silence. 'Of course you must keep the job if it makes you feel good.'

Nina opened her mouth to say thanks, but changed her mind. If she wanted to she would keep it without asking permission. Soon the month would be up and she fully expected that Joy would ask her to stay on.

Choosing her words carefully, Nina replied, 'I like my new hairstyle. The long hair was holding me back, it wasn't letting me leave behind things that needed leaving behind. You know.' Again the silence but this time it was filled with expectancy, for there was more for her to say. 'It was so long they could w-wind it round their wrists and hold me tight so I couldn't get away.'

She began to sob, quite quietly at first, but then it overcame her and she wept like she'd never wept before. Valentine took hold of her, rocking her back and forth, helplessly murmuring words of comfort and this time, held tightly in his arms, she didn't flinch.

The whole of her inner being was laid bare to him and he sensed he wasn't man enough to help her through the crisis. He quite simply did not have the words nor the empathy to feel it along with her and help her heal. He despised himself for the poverty of his understanding.

When Nina woke the next morning, the loss of her hair came to her immediately as she turned over on to her back. There was no longer the heavy dragging of the long plait, and straight away she recollected the lightness of heart that came with the loss of it. Why had she never thought to cut her hair before? Was it because she actually enjoyed being ensnared by the horror of her experiences? Was she fundamentally afraid of being 'normal'?

Nina turned to find Valentine on his side facing her. He looked so good even at this early hour. Was there a time when he didn't look good? Not really.

Without warning his eyes sprang open and they lay studying each other deeply. Only thirty centimetres away, she could see in his eyes the memories of what had been said the previous night and she blushed when she remembered the plate smashing on the tiled floor. Nina couldn't look into his eyes any longer. It was too much, that kind of deep concentration, seeing into each other's souls like that; it was something they didn't do.

The alarm went and broke the spell. Nina turned it off and sat upright on the edge of the bed, her bare toes searching the rug for her slippers. She yawned and stretched.

'Five more minutes in bed, Nina?'

'No, things to do.'

'Two more minutes in bed?'

Nina fell backwards onto the bed so her head came to rest on his stomach. 'Oh! Sorry!'

'Stay where you are. When I looked at you just then I decided I like your hair. It's much better and a lot less trouble for you.'

'Exact!'

'Exactly. Not exact. Makes you look carefree.'

He surprised her. He hadn't corrected her English for months. No, years.

'Exactly.' She looked up at him and smiled, and they had another of those silent soul-searching moments.

They lay there saying nothing more until Nina saw that she would be running late and leapt out of bed. While she was in the bathroom she heard Valentine speaking on his mobile and, from the tone of his voice, she knew it was Eleanor. But this time her spirits didn't take a plunge; she wouldn't let them.

*

When Nina walked into the reception area that morning at seven fifty-five precisely she was greeted by welcoming shrieks of delight.

'Nina! Wow!' from Annette.

'I say! Magnificent, you look great.' This from Joy, who was pulling her uniform over her head and emerged smiling at what she saw.

Annette burst out with, 'Whatever made you do it?'

Their delight made her glow with pleasure.

'My hair was ridiculous old-fashioned. I looked like milkmaid in an Austrian musical with that long plait wound round my head, and I thought no, this is twenty-first century. So I did it.' She tossed her head, just for the thrill of feeling the freedom.

Valentine came in right then and Joy asked him, 'What do you think about Nina's new hairstyle?'

He looked embarrassed, a rare emotion for Valentine, and muttered, 'I think it's excellent.' He beamed at them all and went immediately to his consulting room, shutting the door.

As it struck half past eight, Joy said, 'I'll give Virginia a ring about that call that's just come in, she'll need to know what's happened.' So she rang Virginia's mobile but it was switched off. 'That's funny.' Joy stood looking at the phone, wondering why she couldn't make contact. 'I know, I'll ring—'

But just then the phone rang and when she answered it proved to be Kate asking if Virginia was all right as she hadn't called yet to pick her up. 'I've rung her flat but there's no reply, and I've rung her mobile and—'

'So have I. Come in, Kate, and we'll sort something. It's not like Virginia not to be in contact. Maybe she's gone to feed the guinea pigs.'

'No, she hasn't. Ben and Gideon are doing the mornings and Virginia and I are doing the evenings this week. So unless there's been a crisis I can't see why she should. I hope she's not ill in the flat.'

By the time Kate got to the practice Joy had received an enigmatic message from Virginia on her answerphone. She was terribly sorry but she wouldn't be in today and possibly not tomorrow, as she had some urgent family business that had to be attended to. She'd be in touch before the weekend. She thought. Perhaps.

They were all concerned about Virginia, although Joy could do nothing about it but reorganize her calls between Dan, Scott and, though he was reluctant, Colin.

But before lunch there was an incident which thrust all anxiety about Virginia out of their minds.

Through the main door, looking bedraggled and quite unlike her usual well-dressed self, came a hysterical Eleanor Eustace, carrying little Choo in a towel streaked with blood.

'She's cut herself! Help me, please, she's b-bleeding to death!'

Annette got her to sit down and, in the circumstances, suggested that Rhodri should see her. There was no way she should be seen by Valentine. Enough was enough.

Eleanor jumped up, almost knocking Annette to the floor. 'I want Val to see her, do you hear me?'

As though on cue, in walked Nina, back from a trip to the convenience store. She took in the situation at a glance. So here she was again, this Eleanor person, begging to see Valentine. By the looks of it, it was genuine enough; the cat did look ill. But how dare she?

Annette swiftly said, 'Rhodri's been alerted. He'll deal with it.'

Nina nodded her agreement. Now she'd got Eleanor at a disadvantage she tried to remember all the things she'd thought to say at home when she brooded about the woman. But nothing sprung to mind and she stood speechless, so very angry with herself.

Rhodri came into reception, saying in his wonderful rich Welsh voice, 'Choo Eustace, please. Come along, let's see what's happened, then.'

Eleanor didn't move a muscle. She sat rigid, clutching Choo and saying, 'It's Val I want to see. You stupid bitch, get me *Val*. Do you hear me? *Val*.'

Joy emerged, brushing the crumbs from a sandwich off her lips.

'Your cat is the crucial thing at this moment and if Val is busy, Rhodri will do very nicely, thank you. Give it to me. I won't have this hysteria in my waiting room a moment longer.' She masterfully carried Choo to Rhodri's consulting room, kicking the door shut behind her with her foot, leaving Eleanor bellowing with temper.

Annette suggested a glass of water. Nina thought a bucket of water poured over her would be a better idea like they used if dogs began fighting, but she couldn't have gone to get it if she'd tried, she was so distressed by Eleanor's presence.

Eleanor was giving a very good impression of a toddler in a tantrum; hammering her feet on the floor, beating her fists on her thighs, shaking her head from side to side so vigorously her long blonde hair was flailing about her head.

Just as they were thinking medical help might have to be called in, Mrs Bookbinder arrived in reception. Her arrival silenced the tut-tutting in the waiting room but had no effect on Eleanor.

Mrs Bookbinder whispered sensitively, 'Has her cat died or her dog or something?'

Annette shook her head. 'She wanted Valentine to see her cat, but he can't, he's busy. She hasn't an appointment so Rhodri's attending.'

Mrs Bookbinder's powerful voice reverberated round reception. 'My dear, I know the feeling. He makes me want to scream if I can't see him; he's so clever and such a darling, darling man. Fortunately, I have self-control, which you are apparently lacking. Now drink that water . . . did you hear me, *drink that water* and stop howling like a banshee, it's too upsetting for my new baby here.' She peered through the bars of the carrying cage in her hand at the most charming Burmese kitten anyone could hope to see. 'When I say *drink* I mean *der-rink*.' Mrs Bookbinder must have forgotten she was no longer on a parade ground (she'd once confessed to Joy in a weak moment that she'd been an army officer) for her voice seemed to bounce off the walls several times.

Eleanor cringed and obediently sipped the water Annette had brought her, stifling her shrieks as best she could and hoping no one realized the shrieks were not caused by fear for her cat but because she wasn't allowed to see Val. This wasn't working out a bit like she'd intended. She'd imagined staggering into Val's consulting room, moaning and weeping, and finding Val's strong arms around her and getting a delicious hormone-triggering burst of his aftershave. Instead that harridan was shouting at her, her hair was a mess and her mascara was running, and damn it, she wanted to see him and why shouldn't she? She *paid* to see him, after all.

Joy emerged from Rhodri's room, her face very grim. They all noticed it, even the clients, and they were desperate to find out why.

'Miss Eustace, would you kindly come with me into my office? I'd like to discuss your cat with you.'

She shot to her feet. 'She's not died, has she?'

Joy didn't answer.

Eleanor brought the water with her and stood it on Joy's desk, slopping water over the pile of newly printed rosters, which Joy impatiently moved away.

'I'm sorry your cat — Choo, isn't it? — has been hurt. Do you have any idea how it happened?'

Eleanor shook her head. She could see it was going to be an afternoon of telling lies . . .

'You see, she's been quite badly hurt. We wondered if there was anyone with a grudge against you, because it looks quite deliberate. When cats are allowed to run free, cuts are usually more jagged, you know, more-rough edged because they've caught themselves on barbed wire or something similar.'

She waited for a reply, but didn't get one.

'Is she a house cat, then?'

Eleanor shook her head. 'No.'

'She's going to need stitches and Rhodri thinks it's best if she stays in overnight, because the cut is in a difficult place, right behind her front leg, kind of behind the elbow. It could pull open very easily.'

A slight groan escaped. 'That bad?'

Joy nodded and left a silence.

'Are you serious? I can't leave her here, she needs me.'

'We have all-night staff. She'll be fine and well cared for.'

'I didn't think . . .'

Joy leaned forward, 'You didn't think . . . what?'

'Nothing. Has Val got a free moment?'

I'm not having that, thought Joy. 'No, he's fully booked until we close. Busy day. One of those things. Rhodri is excellent, equally as good as Val. Choo will have every attention, I assure you. How about going home now? We'll take great care of your cat.' She pushed her chair back and squeezed behind Eleanor's chair to open the door. 'Must press on.'

'I'll pop in to see him between clients, I know he won't mind.'

'I'm sorry. Like I've said, he's busy.'

Eleanor, hating the fact she couldn't have her own way, tried a quick dodge towards Val's consulting room, but Joy grabbed her back, almost manhandled her out of the front door and shut it tightly.

So the whole scheme had achieved nothing except a large vet's bill. Eleanor could have screamed her anguish out loud except that damned shouting woman was still on the premises and she couldn't face another session with *her*.

From behind the reception desk, dealing with paying bills and making appointments, Nina was hating herself for being a coward. She had the uncomfortable feeling that the cut on poor Choo had been done by Eleanor to secure time with Val. She was almost sick with disgust at the strength of Eleanor's determination to keep Val for herself.

Later that morning, Valentine, having been asked by Joy to examine Choo, blanched when he saw the cut. His first unnerving thought was that Eleanor had deliberately cut the cat as a reason for getting his attention. If he was right, she must be completely mad. Not only mad, but cruel in the extreme. Where, now, was her love for Choo, that passionate, all-adoring love she exhibited? Where now was he placed in relation to her? He'd rung her that morning to tell her he couldn't keep their date that night. Why he'd done that he didn't know. All he knew was that he needed to sort his head out about her before he saw her again. There'd always been that feeling of uneasiness in their relationship, her driving the pace, her twenty-four/seven demands on his time. But to go to such extremes indicated a seriously unbalanced mind.

Valentine went into Joy's office and closed the door. 'Are you, like me, thinking she did it deliberately?'

Joy answered that Rhodri thought the same, then she looked up at him and felt appalled by the look on his face. He looked like an old man. His face was drawn, his eyes dull, his shoulders drooping. He needed her to talk straight. 'I do think she did. She's poison, Valentine.'

'Joy, she's raving mad.'

'Very possibly. Whatever caused it, for God's sake, *be careful.*'

'I'll take another look.'

He went to the intensive care room to look at Choo again, lifting her out of her cage and placing her on a worktop, watching her, looking, assessing. Valentine admired the way Rhodri had stitched the cut. It was so precise, almost a work of art, and such a difficult place to stitch, too. Valentine couldn't have done any better.

He placed Choo carefully in her cage and kissed the top of her head as she peeped up at him. Then, locking her in, he went to find Joy.

'I'm sure I'm right. I'll see Mungo. Ask him if he wants to prosecute.'

'You feel as badly as *that*?'

'I do. It's my professional opinion, not an emotional kind of revenge, believe me. Will he want to, do you think?'

Joy patted Valentine's arm in sympathy. 'Never come across this before.'

'What's the alternative?'

'Take the kitten from her. Otherwise you'll tell the police.'

'I'll see Mungo, Joy, see what he thinks.'

Mungo favoured taking the kitten from her. 'It will leave a nasty taste in people's mouths if *we* prosecute. It's no good thinking no one will know what we're doing, they will. They saw her exhibition in the waiting room for a start. We can't afford to damage the practice reputation, can we now? And about you? She's obviously mad, and what she's done repels me. If she'll do this to a beautiful—'

'You've seen Choo?'

'I have. She must have a block of concrete for a heart. It's despicable.' He looked at Valentine over the top of his reading glasses, 'You've been a fool. Will you never learn?'

Ruefully Valentine said, 'Maybe.'

'If there's any nonsense from her, tell her we'll get the RSPCA to prosecute and then see where her friends are when she needs them. You and Rhodri'd better make a detailed report of what you consider has happened just in case it goes legal. We'll keep her here for a few days while we have a think about what to do. It would be wrong to let her take Choo home. Heaven alone knows what she would do.'

'OK. It's not life-threatening, so a few days—'

'Good man. You see to it, then? We'll delay telling the RSPCA while we have a think.'

That night there were endless messages on their land-line from Eleanor, hysterical, sometimes screaming calls, which they couldn't decipher. But whatever she was saying, she was clearly unhinged.

The next morning Eleanor was at the practice as the clock struck eight. 'I want my cat. You said overnight and so I've come.'

There was only Annette on duty because Joy had an early-morning appointment at the doctor's and wouldn't be in until later and it was Nina's day off.

'Appointments begin at eight-thirty, I'm afraid. But take a pew and you can wait.'

'I want to see her now.' She stood belligerently, close up to the counter and glaring at Annette, who discreetly placed her finger on the alarm bell under the counter, ready to press if the need arose.

'I'm afraid not.'

'In that case I'm going in the back to find her.'

'I'm sorry, clients aren't allowed in the back, it's strictly against the rules.'

'I'm no ordinary client.' Eleanor dumped her bag on the counter top and set off down the corridor. Fortunately Sarah One had had the instinct to lock the intensive care room when she'd finished attending to the dog in there, for whom there was not much hope, and to Choo.

Eleanor rattled the doorknob, banged on the door with her fists and shouted for help. Mungo came down the stairs to find the reason for the noise at that time in the morning.

He was horrified to see the dishevelled Eleanor hammering on the door in such a hysterical way. Miriam had followed him down and, knowing the history of Eleanor and Valentine, was filled with compassion.

'My dear! We have a very sick dog in there, you'll be alarming him. Let me take you upstairs to our flat. Have you had breakfast?'

The tenderness of Miriam's voice finally broke Eleanor, and she all but collapsed onto her. Mungo took most of her weight and between them they got her up to the flat.

Miriam said, 'Head for the kitchen, we'll sit her in my chair.'

It was a wooden Victorian chair Miriam had found in an antique market one day when she was feeling low and wondering how she would ever get over the deaths of her children. It looked like the kind of chair which would bring comfort to anyone who was sad. She'd made cushions for it, a big thick one for the back rest and a solid square one for the seat. It always managed to still her pain, and Miriam thought it might do the same for Eleanor.

'Sit there, my dear, and have some coffee. Cream and sugar?'

Eleanor nodded.

'One or two?'

Eleanor held up one finger.

'Have you had breakfast?'

Eleanor shook her head.

'Toast? I know! A toasted teacake with butter and homemade raspberry jam. Does that sound good?'

Eleanor nodded again.

Miriam didn't speak a word until the toasted teacake and the coffee were finished. Then, and then only, did she sit down and say, 'Now, tell me everything that is wrong with you.' She handed Eleanor a tissue from the box on the window sill, tested her African violets to see if they needed watering and then gave Eleanor her whole attention.

The whole sad story of Eleanor's infatuation for Valentine came pouring out, sometimes incoherent, sometimes lucid, sometimes simply self-pitying nonsense. When she'd finally admitted to harming her kitten just to hold on to Valentine's attention, she laid her head back against the cushion and stared with desperate, glistening eyes at Miriam.

Miriam, stunned by her confessions, was momentarily at a loss. Not a single word of comfort could she find to say. Then she remembered something she'd heard about Eleanor and decided to get to the truth. 'Is it correct that you are so well-heeled because of an inheritance that you no longer need to work?'

Eleanor gave a funny squeaky 'yes,' but didn't enlarge on it.

'I see. Do you do any charity work to keep busy?'

The expression on Eleanor's face changed to one of horror. 'Me? Charity work! My God, no!'

'So you do nothing but indulge yourself with shopping and men?'

The silence which followed made Miriam think she'd blown it, but suddenly Eleanor agreed. 'Yes. What else is there to do?'

'Exactly. What else is there to do? That's your problem. What were you before you had the misfortune to come into pots of money?'

'I was an editor with a large publishing house. Busy. Busy. Long hours.'

'But did you love it?'

'I did. Every day different. Every day the chance that you might find that author with that extra bit of something which would make them a bestseller.'

'So you've gone from that kind of high state of expectation, that heavy demand on your skill, on your perception of what the public will want to read eighteen months from now, to absolutely . . . nothing.'

Eleanor nodded.

'My dear, that's your problem. You've a sharp brain and you're clearly bursting with energy, with ideas. That's what you're missing. Get back to work. Find a challenge out there in the hurly-burly of the publishing world. You never know, the novel that will make your name could be just round the corner. You don't need the salary but the *challenge* can be your reward. Then Valentine will fade into insignificance. Believe me, he will. He always goes back to Nina, always. His affairs don't last much longer than six, maybe eight weeks, and then they're over. It doesn't matter how beautiful the women are, how sparkling, how dazzled by him, he always drops them like a hot potato.'

'But Nina is a fool. A waste of space. He told me she was a secret service person, when all the time she's a receptionist in a veterinary practice. I mean—'

'Nina had the most terrible time in her teens, and it was Valentine who married her so he could rescue her from it and bring her to England. She saw her parents and brothers murdered in front of her and thrown into a mass grave, and what happened to *her* afterwards doesn't bear telling. That's why she's here. Not because it's the only thing she's capable of, but because at the moment it's the biggest thing she's been able to do in years. And it's not for you to criticize her for it. Just be grateful it wasn't you.'

The only response Miriam got was, 'Can I sit here a while longer?'

'Of course. I've the dog to take out. Stay as long as you like and shut the flat door behind you as you leave. But no more scenes in reception, please, I don't want Mungo getting upset, he has a busy day.'

Miriam didn't need to call for Perkins; he was already at the kitchen door, tail wagging, having sensed she was ready to take him out. She fastened his collar on, as he always slept without it, and the two of them went downstairs and set out across the car park to go up Beulah Bank Top.

She walked much further than normal that morning while she dwelt on Eleanor's problems and tried to rid herself of the exhaustion of counselling her. What a fool the girl had been. The higher Miriam got the stronger the wind blew and it came as a relief from the ever-climbing rise in temperature down in the town. With the wind blowing in her hair, her heart filled with the pleasure of the open space and the joy of seeing Perkins running freely about the hill. Her spirits soared. When she finally turned to go back home, and she could see the roof of the practice building gleaming in the sun, she felt restored, and able to count her blessings.

Back at the practice Miriam rubbed Perkins down with a towel kept especially for the purpose, then opened up the flat door and called out, 'Eleanor!' There was no reply, but when she got in the kitchen she was still sitting there, staring straight ahead, not moving.

Miriam put the kettle on. Perkins went to sit close to Eleanor and put his paw on her knee, looking up at her face, waiting.

Her hand went out to stroke his head. After a few moments Eleanor looked at Miriam and said, 'You're very wise.'

'Oh, I don't know about that. I just say what comes. If it's of use then—'

'I'm going home to think about what you've said. Thank you for saying it. At bottom Valentine is a . . . well, pardon the expression, he's a sod. A complete and utter sod. I'll collect Choo on the way.'

'Ah! I don't know if she's fit to go home.' But Miriam looked at her with a different message in her eyes.

'Oh! I see. You mean, they daren't let me have her?'

'Something like that.'

'Perhaps not, then. I'll come in tomorrow.'

Miriam switched off the kettle. 'Ask to see Rhodri. He did the stitching.'

The unspoken message reached Eleanor and, instead of demanding her own way so she could see Valentine, she accepted the wisdom of Miriam's words and left. Frankly she was well shot of him . . . but her heart bled at her loss. As she walked towards her car she braced her shoulders.

Chapter 15

First thing the following morning, Joy and Kate went to the practice flat to see what had happened to Virginia. They went in Joy's car full of apprehension.

Joy checked before turning right into the road where the flat was. 'I always think Terminus Street an awful address.'

'It is, but the old tram depot was at the end, you know.'

'How do you know that, a young slip of a thing like you? There hasn't been trams in Barleybridge for more than fifty years.'

'My dad told me. He knew all the history of the transport in Barleybridge, being keen on model trains. But the trams didn't last long, I think the town woke up to trams just as buses were becoming popular and some bright spark on the council fancied Barleybridge being up to date.'

'Of course, I'd forgotten. How's Mia getting on now she's a widow?'

'Exceptionally well, thanks. Bit lonely when I'm at college, though. Here we are. Nice flats, aren't they?'

'Oh, yes. Miriam found it and persuaded Mungo to buy it for the practice. It's hardly been empty since. Kate, do you suppose Virginia really does have urgent family business?'

'I don't know. Got the key?

'Yes. I don't like using it, but we have tried to ring. We'll knock, to be sure.'

There was no answer to their knock so Joy let them in. She bent down to pick up Saturday's post, laid it on the hall table and went in first followed by Kate, who remembered the last time she'd been here was when she visited Scott after he'd been trampled by Phil Parsons' old bull. The emotions she felt then! Wow! Sitting on the sofa – still the same one, she noticed – beside him, talking quietly. How full she'd been with love that day. Instead, today, she was filled with anxiety.

Joy gasped at the beautiful decoration of the sitting room. 'My word, what a difference. Why, she's made it quite beautiful, hasn't she? Her pictures are gorgeous! Try the bedroom, Kate.'

The bedroom was decorated in a very subtle lavender. Facing south, it was just beginning to fill with sunshine, but there was no Virginia. It was immaculately tidy, though, with no signs of hurried departure or even an unexpected departure. She tried the kitchen and found Joy already in there admiring its pristine cleanliness and its selection of top-of-the-shop kitchen equipment. 'My word, this is fantastic! I wonder if she uses any of it?'

Kate, suffering a moment of lurid imagination, tried the bathroom, thinking there might be something gory in there, but there wasn't, no slashed wrists, no bloodied bathwater then.

'I'll try the wardrobe, see if her clothes have gone.' Kate flung wide the wardrobe doors and found Virginia's clothes neatly hanging in regimental order – skirts, then tops, then dresses, then evening clothes. Outdoor clothing in a smaller section with cashmere jackets, a Barbour jacket and Aquascutum rainwear. Expensive, scarcely worn shoes carefully lined up along the bottom shelf, grouped by colour. On the top shelf a selection of expensive scarves were carefully folded, silk, mohair, cashmere. She had money, did our Virginia, but that didn't tell them where she'd gone. So Joy and Kate left her flat no wiser about her whereabouts, but much wiser about her financial status.

As they drove away Joy said, 'Another twenty-four hours and it's the police. We can't just ignore her disappearance. Where on earth do you think she'll have gone? You've spent a lot of time with her. Have you any clues?'

'None at all. She never discusses anything personal, so I'm no closer than you. If she's all right why hasn't she phoned since yesterday? She's gone in her car, it wasn't in the car park, 'cos I looked from the bedroom window and couldn't see it.'

'Stranger and stranger. I mean, where is she? Why should she disappear? With a job and responsibilities, I mean what the hell.'

Mungo was equally at a loss. 'The stupid woman. What is she playing at? As if she hasn't been enough trouble already. I also understand she's done a call at Tad Porter's and didn't record it. She knows that's forbidden.'

Joy told him she thought they ought to tell the police. 'Or we could ring the hospitals.'

Mungo stopped his incessant tapping on his desk with his pen and thought for a moment. 'If she'd been run over she'd have had all her official things with her, like credit cards, driving licence and such, therefore she'd have been identified. No, it can't be that.'

'It's putting me in a real mess for the weekend if she doesn't turn up. I've worked in veterinary practices for more years than I want to remember, and this has never happened before. Missing for a few hours, idling their time away fishing or something, yes, but never this. First thing tomorrow I'm ringing the police.'

Mungo nodded his agreement. 'Best to go in there with a photograph.'

'Have we got any? I don't think we have.'

Kate volunteered to go back to the flat and look for one.

'Tomorrow, if there's no news, you can, Kate. We're informing the police . . . quite definitely.'

'OK. I'll ring the flat and her mobile at a quarter to eight in the morning and see if I get a reply. If not I'll ring you and then you can go to the police.'

But at seven-thirty the next morning Virginia rang Kate, who was in the bathroom cleaning her teeth and wondering if she might turn up today. She got a shock to find herself talking to her.

'Kate! I've checked my calls – I haven't many. Come round to see me at the flat and we'll have a late start.'

'Oh! Right. Virginia, we've been so worried about you.'

'I expect you have. But come. Have you had breakfast?'

'Yes.' There was no reply, so Kate followed on with, 'I'll see you at your flat, then?'

'Yes. See you.'

Kate fully expected to see a devastated Virginia in need of TLC. Nothing could have been further from the truth. She was full of light and positively glowed.

'Hi! I've rung Joy, told her we're doing your calls as usual. I said it would be a bit of a late start.'

Virginia nodded. 'Come in. I have showered. Just got to dress and put my make-up on.'

As Virginia never wore make-up when she was working this came as something of a surprise to Kate. 'Oh! I'll wait here, then.'

She sat facing the window, looking out over the road where traces of the old tramlines could just be detected in the tarmac. There were flats opposite with people moving about getting ready for work, some slothful, others rushing. She could hear Virginia slamming wardrobe doors, and then silence. Maybe she was doing her face. It rather intrigued Kate thinking about Virginia in make-up. When she finally appeared Virginia looked very different from her normal self.

The unusual circumstances in which she found herself emboldened Kate and she remarked very genuinely, 'What's happened? You're so different. Where've you been? We've been worried sick about you.'

'Have we time?' Virginia glanced at the clock. 'No, we haven't, but I'll tell you. You're the only person I know at the practice, the only one I've really bothered with. Will you be bored, are you perhaps not interested?' She almost begged Kate not to be bored, she so obviously wanted to tell all.

'Please tell me. I promise I shan't be bored.' How could she be? thought Kate. It was all so bizarre.

'Two and a half years ago I was engaged to the most terrific chap anyone could hope to meet,' Virginia began. 'Simon Carter, he was called. He wasn't good-looking, he wasn't charismatic, in fact, no one noticed him very much, but he was highly intelligent, highly paid and, best of all, he adored me, and I him. We were having a family party two nights before our wedding, his family and mine. I was called out so I asked Simon to pick up my parents and take them to the hotel for the party and I would follow on.' She stared out of the window for a moment, no doubt watching those in the flats Kate had seen earlier. 'I actually passed the road accident on my way to it. One of those huge continental lorries had gone completely out of control, overturned and landed right on top of a car. I couldn't see the car because it was completely c-crushed under it. I remember thinking, there won't be much of them left to r-rescue.' Words failed Virginia and Kate couldn't bear to look at her and witness the pain she was evidently going through, so she waited and waited. Virginia cleared her throat and said softly, 'The traffic was being diverted and I carried on to the hotel.'

She paused and Kate asked, 'You're not telling me . . . it was them?'

Virginia nodded.

Kate felt her scalp prickle at the horror of the whole shocking story. 'If you don't want to tell me any more—'

'I've got to, to explain why I've been missing. Of course, they never arrived. The party was a funeral wake not a pre-wedding party, though we didn't realize it. It was horrific. The police came, I fell apart and had to be sedated for an eternity. My life was a living hell. Their deaths left me very well off. I got all my parents' money and assets, as I'm an only child, and Simon had made his will and left his house, where we were going to live, and all his worldly goods to me, but it was hell to be alive – and still was until Monday.'

'So what happened Monday?'

'I went to check that the guinea pigs had been attended to. Couldn't quite believe that Ben and Gideon would be loyal – no faith in anyone, you see. But instead Gab was there.'

'Ahh!'

Virginia tucked her legs up onto the sofa. 'I'd no idea you could meet someone and instantly feel such amazing rapport.' She stared at the fashionable leather rag rug in front of the sofa, looked up at Kate and said, 'He's the reason I've been missing.'

Kate smiled. 'Well, he's a very good reason to go missing, I suppose, if you like that kind of thing!'

Virginia abruptly reprimanded her for her frivolity. 'I'm serious, Kate. He's a very different person from the one you all think he is. He reads philosophy.'

That did it for Kate. It was impossible to think of Gab Bridges reading a book, let alone a serious one. 'Gab? Reading a book? Pull the other one!' She burst out laughing.

Virginia protested, 'You see, you're just as bad as everyone else. Everyone gets him completely wrong.'

'Sorry. If he floats your boat, then so be it. So where have you been these last few days?'

Virginia told her about going home to supper with Gab, and how lovely his mother was and how delighted she was that he'd brought someone home, even if that someone was taut with anxiety and the unfamiliarity of a large family, predominantly male. They had an uproarious supper, which lasted two and a half hours, and Gab and she left when the late-night farm jobs took over. He drove behind her all the way to her flat, but when he saw it he didn't feel at home and suggested the White Hart for the night, neutral ground and all that. She told Kate they didn't sleep all night, whereupon a wicked grin came over Kate's face, which had to be quickly smothered when she saw how serious Virginia was.

'No, we didn't share the bed,' she said. 'We sat up and talked like neither he nor I had talked in all our lives. We each told our whole life histories – he even told me about Megan Hughes. I told him about Simon and somehow he healed the whole grieving process for me. He was so understanding.' She swallowed hard and couldn't speak.

Kate burst out with, 'I . . . find it . . . hard to believe. He's always been so sexy, that's how everyone thinks about him. Gab and sex. Sex and Gab. He's been through dozens of girls . . . Sorry, I shouldn't have said that.' Kate raised her hands as an apology for what she'd let slip and wished she'd kept her mouth shut.

'That's all right, he's told me all about his sex life.'

'So you spent *four* nights there? Talking?'

'That's right. Talking and talking. I know it sounds peculiar of us, but we've both benefited. We've talked about the future, our own futures. He's coming here tonight for a meal. Just talking to him has filled me with joy, learning about him, laughing with him. What the outcome will be . . .' Virginia shrugged, then leapt to her feet and said, 'Let's be off. Guinea pigs first, then visits.'

Kate felt very humbled and said so. 'I'm so glad for you and sorry about that dreadful time you had . . . you know. No wonder you've been so sharp-tongued and unbending. Anyone would be after losing parents and fiancé all in one night. Perhaps this is the start of a whole new life.'

'That's what it feels like, but we'll wait and see, shall we? I know I feel completely different from how I felt at the beginning of the week.'

'You look different. You *are* different. I'm just amazed it's Gab who's brought it about.'

Virginia grinned at her. 'So am I. He's the most unlikely person, isn't he? We're not exactly compatible, are we? You know, not the same type of person, but underneath we must be. He has such *strength*. I don't mean he's a bully, just honest-to-goodness strength in his body and in his mind. If you were shipwrecked and he was with you there's no doubt in my mind you'd survive.' She looked into the distance and a smile crept over her face, which, to Kate's eyes, made her, for once, quite good-looking.

When they reached Bridge End Farm Virginia asked Kate if she'd make a start on the guinea pigs while she went to the house to see the Misses Patterson for five minutes. Kate nodded and set off for the stables. She opened up the doors to freshen the air after the steaming night it had been and found the guinea pigs all looking perky and bright. All they'd needed was food and water, and cleaning out. Such a pity they were all in hutches. Nowadays, space for running about would be a priority, not this total incarceration.

In the farmhouse Virginia was discussing business with Emily and Louisa.

'You know Miriam Price, do you?' she began.

They nodded.

'Well, she's remembered the name of a man in the same business as you, and we've made contact.'

Emily's eyes sparkled. 'You don't mean he might be interested in buying us out?'

'He's interested in buying your guinea pigs, not the property. He's not going to pay a great deal but the offer is there. He's called Desmond Denning. He lives over Yeovil way. I've told him I'll speak to you about it, and I've promised him if he decides to take them that they'll be very fit by the time money has exchanged hands. Frankly, I think we have to be grateful to have found someone, don't you?'

'Oh, we are, aren't we, Louisa, dear?'

'I shall be sad to see them go, but on the other hand I can't do the work any more. I'm so grateful to you, Veterinary, so grateful. Such a burden they are for you and those two nice boys who come in the evenings. Or is it the morning when they come?'

'It's a pleasure to be of help, believe me.' Virginia had to broach the other idea she had. 'I've an inkling that I might like to buy the property. How would you feel about that? Full market price, of course.'

Louisa looked appalled. 'Oh! I don't think so. We were born here, we can't move. No, father wouldn't like that. He'd be horrified. It's been in our family since the 1750s. No, my dear, I'm sorry.'

Emily appeared not quite so sure. 'When I think of the repairs, the roof, the decorating which we shall never be able to afford . . .'

'We could use the money from selling the guinea pigs to do that,' Louisa said triumphantly as though she'd solved all their problems at one stroke.

Virginia said nothing. She knew full well, though no price had been quoted, that the money from the sale would scarcely pay for the cans of paint. The man was taking them out of pity not for commercial reasons, and Virginia had to smile when she remembered Miriam's persuasive tongue when she rang Desmond in her hearing. Desmond Denning couldn't have refused if it had been a herd of elephants she was asking him to take on board. That was just like Miriam. Sweet wasn't a word she liked, but it so fitted her.

Emily patted Louisa's hand. 'We'll have a little talk, dear, sort ourselves out.'

Virginia decided to open their minds up to the advantages of moving. 'You could buy a ground-floor flat close to the shops with some of the money. It would make life so much easier for you both.'

'You're quite right. And we could find somewhere near the doctor's and the bus stops.' Emily saw the common sense of the idea and suddenly Louisa caught the spirit of it. She suggested they could buy a flat close to the railway station, then they could visit their niece Toria and her family.

Virginia's idea had apparently sprouted wings. 'Think about it,' she said. 'I'll go help Kate with the guinea pigs and then we'll be off. If you decided to sell I'd buy the farm land, too, of course.'

'It's good land and the Ministry would be glad for it to be farmed properly. We used to rent it all out but, with farming being what it is, that fell through. That's another reason why we're in such a mess.' Tears flooded Emily's eyes and Virginia decided to beat a retreat. She'd experienced enough emotional see-sawing this week and couldn't take any more.

As she went out into the sunshine she looked up at the heavens and her heart raced with joy. How could the world be so beautiful? Just looking up at that brilliant blue sky, with birds lazily wheeling about trying to catch the thermals to make life even easier, the trees still as still and the sun pouring into every nook and cranny was such a pleasure. Was there anywhere on earth more beautiful?

Kate appeared with the wheelbarrow filled with used bedding from the hutches and Virginia had to laugh. Sun or no sun, joy or no joy, the workaday things of this world had a habit of intruding. She called across, 'Never fear, Ginny's here,' took the barrow from Kate and wheeled it away to the midden, her head filled with the thought that she'd see Gab tonight.

They had a message on Virginia's phone to call in to see Mungo any time after four o'clock. Virginia looked grimly out of the windscreen. Another hurdle to jump. But then she smiled and decided that the new Virginia could sail through this confrontation. Yes, of course she could. 'We'll go straight up at four. You make us a pot of tea while I see Mungo. Better still, we'll have bottled water, too. Tea to revive, water to stop us getting dehydrated.'

Kate smiled. 'You don't seem very bothered about Mungo.'

'I'm not. I shall take my days off as holiday, then he can't complain.'

'Joy will go ballistic.'

'Let her. There're worse things in life.'

'There are.' Kate thought about Virginia's tragedy and wondered if she could have pulled through such horror.

Mungo was overheated after a difficult spat with a client, who had seen a documentary on TV and thought he knew it all. Mungo's advice had been that they went back to the breeder from whom they'd bought their pedigree Labrador puppy and claim compensation to help pay for the surgery he needed.

'But we can't, they're friends of ours,' the client had said.

'Frankly, they have an obligation to be honest with you and they weren't,' Mungo had replied. 'I honestly believe they knew about the problem and kept mum, thinking, no doubt, that you were inexperienced in the way of dogs and you wouldn't notice. It's a common fault with Labradors, less so than it used to be, but it still crops up from time to time. Other than that, I'll do my best to sort it with an operation.'

The clients were scandalized at the thought of telling their friends, and decided to go home and think about it. They'd left Mungo with a flea in his ear, saying they'd paid to see him because of his reputation and here he was saying he would do his best – well, maybe his best wasn't going to be good enough. So when Virginia walked in, he had run out of the milk of human kindness.

'Virginia, what have you to say?' He glanced up at her and recognized this was a different Virginia, a Virginia full of bonhomie and lightness of heart. Did he see lipstick? He did. My God!

'I have to apologize and say yes, I did take three days' holiday without first informing the practice manager, which I am about to do. I'm very sorry, it won't occur again.'

'Another thing: what made you think you could dispense veterinary expertise without charging for it? Tad rang me and told me you hadn't charged him for a visit and some drugs. Do not do that again. He was upset that you thought he was willing to accept charity.'

Virginia began to say, 'You know what it's like for hill farmers at the moment, so I thought just this once—'

'What with that and being absent without leave I should . . . ' He broke off surprised by her disarming smile.

'I'm sorry about Tad Porter. But this week something came up and I got carried away. But here I am, all in one piece and glad to be alive.'

Mungo saw she was different, but he couldn't understand how or why. 'Well, all right then, we'll let it go this time, but don't do it again. Let Joy know it's three days' holiday, with my permission – even if it is belated.'

'Of course. Thanks, Mungo, for being so understanding.' She patted his hand as it lay on the desk, and left him more puzzled than ever.

Joy was not so easy to persuade, but by being charming, a state of affairs she was unaccustomed to, Virginia won her over.

'Well, all right then, but don't make a habit of it. I'm afraid you'll be on call over the weekend. Mungo and Dan did yours for you, which I thought was heroic on their part at such short notice and in particular with no explanation as to why. What's happening about the guinea pigs?' Joy thought she saw a slight blush on Virginia's face, but she must have been mistaken.

'We look as though we've found a buyer. He won't be paying much, but at least it gets rid of the problem for the Pattersons.'

'Good. It's important to see them well looked after. Are the Bridges boys still helping?'

'Oh, yes. Kate and I couldn't manage without them', Virginia said hastily, adding, 'Cup of tea waiting,' and escaped as fast as she could.

Kate and Joy had been wrong about the state-of-the-art kitchen equipment in Virginia's flat. It was in daily use, and the meal she prepared for Gab that night was superb because of it. Finding Virginia's cooking matched, if not excelled, his mother's farm house food, when he finished his main course Gab laid his knife and fork together and rejoiced. 'That was wonderful.'

'Wait till I bring the pudding.'

'There's pudding? I haven't room.'

'Wait till you see it. Have another glass of wine while I put the finishing touches to it.'

It was the hint of kirsch in the pudding which triggered Gab's tastebuds. The pudding appeared light and delicate, just right for such a hot night, but it was filling and all he wanted to do when he'd eaten was fall asleep, but Virginia had made espresso coffee and he guessed that would keep him awake.

They left the table, Gab sitting in the big squashy armchair and Virginia on the sofa, looking out at the flats opposite. The air conditioning was on and Gab was grateful for that.

'Not much of a view, I'm afraid.'

'No.' He eyed her surreptitiously from half-closed eyes. Her defrosting process had already begun, he could sense that, but this time, because he was serious, he wasn't having any of that business of sex for breakfast, lunch and supper. This time he was getting it right. She knew he was observing her and flushed. It caught him off guard. He couldn't remember the last time a girl blushed because of him. They were usually so up for it there was no time for the niceties. He found it endearing. When he saw her features soften, he thought: Yes, this is great, this is how it should be.

Virginia yawned loudly. 'I'm sorry, it's awfully rude of me but I feel as though I haven't slept for weeks. I'm going to have to go to bed. Sorry and all that.'

'In that case, I'll bung everything in the dishwasher and tidy up in the kitchen. You go to bed. I'll make sure the front door's locked.'

'Are you sure?'

'Certainly I am. I'm good at it. We all have to get stuck in at home with so many of us.'

'Of course. I'll go to bed, then. Thanks for a lovely evening.'

'Thank *you* for a lovely evening. I'll say goodnight before I leave.'

She could hear him tramping about in the kitchen, and then calling out, 'Are you decent?'

'Yes, come in.' She wondered what he would have in mind and hoped he would be sensitive enough to know she wasn't wanting sex with him – well, not yet anyway.

He leaned over the bed and looked deeply into her eyes from only a foot away. He was so close she could smell his aftershave, see the abounding health in his smooth brown cheeks and clear frank eyes, and sense that blatant sex appeal which was so much part of him.

He said, 'You're special, d'yer know that?' Then kissed her sweetly on the lips, straightened up and stood looking down at her. Because of the heat she had only a sheet covering her and felt very vulnerable, and disappointed too, that he looked as though he was expecting more and she'd have to say No. But Gab just said, 'Goodnight, Ginny. Suits you, does "Ginny". I'll ring tomorrow, very first thing.'

He stood at the door giving her a long, penetrating look as though memorizing her face to keep him going through the night, and then left. Ginny heard the front door slam, thought how precious to her it was that he didn't expect . . . and immediately fell asleep.

Chapter 16

No one but Kate had a clue to what had caused the change in Virginia, but they all observed it.

Never before had Joy so willingly accepted an apology from a member of staff for not giving notice of a three-day holiday. She'd surprised herself and said so to Mungo. 'Did she tell you why?'

'No. I didn't ask. I was too flabbergasted. She's not the same, is she?' He looked over the top of his reading glasses, hoping Joy had the answer.

'Don't look at me. She even told me this morning that she preferred to be called Ginny from now on.'

'It's a man. That's what. It must be.'

Joy contemplated this idea. 'You could be right, but who the blazes is it? It's not Valentine, is it?'

'No, she's not his type. He likes them slender and fluffy with dazzle, and that's not Virginia. Does Kate know? They've worked together quite a bit.'

Joy shrugged. 'Claims she's no idea, but I don't believe her.'

'I'll ask Miriam at lunch-time.'

But Miriam hadn't a clue, either. 'He'd have to be tall, he'd have to have money, he'd have to be intelligent. Sorry, I don't know who fits the bill unless it's you.'

Something on the Radio 4 news caught Mungo's attention, and he replied, 'Yes, possibly.'

Miriam, with a wry smile, asked, 'How has she looked after the flat? Does it look clean and smart? My six-monthly inspection is about due.'

'How should I know how she's got the flat?'

Miriam began laughing. 'Honestly, I do love you.'

'What's funny?'

'Never mind, eat your lunch. I wonder who it is? I bet Kate does know.'

Kate was spending the day with Scott and loving it. She hadn't much longer left at the practice and she was wishing she could stay on for ever.

'Well, who is it?' Scott asked as he stamped on the brakes to avoid a stray dog.

'Who's what?'

'Don't pull my leg, I know you know. I can tell.'

Kate said, 'My lips are sealed. Sorry and all that, but she confided in me because she'd no one else to confide in and I was privileged . . . yes . . . privileged to hear what has happened to her these last few years. It explains a lot, and I'm not prepared to tell any one. If you want to know, ask Ginny.'

Scott took a moment to glance at Kate. 'Ginny, is it now? Well, well.'

'You're just as bad as everyone else. Gossips, that's what you all are, gossips. Who says it's a man anyway?'

'No one, but we all think it is. Zoe's convinced it's someone like Gab Bridges. We fell about laughing at that. Him of all people!'

'You're both heartless, you two. As if . . .' But Kate couldn't help smiling at how close Zoe had unwittingly been.

But Scott wasn't laughing today. He and Zoe had the most tremendous row afterwards about their ongoing difficulty with conception. He still hadn't told her that he had an appointment at the fertility clinic and held out through the whole argument, never letting on. He knew that if he told her, and he knew she knew he was there, he'd never be able to 'perform'.

Zoe, distraught because, during the next few days she'd know whether or not they'd succeeded this month, let fly with the wildest display of temper he'd ever seen. She'd just reached the throwing things stage when she collapsed in tears, heartbroken. Scott knew then he should have told her but still he held back. It was the idea of the shame if it were he at fault. The utter, utter shame. If you weren't firing on all cylinders, what kind of a man were you, eh? A nothing. If that was what he was, would she still love him with that stormy, tempestuous passion she always displayed to him? He didn't know. He honestly didn't know. He swung the car into Applegate Farm and felt a deep and abiding ache for Zoe at that very moment, this instant, right now, his arms encircling her, loving her, relishing the sweetness of her, sensing the passion rising in her. He vowed to tell her about the appointment that night as soon as he got home, definitely, tonight, because he couldn't keep his secret any longer. If he . . .

Then Kate brushed against his shoulder as she knelt up and twisted round to the back for her boots, and he didn't know quite how it happened but in a trice she was in his arms and they were kissing.

Kate struggled against him at first, and then responded with a freshness and an alacrity which clearly demonstrated the love she'd been keeping under wraps that long hot summer. But it was Kate who struggled free, Kate who forced him away, Kate who got out and opened the back door to reach her boots, Kate who marched off across the yard and Scott who sat appalled at what he'd done. If she hadn't taken the initiative and got out of the Land Rover, heaven alone knew what might have happened, and in daylight, too. Scott was horrified at himself.

As Kate crossed the yard, hysteria began to rise in her and, try as she might, she couldn't make herself feel normal. How stupid she was. She must have gone mad, but how she'd longed for a glorious conclusion. Worst of all, he'd called out, *'Zo! Zo!'* and hadn't realized it. *Twice, he said it.* That was when she fought to escape his embrace. She now knew for certain that he loved Zoe first and foremost, and that no one else had a chance.

Scott followed her across the yard and was beside her when she was shouting for the third time, 'Phil! Blossom! It's Scott and Kate here!' at the open farmhouse door. Kate daren't look at him. Her heart was still beating fast and her face was flushed, but that she could blame on the heat of the day.

There was no reply. Scott spoke for the first time. 'What's happening here? Where the blazes are they?'

Then they became aware of a heavy, lumbering, thudding noise approaching and Star, Phil's bull, careered into the yard, out of breath, steam rising from his body, his temper out of control. Scott and Kate had to leap to one side to avoid being run down. He filled the whole of the yard with his stamping feet, his snorting, his pawing at the cobbles, his furious circling about. In close pursuit, Phil appeared, panting heavily. Racing round the corner into the yard he staggered into the open door of Star's stall, apparently so fearful of what might happen next he screamed, 'It's Hercules! Watch out!'

The genuine fear in his voice prompted both Scott and Kate to leap into the cowshed doorway. Apparently this was no joke. Scott only had time to ask, 'Who's Hercules?' when Hercules roared into the farm yard. Scott paled at the sight of him and pushed Kate behind him.

They thought Star was big now he was fully grown, but they'd seen nothing. This massive, majestic Hercules was surely the biggest bull any of them had come across. Jet-black with a white crescent on his huge forehead, he heaved himself towards Star and they rammed their heads together time and again, the sound bouncing off the buildings surrounding the yard.

Kate was petrified. She shook from head to toe as the two bulls played their power game. They backed off and Hercules thrashed himself about the yard, endeavouring to lay hold on Star again, but Star knew a trick worth two of that and took the decision to head for the security of his stall. Phil, being in his way, hastily stepped out on to the cobbles and Star hurtled in, seemingly admitting he was terrified of this mountain of a bull. With the door shut and bolted on Star, and his prey apparently having vanished, Hercules began trashing the door to Star's stall.

Time and again he backed off and then attacked it with his huge head down, thundering towards it, crashing into it with all his might.

Kate whispered to Scott, 'You've got some sedative in your bag, can't you stick it in him?'

The heavy door began to shudder under Hercules' frantic onslaught, and Kate said, 'Be quick. If he gets in there . . .'

Just then Blossom appeared in the house doorway, streaming water and wrapped in a towel. When she saw Hercules she gave one long scream and passed out on the doorstep.

Phil, his face white with terror and his back to Star's byre wall, stood spreadeagled and moaning.

Kate prodded Scott and muttered fiercely, 'Do something!'

Phil's sheepdog, Tyson, came scurrying in from the fields, his long tongue hanging out, his barks hoarse, and his anger at Hercules knowing no bounds. Some ancient memory made him try rounding Hercules up by nipping at his ankles as though he were a sheep, which infuriated Hercules and made him threaten to toss his attacker, but Tyson was too nimble for a lumbering great bull.

'Some good that bloody dog is,' shouted Phil. 'Come!' he bellowed, but Tyson wouldn't listen.

Quietly, Scott slid forward out of the cowshed door, armed with a syringe charged with sedative. He'd made a hasty calculation how much he would need to slow Hercules right down without killing him, but it wasn't an easy thing to do with that massive great beast running free and his own heart booming with panic. All he could hope was he'd got it right, and that he'd avoid injecting himself in the possible furore.

Tyson, conveniently, kept Hercules' attention while Scott made his way across the yard with his back against the stone walls. He stepped carefully over Blossom, who was still unconscious, noticed Hercules eyeing him up, prayed to be ignored, watched him deciding whether or not Scott was a prime target, then, feeling he was leaping into the jaws of death, Scott paused while Hercules turned towards him, before he leapt forward and plunged the syringe into him releasing the whole of its contents.

A strange silence fell. Tyson, Kate, Scott, Phil and, naturally, Blossom didn't make a sound. Hercules felt the effects of the sedative almost immediately and, for one terrible moment, Scott wondered if he'd miscalculated. His brain saw headlines in the paper: 'VET MASSACRES PRIZE BULL'.

Kate broke the silence. 'Well done.'

Phil, still ashen-faced, shouted, 'He's come across three fields, broken down the fences. There's cows all over the place. What a mess.'

Scott croaked, 'Whose is he?'

'Benny and Laura Taylor's new bull. They put him out; he must have spotted Star out with my cows and set off after him. I've never run as fast in my life. Them fences are a waste of time.'

They heard a vehicle approaching across the fields and in moments Laura and Benny were in the yard.

Scott shouted, 'Watch out. I've sedated him and he's not quite under properly. Be careful.'

Benny, looking appalled, addressed Scott and the others as though they were his board of directors in the City. 'I regret to say that I do not appreciate you sedating my bull without first informing me of your intention.'

Scott stood open-mouthed.

Benny continued. 'I'm sorry but I'm afraid I'm prosecuting you, Scott, for treating my bull without . . . I say, is he going to be all right? He's almighty quiet.'

Scott pulled himself together. 'I had no alternative, it had to be done. He was a serious threat and rampaging about. We've partly solved the situation by getting Star into his stall. If it wasn't for Phil doing that there would have been untold savagery. I wasn't prepared to allow him to continue putting people's lives at risk.'

Phil wasn't quite so polite. He went up to Benny, squared up to him and, standing only about a foot away and in measured tones, told him a thing or two about his failings as a farmer. 'You come here with your blankety-blank money and your book-learning and think you know it all. You don't know what makes 'em tick in here.' Phil prodded his temple with his finger. 'You put him out far too soon before he'd got his bearings, you put him out in a field with fences which didn't have a hope in hell of keeping him confined. He saw what appeared to him to be a strange bull in the middle of what he imagined was *his* harem and he wasn't going to stand for that. All that testeroni pumping him up, no wonder he went crackers. I'm going now to sort out my cows and assess the damage. My solicitor will be in contact as soon as maybe.'

He stepped back waiting for a reply from Benny, who though he stood at least a head taller than Phil, was being made to look ridiculous and therefore was not best pleased. After all, he had more brains than all the farmers around here put together, that was why he was making such a success of his farm.

'My fences are well made—'

Phil sneered, 'For a rabbit run.'

'I beg your pardon, they're all new—'

Phil stormed off, shouting over his shoulder, 'When I get back I want that damned bull under lock and key on your farm, not mine, *yours*. Right?' Tyson began following him. 'Tyson! In the house! Don't want a daft ponce of a dog like you helping to sort out the mess.' Horrified by the tone of Phil's voice, his tail between his legs, Tyson swiftly leapt over the still prone Blossom and disappeared into the house as he'd been told.

Laura said quietly, 'Admit it, Benny, you've made a ghastly mistake. Scott, what shall we do?'

'Hope to hell we can lead Hercules back to his stall. I'll get two lengths of rope that Phil uses for Star, and they'll go through his nose ring. Between us we'll lead him home before he comes to properly. And one word from you, Benny, about how angry you are about this incident and, client or no client, I shall more than likely punch you senseless because I risked my *life* to give him that sedative. Understand?'

Benny said humbly, 'Right. Yes. OK, then. I'll get the fences strengthened this week and I shan't put him out till they're done. I'd no idea he'd be so . . . powerful. God, what an animal!'

'Phil has years of experience with his own bull, years of it, he knows his every mood. That's what you've to learn *before* you take even the smallest risk with yours.'

Scott knotted the two lengths of rope onto Hercules' nose-ring, handed the end of one to Benny, and the two of them began the long process of persuading Benny's bull to go home.

Kate went to attend to Blossom. She was on the verge of coming to and a glass of water helped. She sat up with her bottom on the kitchen floor and her feet out on the doorstep.

'Oh, my God! Am I decent?' she said, pulling at the towel now rather haphazardly wrapped about her person. 'Where's Star? Is he all right?'

'He's fine. He had the sense to get in his stall and Phil slammed the door on him. Hercules, fingers crossed, is on his way home. We've all had a narrow escape.'

'That's the trouble with these newcomers, they read a book and think they know everything, and they don't. Though I love Benny, he's an absolute darling. So's Laura, but she's got more common sense than Benny; he's too concerned with his image. Better get up. I've never fainted in my life, but it was such a shock seeing that Hercules there, the great brute. I heard all the hullabaloo when I was in the shower and came down to see. It was such a shock. It's dangerous him having a bull like that. Our Star is a pussycat compared.' Blossom hauled herself up and prepared to disappear inside.

'Believe me, I felt like joining you.'

'There's one thing about you, Kate, you don't get far but you do see life.'

Kate agreed but now she was thinking more about her narrow escape with Scott than the threat Hercules posed. If she hadn't been so bewilderingly disappointed about Scott calling her 'Zo' they could have gone far, too far, and where would that have left her? She still hadn't looked Scott in the eye and didn't know if she ever would be able to again. All she'd done was brush against him as she twisted round for her boots and it had been like putting a flaming torch to a petrol tanker. She allowed herself one single moment of reminiscing about her exquisite enjoyment of his arms wrapped tightly round her and the pounding of his heart so close to hers, then compelled herself to dismiss it. After all, she wasn't prepared to have an affair with Scott. Too many people would be hurt, none more so than herself.

Kate went to sit on the old mounting block to wait for Scott. She thought about phoning him to tell him not to come back over the fields, that she'd go round to Benny's in the Land Rover and pick him up, but decided the ringing of the phone might easily upset Hercules. To get out of the heat, she went to sit in the passenger seat with the door wide open. She took a long drink of mineral water from her bottle and contemplated life.

Kate was so deep in thought that she was unaware that Scott was back from Benny's and already crossing the farm yard to the Land Rover still parked in the lane. She looked up at the sound of his footsteps on the hard ground – dry after so many weeks without rain – and saw someone quite different from an hour and a half ago when they'd first parked up. Here was a man soaked with sweat, his face lined where once there were no lines, a man bowed with exhaustion, all his natural vibrancy gone. He went to the back, opened it up, took off his boots, slung them carelessly in, put his sandals on and came round to the driver's door and climbed in.

Staring through the windscreen, Scott said, 'I'm getting too old for this lark.'

'You're not. You did brilliantly, with a bit of prodding from me.' Kate grinned at him to show she wasn't being serious, but even his profile showed his extreme fatigue and she got no reciprocal smile. 'How's Hercules?'

'Docile as a lamb, for now.'

'And Benny?'

'Off his high horse and humbled. He's a damn fool for buying that bull, but there you are.' He switched on the ignition, then turned it off again and found his bottle of mineral water and took a long swig. A lot of it swilled down his chin and on to his shirt but it felt welcome. 'Hell, Kate, when's the weather going to change? Sorry about being so sweaty. I'll have to go home to shower and change.'

'Home' reminded him of Zoe and then how close he'd come

. . . He paused to stare through his side window then remarked hesitantly, 'I can't . . . can you forgive . . . I'm trying to apologize about earlier. It should never have happened. And it won't happen again. I'm deeply sorry. I just hope you can forgive me.'

Kate didn't even look at him, just said quite calmly, 'I blame the weather. When it rains, I shall be so grateful I shall stand outside in it, stark naked.' and meant it.

'Exactly. We'll put it down to that. Thanks.'

'But we've forgotten about Pearl and the other goats. We were supposed to be putting them to sleep.'

'Blast it, so we were. It'll keep till tomorrow. The Parsons have had enough trauma for one day.'

They spent the rest of the day as a team, without the explosive undercurrents Kate had always been aware of when they were together. First they called in at Scott's home for him to shower and change his clothes, and she sat with Zoe while she waited and they had a long companionable chat in the shade of their beech tree. When Scott reappeared looking refreshed Kate watched Zoe's face; it lit up with such joy it was almost embarrassing to witness. He leaned down to kiss her *au revoir*, his hand gently caressing her shoulder, and as he did so, Kate found her passion had been extinguished all because of that one intimate word: 'Zo'.

Chapter 17

In the staffroom the following lunch-time they were full of Scott's experience with Hercules and Star, and weighed up the pros and cons of Benny being in charge of a prize bull of that size.

Colin said he'd met Benny at a local veterinary meeting and liked the chap very much indeed. Got his head well screwed on, he thought, and couldn't see why Scott thought Benny was mad to have a bull in the first place and even madder to buy a prize bull of such a size.

Scott said, most emphatically, 'I'll tell you why – it's a vast brute and very unpredictable into the bargain. Anyone gets called to him, just watch out. If it's me I shall go sick and not turn out.'

They all looked at him, and saw he was not himself at all.

Dan said, 'That's not like you, Scott. What's the matter? Not feeling well?'

'No. It's not that, just a bit under the weather. You know how it is.'

Not for anything would he admit the real reason; that this afternoon he was off to the fertility clinic and he wasn't looking forward to it. He never did tell Zoe, couldn't bring himself to do so, especially after the shock he had when he kissed Kate with such enthusiasm. God! That was so embarrassing, and somewhere he had a vague recollection that he'd called her 'Zo'. He wasn't quite sure, and obviously couldn't ask Kate, but he wondered if that was why the spark between the two of them had gone out that day. It was a good thing it had. He was no good for a girl her age. What was he? Ten years older than her? Oh, God, surely not. But he guessed he was right; yes, that was it, at least ten years older. He'd looked in the mirror when he'd popped home for a shower and a change of clothes after the bull incident and seen the exhaustion and the lines on his face he'd never noticed and had felt his age like never before. The Barleybridge Romeo had perhaps had his day.

Ginny, as she now preferred to be called, said she agreed with him. 'Benny is an over-confident idiot. His animals are numbers on a spreadsheet and not close to his heart, like Phil Parsons. I admire him, Phil that is.' Very casually, though it was extremely difficult, she said, 'Oh, by the way, you'd better be the first to know: I'm buying the Miss Pattersons' farm – you know, Bridge End. Take a few weeks for it to go through but then I will be joint owner with . . . well, with . . .' She cleared her throat and tried again, 'With Gabriel Bridges.'

If she'd said she'd been chosen as team leader on the next manned space flight they couldn't have been more stunned. First there was complete silence and then an outbreak of astonishment. Buying the farm didn't appear to be outrageous, but buying it with Gab?

'Gab?' asked Joy, thinking Ginny must have taken leave of her senses.

'*Gab Bridges!*'

'Gabriel Bridges, as in Gab Bridges the most popular sex symbol in Barleybridge?'

'I don't believe it. I didn't know you knew him.'

Ginny nodded vigorously. 'Just let anyone try to persuade me differently. I am. With Gab. The two of us are together and we shall be getting married eventually. Well, fairly soon. Love at first sight, across a crowded room, except it was across a farm yard and Gab had two dead guinea pigs in his hand.' She gave them all a beaming smile.

'Well, I never.' Scott slapped his mug down on the table and looked straight at Kate. 'Did you know about this?'

Kate nodded.

'Didn't you try to dissuade her?'

'No. I think the words I used were: "If he floats your boat, then so be it." That right, Ginny?'

Ginny nodded.

'Might I point out,' said Joy selecting her words very carefully, 'that you haven't known him very long. How long? Is it a matter of weeks, or days? Is it wise? You do know his reputation?'

'Yes. And I'm a grown woman and have every intention of marrying him. I came to the conclusion the other night, I simply can't live without him. We're going to put the house and the buildings in good order and farm it well.'

Colin asked, 'What about your job here? Will you still be a vet?'

'Nothing on earth will stop me being a vet. Working here has reignited my enjoyment of the job and so long as Mungo wants me to work here I will.'

Joy appeared to want to put stumbling blocks in her way. 'But what about the two sisters. Where will they live?'

'We've found them a new-build ground-floor flat in Terminus Road and they can't wait to move in. You know that new block they've just finished building halfway down the road on the other side from my flat? It's absolutely right for them. They can reach the shops, the doctor's and the station in no time down a public footpath that runs along the back of the block. They'll have the money to buy it when our purchase goes through.'

Joy nodded. 'Ah. And what does Gab think to your grand design?'

Ginny smiled a lovely, sweet, thoughtful smile like they'd never seen on her face before, and they recognized what a huge change there was in her. 'It's not *my* design, it's mine and Gab's. He's thrilled to bits, and as for his mother . . . well, she's delighted. She's a very soft spot for Gab since his suicide attempt – yes, I know all about that, too; he's told me everything, and I've told him everything about me too – and his mother, well, she just wishes I had some sisters that she could marry the rest of her sons off to.'

'In that case, congratulations are in order.' Joy got to her feet and reached up to kiss Ginny, and got hugged for her thoughtfulness, as did anyone who showed their pleasure at her surprising news. It had taken a lot for Ginny to tell them, mainly because she thought they would all think she was mad, which she probably was, but it was the nicest kind of madness she'd ever experienced and it was staying that way.

As she walked out to her car she thought about Gab and his deep hurt over Megan, which, to her, signalled a loving heart; to try to kill himself over her he must have been desolate. She'd like to meet Megan to see what sort of a person she was. As she approached her car she gave a little skip of joy, which was witnessed by Miriam alone, who was looking out of the flat windows and contemplating taking Perkins up Beulah Bank Top. It was so unlike Ginny that she smiled and wondered what had brought that about. But Miriam liked the joy in it, yes, she approved of that.

When Mungo went up to the flat at the end of his working day and she found out the reason for Ginny's delight, Miriam couldn't believe it. 'Gab Bridges? *Gab Bridges.* You must have misheard, surely?'

'No, it's absolutely true, Joy told me.'

'Well, I never, so that's what that little skip was about this afternoon. Isn't that lovely. I'm so pleased. What a risk she's taking, though, what a challenge.'

'I don't know what the hell he sees in her, but at least it's made her more normal. I couldn't take much more of her as she was.'

'Mungo!'

He grinned at her over the top of his newspaper. 'Love you, Miriam. Always will.' Then he returned to his newspaper, amused by the apparent taming of Gabriel Bridges, who had the choice of every unmarried and married woman in Barleybridge, by Ginny Havelock, of all people. Maybe it was her money he fancied and the thought of a farm all his own, or was he being uncharitable? Maybe he was.

The news bubbled round the practice for the rest of the day; the clients in particular were dazzled by the whole idea. There weren't many of them who hadn't at some time brushed with Gab, either going out with him themselves or knowing someone else who'd experienced the delights of his attention.

'Well, that'll give all the other men a chance; they couldn't win against Gab on the loose.'

'Ah! But who says he'll never play away again?'

'You've got a point,' said one client who remembered her days with Gab and the sheer thrill of being seen out with him. She slapped her three-year-old for poking his finger in someone's gerbil cage and getting a nip for his pains, lifted the baby out of his pushchair to stop him crying and was filled with nostalgia for those halcyon days. It seemed to her like the end of an era.

That afternoon Scott honestly felt that he too was at the end of an era. One session at the fertility clinic had finally brought it home to him that he was no longer the catch of the year, a state of affairs he'd subscribed to all his adult life – come to think of it, all his teens too. Now, somehow, he'd been humiliated by having to talk about the most intimate of matters with a person he'd never met before and hoped he would never see again. After it was all over he dallied in the nearest pub for over an hour, desperately trying to piece his life back together again and didn't succeed very well.

By the time he got home to Zoe his spirits were at a very low ebb.

'Scott? Why, what's the matter? You look dreadful, are you ill?'

'No. Tired, that's all. It's the heat, you know.'

'Sit down before you fall down. A glass of lager?'

'Yes, please.'

He slumped down on a kitchen chair. He watched Zoe go to the fridge, get a bottle out, open the top, find a glass, pour out the lager and place it in front of him on the kitchen table. She did it with such zest and enthusiasm he envied her *joie de vivre*. He positively envied it, because he'd none at all at the moment. 'You're not having one?'

'No.'

'Oh!' Scott downed half the glass in one long, lifesaving gasp. 'That was good. I needed that.'

'Scott?'

'Mmm.'

'I'm four days late.'

He looked up at her, puzzled. 'For what?'

'You know . . .'

He saw the most amazing expression on her face; it positively glowed with joy.

'I know it's early days, but I'm never, ever late. I nearly told you this morning but I thought no, better wait.'

'You mean . . . ?'

'Yes.'

Scott began to laugh. He laughed so much she thought he'd gone mad. His laughter roared round the kitchen, and sweat glistened on his face. Then he leapt to his feet and, flinging up his arms, he shouted, 'Hallelujah!' Then he grabbed hold of her and hugged her so tightly she couldn't breathe.

'Scott! Darling! Please.'

'Just say it in plain words. Go on, actually *say* it.'

'I-think-I am-pregnant. There. I've said it.'

Scott laughed again. 'You've no idea. Oh, help.' He sat down again, drank down the rest of his lager, patted his knee and invited Zoe to sit on it.

With his arms comfortably linked around her waist he kissed her and said, 'It's wonderful. Just wonderful. I'm so thrilled. My dad will be thrilled, too, he's been longing for some more Spencer grandchildren to arrive.' He paused to give her a big grin. 'I think I'll give them a ring first thing and say don't bother with the tests, everything is in full working order.' He grinned again.

'What are you talking about? What tests?'

He winked at her, but she still didn't tipple to his secret. 'Well, I went for an appointment at the fertility clinic this afternoon and—'

'Scott! You didn't. I *love* you for that, I love you so much for that you've no idea. I'm so proud of you. Why didn't you say?'

'I knew if you knew I was there I'd never manage it, so I didn't tell you. I didn't want to take the risk that I couldn't perform and have to brace myself all over again for another appointment. And I shan't be going there ever again.'

'Honestly, and you never said. Love you. I know it's early but it does look promising, doesn't it? There was I, having given up all hope, thinking I'd offer to do some part-time work at the practice to keep my hand in.'

'We won't tell a soul, not a soul, until much later, right? And you've to take care of yourself, every minute of every day. We shan't tell Oscar yet, either; it's too long for him to have to wait. Where is he, by the way?'

'I'm just going to collect him from his trampoline class.'

'We'll both go. No, I'll go and you rest till I get back.'

'Don't be ridiculous, I'm coming.'

'All right, then, but I'm driving.'

Zoe followed him out of the house, smiling to herself at his spectacular reaction and almost more so because he'd gone to the clinic for her sake when he loathed the whole idea; she felt so intensely happy.

Scott, trying hard to concentrate on his driving when he was so utterly delighted with himself, said out of the blue, 'That'll be it.'

'What will?'

'You giving up hoping. You've relaxed and it's worked. That's it, I'm sure I'm right.'

Zoe patted his knee and left her hand there, squeezing his leg every now and again to remind him how happy she was.

Chapter 18

Next day Joy found herself reading an email addressed to her from Eleanor Eustace. The email read:

Joy, Hi!

I talked to Miriam a few days ago. She pulled me up short and gave me a lot to think about. As a result of our indepth discussion I have positively decided to sell up and go back to London to get back into the thick of things in the publishing world. The gift of my aunt's money, kindly and generously meant, has given me far too much time with nothing to do in it, and I've decided it isn't me at all.

I am intending to rent a flat in London until I sell this one here in Barleybridge, which will be entirely unsuitable for an energetic kitten like Choo. In any case, if I get a job it would mean her being left on her own all day, which is not a good idea. I adore her, but for her sake I need someone to take her on who can do what is right for her. I do not require payment for her. Can you help me with this?

Sorry about such short notice, but out of the kindness of your heart I hope you can find her a lovely home.

I have behaved like an idiot to Val and to Nina, but have now dug myself out of the pit and am behaving more like a real human being should.

Use my email to send me news of Choo.

Many thanks.

Eleanor

Joy sat back in her chair and read the email through again. Miriam! How did she do it. From the remnants of Eleanor's life she'd pulled her together and completely changed her outlook. Hang the money, it might be lovely to have but it had almost destroyed Eleanor. Briefly Joy gave a thought to Valentine and wondered if he'd had an email, too, but she didn't care whether or not he had. Eleanor was leaving, that was the important bit, thus giving Valentine and Nina a chance. Joy printed out the email and hurtled upstairs to find Miriam.

'Look! Just found this in my inbox. Read it.'

Miriam gravely read it through, re-checked the part where Eleanor said she was going to London, and then handed it back to Joy.

'That's excellent. I didn't do anything, I only pointed out her present situation to her. Her days were too empty, that was the core of the problem, so she had to invent things to do and men seemed like a good idea.'

'I say good riddance. She was a bad apple, a really, really bad apple. I'm glad she's going. What she did to that kitten . . .' Joy's eyes filled with tears. 'It doesn't bear thinking about.'

Miriam sensed the depth of Joy's sympathy and, raising her eyebrows in surprise, she asked, 'You're not thinking of taking her on, are you?'

Joy sprang off the kitchen chair. 'Certainly not. No, we've enough with Tiger and Copper.' Joy wagged a finger at Miriam. 'And don't mention Choo to Duncan, please, or he'll do his lame dog act and I shall not want to disappoint him and then we'll have three, and three's a crowd.'

What Joy had not bargained for was Eleanor appearing that same afternoon carrying Choo's bed, grooming tools, tins of meat and dishes, as well as her toys. She'd spent lavishly on her kitten and was positively staggering under the load.

Joy was called out from her back office and Eleanor's first words were: 'Please, these are for Choo. No point in me keeping them, so I've brought them for whoever it is who takes her on. Where shall I put them, Joy?'

'Bring them in the back. I got your email but I haven't had time to do anything about it yet.'

As she packed them into a huge empty cardboard box in Joy's office, Eleanor said softly, 'I'd love to see Val? May I, do you think?'

When she straightened up Joy looked seriously into her eyes. There was a difference in them. The bold, confrontational, 'come hither' gaze had been replaced by a calmer, more frank look. Joy smiled at her and Eleanor smiled back. 'I've caused trouble and now I've come to my senses after listening to Miriam. I want to apologize. I imagined I should have all my own way about everything and of course one can't. I've an interview on Thursday with a publisher and it seems I'm in the right place at the right time with the right skills, so I'm very hopeful.' She stopped speaking and looked directly at Joy. 'Is Nina in today?'

'As it happens, she's on her day off, Val is in. But there's to be no theatricals, OK?'

Eleanor nodded. 'No theatricals. Promise.'

Joy noticed Eleanor's hands were trembling slightly. When Eleanor saw Joy had noticed she smiled ruefully and hid them behind her back. 'I still think he's wonderful, but I know it's no good. He's devoted to Nina.'

Joy would hardly have described Val's intermittent faithfulness to Nina as 'devoted' but she didn't comment. 'I'll find him for you. He's just finishing an emergency Caesarean on a cat. Sit down while I get him.'

Valentine came in smelling of the operating theatre, all cleansed and fantastically heroic, Eleanor thought.

Before he could speak she said, 'Successful?'

'Indeed. Three live kittens and a happy mother.'

'What more could you ask? What else would I expect of someone as clever as you?'

Eleanor heard the anger in him when he replied, with a sound like crushed ice in his voice, 'I don't need that kind of flattery.'

'Sorry for all the trouble I've caused. Sorry for hurting Nina. Now I've come round to common sense and a purpose in my life I know I must have hurt her and that's not fair. I admire your devotion to her. After what she's been through she deserves you and I'm glad, yes, I'm glad I spoke to Miriam and took on board what she said. I'm going back to London to work. Will you tell Nina I'm sorry? Tell her for me, please.'

'Maybe. But I cannot forgive what you did to Choo. You gave her something to make her sick, didn't you?'

Eleanor nodded. 'Yes.'

'And the cut, too? That was you?'

'Yes. It was my desperation to see you that made me do it. A legitimate excuse, you see. You are the most stunning man I have ever met and I want you like crazy.' When that frank remark brought no response Eleanor changed tack. 'I've decided I shall never have another pet again. That's not the real me to do a thing like that. I must have been—'

'Unbalanced? Or mad?'

Eleanor recoiled at the venom in his voice, and some of her colour drained from her face, but he didn't appear to notice.

'I devote *all* my working hours, all my study, to the relief of pain in one way or another, and I am outraged by what you did to Choo. It was so cruel and . . .' he paused while he found the right word and when he did he spat it out, '*despicable*.' He leaned against Joy's desk, arms folded, staring at her.

She placed a gentle hand on his bare forearm, intending to give him the final kiss for which she longed, but he shrugged her hand off.

'I can't believe I was captivated by you. Can't believe you made me hurt Nina so terribly. It was all so . . . unwholesome.'

She saw the disgust in his face and hated him for it. 'Well, there you are, then. I was going to give you my London address, so if you came up sometime we could . . . meet, perhaps . . .'

Valentine shook his head vehemently.

Eleanor saw red. 'It wasn't only me, you know. You leapt *willingly* into bed with me. You weren't forced.'

'To my shame, that is true. I must have been intoxicated by your *desperation* to get me in to bed, but not any more.' He looked straight into her eyes and for a brief moment she thought she caught a glimmer of interest in them. *He doesn't mean it, he doesn't mean it!* But it must have been a trick of the light, for then he said, 'They're just preparing a dog for me for another emergency operation, so I'll say goodbye and good luck.'

She hadn't expected this. In her mind she'd imagined tears, regrets and disappointment and, maybe, even sorrow, but not this hatred. Not this feeling of him being revolted by her. It reduced her to nothing. Rallying her resources, she said hopefully, 'One last kiss,' looking up at him, pleading with him, longing for him, but it wasn't to be. He stood away from the desk, reached out to open the door for her and turned his back. Eleanor paused for a moment, trying to come up with some hugely cruelly damaging remark to hurt him, where it would hurt a man like him the very most, but it wouldn't come.

Eleanor left Joy's office, feeling like dirt beneath his shoes. But in the reception area she automatically turned on the charm as only she could, smiled, waved to Joy and left; a survivor if ever there was one.

Valentine immersed himself in operating on the Norfolk terrier that had just been brought in after being involved in a car accident. The X-rays showed a broken leg and he began working on it with Bunty's assistance, losing himself in his work. By the time the broken leg had been repaired and he'd handed the dog over to Bunty for safe keeping, Valentine knew that his whole life needed a massive re-think. He went home to do just that.

He was disappointed to find Nina was out. She'd left a note to say she'd gone to Bournemouth shopping and would be back by six. She'd signed it 'Love, Nina', followed by four kisses.

For several minutes Valentine studied her message and felt humbled by it. This kind of love he didn't deserve. It ran sparklingly bright, in vivid colours, all the colours of the rainbow, brilliant and glowing. By comparison, Eleanor's love was greedy, dark and obsessive, deeply hidden in the very depths of her soul, not flying free like Nina's. Why had he not perceived that at the beginning? Or that night she'd found a temporary new lover and flaunted him in the White Hart, why had he not seen then what she was truly like? The things she did demonstrated her shallowness, her selfishness, her twisted soul. Worst of all was what Eleanor did to her kitten, just to keep his attention. Nina had first-hand experience of the very depths of evil, but it hadn't touched her spirit; that was still beautiful.

He heard Nina parking her car and rushed for the stairs and a shower to clean off any trace of Eleanor. As he undressed he shouted down to Nina, 'Having a shower, won't be long. Had a good shop?'

'Indeed I have. Wait and see!'

Well scrubbed, shaved and shining, Valentine came down the stairs to find Nina in the sitting room, laying out a display of clothes she'd bought for him. Occasionally she did this when she felt he was neglecting himself but this time somehow the things she'd bought were extra-special in his eyes. 'I prepare for winter! See!'

'But it's boiling hot!'

'But the right time to get the best choices for cold weather.' He carefully studied the things she'd bought. 'Here's a cashmere V-necked sweater with a matching blue shirt and a spectacular tie. At last something to wear with those light-grey trousers you never wear.' Next chocolate-brown trousers, with a mustard, polo-necked sweater and chocolate-brown suede waistcoat. 'From that man's shop you like.' She stood back smiling delightedly at him and he saw for himself, shining in her face, that splendid love she had for him. How could any man in his right mind spurn love like that? It had a value above . . . At a loss for words, he compared it, rather lamely, to rubies.

'They're great. If I'd been with you they're exactly what I would have chosen for myself. Have you bought anything for yourself?'

Offhandedly, she waved a vague hand at a collection of carriers in the armchair. 'They're mine. I open later.'

Valentine was so eager to tell her how he felt that he hadn't time to wait for the right moment. 'Nina, I need to talk. Seriously.'

The light went out of Nina's face.

Valentine ran a forefinger along her cheek and smiled. 'Not serious. Well, it is, but it's positive. Sit down, here, look, on the sofa.' He sat beside her. 'This afternoon Eleanor came to see me.'

This was what Nina had been dreading, him saying he was leaving her and going to live with . . . that woman. She was determined not to let him think his news devastated her, but she couldn't control the shudder that went from her shoulders right down to her feet, because she knew she couldn't live without him and that there was only one answer for her, and that was killing herself.

'She's leaving for London and never coming back.'

He got no response from Nina, at least, not what he'd expected. He thought she'd hug him, kiss him, perhaps. But no, she sat quite still; silent and withdrawn.

'I've told her I am ashamed of what we did. Absolutely ashamed. To be honest, I wish I'd never met her. I know now what a terrible influence she had on me.' Valentine gave her a gentle shake. 'Do you understand what I'm saying? I've finished with her for good. I'm free of her.' He smiled into her face, imagining his apologies were complete and confident she understood what he was struggling to convey. He put his hand under her chin and turned her face towards him, bending his head, intending to kiss her – very, very gently so as not to alarm her – but she pushed his hand away and got to her feet, then looked down at him with disdain in her eyes. 'I dare not count number of times I hear this story, not same, but almost. Time and again, Val. Until next time.'

'But it's true. Really true this time. I hate myself, absolutely hate myself for what I've done to you. For what she's done to

225

you. For how dirty she has made me feel. It's over with for ever. I'm yours, don't you see?'

'You think I run straight to your arms and be good wife? Immediately? After this last weeks and past?'

Nina's ability to speak English crumbled in the wave of distress his words had brought about. She was devastated. Although he sounded more genuine than ever before, she couldn't, wouldn't believe him after so many broken promises. Now at this moment she felt there'd been a tremendous change in her and for the first time ever she wanted to have him make love to her like he should, but that step forward was the very one she could not take, because if he broke his promise after that, the pain of his unfaithfulness would be too terrible to bear.

She walked out and left him standing there totally confused. Her footsteps resounded in his heart and the locking of their bedroom door felt like a death knell. He felt further away from a complete marriage with her than he'd ever been.

An hour and a half later he called upstairs to tell her that their evening meal was almost ready. 'It's steak, just how you like it.'

But Nina never came downstairs, and Valentine slept in his computer room on the put-up feeling abandoned and mortally afraid that she'd finally lost all faith in him.

First thing the next morning Nina asked to speak privately to Joy, immediately. She looked as though she hadn't slept all night, was haggard with great dark shadows under her eyes.

Joy's heart sank. Oh, no. Surely Val wasn't going with Eleanor to London? Surely not. What this dear girl would do if he did she couldn't even begin to imagine.

'Yes, of course. Go and wait for me in my office. I'll just get everything started, and Annette can hold the fort at the desk. Go on! I shan't be long.'

Nina opened the windows in Joy's office and stood staring out at the clients arriving for the morning surgery. After a night like she had experienced, their problems appeared trivial. But how she loved them all! Every single one. Valentine was off today. Strange how they never had bothered to get their days off synchronized; perhaps there was something significant in that.

The door opened and in bustled Joy. 'Sit down, Nina, you'll be on your feet long enough today. Now, my dear, what's the problem?'

'For a while, or perhaps for ever, I'm leaving Valentine. He doesn't know yet, I'll tell him when I get home.'

She'd said it so casually that Joy, for a moment, didn't get to grips with what she meant. '*You're* leaving *him*? Valentine?'

'I worship him, he is my *raison d'être*, but I can't—'

'But Eleanor's gone to London, she's right out of your way . . . isn't she?'

Nina nodded. 'So I understand. I'm going home to Vukavar. A pilgrimage, in a way. To see people I know, lay flowers on my parents' grave and those who died that same day, visit the university I attended, catch up with old friends, see how they have survived, and perhaps finally put all of that behind me. Then I move on.'

'Yes, but what then? What about Valentine?'

'I don't know.' Nina looked grim, but it was possible to see a strand of steely determination in her. 'Now I make the decisions, not Valentine. He will have to wait until *I* decide what *I* want to do. These five years I have been here, my life been ruled by his love affairs. I go, I weep, I despair, I return. All that is finished. I am taking charge of my life.'

Fearful for the sweet running of the practice, Joy asked tentatively, 'When will all this happen, exactly?'

'Only when you find my replacement. But I met receptionist from the High Street practice in the Red Umbrella Café in the High Street two days ago, and we talked. She only has one more week of notice because she is bored, so little work to do, and she's looking for a job. She's rather jolly, you'll like her. Her name is Dorothy Pilgrim but she calls herself Dodie because she hates Dorothy.' Out of her uniform pocket she pulled a piece of paper. 'Here is her home number. I hope you're not angry with me.'

'Angry? Of course not. It's you I'm concerned about, Nina. So long as you're sure you're doing the right thing.'

Nina stood up. 'I no longer know what is right and what is wrong between Val and me. I do know that I need to go back home and see for myself what is going on, to put a close on it. Maybe.'

'You do that, and if you want your job back when you return . . . you are returning, aren't you?'

'Perhaps.'

'Oh! Right. Anyway, if you want your job back I shall do my best to accommodate you. Keep in touch with Valentine, though, won't you?'

Nina shrugged her shoulders and went.

Something that Valentine never did was come into the practice on his day off. He had done once when a dog he'd operated on had taken a turn for the worse; then they'd rung him for advice and he'd come immediately. But that day he called for no apparent reason. Joy, knowing what she did, was alarmed for Nina.

'Hi, Valentine! This is a pleasant surprise.'

'Has Nina gone for lunch?'

'Five minutes ago.' Joy decided to give him one last chance. 'She's calling for a packed lunch from the delicatessen and going to the park to eat it. She has a spot that she declares is "the coolest place in town", as in, out of the sun, under the beech trees near the pavilion.'

'Right, thanks.'

She was at the front of the queue in the shop and he pushed forward to join her. 'Can we have that twice, please? Have you ordered a drink?'

Nina swung round to face him. 'Iced orange juice.'

'Make that two iced orange juices, please.'

Nina showed no surprise. She'd run out of emotions, what with last night and this morning with Joy. Valentine took her elbow in one hand and the carrier in the other and they went out together, a picture of married bliss to anyone who didn't know their story.

'You're right, this is the coolest place in town,' Valentine said as they approached the beech trees near the pavilion. 'End of August and not a drop of rain for almost eight weeks. One day it will begin to rain and never stop. Is this where you'd like to sit? Or further along?'

They chose a bench and sat. He dug in the carrier for the napkins and presented her with her box of sandwiches and her drink, which he balanced carefully for her on the seat the other side of her. 'There. OK?'

'How did you know where I was?'

'Joy told me.'

'Oh! What did she say?' If he knew, so be it, she didn't really care.

'Just about where you were having lunch. I'm sorry I missed you this morning. I hadn't slept and then of course I did. I really meant what I said last night. It's all over and done with and I want to say again all that is finished. I shan't be straying again . . .

'Straying? What is straying?'

'Just a kinder way of saying I shan't be . . . I've stopped looking at other women. I want you and me to make a go of it. You and me will make a real marriage, at last. Slowly, you know, for your sake.'

He looked so lovingly at her, with the beginnings of desire in those fascinating eyes of his, that her resolve almost left her. She stroked his cheek, looked into his dark-brown eyes, stroked his hair by his temples and then recollected her decision.

Nina sighed. He kept saying the same thing time and again. She'd heard it so often. She took a deep breath, filling her lungs with air to brace herself to say what she had to say. 'I've decided I'm going home,' Val looked horrified, 'to look up my aunts and uncles, my cousins, my friends, to see what life like for them now. See my school, the university, the mountains where my brothers and I used to ski. Maybe to stay a while, maybe come back, maybe not.'

Valentine had been about to take his first bite of his sandwich when she started speaking, but stopped abruptly, absolutely appalled by her decision. 'Maybe not come back? Whyever not? You can't do that. Not leave *me*. On my own. Have you not heard what I've said? I'm yours for evermore. I can't say more than that, now can I?'

It was as if he'd hadn't spoken. 'Don't worry about the money. I shall get a job and support myself.'

'I . . . I *shall* support you, you're my *wife*. You'll have no worries about money. After all, you're not really staying there for a lifetime, are you?'

'Who knows?' She didn't even look at him when she said it; he didn't appear to matter.

Her voice reminded him of that night when she threw his dinner at him. There was that same empowered tone, that same courage. She meant it. The tables had been very neatly turned on him and he deserved it. He began to eat his sandwich, abandoned it on the seat, and then said quietly, 'I can't bear this. Please, always tell me where you are. You might need help. If you do I'll come straight away. I shall need your address to send the money, of course.'

'Strange you should be so concerned . . . when it's all over.'

'It isn't all over, don't even think that. I told you I'd finished with other women. Why can't you accept what I say? There's no need for you to go.'

Nina stood up, crushed her sandwich carton into the carrier bag, drank the last of the juice and said, 'I might go early next week, depend Joy finding replacement. I'll not move out till then. We will be good-mannered to each other.' Placing her hands either side of his face, she tilted it up so she could look into his eyes, eyes that were clouded with bitter disappointment, and very gently kissed his lips three times, at the last remembering her withering love for him and reluctant to let him go.

Chapter 19

For her last week at the practice, Kate was shadowing Rhodri. It was entirely different from watching Valentine. Rhodri was so considerate, had no problem boosting his reputation and sought neither praise nor admiration from his clients as Valentine did. Kate learned a lot, but she couldn't quite believe that two vets doing the same job could be so different. Learning that Nina had decided to leave Valentine for a while, and seeing the impact it had had on him, Kate was grateful to have a less emotional time. She'd never seen Valentine so drained of energy, of passion, of sex appeal. These days he appeared at first glance a very ordinary man.

Nina was leaving on Friday, sooner than she had expected because Joy had taken on the receptionist from the High Street practice whom Nina had met and she was starting the following Monday. They were all concerned about Nina going 'home', as she called it, but were on her side when they remembered how badly Valentine had treated her in the past.

Miriam, in particular, was deeply worried and asked her up for coffee the day before she left.

Instead of drinking it in the kitchen, where a great deal of Miriam's and Mungo's life was spent, they sat in the sitting room with Perkins in attendance. He was hoping for a biscuit and was sitting with that in mind close up to Nina and looking soulfully into her eyes. He knew what a complete waste of time it would be looking hopefully into Miriam's eyes; Mungo's perhaps but not Miriam's.

Nina broke off from speaking and popped a corner of her

biscuit into his mouth. He rapidly chomped on it and recommenced his campaign.

'No, Perkins, not another one. How can you resist him, Miriam?'

'That's easy. I remember how many miles I walk to keep him fit, and I can resist him quite easily!'

'I shall miss you all, so very much.'

'We'll miss you. But you know, if you are overcome with longing for Valentine and for us, you will be welcomed back. You are sure, Nina, this is what you want? You know, going back home?'

Nina nodded. 'I have to go, though I do believe he means it this time when he promises Eleanor is the last, but I not giving in. He's given me a great deal of money to take with me, just as though he loves me, but he can't, can he? To do what he does. Truthfully, you see . . . it is my fault.'

Miriam left a silence, quietly sipping her coffee while she waited.

'You see, I've never told anyone this before, but we've never . . . he and I, we've never made love. I can't. Not since w-what happened to me. That's one of the reasons he . . . well, you know . . .' She hunched her shoulders and didn't look at Miriam.

'My dear. I didn't know.' Shocked to the core, Miriam couldn't say anything more. It was too appalling to contemplate. A man so overtly sexual like Valentine. My God! What a situation.

Nina put down her cup too quickly and, as she did so, her remaining piece of biscuit shot off her saucer and was snapped up by Perkins almost before it hit the carpet.

Horrified, Miriam growled fearsomely, 'Perkins, in your bed, this minute.'

He gave Nina an apologetic smile, exposing the smallest of his front teeth, and slowly waved his tail, then, glancing at Miriam's outraged face, he slipped out silently and quickly. Somehow it broke the tension and Miriam said, 'That is something which can be cured, you know, but it's entirely up to you. Only you can solve it. Tell me, if you hadn't got Valentine what would you do?'

Nina uttered one word, 'Die.'

Miriam swallowed hard. She was normally very good at getting people to understand what they needed to do to solve their problems, like she had done with that Eleanor, but this. Oh, my God!

'So you do love him?'

'I adore every inch of him, but I can't compete with all his women friends. These last few days I want him like a wife should want her husband, but I daren't in case he doesn't mean it, and then I have slept with him at great cost for myself, only for him to find another woman. That pain is too terrible to contemplate.'

'If you could bring yourself to . . . let him love you then he might not turn to other women. It must be hard for him, an attractive man like Valentine, but loving is giving and *not* counting the cost, surely?' Everything she said seemed to be coming out in funny, short, sharp, meaningless jerks, and Miriam was beginning to lose her grip. 'But I can fully understand your problem . . . though I've never been anywhere near being raped so it's not easy for me *really* to understand . . . but I can see your problem all too clearly. You're terrified of it bringing back frightful memories. But it wouldn't, would it, with Valentine, because you love him. A sense of proportion is needed. To marry you to save you he must love you in his way. Imagine what your life would have been if Valentine *hadn't* married you and brought you here, where you feel secure, where you have enough to eat, where people care about you? If you hadn't met him and hadn't loved him, *you* could have been in a mass grave, or pregnant in the most horrific way any woman can be, or living in unbelievable fear every single day, with no Valentine to protect you. Then what? Mmmm?' Miriam got up and opened the window that overlooked Beulah Bank Top. 'My word, it's very hot this morning, I hope you don't mind me . . .'

Nina, lying back against the sofa cushions, shook her head. 'Go ahead. I've no emotions, they've been slowly destroyed. I need to get away, to stand away from myself, to stop and think. He must love me, I suppose, but his love hard to find most days. Though he never hits me, never swears at me, he is always, always, the gentleman. Generous with his money – to all his women, but especially to me.'

She appeared to make up her mind about something. 'I'll take no more of your time. Thank you.' She got to her feet and joined Miriam at the window, putting her arms around her and hugging her almost breathless.

Miriam hugged her back and said, 'Please keep in touch with me and I will with you.'

Nina let her go. 'I will. You are so wise. What you said is sensible, but still I must go to my roots, for a while. I'll let you know. OK? Thank you.'

She left Miriam in pieces, emotionally exhausted and with the most incredibly painful headache. But, being Miriam, she didn't begrudge the time nor the effect it had on her. She just hoped she'd done some good, though she couldn't believe she had. Perkins crept back into the sitting room and leaned against her legs to let her know he wished to make amends for his bad manners.

A walk, that was what she needed, a long walk to clear her head and rejuvenate her nerves. She wouldn't need a cardigan, for certain, even at the top of the Bank, for the day was already too humid for comfort. Perkins, of course, knew exactly what she was thinking and was standing at the door waiting to go down even before she'd picked up his lead.

On the Monday after Nina had gone and they were all tiptoeing around Valentine because he was so obviously distressed, the question of Choo, Eleanor's kitten, who was still being looked after at the practice, became paramount.

Joy said to a crowded staffroom, 'Has anyone any ideas about what we can do with Choo? A home has got to be found. It's not good for her here.'

Valentine offered to give her a home. His offer was greeted by an uncomfortable silence. It was Joy who finally said she didn't think so, but Valentine was persistent: 'I need the company. I've never known our house so still. She'd do me good.'

'Well, Valentine, she certainly wouldn't do Nina any good when – if – she comes home. A constant reminder, for heaven's sake . . .'

'Nina's not like that.'

'No, but she might be about Eleanor's cat. It simply wouldn't do. Just think how you would feel in her circumstances.'

Valentine thought for a moment. 'Maybe you're right.'

'I am right, there's no maybe about it.' Having crushed the idea of Nina coming home to find Choo in residence, Joy looked round the others but they all avoided her eye. 'Well, someone's got to do something. Have we a client who's just lost their cat? Mmm?'

They all shook their heads.

'In that case,' Joy said, 'maybe I should ask Duncan what he thinks.'

Rhodri, who wasn't always the most subtle of people, suggested that he thought Duncan believed animals to be excessive in the trouble stakes, and totally pointless.

'He did, till he got Tiger and things have gone downhill ever since. First Tiger, then Copper. But if he did take this one on he'd never allow her to be called Choo. That would have to be changed.'

If he did want her would it upset the poor homeless creature calling her something different? someone asked.

This statement was met with scorn from the vets, but was given some credence by the lay staff.

'Well,' said Bunty, 'it would upset *me* if my name got changed.'

They then all focused their minds on choosing a new name for Choo which sounded remarkably like Choo, but wasn't actually it. Scott made a list but they never got anywhere with it so it was left to Joy to suggest to Duncan that they adopt her.

Duncan opened his mouth to say, 'definitely not', but instead he said, 'What kind of a cat is she? A moggy?'

'She's a very charming Siamese.'

Duncan almost leapt from his chair. 'I've always wanted a Siamese! I'll come round tomorrow after work.'

'You don't mean it.'

'I do. Don't like the idea of her being abandoned, it's not right.'

'If I agree, I want it to be known that Choo, or whatever, is the very last one. Agreed?'

Duncan nodded. 'The very last one. But I've got to see her first.'

'There's no way you'll say no when you've seen her. She is a darling.'

Of course, Duncan fell in love immediately he saw Choo, and this was he who at one time thought Mungo must be mad, loving Perkins as he did. 'I shall simply call her Coffee,' he said. 'That seems to me to be the most appropriate name considering her colour.'

So Choo found someone who truly loved her and she gave all her devotion to Duncan; as far as she was concerned, women were not to be trusted.

Kate suddenly and almost unexpectedly came to the end of her practice work experience and knew without a doubt that she didn't want to leave. But she had to, there was no way she could avoid it. Deep in her heart she was glad she'd come to the stage where Scott meant much less to her than he had done. Gone for good were the days when her heart thumped away in her chest when she saw him, or one glance of those splendid blue eyes of his could set her blood racing. The day they'd been locked in each other's arms, kissing and clinging to each other, had faded into insignificance. There was no way she could overcome his powerful desire for Zoe, obviously the love of his life, so she could go back to college free of her passion for him and concentrate on her work, knowing how right she had been in choosing to be a vet.

Valentine had sobered down so much he was almost unrecognizable as the Omar Sharif of any right-minded female. He never mentioned Nina, though they could tell the days when he'd heard from her because for the whole of that day he was slightly happier than normal. In a kind of a way Kate felt Valentine deserved Nina turning her back on him for a while, but she hoped desperately, for Nina's sake, that they would get back together again.

The Friday night of Kate's last week was party night in honour of her, and everyone gathered at the Fox and Grapes to celebrate. Joy suggested that Mia might like to come, too, but apparently Mia had a prior engagement and was very cagey about telling Kate where she was going.

'I'd love to but I can't. Got to keep my promise. Sorry. Give everyone my best regards, won't you?' Mia had said, then turned away without offering any further explanation.

It left Kate wondering what on earth she was up to. Then, like a flash, she thought: It's a man! She'd been different this last week or two. Staring into space sometimes, laughing a lot, much happier. Yes, it was definitely a man. It couldn't be, could it? No! But whyever not? For a split second Kate was staggered by the prospect of Mia being involved with someone, because up until now she, Kate, had always been the centre of Mia's universe . . . Just in time Kate pulled herself together, and decided that, of course, she was glad for her. After all, Mia had devoted years and years to looking after her, so why shouldn't she have a chance of a life of her own?

A farewell party, then back to college in a few weeks and lots of hard work to follow. So she went to the party by herself. As she pulled up in the car park, Scott and Zoe drew up alongside her.

Zoe burst out of their car and, flinging her arms round Kate, said, 'I can't believe you've been here six weeks. I kept meaning to ask you for supper but never got round to it. At Christmas I shall do that very thing, ask you round and get all the info about college and which of the tutors are still there and things. Are you enjoying it?'

'I most certainly am, every minute. My God! Isn't it hot tonight? I swear it's hotter than ever.'

Scott interrupted their tête-à-tête by kissing Kate's ear and squeezing her arm. 'Sorry to be saying goodbye. It's been lovely seeing you all summer. Like Zo says, at Christmas you'll have to come to Bridge Cottage and have supper, so the two of you can talk shop.' He smiled at her, not his usual sparkling, all-consuming, I-am-an-astounding-member-of-the-male-species smile, but in a comradely way, warm and genuine, and when she reached up to return his kiss, her heart didn't even go into a spin.

Zoe put her hand in the crook of Kate's arm and steered her into the Fox and Grapes.

In one of the downstairs rooms was an enormously long dining table. Hugely long, in fact, one which could only have been accommodated in a vast medieval hall, its age obvious in the wonderful patina where thousands of revellers had leaned their elbows, stood their tankards and smoothed their hands over its surface, enjoying the glow of the wood. Tonight it was difficult to see the wood, however, because the table was covered from end to end with place settings for a meal, to say nothing of the food. Vast baskets of fresh rolls, huge platters filled to overflowing with cold meats and stand pies, vast bowls of salad, enormous jugs of beer almost too heavy to lift, of iced water, of juice, of mead, so tempting, so carefully thought out.

'Oh! Just take a look at that! It's wonderful.' Kate didn't think she'd seen a more tempting lay-out for a meal in her life. They were the first to arrive. But within minutes the others began piling in, all of them staggered by the sight of the food.

Zoe said softly, 'Mungo's providing *all* this. We've nothing to pay, would you believe! We must remember to thank him.' She let go of Kate's arm as Mungo shouted above the rabble, 'Free bar till ten, OK?'

They all climbed over the old refectory-type benches and seated themselves, a swathe of waiters and waitresses appeared, and the fun began. This was half past eight and by ten o'clock vast inroads had been made into the food, and Mungo decided it was time he stood up to make his speech.

'Ladies and gentlemen, unaccustomed as I am to public speaking,' he paused for the snigger that went round the table, 'I would like to begin by saying how delighted we have all been to welcome Kate to the practice for six weeks this summer. It's been the hottest summer in living memory, in more ways than one. There's have been various requests at one time or another asking for air conditioning due to the impossibility of working in such high temperatures. Those of you who have air-conditioned cars won't have suffered like the reception staff who—'

Dan shouted, 'I don't have air conditioning!'

Scott shouted, 'Neither do I. My Land Rover's so old I shall be needing foot pedals fitted to make it go at all!'

Mungo had to laugh. 'OK, OK! I'm sure you'll all be delighted to hear that air conditioning will be fitted straight after Christmas right the way through the building. Then I suspect we shall have the worst summer with the heaviest rainfall ever and whose fault will that be? Eh?'

Joy punched the air and bellowed, 'Hallelujah!!'

'Dan and Scott will be pleased to hear that their new vehicles will be delivered before the winter sets in . . .'

The room filled with cheers, Kate got pushed off the end of her bench and had to be rescued from the floor, and Ginny, enthusiastically hugged by Gab in the excitement, went over backwards off the bench and laughed so much it took two of them to pull her back up again.

'OK, everyone, calm down. Now for the serious bit. Errol Spencer, known by all as Scott, is to be a full-blooded partner from the first of January next year, now that marriage appears to have sobered him a little but not too much, Scott. We can't manage without your sense of fun, and all those women fancying you like fury. Other than that, the practice is going from strength to strength and I am very, very pleased to tell you that we are envisaging building an extension to provide one more operating theatre and two more consulting rooms as well as enlarging the intensive care room.'

A great cheer went up and an extra buzz of excitement surged through the room. Scott received several hearty claps on his back in congratulation and more than one lifted their glasses to salute him.

'All in all, we have had a very successful year so far, a few hiccoughs,' he took care not to glance in Ginny's direction, 'but we've surmounted those and are riding straight into the sunset full of vigour and ready for any challenges that are thrown at us. I ask you to all raise your glasses and toast Barleybridge Veterinary Hospital; may it go on being as successful as it has been this year, if not more so.'

When the hubbub had died down and everyone was seated again, Mungo proposed a further toast. 'This second toast is for Kate, who has spent such a successful six weeks with us that we don't want her to go back to college, and we hope that one day she will be back here, qualified and working for us, so you've all to make sure everything goes well from now on, as she'll need the practice to be here and functioning well when she joins us as a fully fledged member of staff. Thank you, Kate!'

At that moment there was the most enormous flash of lightning followed by a clap of thunder immediately overhead which almost made the table tremble.

'Wow! Would you believe it!'

'Shall we take that as a warning *not* to have Kate back?' someone said.

'Listen to that blessed rain!' Miriam held up her hand and they fell silent. The rain crashed down onto the glass roof they were sitting under and it became almost impossible to hear oneself speak.

Someone remembered then that Kate had said during the heat of the summer: 'When it rains I shall be so grateful I shall stand outside in it stark naked.'

'Right! Now's your moment, Kate. Come on, let's be having you.' Ginny stood up and set off round to Kate's side of the table, followed by Gab and then Scott. They bodily picked her up and raced her off through the garden door, then stood her up under the porch saying, 'Well? Come on then!'

Never one to refuse a challenge Kate said, 'I will, but with my clothes on.'

So she dashed out from under the porch and stood with the heavy rain beating down on her, did a sailor's hornpipe round one of the garden tables, raised her arms to the sky and roared, 'Hurrah! Hurrah! Hurrah!' her voice drowned by the sound of the rain falling on her, and all of those watching her from the safety of the Fox and Grapes shouted their approval.

Love in the Country

LIST OF CHARACTERS AT BARLEYBRIDGE VETERINARY HOSPITAL

Mungo Price	Orthopaedic Surgeon and Senior Partner
Colin Walker	Partner - large and small animal
Daniel Franklin Brown	Partner - large animal
Scott Spencer	Partner – large animal
Virginia Havelock	Large animal vet
Valentine Dedic	Small animal vet
Rhodri Hughes	Small animal vet
Sebastian Partridge	Large and small animal vet

NURSING STAFF
Sarah Cockroft (Sarah One)
Sarah MacMillan (Sarah Two)
Bunty Bird

RECEPTIONISTS
Joy Bastable (Practice Manager)
Lesley Jennings
Dodi Pilgrim
Annette Smith

Miriam Price	Mungo's wife
Duncan Bastable	Joy's husband
Letty Walker	Colin's wife
Rose Franklin Brown	Dan's wife
Zoe Spencer	Scott's wife
Megan Hughes	Rhodri's wife
Nina Dedic	Valentine's wife
Dicky Bird	Bunty's husband

THE BARLEYBRIDGE PRACTICE

BEULAH BANK MOOR

ASKEW NEWTON

LORD ASKEW'S

BEULAH BANK TOP

NEWTON NEW ROAD

BRIDGE LANE

BARLEYBRIDGE PRAC

RIVER FARM

RIVER CHESS

BRIDGE END FARM

BARLEYBRIDGE

BRIDGE FARM

BRIDGE LANE

WOOTTON CAUSE

WOOTTON CAUSEWAY FARM

LOWER KIRKSTALL

WOOTTON CAUSEWAY TROUT FARM

CHESHAM CRISPY CHICKEN CO.

KIRKSTALL HILL

Chapter 1

Seb checked his watch. Ten minutes to eight. He was in good time for the first day of his new job. It was two years since he first qualified, yet he still felt a thrill.

A strong draught told him the rear door to the animal hospital had been opened and into the reception area came Joy Bastable the practice manager.

'Seb! You're here. You've found your way. Well, of course, you must have, and to prove it you're standing in front of me!' She put down her bag on the reception desk and turned to study him. What a lovely chap he was. Not handsome in the modern manner, but sweet and kind like her Duncan. Very like Duncan, in fact. 'Look! Here's your name-plate. This morning you'll be in this last consulting room here, newly built just in time for you to use. It slots in here. Look.' She held up the name-plate for him to see. It read: '*Sebastian J. Partridge* B.Vet.Med.,M.R.C.V.S.' Seb almost burst with pride.

'You put it in,' Joyce said. 'It moves with you, you see, to whichever consulting room you're in.'

Seb dropped it into place and stood back to admire it. This was his reward. Despite his family's opposition he'd stuck to his guns, determined to be a vet and not the farmer the rest of them assumed he would be. Living on that isolated family farm for the rest of his life? Absolutely not. His dad had been bitterly disappointed, but Seb couldn't help himself. He knew his brother was neither physically nor mentally capable of making a success of the farm, but a lifetime incarcerated there with nothing but bleak hills for company ... well, he couldn't. So here he was, ready to begin.

The emptiness of the reception area was disturbed by another blast of air and down the passage from the back door came a tall man with brown hair lightened by the sun. He wore a bush hat, an open-necked khaki shirt with pockets and epaulettes, and suede Timberland boots. Round his neck was a gold chain with a thick wedding ring threaded onto it.

Joy introduced him. 'This is Scott.'

The said Scott held out his hand. 'How do you do. I'm farm animal, not small.'

The accent gave him away. 'You're Australian?' asked Seb.

'I am. Australian by birth but English by inclination. Welcome to the practice. Best place on earth to be working. He looks as though he might turn out quite well, doesn't he, Joy?' Scott grinned broadly and play-punched Seb on his shoulder.

Joy looked Seb up and down. 'Indeed he might.'

'Is my list ready?' Scott asked.

'Of course. Busy day. But that's what you like. How's the baby doing?'

'Very well indeed. Three children keep Zoe very busy so it's a good thing the baby's better behaved than the last one was.'

'Well, Zoe deserved it to be so.'

'She's a glutton for punishment; she's decided four would be a good idea.'

'Heaven help us!'

'That's what I said.' Scott smiled.

Suddenly there was an influx of staff arriving. Scott collected his list and left to begin his busy day. The introductions flustered Seb, and he got names and faces all mixed up. Then a woman arrived in their midst, with dark curly hair and a generous smile, her hand outstretched in welcome. 'I'm Miriam Price, Mungo's wife,' she said. 'I've got a pot of coffee waiting in the flat upstairs; come up and have a cup before your day begins. I shan't keep him long, Joy.' She tucked his hand into the crook of her arm and led him down the passage. 'Mungo's just finishing breakfast.'

They climbed the stairs to the Prices' beautiful welcoming kitchen, and he felt immediately at home. Mungo was reading the paper and looked at him over the top of his reading glasses. 'Morning, Seb. Welcome to Barleybridge Veterinary Hospital.' He reached a hand round the edge of the paper and shook Seb's vigorously.

Miriam asked, 'Black? Milk? Sugar?'

'Milk and sugar, please.'

'I've a full list of clients this morning, Seb, so drink up and I'll go down with you and show you the ropes before I begin.'

'Thank you.' Seb, remembering an incident that had occurred when he'd come for his second interview, recalled Mungo's explosive temper and was grateful for his warm welcome.

Miriam anxiously enquired, 'Flat all right? I made sure the boiler was on in good time. Are you pleased with it?'

'Yes, it's lovely. Thank you.'

'Anything you need, just let me know. I look after the flat, you see.'

'There's nothing I can think of at the moment. I hadn't expected two bedrooms; it feels luxurious.'

Mungo rattled his paper and Seb took the hint and drank his coffee right to the bottom. 'Ready when you are, Mr Price.'

Mungo stood up, folded his newspaper and headed for the stairs. 'You're lucky to arrive when the building work is finished. It's been hectic here this year, but finally it's done and now we've to earn the money to pay for it all. Ah! I see your name-plate is up already.

The scene in the waiting room was transformed. The empty chairs were filled with clients holding cages housing gerbils or hamsters or birds, cats in baskets and dogs on leads. There was a general air of anxiety and activity to which, Seb realized, he *belonged*.

A consulting-room door opened and a voice called out, 'Lucky Campbell'. It was immediately followed by a sharp click of the heels and a nod of the head. The client got to her feet and said, 'Good morning, Mr Dedic.'

'That's Valentine Dedic,' said Mungo. 'Don't be fooled by the clicking and bowing; it may look amusing but never under-estimate him. He's the sharpest knife in the drawer. Remember that.'

Mungo ran through the equipment in the state-of-the-art consulting room which was to be Seb's for the morning. Seb's head whirled with detail and he desperately hoped he would remember it all.

'Right. Time I wasn't here,' Mungo finished. 'Immaculate

4

scrubs at all times. Only the best for our clients, with the highest standards of diagnosis, of course. Absolute integrity. No free consultations, much as some of them would like to get away with one. We have expenses and are not a charity. But do not over-charge. If clients feel that's what you've done they'll be resentful and it doesn't do the client–vet relationship any good at all. Here in this folder is our list of statutory charges. Ask for advice whenever. You're bound to need it at first and no one minds helping you out. Must go. Have a good morning.'

Seb took a deep breath, put on his scrubs, hung his stethoscope round his neck and looked at his list. So this was where it all began. The very first real step up in his career. This was the start of a new life, leaving behind, he hoped, the horrors of his first two years in practice, where he'd been marginalised and made to feel useless. Here he could prove just how good he was.

His first patient was a canary called Nellie. Problem? Removal of band. It all appeared too easy for words.

He opened his door and called out, 'Nellie Smithson.' A huge man got to his feet with the canary apparently in the cardboard box in his large fist.

Seb held out his hand. 'I'm Seb Partridge. I'm new.'

'Student, are yer?'

'No, qualified but new to this practice. Can I see the bird?'

'This 'ere is Nellie. Good name for a canary, don't you think? Have to hope she'll sing well, else I shall look silly.'

Seb had to acknowledge he didn't know why.

Seemingly surprised by Seb's ignorance, Mr Smithson said, 'You know – Dame Nellie Melba, the famous Australian singer from way back. This 'ere canary, I bought her yesterday. Took a right fancy to her, but I don't like this band round her leg. She's not fully grown, I'm told, and I'm frightened her leg might grow more and the band be too tight. You can hardly move it as it is now. See what you think.'

He withdrew Nellie from the cardboard box with the greatest of gentleness despite his large hands and thick fingers. She was a vivid yellow, with every feather well groomed and aligned.

'She's a great specimen.' Seb tried moving the band on her leg and agreed that it was already tight. 'Best off, I think. Would you like me to do it for you?'

'That's what I've come for, to have it cut off.'

It was the work of a moment to snip off the band. Seb held it out for Mr Smithson. 'Want to take it? Keepsake?'

'No, thanks. That's it, then.'

'Where did you get her from?'

'Chap down the market. He included the cage, too.'

Seb took the opportunity to examine her while she lay so quietly in his hand. While he was looking at her feet he asked, 'The perches in the cage, are they covered with sandpaper?'

'Yes, they are. Gives the bird a better grip, he said.'

'Will you take my advice? All they're going to do is make her feet very tender and sore. She needs smooth perches. Imagine if you had sandpaper lining your shoes. You wouldn't get far, would you?' Seb said this as gently as he could so as not to give offence. With Nellie resting on her back on the palm of his hand, her head held securely between his finger and thumb, Seb held her feet out for inspection. 'Look, they're becoming inflamed already.'

Mr Smithson was appalled. 'They are. They are. Well,

young man, you do know your stuff. I shall be back with my Nellie should a problem arise. Thanks for telling me. I'm straight back down the market to give that chap a piece of my mind. Now, how much do I owe?'

'They'll deal with that at the reception desk, Mr Smithson.'

'Right. Thank you very much.'

Seb glanced at his statutory charge list and tapped the price into his computer.

Next was a dog for its annual booster. Well, that was easy enough, except Rex bit him good and hard and the client almost collapsed with apologies.

'That's fine, Mrs Evans, I've kept my tetanus up to date so—'

'Are you inferring my Rex has rabies?' She hunched her shoulders defensively.

'No, of course not, but every vet has to keep their tetanus up to date. One never knows.' He smiled sweetly at her and that did the trick.

She beamed back at him. 'Of course, it's only sensible. You'll go far, Mr Partridge. I shall ask for you next time.'

For one brief moment Seb thought she was going to kiss him, and he blushed. She noticed the blush and smiled at him, gave him a wave and left. Another satisfied customer, thought Seb. In fact, that morning he had a legion of happy customers and felt well pleased with his first morning's work. In the afternoon he assisted Valentine with three operations and was complimented on his intuitive help.

'You've a good instinct for surgery, Seb, congratulations.'

'Thank you. I always enjoyed surgery at college.'

'Why don't you ask Mungo if you can watch his last

7

operation this afternoon; it's very complicated and interesting.'

'Would he mind?'

'He likes enthusiasm. Try him and see. It's a badly smashed jaw.'

'I will then.'

Seb found Mungo in the orthopaedic operating theatre, newly built along with the extra consulting rooms and the increased accommodation for intensive care.

'Of course. Come in,' he said in reply to Seb's request.

Mungo didn't speak again except to ask Bunty the nurse for instruments or mutter furiously about the owner who'd given this dog such a savage beating that his jaw was broken in three places. Most vets would have suggested the dog be put to sleep but Mungo, despite knowing he most likely wouldn't get paid for his efforts, with his exceptional skills and his intense compassion for animals in pain, was willing to operate.

After two hours' intense concentration he straightened his back with a great sigh. 'Bunty, thanks for your help. It's worked out better than I'd hoped. Take care of him. Enjoyed that, Seb, did you?'

'I most certainly did. Thank you for letting me watch.'

'Perhaps next time you might like to help?'

'That would be a privilege.' Seb helped Bunty lift the dog onto the trolley and wheeled it into the intensive-care room for her.

As Bunty settled the dog in a cage with a drip and a fleece over him to keep him warm, she asked, 'You do realise you've just been watching a genius at work?' Seb detected a note of passionate devotion in her voice but he was tactful enough to ignore it.

'Of course I do.'

'I've worked for him for ten years and he gets better all the time. People come from miles around, you know. He doesn't turn up his nose at mongrels or moggies; if they need his help they're all the same to him. A scruffy mongrel gets the same attention as a top show dog. We've a mongrel in next Monday from eighty miles away, coming on the recommendation of a grateful client of ours. I wouldn't change my job for anything. I've told Dicky he needn't think when he retires from the police that we're moving away because I couldn't. Not a single mile.' Bunty gave him a trembling smile that Seb put down to fatigue, but he felt a mite of pity for poor Dicky.

He'd been lent an aged Land Rover belonging to the practice until a permanent vehicle was available, but the fact didn't diminish his high spirits; he'd had such a spectacular day nothing could dishearten him. What finally put the icing on the cake was Scott saying, 'I've got a call-out – want to come?'

'Yes, please, I'd love to.'

'It's not far. A sow in trouble. Owners are Francesca and Cecil Goodwood, and a more peculiarly matched pair it would be hard to find. Lovely people, though. Come on, be sharp. They ring up and expect me there within five minutes.'

Scott paused to put his head round Joy's office door. 'Joy, I'm taking the mobile scanner, OK? I'll bring it back before I go home.'

The moment Francesca Goodwood saw Seb, she beamed at him. 'Well, young man. Seb, you say? I hope you know how lucky you are to be watching Scott at work. His veterinary skills are top of the shop and if you do as well as him you'll do

9

all right, believe me. You look a grand chap to me. This way. Cecil's brought Constantia in to give her a bit more comfort; she's in the farrowing stall in the barn – more room for you, you see. She's a favourite of his.'

'Cecil?'

'Yes, Scott, like I said, believe it or not, Cecil is in there with her now.'

The barn was mainly used for storing the straw used for the pigs' bedding but Cecil had organised some bales to form a compact area for housing Constantia and the three piglets she'd managed to give birth to before her trouble started.

'Evening, Cecil. I can see why you've taken a fancy to her. I've no doubt she's a winner.' Scott was instantly on his knees examining Constantia. 'Fancy name, lovely sow. My stethoscope, Seb. Thanks.'

Seb watched while Scott examined Constantia, and to him there was something rather disturbing about Scott's careful examination. It felt rather over the top.

Eventually Scott sat back on his haunches. 'Have you any other sows just pigged?'

'Why?' Cecil asked, looking panicked for the first time.

'I'm not happy about her, things appear very wrong. I was thinking of handing her three piglets over to another sow, just in case.'

Francesca choked on her words. 'Just in case what?'

'How long has she been at this?'

'Well, we didn't notice until about an hour ago that she'd started, by then she already had the three, so we don't really know.'

Cecil began to shake. 'Not my Constantia, not her.'

'First litter?'

Francesca nodded.

Scott slowly shook his head. 'She's completely stopped having contractions.'

'Can't you give her something out of that magic bag of yours? You've always worked the miracle before.' By this time Francesca was kneeling in the straw beside Scott, a trembling hand resting on his shoulder.

'I'll give her some oxytocin but we'll use the scanner first and see just exactly what's going on in there. Hopefully the injection will start up the contractions again. She's definitely got more piglets inside – a good number, I should say.'

Cecil rubbed a hand across his eyes. 'Well, let's get on with it then. No point in hanging about.'

'I agree.'

Fascinated, Seb watched the screen. The piglets were lying head to tail in the womb. But at the same time he could feel Scott's anxiety.

'I'll have to reach inside and get out the first one. Here, look down this side – it's big and it's stuck fast. That's what's holding everything up, I think.'

Scott stripped off and put on his calving gown. He rolled up the sleeves as far as he could and, almost lying down on the barn floor, reached inside. The other three stood breathless, waiting for a result. It seemed an age until Scott grunted his satisfaction and managed to release the piglet. Out it popped and Scott gave it to Francesca to clean up and get it breathing.

'It's a whopper! An absolute whopper! Never seen one as big.' Cecil was beside himself with joy. 'He's a Goliath, he is. My God! No wonder she was having problems.'

The oxytocin gradually began to have an effect on the sow's

contractions, and slowly but surely the rest of the litter made their appearance. The piglets burst into life with astonishing swiftness and were searching for their mother's teats in no time at all. Seb was full of admiration for Scott; there was no sentimental tosh, simply the drive to get the matter dealt with and have a successful conclusion. Whereas Seb could have wept tears of joy as each piglet appeared. They were such jolly little things with lovely curly tails and sweet little faces.

'Just look at them! Aren't they all wonderful? Well done!' He stopped his tears and took a tight grip on himself as Scott spoke to Francesca.

'There we are. Thirteen safe and sound. They all look as though they'll thrive.'

Cecil fetched a bucket of hot water, a bar of soap and a clean towel. 'There we are. Thanks very much – she'd have died without you.'

'All part of the service.'

Cecil pulled up a box and sat on it to watch the litter. 'It's grand, is this. Thirteen. Good old Constantia.'

As Scott revved up his Land Rover, Seb said, 'Why was one of them so very big?'

'It happens. Frankly, I think we got there just in time. She was beginning to flag, and with a piglet that size I'm not surprised. Been in labour a lot longer than they realised, I think. Newborn piglets are pretty mobile virtually immediately, but those first three little beggars were stronger on their feet than I would have expected.'

Scott dropped Seb off at the practice, returned the scanner and left Seb to make his way home in his old Land Rover.

On his way back to the flat Seb took a wrong turning and

spotted a fish and chip shop with a queue of customers inside. He decided to pick up his supper, but he was the sixth in the queue and had a while to wait.

Someone roared in shouting, 'Three plaice and chips a.s.a.p.! Who's driving that old Land Rover outside? Eh?'

Seb put up his hand. 'Me.'

'You the new vet, then?'

Seb nodded.

'Thought so.'

Seb smiled. 'I'm Seb Partridge, and you are?'

'I'm Phil Parsons, Applegate Farm. Pleased to meet you.' He offered his hand to Seb and shook his vigorously. 'You'll have some good times there. They're a great bunch.'

'Thanks. I'm sure I will.'

'That other vet in the High Street packed up two weeks ago. Miserable beggar, he was. I don't wonder he lost all his business to your practice. No wonder at all.' There followed an in-depth discussion about which animals each of the customers had taken to the Barleybridge practice at some time or another, and suddenly, all over again, Seb felt he belonged. There was an outbreak of hand-shaking and back-slapping for Seb, followed by free fish and chips. He held out his money but it was sturdily refused.

'By heck!' said Phil Parsons. 'You're favoured. Take 'em while you can, it won't happen again.'

The whole queue dissolved into laughter.

Someone else shouted, 'Don't miss out on your salt and vinegar! Put plenty on, them's free, and they'll taste even better than normal. You're favoured, you are.'

The man behind the counter took their teasing in his stride. 'You lot can shut up. You're all here because I sell the best fish and chips for miles, and well you know it.' The till rang and the fish and chips were served sizzling and crisp as fast as he was able.

Seb left to a chorus of 'goodnights', greatly moved by the enthusiasm of the queue. So this was what being a vet in a country market town meant; people knew you and, not only that, accepted you immediately.

Seb watched TV while he ate his supper. Kindly provided by the practice, the set wasn't very up to date, but it was satisfactory. This then was the life he had always longed to live, and the time spent observing Mungo Price repairing that dog's jaw had been absolutely fascinating. He was obviously a very skilled surgeon and fired Seb into wondering if he too could reach that level of skill.

He'd always enjoyed surgery when he was at college but at his first practice he hadn't had the opportunity to observe that level of expertise. If serious orthopaedic work was needed then it was given to a referral practice and Seb had never had the chance to watch. Three breaks in the jaw, but with clever drilling and pinning it had been restored to almost perfect condition.

In fact, come to think of it, he'd never been trusted with anything that required diagnosis or research or the use of his brain. He'd always been given the routine stuff, like boosters and nail clipping, and he'd become thoroughly disillusioned about his veterinary prospects. For two years he'd laboured on, then one bright shining morning he'd seen the light, as his mother would have said, and decided to find a new job. He'd even got a flat, too. At the other practice he'd found his own accommodation and it had been grotty, cold and depressing. But here! Seb glanced round the flat, admiring the comfortable terracotta-coloured sofa, the light cream walls, the luxurious sheepskin hearth rug and the black stove glowing behind the glass doors and throwing out enough heat to warm his flat and the next-door flat, too. He'd have to turn it to low.

For over an hour Seb dozed, relaxed and happy. The TV programme had changed twice by the time he woke and he had to smile at himself. One day at work and he was so tired he'd fallen asleep like an old man. The phone rang. That would be his mother he was sure, but it wasn't. It was Dan, one of the farm vets he'd spoken to at lunchtime, ringing to see if he'd come round to their house for a drink.

'I'd be delighted.'

'Scott's coming and Ginny and Gab. It'll give you a chance to get to know them.'

'Lovely. Where exactly do you live?'

'The address is Rose Cottage, appropriate as my wife is called Rose, and we live down Newton New Road, it's—'

'Don't worry, I have a map.'

'It's called New Road but it's ancient, about two hundred years older than most of the roads round here.'

Seb had to laugh. 'Right, I'll be there. Won't be long.'

Sometimes Seb had difficulty with small talk and though he was glad to be invited, that nervous edge which always beset him when meeting new people manifested itself. But he needn't have worried because he was welcomed like a long-lost brother.

Rose, with her American accent, embraced and kissed him as though she'd known him all his life, and that broke the ice for him. Ginny shook hands rather more formally but Gab, her husband, shook his hand vigorously, clapping him on the back and saying, 'Welcome, Seb, to the Barleybridge Veterinary Hospital. I can tell you'll fit in brilliantly.' He was only too obviously an outdoors man; weather-beaten with the air of a farmer about him. A very good-looking son of the soil, Seb thought.

'Ginny and I own Bridge End Farm,' Gab continued. 'Been there two years now and we're really beginning to turn it round. In a very poor way when we bought it, but with Ginny's veterinary skills and my farming experience it's going from strength to strength. Not to be confused with Bridge Farm, which my father owns; they're very close. But you're not farming, are you?'

'I only have experience with small animals but I am intrigued by farm animal work.'

Ginny interrupted. 'Don't believe a word he says. I happen to know he spent a blissful couple of hours watching Mungo at work this afternoon. Seb's much more interested in surgery.'

'Surgery?' Scott looked appalled. 'Surgery? Oh, my God! Surgery? Mungo's minute, detailed orthopaedic work? Heavens above. In the open air, in a field or a barn – now that's *real* surgery.'

Seb, a little taken aback by Scott's remarks, hesitated for a moment and then replied, 'Yes, I love it. You should have seen—'

'Stop this minute! Dan, get the man a drink immediately; his need is greater than mine.'

They all settled down in comfortable chairs around a blazing fire in the huge inglenook fireplace. Genuine horse brasses lined up on the brickwork and brass fire irons shone as though they'd been polished that very day. With a good drink in his hand, Seb began to relax.

Above the noise of everyone's voices the wail of a very young baby floated downstairs. Rose sprang to her feet. 'That's James. Sorry. Feed-time. Anybody mind if I feed him down here? Otherwise I shall miss all the fun.'

They all agreed she mustn't miss the fun and Rose returned down the stairs carrying a baby so like Dan there was no doubting who his father was.

Seb had to say so and Rose replied that Serena was like her and the two boys like Dan – 'Thank goodness.' She laughed at Dan, who grinned back, and settled down like an earth mother to feed the baby. No one minded, no one was embarrassed, and the conversation flowed as before until someone mentioned the Hunt, which would be leaving from Barleybridge town square the very next day.

Seb had reservations about hunting, so he held back from any comment until he had a chance to see how everyone else felt.

Gab only too obviously approved, Scott kind of half-approved, and Ginny was so against it that Seb was surprised the other vets were still speaking to her.

'Well, Seb, where do you stand with hunting?' Ginny asked.

So Seb had to declare, 'The Hunt at home goes over our farm fields. I've grown up with it, accepted it, and although I have never hunted myself I cannot say I disapprove; it's all part of country life to me. When I see our chickens dead because the fox has been past on his nightly inspection and discovered that the chickens have not been locked up for the night, and they're slaughtered right to the last one, then I think the fewer foxes there are the better.'

'That's not the fox's fault; it's your fault for forgetting to lock them up,' Ginny protested loudly.

Seb spoke up in defence of the chickens. 'If the fox took just enough food for itself, then I suppose it wouldn't appear so cruel, but slaughtering them all needlessly is ... well, not fair.'

An explosion of opinions flooded the room and baby James took fright.

Dan said, 'Remember the baby!'

The argument, now far too fierce to be called a discussion, continued, but Seb kept silent and didn't join in again. As the new man of the party he decided that was more diplomatic. Eventually, at half past eleven they decided to agree to differ and they all dispersed.

As Seb was getting into his Land Rover Dan came to speak to him. 'Stick to your own opinions, Seb, it's your right. They all get worked up about it. They forget the number of times the Hunt goes out and never even sees a fox. Goodnight. Thanks for coming. You should do well. If surgery is your passion you couldn't have a better teacher than Mungo.'

'That's right. Thanks for inviting me. Sorry I stirred things up, but that's how it strikes me.'

'Well, at least the death is quick with the hounds whereas shooting them can leave them dying in agony for days. Goodnight.'

Chapter 2

Full to the brim with enthusiasm, Seb got to the practice even earlier the next day, but it gave him a chance to talk to Scott, who invited him to visit a couple of farms with him that afternoon if he was free. 'I'll be here at lunchtime because Zoe's lunching with Rose and exchanging baby talk so we'll see if you're free. I'll mention it to Joy.'

'Thanks, that'll be great.'

'You'll love it here when you get settled in. Lovely staff, great clients. Wonderful place to live. Wouldn't be anywhere else in the world.'

'Don't you miss the sun and the wide open spaces?'

'And the flies and the boiling heat and the thousands of sheep to shear and the million miles to see a neighbour? No, I do not. A quiet trundle down to the Fox and Grapes, a pleasant chat over a pint with country people is much, much better. Right?'

Seb laughed. He had thought Australia would be too captivating to leave, but apparently not.

His first client that morning was Miranda Costello. He flicked through the on-screen notes and saw that Valentine had added 'difficult client' to them. A rabbit named Lettice was the patient.

'Lettice Costello, please.' The dazzling Mrs Costello rose to her feet and sailed forthwith into his consulting room. Musk! That was it, she was wearing musk perfume and he didn't like it. Still, she was a client and smiling broadly at him.

'Why is it that all the vets who work here are good-looking?' she said. 'There's Valentine, there's Scott, there's that Rhodri with the Welsh accent, and now you.' She put her head on one side and looked up at him beguilingly.

'I'm Seb Partridge. This is my second day at the practice. What can I do for you, Mrs Costello?'

She patted his forearm. 'Miranda to everyone who knows me.'

'What seems to be the problem?'

Miranda's eyes welled with tears. Two large ones spilled down her rouged cheeks. She sniffed loudly. 'Sorry. It's Lettice, you see. In my bones I know there's something wrong with her. What, I don't know, but there is. I've tried to ignore it, pretend it isn't there, but it's no good. Yesterday I had to face up to it. Now if it's too much for you I'll see Valentine instead; he'll know what to do.'

'Let me try first, Mrs ...' She wagged a finger at him. '... Miranda. I kept rabbits when I was a boy at home. Come to think of it, I kept almost every pet you could name. I might have known I would turn out to be a vet. You get her out.'

Seb placed Lettice on the examination table. 'What is it you had to face yesterday, exactly? Tell me in your own words. Take your time.'

A pathetic smile flickered at the corners of Miranda Costello's mouth; she was so grateful for his understanding. 'At first, like two or three weeks ago, I thought she must be pregnant, though I couldn't see how. I only have girl rabbits, but then you never know. I was so excited. Baby rabbits! Would I be able to part with them? Should I keep them all?' She paused to gain control of her voice. 'But I realise now the swelling is bigger, and she'd have had the babies by now, and . . . she's almost stopped . . . eating, and things are not working their way out at the other end, if you get my meaning.' A long, heartfelt sob halted any further conversation.

Seb knew precisely what the matter was the moment he examined her. The lump was monstrous and beyond veterinary care. 'Are you brave, Miranda?' he asked.

His answer was a nod. 'You mean you need me to be brave now?'

Seb nodded, too. 'You love her, I know, and so we must decide what to do. You see she's probably in pain, and we can't have that, can we?'

Miranda shook her head.

'We've got to take the pain away, haven't we?'

'You mean you could operate?' A gleam of hope shone in Miranda's eyes.

'No, I'm afraid not.'

'You mean she's too old?'

'How old do you think she is?'

'I don't know. So she's not pregnant?'

'No, it's a swelling that shouldn't be there and it must be causing her pain right now. If you like I'll get a second opinion from one of the other vets. Would you like me to do that?'

'It's not that I don't trust you, because I do, but . . . yes, seeing as you're new. Yes, I would.'

'Hold her. I'll get someone.'

Rhodri had a short gap in his appointments and was about to sink his teeth into a tempting sandwich Megan had made him for his lunch, even though there were three more hours to go before his lunch-hour.

Carefully wrapping his sandwich up to keep it fresh Rhodri followed Seb and greeted Miranda like a long-lost friend, shaking her hand and patting her forearm. 'Miranda! Long time no see. How are you?'

Bravely Miranda smiled at him. 'Not too good today.'

'I expect not. Seb says you'd like a second opinion on Lettice?'

Miranda nodded.

Rhodri took over at the examination table and gently examined Lettice, his face grim. 'I'm sorry, Mrs Costello, but ... Seb is absolutely right. I'm afraid it's all too late. Lettice is in pain and the very kindest gift you can give her at this moment is to have Seb put her to sleep and out of her misery. It's a massive growth and will only get worse. The pain will become indescribable; in fact, it is at that level now, I should imagine. Poor old thing.' Rhodri gently scratched Lettice behind her ear.

'I see. I'd be doing her a kindness, you mean?'

Rhodri nodded. 'I'll leave you to it.'

After he'd gone Miranda said, 'Same thing happened to my mother. She never told us she had a lump and when she couldn't stand it any longer she admitted it and we had to watch her die filled to the brim with morphine and still she had pain. At least I can put Lettice out of her agony before she gets even worse.'

Seb watched the decision being made and regretted he had it to do, but do it he must. 'Believe me, it's for the best. She'll know nothing about it. Nothing at all. You sit down there in the chair and we'll put her on your knee and you can cuddle her while I get the injection ready and then she'll fall quietly to sleep.'

'For ever!' Miranda gave a strangled sob, which struck Seb right to his heart. But he gently laid Lettice on Miranda's knee and turned away to prepare the injection.

Lettice was given enough cuddles to last her for weeks as Miranda stroked and stroked her from head to toe, whispering sweet nothings to her with tears pouring down her face.

Lettice fell asleep for ever within seconds and Seb left Miranda to cuddle her a while longer.

'Now shall you take her home, or would you like me to dispose of her for you?'

Seb knew instantly he should have phrased that better, but Miranda didn't appear to notice how clumsy he'd been.

'I have a graveyard for my pets, in a quiet corner of my garden. Did I say garden? More like a tip but there's loads of wildlife. I'll take her.' Completely forgetting she'd brought Lettice in one of her cat baskets, Miranda stood up and shuffled out into the waiting room with Lettice in her arms before Seb could stop her, so every anxious pet-owner witnessed the departure of Lettice, who was so obviously dead it brought a gasp of horror from them. Seb followed her out with the cat basket but too late to prevent the clients from being shocked.

Silence fell in the waiting room. Dodie Pilgrim the senior receptionist almost collapsed at the sight of a dead rabbit being carried through reception. Miranda came to a halt and declared loudly to anyone who cared to listen, 'This is Lettice, out of her pain and gone to the rabbit heaven in the

23

sky where all the carrots are juicy and fresh, the grass as green as green, and the burrows warm and cosy.'

This highly romantic picture of a bunny heaven left not a dry eye in the waiting room. Hankies came out and were swiftly put to use, loud sniffs were heard, and there was an outbreak of patting and stroking of the animals awaiting their turn.

Seb raced outside with the cat basket, saw Miranda safely installed in her van and waved her off. He returned feeling drained by his experience of putting a beloved animal down in front of its owner, only to find himself, when he went back in, facing the stern, beckoning finger of Dodie Pilgrim. She nodded her head in the direction of the back office and Seb followed her, puzzled as to why she needed to speak to him.

Between clenched teeth Dodie said, 'Dead animals go out through the back. It's a wonder our clients haven't collapsed *en masse* with the horror of what happened just now. You remember that, right? Dead – out the back, no messing. Alive – out the front. OK?' She emphasised her point by prodding his chest vigorously with a very sharp finger.

When lunchtime came Seb wondered whether he should eat his sandwich and drink his tea somewhere other than the staffroom because he couldn't face the wrath of Dodie Pilgrim. Someone had mentioned her a couple of times when he came for his second interview but he hadn't imagined that she could be so ... well ... vicious. He felt so depressed about Lettice he went to sit outside on the bench by the back door to eat, all alone, looking up at the cold, unwelcoming foothills of Beulah Bank Top. Was that snow he saw on the top-most peaks? Surely not. His spirits plummeted even further.

The back door opened and Dodie came out. Seb stood up. 'Sit down, boy.' She joined him on the bench, a vast mug of steaming coffee in her hand. 'She also left without paying. Cardinal sin, that.'

'I'd forgotten that. The last place I was at sent out monthly accounts. I just didn't think.'

'Obviously.'

'It seems so thoughtless to ask for money in those circumstances.'

'It isn't. They know it and expect to pay. Chasing unpaid accounts takes up too much time and the bad debts that arise … You see, when you've been here a while your earnings will cover your salary and allow us to make a profit to pay for the upkeep of this place, but at the moment, with no clients of your own yet, you don't earn your salary. Understand?' She turned her head to smile at him.

'I understand. It won't happen again.'

'Good boy. The clients you dealt with yesterday were mightily impressed, especially that canary man. Keep it like that and you'll do all right.'

'Thanks.'

Dodie disappeared inside, leaving Seb to finish his now almost cold tea and reflect on life. But his mood lifted when he remembered he was going to a couple of farms with Scott after lunch.

'We're going to Applegate Farm first,' Scott said. 'Don't be surprised by anything, right? The Parsons are excellent clients, every bill paid on time, but inclined to be hysterical. You'll see what I mean when you get there. Got your wellingtons?'

'Yes.'

'Good. Believe me, you'll need them.'

'But it hasn't rained for days; it can't be muddy.'

'Believe me, you'll need 'em,' Scott repeated.

They pulled into the farm lane. Phil was in the yard looking out for them. He gave Seb a nod, remembering him from the fish and chip shop the previous night, but was obviously too anxious to say anything. Scott expected to be seeing the goats, or more likely one of the cows, but no, Phil headed straight for the house.

'What's this, Phil? I thought I was seeing a cow.'

'It's Little Scott.'

'Your boots off, Seb.' They both kicked off their boots and left them in the yard.

Seb had something of a surprise when he was introduced to Blossom. Having seen Phil he had not anticipated that Blossom would be so ... well ... so glamorous.

'Oo-o-h!' murmured Blossom. 'You must be Seb. Phil said he'd met you buying your fish and chips. Why, you remind me of Scott when he first came to the practice. Just lovely. Believe me, lovely.'

Scott, anxious to know why he'd been called out, said, 'Why are we here?'

Blossom whispered, 'It's Little Scott; she's swelling up and we don't know why.'

'Swelling up?'

'Yes, she's in the basket by the fire.' She waved a vague finger towards the fireplace and then got out a tissue from the pocket of her skirt.

'But you should have brought her in; this is a small animal job. Seb, step forward.'

Seb pulled the cat's basket further into the light.

'Well,' he said eventually, 'it's my honest opinion that Little Scott is about to give birth.'

'Give birth!' Phil and Blossom said together.

'She can't be!' added Blossom. 'She isn't that kind of a cat.'

'I would suggest she is. Look, she's straining.'

Scott was down on his knees immediately. 'My God! She is.'

Blossom went to the door and shrieked, 'Hamish!' three times. Young Hamish, who'd lived with the Parsons for years, arrived in a rush. Blossom, almost incoherent with delight, told him what was happening. His reply was that he'd told her a while ago Little Scott had been up to some hanky-panky with the tom from the caravan site so there was no wonder.

'But I didn't believe you. She's never bothered about male cats, ever.'

'Bit late now. She must have done.'

Phil slumped down into his fireside chair. 'Kittens. Would you believe it? Is she all right, Scott?'

'Seb thinks so and that's good enough for me. We can spare half an hour and then we've got to go. Clients to see, work to be done.'

Seb glanced up at him. 'I could always stay, if you like. Get back on the bus or something. You could see the other clients. Whoops! There's one coming.'

'There is!' The farm kitchen filled with silence as the tiny kitten was squeezed out onto the blanket. The kitten was the image of its mother. Immediately Little Scott began cleaning the kitten's face, then started on its body.

In no time at all another one began to arrive, head first, and this time it was jet-black with white paws.

27

'It is the tom from the caravan park, like I said. He's black with white legs. It is him. I said so.' Hamish clapped Scott on his shoulder. 'I was right.'

There appeared to be a lull in the arrival of the kittens and Scott decided he had to go. 'Take care of her, Seb, she's my namesake. I'll ring in an hour and find out what's happening.'

Disappointed, Blossom said, 'Can't you stay a bit longer?'

'Sorry, but Seb knows what he's doing. Stick at it, Little Scott.'

Another hour and a highly charged Seb, now quite beyond himself with satisfaction and delight, declared this was the last one. It was the smallest of the four of them and didn't begin to breathe immediately. Seb cleared its mouth and nostrils himself and gave it a quick shake to shock it into breathing. Anxiously they all watched and waited, and eventually Seb's rough treatment worked. He gave the kitten to Little Scott and they sat back to admire the afternoon's handiwork.

'Well, I never,' said Blossom. 'I didn't imagine ... did you, Phil?'

'Never occurred to me. But you were right, weren't you, Hamish? She's a right little devil, aren't you, Little Scott?'

'I'll give her a drop of warm milk and brandy, eh? Just to perk her up a bit.' After she'd administered the brandy Blossom said, 'I'd like to keep the gingery one.'

Hamish declared he liked the black one with white feet, while Phil decided he liked the ones that were like twins, with tabby and ginger markings. 'Shall we keep them all? Just this once and then we'll get Seb here to spay her. What do you say, Blossom?'

'I agree. I mean we've no farm cats at all now, we lost

them all when they got that peculiar virus thing, and Little Scott is a house cat really, so let's indulge ourselves. Thank you, Seb. Now look, Hamish can drive you back to the practice. Never mind about catching the bus; it only comes once in a blue moon. I'm sure there's things you should be doing. Thank you so much for what you've done. Sometime we might have an emergency and you'll come and you can see the kittens while you're here. God bless, Seb. They're gorgeous. Really gorgeous.'

Seb was grateful for the lift but after three minutes of his journey back to the practice he wished himself anywhere but where he was. Hamish was the most unpredictable, mad driver he'd ever met. It was when Hamish went through a second red light that Seb realised his end might well have come and he didn't take a breath from then on all the way back until they finally came to a juddering halt in the car park with the most tremendous screech of brakes and gears.

In a feeble voice Seb asked Hamish how long it had been since he took his test.

Hamish turned to stare at him and said, 'Well, don't let on, please, no one knows, but I've never taken one. Most of us don't bother round here, but you'd never know that I'd had no lessons, now would you? Just learned on the tractor and that.'

'Oh! I see. Well, thanks for the lift. I shall keep your secret, promise.' He clambered out, shook his trembling legs into life, and marched as best he could towards the back door, to be met by Dodie, who'd been watching from the laundry room. She stood in the open doorway, grinning at him.

Very solicitously she asked, 'Cup of tea?'

Seb nodded.

'He's notorious for being a bad driver, I'm amazed you accepted a lift.'

'I didn't know. Anyway, it would have been churlish to refuse and one does have to consider client relationships.'

'You're being pompous, Seb. Go and sit down and I'll bring you a cuppa; you look as though you need it.'

Seb nodded and make a vow that never would be accept a lift from Hamish ever again, not if he wanted to live. He had a feeling that Dodie had added something alcoholic to the tea in his mug, but he didn't protest.

The following day was one of those mysteriously quiet ones which occur from time to time for no apparent reason. It was especially quiet for Seb who as yet had no real client list of his own. Scott had a rather interesting farm call to make, however, and suggested that maybe it could be of value to him.

They drove right through Barleybridge main square, but as they approached they met a traffic jam caused by the Barleybridge Hunt. 'Blast,' said Scott. 'I forgot. Just our luck. We're stuck good and proper. Impossible to turn round and go the other way. Oh, well, there we are. Get out if you like, Seb, and have a look round.'

'OK, I will.'

The pavements were thronging with people waiting for the off. The centre of the square, cleared of traffic, was jammed with horses and their riders. There was an air of excitement which reminded Seb of his childhood when he too had gone down to see off the Hunt. The hounds were milling about and the strong smell of the pack filled his nostrils. There must have been twenty-five or thirty of them, all at the peak of fitness, lean, eager, completely silent and full of anticipation. He found himself being sniffed in the vain hope he might have titbits in his pockets. The Master of Hounds and the whipper-in in their red jackets were keeping them under control without the need to use their whips. Seb noticed two hounds had escaped their notice and were running about between the horses. A crowd of riders wearing black jackets had just come swirling down the road to join the others and created something of a flurry as space was so limited.

One horse, a magnificent, well-bred creature, was spooked by the two loose hounds that had wandered away from the main pack. The woman rider had difficulty controlling her mount as it tossed its head and spun about, with the hounds springing out of its way as best they could. Suddenly it reared and when its front hooves came down it knocked one of the hounds to the ground. Someone shouted, 'Jilly!' Another rider called out, 'The hound!'

The whipper-in made his way across, growling, 'Bracken!'

Seb instinctively went forward to see if he could help. 'I'm a vet. Can I do anything for him? I'm from the Barleybridge Veterinary Hospital.'

Bracken was shaking himself, apparently prepared to carry on as though nothing had happened.

'I see. Well, you could examine him, if you please.'

'Certainly.'

'Bracken! Stay!'

It was a serious pleasure for Seb to examine the hound. He was so alert, so in the prime of life, so full of energy, without an ounce of excess fat on him that Seb's delight in handling him knew no bounds. His ribcage was unharmed, and there appeared to be no sign of pain when he felt down his legs, nor when he put pressure on Bracken's vertebra.

31

Seb looked up at the whipper-in. 'I'm pretty sure there's no harm done, but keep an eye out just in case.'

'Thanks for that.'

Jilly looked down at him from the back of her horse and thanked him. She was haughty with a very clipped accent, one of those strong horsey women, fearless in any situation, and possibly older than she appeared. 'All right, is he? Good. I'm Jilly Askew, niece of the Master. Do you hunt?' She leant down and offered to shake hands.

Seb shook his head.

'Do you ride?'

Seb shook his head again.

'I was going to offer you a ride on the estate, but there we are. I'm here for another two weeks. You're ...?'

'Seb Partridge.'

'Quaint name. Nice to have met you. See you again sometime.' She touched the brim of her hat with her riding crop and joined the mêlée of riders.

In moments the decision was taken that the Hunt should leave. The Hunt Master made a speech thanking the public for turning out to see them off and for their contributions to Hunt funds. Then the Master of Hounds raised his horn to his lips. Every single hound gave itself to the sound and set off at speed behind him, followed by the stream of riders in their stocks and black coats and caps, and suddenly the clatter of horses' hooves on tarmac was a distant memory, the excitement left the square and in an instant life was back to normal; the traffic flowed, the pedestrians wandered away and Seb got back into Scott's car.

'That was brilliant. There's such an atmosphere, it's unbelievable. Someone called Jilly lost control of her horse and—'

'That would be Jilly Askew, Lord Askew's niece. He's Master of the Hunt, I think. Very big chap, white hair, red face?'

Seb nodded.

'Jilly's a well-known rider, always comes for the Hunt. What had she to say for herself? Something bullish no doubt.'

'Nothing, really, except she seemed to dismiss me when I said I didn't ride. It was the hound her horse stood on that was worrying, but I examined him and he appeared fine.'

'It happens.' Scott checked the traffic and pulled away. 'Best not let Ginny know what you did; she'll probably have you hanged, drawn and quartered for having anything at all to do with the Hunt.'

Seb had to laugh. Had he known that before the week was out Jilly Askew would be asking him to go out for a drink with her, and that he was soon to meet the love of his life, he might not have been so carefree.

Chapter 3

'Ready, Seb?' It was Scott waiting to take him home to supper.

They called in first at the Fox and Grapes for a drink to give Zoe time to feed the baby and get the other two to bed. 'Well, not so much Oscar to bed now he's seven and quite presentable to people with no children,' Scot explained, 'but certainly young Jake and baby Amelia. You see, Seb, I adore them but then they are mine and I can quite understand that people without children could find them a complete pain.'

'I like children very much indeed.'

'Oh, well. Maybe it wouldn't have been a bad idea then, but us being here for a while does give Zoe some space. You know, I never cease to be amazed at how well she has adapted to being a mother; she's just brilliant, patient, well organised and contemplating a fourth one, would you believe. What are you having, Seb?'

'I'll have half a pint of Wobbly Boot.'

They settled themselves by the huge open fire that had welcomed travellers for more years than any architectural historian could count.

'I enjoyed going round the farms this afternoon with you,'

Seb said. 'It's interesting meeting the farmers; they're all so different.'

'Indeed they are. But if you're interested in surgery you couldn't have a better teacher than Mungo. He is superb. I've nothing but admiration for him, but it's not for me. I enjoy the hustle and bustle of the farmyard, the lambing, the calving, the equine. Small animals leave me cold.'

'Good thing we're not all the same, then. This beer's a bit strong.'

'Never tried it. Never heard of it even. Must be new.'

'I've had it before but this seems extra strong.'

'Empty stomach, perhaps.'

'Could be. How long have you worked in England, then?'

'Lost count. Came, went back home and then came back again. Me and Zoe got together, married and had babies. Best thing I ever did marrying Zoe. Never thought I'd say that. Independent, playing the field, that was me. But having babies – wow! That's another brilliant occupation. By the look on your face you don't agree.'

Seb hid his feelings. 'I'm too young yet. I'm thinking about my career rather more than marriage.'

'Quite right, too. Just what you should be doing.' Scott looked into the distance and added, 'There's plenty of lovely girls round here. You'll be spoilt for choice.' He checked his watch. 'Let's be off. Ginny and Gab are coming, and Valentine, too, so we can't be late or Zoe's plans will go into melt-down.'

A closer look at Valentine and Seb could recognise blatant charm riding high, and when Gab arrived with Ginny he recollected what he'd noticed the previous day, the rugged attraction of a son of the soil.

As they walked through to the dining room Seb caught sight of himself in a mirror and didn't see any of that in his own demeanour, rather the opposite: he came across as mild, self-effacing and scholarly, and was very depressed.

They had an uproarious meal. Stories were exchanged, with lots of laughter and teasing, and Seb loved it all. At home on his family's hill farm, the pressure of making a profit no matter how small overlaid their jollity, and mealtimes were inclined to be dour but this ... this was how meals should be, and he laughed as loud as anyone. Then Scott's mobile rang and Zoe looked at him, waiting to hear his reply.

After a short conversation he clipped his phone shut. 'Call out. Lord Askew's champion Guernsey cow, the one he's won all the prizes with. Must go. You know what's he's like, leaving it all too late ...'

Ginny stood up. 'Let's all go.'

'All of us?'

Zoe said, 'I can't because of the children. You all go; I'll clear up.'

Gab offered to help Zoe with the dishes. Scott agreed it would be a kindness to Zoe if Gab stayed behind.

So out into the cold frosty night went Seb, Scott, Valentine and Ginny. Scott's new Land Rover made short work of the journey and at that time of night the traffic was minimal.

They roared into the beautiful Georgian courtyard where the stables were, and then through the archway to the cow byres. They jumped out. Valentine had never been there before and was mightily impressed. 'This is beautiful,' he said. 'The cows are kept in here? I can't believe it. There are people living in worse conditions back home. This is luxurious.'

Too late Ginny remembered she was still forbidden to come

36

to the premises after the débâcle with Lady Mary's eventer, so she kept to the back of the group, hoping she wouldn't be noticed.

Scott shouted, 'Keiran! Scott Spencer here. Keiran! You rang.'

Keiran popped his head out of a door. 'My God! What's this? A gaggle of vets? Come in. It's Guinevere. I've put her on her own. She's in a right mess. Aborting. No doubt at all.'

Scott led the way in. There was plenty of room for all of them. One brief inspection was all Scott needed.

'You're right,' he said to Keiran. 'What's brought this about, then?'

Keiran shrugged. 'No idea. She's been straining for hours, I just bloody hope it isn't catching because if the others start, his lordship, the old—' Keiran, alerted by a footstep he knew only too well, quickly touched his cap. 'Good evening, my lord. See ... they've brought the big guns with 'em, so we should be OK.'

Lord Askew came in and closed the door carefully. He briefly nodded to them all, too preoccupied by anxiety to bother speaking to them. He looked directly at Scott. 'She's my best ever. Past showing now but she's having perfectly splendid calves, aren't you, Guinevere old girl? And her milk yield is amazing. Well, is it all too late? Eh?'

''Fraid so, my lord. I should have been called earlier.' He refrained from adding 'as usual'.

Lord Askew looked discomfited. Then he noticed Ginny and went on the attack. 'That woman ... what is she doing here? I forbade you—'

Scott intervened. 'We happened to be at a party together

and she came along for the ride. No offence meant, just co-incidence. But she'll sit in the car, if you prefer, sir. I'm the vet on duty.' Lord Askew dismissed the idea, all too anxious to see his prize cow attended to.

Scott stripped off and put on his calving gown and trousers. 'Seb, you give me a hand. She won't bring this one without help. Ropes, Seb. I brought them in.' He turned to Lord Askew. 'I'm afraid the calf may already be dead.'

Lord Askew stamped his wellingtons. 'Blast it. Surely not.'

Scott nodded. 'I'm fairly sure. But I'll get it out and we'll see. We may manage to revive it. After all, it's almost due, so it's not that early.'

Though it felt too cold in the byre to be stripping off, Seb took off his jacket and pullover, hung them on a convenient hook and rolled up his shirt-sleeves to await Scott's instructions.

'The calf's too big for her, but it is the right way round and what you've got to do is slip this loop of rope round the front legs.' Scott handed over the rope. 'Earn your keep, there's a good chap.'

Seb, rapidly recalling his days at college, did as instructed and managed to get the rope tied round the calf's feet with reasonable speed.

'That's it, well done.'

At a signal from Scott, they began the slow steady pull to withdraw the calf from the uterus.

'He's in a good position. Steady now, Seb, use her straining to our advantage ... that's it, slow and steady when she strains.'

Lord Askew shuffled about anxiously. 'Take care of her; she's the priority. If the calf's dead, so be it, though it's damned annoying.' He scowled at Keiran, stood on Ginny's foot by mistake and didn't apologise, eyed Valentine with suspicion, clamped a cigarette in his teeth and lit it, then swore like a trooper.

But Scott and Seb were making progress. The feet were showing and the nose of the calf had momentarily appeared and then disappeared just as quickly, then reappeared as Seb and Scott used another contraction to its best advantage.

'We're nearly there!' Scott said through clenched teeth.

Lord Askew shouted, 'Come on, you two, put your shoulders to it. Keiran, I don't know why you asked these sods to turn out, you could have done this on your own.' He half bit through his cigarette in his excitement and had to spit bits of it out on to the floor, almost starting a fire in the straw which he stamped out with his big boots.

Seb caught the calf as it slid slowly out and laid it gently on the floor.

Almost hysterically Scott yelled, '*Rub* it. Get some straw and *rub* it. Clean the mucus away. Don't pussyfoot about, just do it, work at it, *go on! Hurry up!*' He grabbed a big handful of straw himself and rubbed the calf's ribcage vigorously, but it wasn't breathing. 'The mucus! Clear its passages; you've not done it right. Go on. *Do it!*'

Satisfied that the mucus had now been cleared, Scott picked up the calf by its legs and swung it about in an attempt to shock it into breathing. Finally his method worked. The calf snuffled and coughed and they could see its narrow ribcage beginning to move rhythmically.

Lord Askew was beside himself. 'Brilliant! The little beggar's going to live! Look at him. Just look at him. A bull calf, and does he look good! He most certainly does. My God he does. He'll be a winner, just wait and see.'

They all watched in silence as Guinevere nuzzled him comfortingly and the calf, worn out with his exertions, met his mother for the first time and began to learn how proud she was of him.

'You're a beauty, young man. You're a beauty!' Lord Askew bent to stroke him. 'I'll call you Arthur. Appropriate, don't you think?'

They were all fascinated by the bonding of mother and calf.

Keiran squatted down and finished cleaning Arthur with another generous handful of straw. 'He's a beauty indeed, m'lord,' he said softly. 'What a privilege to look after him. What a privilege. You're right that he's a champion in the making.'

Even Valentine, who'd never had the slightest interest in tending farm animals, preferring the cleaner and more anti-septic care of small animals, found it in his heart to be moved by the beauty of the calf. 'He's one of the best, isn't he, my lord?'

'Come on, all of you. Scott and this new boy can clean up, and we'll all go to drink a toast to Arthur in my study. Champagne all round.'

Keiran, knowing his place in the scheme of things, didn't follow them out to the house, but stayed in the byre admiring Guinevere's calf, thinking of the show-ring triumphs he would surely bring to the house of Askew.

Seb felt completely out of place in Lord Askew's study. For more than two hundred years it had been the hub of the vast

Askew estate and it breathed money and status. The beautifully panelled walls, the stag heads mounted on the walls and the oil paintings of champion hunters, hounds and lap dogs made it a very masculine room. In the centre stood an enormously impressive desk from which, for generations, Lord Askew's ancestors had overseen the vast estate.

The butler had already brought the champagne from his pantry into the study along with sparkling cut-glass champagne flutes, and was busy opening the magnum as they arrived in the study.

Lord Askew proposed the toast. 'To Guinevere's calf Arthur Askew. To him good health and many championships. Arthur!'

When the second glass had been served Ginny began to study the oil paintings. Mellowed by the champagne his lordship went to stand beside her to talk about the horses. She discussed the pictures with some considerable knowledge and he began to warm to her, having at first imagined she was merely examining them to impress him.

Scott, remembering Zoe, decided it was time to head for home. He cleared his throat and said, 'I'm on call. Do you mind if we leave now?' Valentine and Seb were only too glad to be leaving but Ginny, finding herself making headway with Lord Askew, was reluctant.

'Must we?' she said.

Scott said, 'Yes, we must. Thank you for your hospitality, Lord Askew.'

'Thank you for saving Arthur. Greatly appreciated.' He shook hands with Scott and the four of them took their leave.

Standing together by Scott's Land Rover, the idea was

mooted that they'd all go to Seb's flat, Scott and Ginny to reminisce about the time when they lived in it and Valentine to see it for the first time.

So they went to Zoe and Scott's, picked up their cars, and drove to the practice flat, leaving Scott at home with Zoe.

Seb put his key in the flat door and pushed it open. 'Wine – red or white – or beer?'

'Beer! Beer!'

So Seb got out the only glasses he had and began pouring the beer.

'I say, you've struck lucky, Seb, you've got a new sofa!' This was Ginny taking her chance to examine the flat. 'The one I had was lumpy and like concrete all at the same time. I do believe this is brand-new! It's certainly not Miriam's old one – that was silvery grey. Lucky you. Has the tap been sorted in the bathroom? I had it looked at twice but the damn thing wouldn't stop dripping.'

'No dripping tap now.'

'Ooo, who's teacher's pet, then?' She swung round to examine the rest of the living room. 'And a new bookcase! I don't believe this! When I lived here the bookcase leaned over to one side and one night it collapsed.'

They were all laughing at Seb's red face, and Gab made matters worse by noticing that the hearth rug was very superior compared to the one Ginny and he had rolled about on. Then Seb's face went even redder.

'Give the fellow a chance,' Valentine said. 'He's not been here a week yet, time enough for romance. Leave him be.'

They spent another half an hour joking and teasing, and then Ginny said, 'Time we went. Night, Seb. So glad you're working at the practice, you're a refreshing change from the one whose place you've taken. Arthur Hetherington! God! Was he a misfit! Grumpy old man he was, except he wasn't old, but he was grumpy and lazy to boot. And I'm being polite!'

Seb went to bed that night both exhausted and exhilerated by the kindness of his new colleagues. They all worked so well together despite being very different kinds of people. He hoped it would always be like that. He couldn't bear arguing and back-biting; he'd had enough of that where he'd worked before.

Seb worked hard the next morning. The canary man, Mr Smithson, was one of his clients. He'd been so taken with Seb's apparent understanding of the needs of canaries that he'd been out and bought all the necessary wire netting, the requisite shed and the lengths of wood, and, with the help of a carpenter friend, had made an aviary to accommodate some more canaries. His intention this morning was to ask Seb to visit his home and check his amateur construction before he painted it.

Flattered by the confidence Mr Smithson had in him Seb agreed to fit the visit in during his lunch-hour.

'It's not far, I'll gladly come. You must have worked fast to get it up by now.'

'My mate had measurements taken and wood cut while I was still thinking about it. I've left him finishing the last of the wire netting. It's turned out bigger than I expected, but let's face it, it'll make life sweeter for them, won't it? We haven't got as far as nesting boxes yet. See you about ...?'

'A quarter to one?'

'Great. I don't mind paying. It's my big new hobby, you

43

see, and I'm determined to do it right. See yer then.' Mr Smithson scurried out.

When his last client had left Seb went to have a word with Valentine. 'I'm free to assist with those spays this afternoon, but I'm just popping out first to see a client. Won't be long.'

'Who?'

'Joe Smithson.'

Valentine grinned. 'A year ago he decided to breed gerbils but his wife said they were like rats and refused to allow it, said she wasn't having her conservatory over-run with any damned gerbils. He was bitterly disappointed. What is it this time?'

Seb smiled. 'Canaries. He's building an aviary for them and wants me to inspect its suitability. So maybe they'll fare better.'

Mrs Smithson welcomed him with open arms. 'So glad you've come to see the aviary. Joe's that thrilled with it. I've made ham and mustard rolls for lunch – will you have one? Joe and his pal are having a beer with theirs.'

'Not for me when I'm working, thank you. Just the roll, please.'

'A mug of tea?'

Seb agreed that would be welcome. 'Shall I go through?'

'You'd better; he's been clock-watching since half past.'

The avairy, even in its unpainted state and without perches, looked excellent. Joe appeared to be getting into breeding in a big way.

'Why, it's excellent,' Seb said. 'You'll have to advertise – made-to-measure aviaries. It's wonderful. Well thought-out. What about perches?'

'Them's coming next.' Joe pointed to lengths of dowelling waiting to be sawn. 'It's OK, then? I need to be sure.' He was filled to the brim with satisfaction, was Joe. 'I'm searching out a better class of breeder for my initial stock, and when they're all installed I'll give you a ring.'

They settled down on three old chairs outside the conservatory with a weather-worn table in front of them loaded with beer, tea and bread rolls bulging with ham and mustard. Despite the cold Seb enjoyed his lunch, eaten as it was with such companionable men. They talked canaries the whole time; even the carpenter friend had a contribution to make.

Seb finished his roll, drank his mug of hot tea and got to his feet. 'Must go, I'm assisting at three operations this afternoon so can't be late.'

'On canaries?' asked Joe.

'No, cats.'

'Well, I must say you're versatile you vets. Fur as well as feathers. I admire it in a chap so young.'

'Thank you. Will you thank Mrs Smithson for the lunch? I'll go out by the back gate. Be seeing you soon, I'm sure.'

'Thanks for coming. Wait till it's finished and it's full of the little blighters.'

Seb glanced at the pair of them as he closed the back gate and smiled to himself; he was looking at complete happiness and it gave his heart a tremendous lift.

But what he faced when he returned to the practice annihilated his satisfaction.

'Seb!' It was Dodie holding the reception desk phone. 'For you. Jilly Askew.'

'Who?' Seb mouthed silently.

Dodie clapped her hand over the receiver and said, 'Jilly

Askew. Here, take it!' And she stood, openly listening to his conversation.

'Good afternoon, Miss Askew,' Seb said politely. 'How can I help?'

'You can't, Seb. This is a social call. I'm asking you out for a drink. I'm the one you spoke to at the meet, remember? Are you free tonight?'

'Yes, I am.'

'Good. I'll be in The George about nine. Would that be convenient?'

'That would be delightful. I shall look forward to seeing you. Is your horse OK after the little contretemps with the hound?'

'Oh! Yes, thanks. Absolutely fine. See you about nine then. Bye!'

Seb handed the receiver back to Dodie. He felt a little shell-shocked.

Dodie couldn't resist saying something. 'Well, that's a turn-up for the books. I heard you'd seen off the Hunt and examined one of the hounds.'

'Yes. I wish I'd said I was on call.'

'I could always create an emergency and then you couldn't go. How about it?'

'It was so unexpected. What does she want from me? Someone like her?'

'I daren't enquire!' Dodie was bursting to laugh but for Seb's sake she managed to contain herself. Indeed, he was quite right – what did someone like Jilly Askew want with Seb? 'Where are you meeting her?'

'At The George.'

'In that case, smart casual.'

'But—'

'Jacket and smart trousers.'

'I haven't got anything smart. Nothing. What the blazes shall I do?'

'It's the man she's after, not the clothes. Just do your best.' Dodie had to retire to her office. She closed the door and began to laugh as discreetly as she could. Poor Seb. He was like a lamb to the slaughter. Fortunately for him he'd no idea about her reputation, but ought she to warn him? Perhaps she should.

Seb was still standing in reception gazing into space when she re-emerged. 'Seb, I feel I ought to say something. About Jilly Askew. Are you listening to me?'

Seb nodded.

'She's well known as a hunter of men, to put it bluntly. But past her sell-by date, you know.'

'Ah! Right.'

'So be warned.'

'Yes, of course. I see.'

'And Valentine's about to start.'

'Start what?'

'Operating. Spaying, you know. You promised to help?'

'Ah! Yes. I did.'

'Go on, then, get cracking.'

Valentine was just about to begin his first spay. 'Here you are, then. Get gowned up and you start the first one. Everything all right at Joe Smithson's? No problems, were there? You seem very agitated.'

Seb didn't reply. He put on a gown, a pair of plastic gloves and went to the operating table. Sarah Cockroft was assisting.

47

Seb acknowledged her with a nod and made to pick up a scalpel.

'Just a minute! You're shaking, you can't operate like that. What's the matter?'

'Sorry, I'll be all right in a mo.'

'No, you won't. I'll do this. You can do the second one once you've calmed down.'

By the time the second spay began Seb was under control and did an excellent job in Valentine's estimation.

'That is good, very good,' he said. 'Couldn't have done better myself and I don't give praise lightly.'

Out of the blue, Seb said, 'Do you know Jilly Askew?'

Sarah snorted her amusement.

Valentine looked Seb straight in the eye. 'Why?'

'She's rung up and asked me out for a drink. At The George.'

Sarah's jaw dropped. 'Asked *you* out for a *drink?*'

Valentine, realising that Seb was still at the starting gate as far as women were concerned, said, 'How's this come about?'

'By chance. Scott and I got held up by the Hunt in the main square and I got out to see it, and her horse panicked and booted one of the hounds so I volunteered to check it over.'

Sarah muttered, 'You never did!'

'Well, why not? Animal with a problem. What does a vet do? Nothing?'

Sarah declared, 'But the Hunt ... it's taboo.'

'Is it?' Seb looked at Valentine for confirmation.

'In the circumstances I agree you could do no other, but as a general rule this practice doesn't agree with hunting.'

48

'*Everyone* disagrees?'

'Scott, Ginny, Colin ... Dan and Rhodri could go either way. Mungo, if it meant more money in the coffers, would have us as the official Hunt vets. So there you are.'

'And you?'

'Just don't care. There's for and against, believe me. Is that what your shaking hands were about? Jilly Askew?'

Seb laughed at himself. 'I can't think why she's asked me, I really can't. We barely exchanged more than a dozen words.'

Valentine grinned. 'Never mind, it'll be good experience for you.' He began the third spay on a lovely seven-month-old cat, with long brownish gingery fur. 'Isn't she a lovely cat? Not pedigree but somehow from way back a pedigree has emerged in her genes. The owner is a dear old client of mine, a Mrs Bookbinder. She adores her dog and now she's taken to cats as well. Wealthy, too.' He looked up at Seb. 'You'd do well to cultivate *her*.' Valentine gave him an amused wink and Seb had to laugh.

'That's how you keep your clients, is it, by flirting with them?'

Scalpel in hand, Valentine paused for a moment. 'That's more like it; Jilly's only asked you out for a drink, nothing more, so enjoy, dear boy, enjoy!'

So that night Seb showered, put on his very best clothes and sauntered out to meet Jilly Askew, with Valentine's advice ringing in his ears.

Chapter 4

Jilly was waiting for him in the bar looking so much more relaxed than when he spoke to her at the Hunt. Her thick black hair was styled into a sharp bob level with her ear-lobes, her skin sparkled with good health and she was full of *joie de vivre*. In fact, Jilly was a very different person from the one he'd seen mounted on that magnificent horse.

'Good evening, Seb.'

'Good evening, Jilly. I almost didn't recognise you. That sounds very impolite but ... it's true.'

'I know. On a horse I change my character. I'll get the drinks. What's your favourite?'

'Allow me.'

'No. I invited you, therefore ...'

Seb gave in graciously. 'Just this once, then. A whisky and water for me.'

'Right. Hate whisky myself.' She bounded off to the bar and he could see by the way the barman greeted her that she was someone who carried a lot of social weight at The George.

'Here we are.' Jilly sat down, place her vermouth and lemonade on a mat, crossed her long, slender legs and said, 'I'm not the horsey type at all. I ride because the family expect it of

50

me, but I dislike it. Every single one of them rides, including my aunt, daily in some cases, but if I never saw a horse again it wouldn't trouble me.'

'I see. Why not admit it?'

'If you knew the Askew family you'd know what I meant.'

Seb raised an eyebrow.

'The pressure is unbearable. You're dismissed as a complete outsider if you don't ride. Have you always wanted to be a vet?'

'For as long as I can remember. My parents own a farm in the Yorkshire Dales and fully expected me to follow on, but I couldn't. The urge to be a vet was too powerful and though I knew it would upset them I followed my own star. They've got used to the idea at last, thank goodness, but it was very dodgy at the time.'

'You'd laugh if I told you what I want to do.'

'No, I wouldn't.'

'It's so outrageous that if I mention it in the family they fall off their chairs laughing.'

'Try me. I won't laugh.'

Jilly took a deep breath. 'Promise?'

'Promise.'

'I went to Oxford, like all self-respecting Askews do, got a first in medieval history, and have made no use of it since, no use at all.'

'You mean you don't work?'

Jilly agreed she didn't. 'Good thing I have family money otherwise I couldn't survive as a paid-up member of the unemployed.'

'So what do you want to do that's causing your family to fall off their chairs?'

'Teach history in a secondary school. I'd like to be of value in this world.'

'What does your uncle think about that?'

'He's kindly disposed to the idea actually.'

'If that's what you want to do, do it.'

'But Lord Askew's sons and that bitch Lady Mary are so scathing about it.'

'Have you done your postgraduate diploma?'

'No. They'd think I'd gone stark staring mad if I did.'

'Then show them you mean business.' Seb reached across and patted her hand. 'Go for it.'

Jilly blushed with delight. 'You really think I should?'

'Of course. Why not? I'm a great believer in people doing exactly what fires them up, whatever the obstacles.'

'You wouldn't laugh at me, then?'

'Absolutely not.'

Jilly squeezed his hand and immediately they became friends. Seb guessed she was about ten years older than himself but that didn't appear to matter. She didn't seem ten years older with her bright, up-to-the-minute designer clothes and that fabulous black hair, and her slender figure. Her face hadn't a single wrinkle and her large, dark-blue eyes were full of passion and vitality.

'Do you know, I might do it, I just might. You speak from experience – can you say you're convinced you did the right thing, despite your parents' disappointment?'

'I couldn't be happier.'

'Really?'

'Living on the farm would have been all right, but being a vet makes every day ... well, it makes every day spectacular.'

Seb felt her relief when he said that. How come she was so unsure of herself when she belonged to such a prestigious family and had money and standing in society?

'My turn to buy the drinks. Same again?' he asked.

'Yes, please.'

The bar was filling up now and Seb had to wait to be served. He glanced across at Jilly and saw a man was talking to her, he looked like one of those upper-crust people he was inclined to despise. But he'd moved on by the time Seb had been served with their drinks.

The rest of the evening was filled with the kind of conversation held by people who are endeavouring to get to know as much as possible about each other, and by the time they were parting company because it was getting late, Seb found himself feeling great attraction towards Jilly. She was so different from the woman on horseback he'd first met – softer, more kindly and much more understanding than he could possible have imagined.

'Are you free on Friday night?' he found himself saying. 'We could have dinner this time?'

'That would be great. Thanks. And thanks for coming this evening. It's a real pleasure to speak with someone who doesn't live and breathe horses!'

The following day Dodie made a point of telling Seb they'd had an emergency appointment. 'Will you see her as your first client? It's a dog.'

The client came into his consulting room without her dog, and she was in a dither. 'My dog is out in the car. I've scalded him. Not on purpose, of course, but I have and he's, well, he's ...' She burst into tears.

'Look, bring him in and I'll take a look at him, see what we can do.'

'He got under my feet and I got cross with him and then I tripped and ... the kettle ... it had just boiled ... it spilled all over his head and I ...'

'What breed is he?'

'A dog. Oh! I mean, he's a Welsh terrier.'

'In that case, I can carry him in. Come with me. You are ...?'

'Delia Loveday. He's terrified. I can't persuade him to get out.'

Seb took her out by the back door and discovered the dog cowering in the back of her estate car. The moment he put his hand on the rear door the dog bared its teeth and growled exceedingly loudly, then hurtled round and round the car, barking threateningly.

'What's his name?'

'Dai.'

'Right. Dai, Dai.'

Dai growled, showing his fangs so close to the window that it steamed up.

'My word! He's very upset. Doesn't appear to have damaged his eyes, though, so that's a plus. What's his favourite treat?'

Delia Loveday hesitated and then admitted that a piece of Mars Bar was what he liked the most.

'Mars Bar. Right. I don't suppose you have one on you?'

'Here, in my pocket.' The Mars Bar was in a plastic bag already cut in small pieces ready for any emergency. 'I always have some with me when we go out, just in case.'

'Just in case?'

54

'Well, you see, he can be difficult to handle. Bites, you know, if he doesn't want to do what I say.'

'Bites? But you're his owner.'

'I know. But he does. I have to be careful.'

Seb kept his opinion to himself. 'You open the window at the front just a tiny bit, then shut the door again quick. I'll hold a piece of Mars Bar close up to the gap so he gets the smell of it. Where's his leash?'

'In my other pocket, here.'

'Right. Operation Dai. Now ... you be ready with the leash. While he's occupied munching the Mars Bar I'll get it clipped on to his collar the moment I open the door.'

'It won't work, he's too sharp.'

'We'll try.'

They did Operation Dai three times, and each time he got the treat but they didn't succeed in getting the leash clipped on.

The back door crashed open and out came Dodie Pilgrim. 'I've been watching this ... *pantomime* from the staffroom window. Give me the leash. And you can put that Mars Bar away. Mars Bar, indeed. Whatever next? He's a dog not a person. What's his name?'

Humiliated, Seb said, 'Dai. Mind, he's scalded his head, it'll be very sore. That's why he's so frightened.'

'Right! Watch!' In a voice more suited to Trooping the Colour, Dodie said firmly, 'Dai! Come!' She then opened the rear door and said it again, in a tone that brooked no nonsense. Dai hesitated for a moment and then squeezed between the front seats and patiently stood in front of Dodie allowing her to clip on his leash, with not a single fang in sight, nor even a murmur of a growl. 'Come, Dai!' Dodie said bracingly.

A slight tug on his collar and Dai jumped down on to the tarmac.

'In!' Dodie opened the back door and marched Dai into Seb's consulting room. She picked him up and stood him on the examination table, then gently cuffed him under his chin saying, 'There, that wasn't too bad, was it?' To his owner she said, 'All he needs is firm handling,' and marched out.

The moment Dai realised he'd been out-manoeuvred by Dodie Pilgrim he submitted to Seb's examination. Treating him with the greatest respect when he saw the scald on his head and ears, Seb gently studied the extent of the damage.

'When it first happened what did you do?'

'I poured jugs of cold water over it to take the heat out, like I would have done for the children. That's why he's still damp. Did I do wrong?'

'No, in the circumstances you did the right thing. Because his fur is thick on his head I think he's escaped the worst. There's no sign of blistering, but it's red and obviously very tender. I suggest you remember not to pat or stroke his head, because that really will hurt. Let's keep a close eye on him and if things begin to look worse, then bring him in and I'll reconsider treatment. I'm a great believer in leaving scalds alone, no greasy creams, just nature. It's very red now, but that will begin to fade. I will, however, give him an injection for the pain and shock.'

Dai gracefully accepted the injection without any opposition and looked at Seb as though thanking him. This was noticed by Mrs Loveday. 'He's taken to you, I can see. We used to go to the vet nearer home, but they got thoroughly unpleasant with him because of his bad temper and I had to stop going about two years ago. He'd never have let them near him with a needle, not like he's just done with you.'

'Has he not had his boosters, then?'

Mrs Loveday shook her head.

'I won't do it today, he's had quite enough of an upset already. Bring him in when you're ready and we'll do them then. Here, Dai.' Seb brought out a box of dog biscuits from a cupboard and gave him two. 'They'll be better for his teeth than Mars Bar.'

Seb smiled so sweetly at Mrs Loveday that she didn't take offence. She smiled back. 'Thank you so much. I do appreciate him liking you, and you liking him. I'll make an appointment for next week or earlier if his scald isn't looking good. I don't know your name.'

'I'm Sebastian Partridge. Be seeing you.'

'Mr Partridge. I'll remember that. Thank you very much.'

With no clients of his own to see Seb went to help Valentine, who had a full list.

Valentine went to his door and called out, 'Kiki Beaumont,' accompanied by his familiar heel clicking and bowing.

Apparently the cat and the owner shared the same name because as she charged into the consulting room she called out, 'Hi! Remember me? Kiki? And how is Valentine? Gorgeous as usual? Oh! Who's this? You're new, aren't you?' She came to an abrupt halt in front of Seb and looked up at him, bright-eyed and intrigued. 'Oh! I say! This place does seem to attract the most gorgeous men. I assume you're qualified?'

'Indeed.'

'Are you going to deal with my darling Kiki, then?'

Valentine agreed he could and stood back to watch the performance.

'If you'll allow me.' Seb checked what needed to be done by bringing up on the screen the notes on her last visit. 'Right. If you'd like to get her out of the carrying basket …'

Out of the basket came a Persian cat more splendid than Seb had ever seen. She was pure white, almost dazzlingly white, and every single square inch of her extremely long fur was beautifully combed.

He couldn't find words to express his delight. 'Why! She looks beautiful. You must spend hours brushing and combing. Hours and hours. She's magnificent.'

Kiki, the owner, glowed with pleasure. She clasped her hands together under her chin. 'She is beautiful, isn't she? She's an indoor cat. I don't let her out. She sleeps on my bed, and we lead a wonderful life together. If anything happened to her … well … I daren't even think about it.' She shuddered at the thought.

'Hold her, I'm ready.'

But Kiki asked for Valentine to hold her cat. 'I can't look, you see.'

'That's fine. Valentine?'

So Val held her, and Kiki the cat behaved beautifully and was back in her basket in a moment.

'Thank you. By the way, I'm having a cocktail party next week. Could you come? Help you get to know people in Barleybridge, wouldn't it? I've loads of friends; they'll all love you.'

Behind her back Valentine was slowly shaking his head. Seb took the hint. Searching frantically for a reasonable excuse he invented a girlfriend.

'I'm terribly sorry but my girlfriend is in hospital having an operation this morning and ... well, she'll need looking after when she gets out. Perhaps another time.'

He felt a complete fraud, but it had to be done. Kiki showed only mild disappointment, almost as though she expected a refusal, and floated out, leaving Seb feeling uncomfortable at the easy way he'd invented his lie.

'Why did you shake your head?' he asked Valentine.

'My dear Seb, you'd probably find yourself the only person at the party, or she'd have completely forgotten all about the invitation and gone out. It happened to Rhodri and to Graham, a vet before your time. She invites me often but I always say I'm on call. Your excuse was marvellous, though. How did things go with Jilly Askew, by the way?'

'Ah! OK. She's quite different when not sitting on a horse. Really quite different.'

'Do I detect a hint of further drinks?'

'Well, yes. Actually. Yes, you do.' He almost told Valentine about her ambition but decided against it. After all, it was her secret.

But by lunchtime it was all round the practice that he'd been seen drinking with Jilly Askew because Scott's Zoe had been attending a meeting at The George and had seen the two of them sitting talking in the bar.

Ginny pulled his leg mercilessly in the staffroom. 'So you've become part of the Hunt brigade, have you? We'll be having to pay to speak to you soon. You should know we have nothing whatsoever to do with it as a practice.'

Seb was riled by her attitude. 'Just because I have a drink with someone it doesn't mean I approve of everything they do.'

'Whoops! You're cross with me. Dear, dear. Sorry. We

attend Lord Askew's horses and his farm animals, but we have nothing to do with the Hunt and you should remember that.'

Dan, angered by Ginny's attack on poor innocent Seb, reminded her she had been barred from the Askew estate. 'Is this a case of sour grapes, I ask myself, Ginny?'

The wind taken out of her sails, Ginny backtracked. 'It's better he knows where we all stand, Dan.'

'Speak for yourself. If the Hunt decided to have a new vet I'd be the first to agree to us being chosen. Not that it's likely. Harvey Johnson-Munt is well entrenched there, but the money involved would transform the practice profits.'

'Over my dead body.' Ginny was red in the face with anger. 'It's cruel and barbaric and needs to be stopped.'

'Well, it hasn't stopped and in any case they follow an artificial trail now so there's no question of fox hunting as it used to be.'

'Until by chance they come across a fox. The essence of the Hunt is there just the same, and I for one won't tolerate it.'

Mungo walked in, sensed the charged atmosphere and asked Dan what the matter was.

'Just a clash of opinions, Mungo. Storm in a teacup.'

'Don't you believe him,' said Ginny. 'It's more than that.'

Mungo looked at everyone and no one volunteered a reply so Ginny spoke up and went straight for the jugular.

'Hypothetical question, Mungo: if the Hunt veterinary post became vacant for whatever reason, would you take it on if invited?'

Without a moment's hesitation Mungo said, 'Yes.'

Stuned silence prevailed until Ginny said bluntly, 'In that case I'd resign.'

Mungo remembered the times when he'd wished she would and replied, 'So be it. You're not a partner and while I take into consideration all my staff's wishes, such a huge opportunity cannot be turned down, believe me.'

'I see. So my opinions count for nothing.'

'For God's sake, Ginny, you wouldn't be tearing the foxes to pieces yourself, now would you? Simply attending to the good health of the animals involved. I don't want to hear anything more about your principles, nor anyone else's. As you said, it's all hypothetical. Just came to say we're having an Open Day. We haven't had one for three years and it's time we did. It'll be the last Saturday in November. Everyone on parade, OK? By the way, you'll be pleased to hear that Kate Howard is starting on Monday so we shall have plenty of veterinary expertise available ... should we ever be invited to be the Hunt vet.' He glared at them all, then escaped as quickly as possible, leaving behind a staffroom heaving with unspoken thoughts.

Dan, determined to lighten the atmosphere, turned the conversation to Kate. 'Kate! A vet at last! Wonderful! You haven't met her, have you, Seb?'

'No. I've heard about her, though.'

'She's great. We all love Kate, don't we, Ginny?'

Ginny, still tight-lipped, muttered, 'Yes,' and left the staff room.

'Bit younger than you but don't imagine she'll be wet behind the ears. Sharpest knife in the box, is our Kate. Prize-winner, don't you know!'

'Help!'

'No need for you to worry. You're bright enough as it is, and doing so well already.'

'Thanks.'

'If you've a quiet day come with me on my rounds, Seb. OK?'

'Thanks, though I am just beginning to get busy.'

'Good. It takes time.'

Seb, horrified by Ginny's blunt attack on his drink with Jilly, had been on the verge of telling them what she was really like, but held back just in time. He wasn't the kind of person to enjoy controversy but if he wanted to see Jilly then see her he would. He was looking forward to that meal on Friday. But he realised that the veterinary world was a small one, and trying to conceal one's social life would be a waste of time. So maybe he'd have to put up with being taunted by Ginny. Did he care? No, he did not.

Chapter 5

On the day of his second date with Jilly Askew, Seb had been given a routine job to do on an old dog called Chuck. His breath smelt apallingly, caused by his teeth being coated in tartar and food debris. Bunty had taken upon herself the task of assisting him, and pointed out a back tooth which was breaking up with decay.

'That must be painful. Bits have fallen off it,' she said.

'You're right! What a mess for the poor old chap. Why don't people take more care of their animals?'

'Well, Seb, in this particular case, the owner is an almost blind old man who is devoted to poor Chuck and relies on him for companionship.'

Seb felt embarrassed. 'Sorry, Bunty, I didn't know. I'll remove the tooth.'

'No, you won't. Not till I've asked the owner. If more has to be done than first mentioned then we have to get permission, although it's not often refused. I'll be a minute or two. He takes ages to answer the phone.'

Seb carried on taking the tartar from Chuck's teeth, thankful that Bunty knew the rules.

She came back in after a while. 'That's fine by him. He's worried sick. I feel so sorry for him. He manages with the minimum of help, but he does have a neighbour who takes the dog out every day so that's a blessing. Finished?'

'Just got the tooth to remove. What do you think? They were bad.'

'Look, you've missed a bit, down here by the gum on the small teeth at the front.'

'So I have. Let's hope it improves his breath; it was disgusting.'

Valentine was called in to see what he thought after they'd done the extraction, and liked what he saw. 'You're very good, you know, despite not being allowed to spread your wings at your last practice, Seb. Excellent job. Thanks. Why don't you ask Mungo if you can watch him do an operation after lunch on a cat involved in a road accident? Sounds a really complicated job. That is, if you've nothing else on at the moment.'

Seb's mind was immediately seized by the idea and he sacrificed his half-day. By closely studying the X-rays Seb could see what a difficult operation it would be. His practical approach to life made him ask Mungo if in fact it would be kinder to put the cat to sleep.

'Yes, I suppose so, in a way,' Mungo replied, 'but she's only a year old with lots of life still left to live and I *know* I can do it. The owners are willing to pay for my time, and if the result gives her years of enjoyable life then ...'

'But it is a bad break. Let's face it, the thigh bone is in *pieces*. Maybe you won't be able to make it right.' The moment he'd finished speaking he could have bitten his tongue out, and he got the broadside he deserved.

Mungo's face grew pinched with annoyance. 'I have years of experience in this field. Sometimes I do have to say that what you've suggested is the right thing to do, but not this time and don't ever, *ever* question my judgement again.' Mungo gave Seb a tight smile, which went some way to softening his criticism but not entirely, and Seb vowed never to doubt Mungo ever again.

By the end of the afternoon Seb decided that Mungo was right to have confidence in his own ability, because what had been a shambles of shattered bone, nerves and muscle was patiently sorted out, pinned and braced so wonderfully well that Seb was left in awe. A final X-ray of the completed operation showed a thigh beautifully aligned; only time would eventually prove whether or not the cat would have full use of its leg, but Seb was so impressed he just knew she would.

Bunty, with adoration on every inch of her face, wheeled the cat away to intensive care. Mungo called out after her, 'Someone to stay the night, please. Check every two hours.'

'I'll organise it.'

'Thanks, Bunty.' Mungo turned to Seb. 'She's an excellent nurse – efficient, conscientious, dedicated. Where would we be without them?'

'We wouldn't. Thank you for letting me watch. I've learned a lot.'

'Good.' Mungo stretched and yawned. 'That's me for the day. Be seeing you, Seb. You appear to have made a good start. Dodie keeps singing your praises. We've someone rung in who's got a herd of alpacas, and is not awfully pleased with their current vet. Would you be interested?'

'I've no experience but I can always learn.'

'That's the way. I understand from the veterinary grapevine that they have used about four different vets in the area and we're their last hope, so it sounds as though they might be difficult clients.' Mungo walked away looking drained and so too was Seb. It was the level of concentration needed and the meticulous exactness of the work over a long period of time that was exhausting. Never the less, he'd thoroughly enjoyed his afternoon.

When Mungo had gone up to the flat, exhausted and longing for Miriam's warming presence, he found she was out and so too was Perkins. He stood at the window from which he could see Beulah Bank Top and thought he could see her coming down from the top. It *was* Miriam. He watched her striding home and shockingly for a second he could also see the shadows of their two children either side of her. If they'd lived they'd have been … what? … ten and eleven. Would one of them have wanted to be a vet? More than likely. The screaming pain of their deaths within six months of each other roared through him again. He turned hastily away from the window and went to put the kettle on to make tea for him and Miriam. He hardly ever got the chance to do things for Miriam; she was always doing the caring.

When he heard Perkins pushing the flat door open with his nose, he filled up the teapot, added it to the tray and carried it into the sitting room. Perkins followed closely and sat down bolt upright waiting for a biscuit.

'Perkins! No,' said Mungo.

Perkins' ears drooped and he looked exceedingly sad as only he could. Miriam came in.

'Tea, darling?'

'Oh! That's wonderful. Good outcome?'

Mungo nodded. 'Took a while. In fact, I've only just finished. But yes, I think we're going to be all right. Seb's a good chap. Going to be very good, actually. I'm glad you persuaded me to take him on.'

'Well, he's different from the rest. None of that overt sexual charm like the others. In a way ... he reminds me of Duncan.'

'Joy's Duncan?'

'Yes. He could almost be his son. Maybe that's why Joy is so taken with him. He's got that quiet I-need-mothering look just like Duncan.'

'Here, sit down.' He dropped a kiss on her forehead as she helped herself to a biscuit. 'He's astute where operating is concerned, very methodical and precise. Good attributes. Time will tell.'

Mungo couldn't withstand Perkins' pleading eyes any longer and dropped, accidentally on purpose, a corner of biscuit in front of his paws. It was swiftly gobbled up but not so swift Miriam didn't notice. 'Mungo! If you had to exercise him every day you wouldn't be giving in like that. He knows it's no good looking at me for biscuits.'

'He deserves some treats at fourteen. He's not so sprightly as he was, you know.'

'Actually, you're right. He isn't. He's glad to turn for home sooner than before.'

Perkins knew he was being talked about. His ears drooped again and he began to look guilty of he knew not what.

Mungo ruffled his ears. 'Never mind, old boy, it happens to all of us.'

Miriam protested. 'Don't say that. I don't want him to die.' Her eyes filled with tears.

'Darling, he will, you know. It's inevitable and you'd better face up to it. Now rather than later.' He made it sound as

67

though he'd faced up to it himself but in fact he hadn't. Not his Perkins. Not the dog who'd given them comfort when ...
'We'll get another one.'

'Another dog will never replace Perkins.' The tears welled in her eyes again. 'I love him so.'

'Come and sit on my knee.' So she did and they comforted each other, one remembering the miles Perkins walked with her when she couldn't bear being in the house with her memories another minute, the other what a stout companion Perkins had always been to him.

'In any case, Mungo, we couldn't have a puppy in a flat. Perkins only manages because I take him out a lot, but he's old in dog terms. A puppy would go mad in here.' She stood up and went to look out of the window, suddenly desolate, her soul meandering without purpose in some distant wilderness. With a devastatingly sad tone in her voice she said softly, 'Sometimes, you know, like today, the two of them ... they're with me when I'm out with Perkins, like they used to be. You remember?'

Mungo stiffened. The shock was almost too much, that they both had been aware of them at the same time. It was more than flesh and blood could stand. Mungo felt her isolation and went to stand beside her with an arm round her waist. Frantically searching for something to say to lift the gloom they both felt he came up with, 'It's been ages since we had a dinner party here in this flat. How about it?'

'For the staff, you mean?'

'Yes. Not the lay staff, just the others. How many would there be?' he counted on his fingers. 'Rhodri and Maggie, Dan and Rose, Valentine, Seb, Colin and Letty, Scott and Zoe, Ginny and Gab. There'd be fourteen of us.'

Not at all inspired by Mungo's enthusiasm Miriam replied, 'Too many in this flat. We haven't even got enough chairs. Nor plates. And what about Joy and Duncan?'

'We could always bring some chairs up from the waiting room.'

Miriam shook her head.

Perkins got up and went to sit beside her, leaning his body against her legs to let her know he was there for her.

Mungo, not knowing what to say next, muttered, 'Got to go check on my cat. I won't be a minute.'

He stood in the intensive-care room contemplating the cat. She was coming round, stirring a little, puzzled, trying to make sense of her surroundings.

'Now, Kitty, how's things?'

But how were things for him? More so, how were things for his Miriam? He had no answer to that.

Bunty burst in. 'Is she all right? When I saw you coming in here I thought the worst?'

'She's doing fine.'

'I couldn't bear it if she died. She's such a lovely cat, not an ounce of nastiness in her, not even when she's in awful pain.'

'She's young and healthy, should be fine, though it was a long operation. Do her owners know?'

'Of course. First thing I do. Sarah Cockroft's volunteered to sleep in. We can rely on her.'

'Yes, of course. We're lucky, you know, having those two girls. They're so reliable.'

Longing for recognition, Bunty asked, 'And me?'

'And you. Goes without saying. Thanks.' Mungo patted Bunty's arm in appreciation as he left.

Mungo went to sit in his office for a while leaving Bunty glowing with his approval. Suddenly he leapt to his feet and dashed upstairs to the flat.

'Miriam! Let's have it at The George! How about it? Celebrating the real conclusion of our extension now the building work is finished. Eh!'

Not wishing to disappoint him Miriam turned from the window with a smile. 'What a good idea. yes, that will be lovely. A really posh do. No skimping. Posh frocks. Smart suits. Something we can all look forward to.'

'Excellent! Love me?' He swung her round and kissed her.

'Of course. I have no one else but you to love. Loads of people love *you*. For a start, all your clients with pets they'd have had to have put down if it hadn't been for your skill.'

Wickedly he added, 'And Bunty.'

Miriam smiled. 'Oh! I've known about Bunty for years. We all know how she feels about you. I should be jealous but I'm not. It's her husband Aubrey I feel sorry for. Fancy getting married knowing you're a second choice.'

'There's never any need to feel jealous; there's only you for me.'

'I know that, my darling.' Brightening up, Miriam added, 'We'll have this dinner party a month from now, so they've all got a chance to find babysitters.'

At 8 p.m. precisely Seb left for his second date with Jilly in high spirits. He was the first to arrive so he sat quietly in the bar thinking about the wonderful day he'd had. Someone came to ask if they could help. 'Name's Partridge, a table for two booked for eight-thirty.'

'Ah! Right. We're busy tonight; shall I bring you a couple of menus? Might save you time.'

'Thank you, that would be good.'

He couldn't have been there for more than five minutes when in walked Scott, carrying a beer. He spotted him immediately and came across. 'Thank God! Someone I know.' He plonked himself down with his drink. 'Got out of the habit of drinking alone, but Zoe's got schoolfriends coming for a meal tonight and I'm banned. So here I am. Don't mind, really. Eating here is better than listening to all the girl gossip, don't you think?'

'Absolutely.'

'Can I get you a drink?'

'No, I'm fine.' Seb paused. Would he get another shooting from the hip like he'd had from Ginny earlier in the week? No, perhaps not. 'I'm waiting for Jilly Askew.'

'Ah! Right, of course. Zoe said. Second date in a week. Mmm.'

'Look, I took a real blasting in the staffroom about her. I know the opposition but there we are.'

'Seb, you go out with whom you please. If she's OK with you, she's OK with me.'

'Thanks. Are you opposed to hunting?'

'Not personally, but Zoe is. Nearly got arrested once for protesting. However, it's up to you. Your choice.' He grinned.

'Thanks. She's much nicer off the horse than on.' He smiled and Scott agreed that well she might be. 'Here she comes now.'

Seb got to his feet and so did Scott. Jilly looked perfectly splendid and Seb was proud it was him she'd come to meet. He introduced Scott.

'Ah! You're Scott the Australian,' she said. 'My uncle is full of admiration for your expertise.'

'Thank you. He has wonderful animals. I'm glad to have the opportunity to look after them. It's a privilege. Must go, I'm expected elsewhere. Have a good evening.' Scott melted tactfully away but not before, behind Jilly's back, he gave Seb a huge wink accompanied by a thumbs-up. Seb had to hope that Jilly didn't notice him blushing.

He handed her a menu while he calmed himself down. Scott was only being friendly and where would one be without friends like him?

'Scott seems a lovely chap. Is he married?'

'He is. Well married with three children and his wife wanting a fourth. I understand they're very happy together.'

'You're not warning me off, are you? I'm not that kind of person.'

'Of course not. Sorry. It's just that he doesn't appear to be a settled kind of person, that's all. What do you fancy from the menu?'

'Haven't decided. I'll have a drink first, please. My usual.'

Seb's mind went blank. 'Your usual?'

'Vermouth and lemonade.'

'Ah! Yes, of course.' Seb went off to the bar. He felt anxious that they wouldn't be seated by eight-thirty as it was already twenty-five past. Being the sort of person he was, that worried him.

As he handed Jilly her drink she said, 'I can see you're on edge because I was late and we shan't be sitting down at eight-thirty. Don't be. They are here to serve people like you and me; that's what they're paid for.' Looking round the room, Jilly sounded surprised when she commented about how nice it was. 'Smart but very comfortable. Uncle wouldn't be seen dead here.'

'Why not?'

'Not expensive enough. He sets great store by cost. Believes it means quality and nowadays I'm afraid it doesn't, not always.'

'I see.'

'What?'

Seb came out on the side of the badly paid. 'It's all right to have that opinion, but not all of us can afford to dine at The George.'

Jilly looked offended. 'You're not one of those damned socialists, are you, envious of people with money?'

'I beg your pardon. I'm so sorry if I've given offence, that wasn't my intention.'

'I should hope not. It's his money, from his land, and he works hard for it, contrary to public opinion. People always have the wrong idea about Uncle Fergal. He is the kindest and most understanding of men, but he is painfully shy.'

'Shy?'

'Yes. I think it's because he was kept in the nursery all the time when he was a child and then sent off to board at a prep school at eight years old. He's never quite recovered. Imagine being sent away to school at eight years old? Unbelievable.'

'How have his own children been brought up?'

'They all went to school locally and then on to public school at thirteen, then university, naturally Oxford, and then made their own choice of careers. They're expected to fend for themselves financially which can be nothing but good for them.'

Seb was tempted to say, 'Not the same for you, then.' But he didn't, he'd offended her once already.

Instead he asked her if she'd done anything about applying for her postgraduate diploma.

'I thought I'd talk to you again. What do you really think?'

'From my own experience I would say do it or you will regret it for the rest of your life. Do it before it's too late.'

'But what about the family? They'll laugh.'

'Let them. You'll have the last laugh because you'll be doing exactly what you want with your life, just as they're doing.'

Jilly raised her eyebrows at the vehemence in his voice. 'You mean it, don't you?'

'Yes. Whose life is it? Yours or theirs? Ask yourself that.'

Jilly looked hard at him before she replied. 'You look very meek and mild, but underneath you're damn tough.'

'You don't struggle through five years at veterinary college without getting tough. Academically it's hard, and proving yourself in front of clients can be shattering. And I also had to make tough decisions, knowing as I did from an early age that I was expected to take over the farm.'

'Who helps your father then?'

'My brother. Lovely chap but not absolutely A1 up top. Couldn't manage the farm himself without help.'

'I see. Then you were brave.'

'I'm certain you've got the same kind of bravery.' Seb smiled at her and she smiled back. They held the glance for a moment and then both lowered their eyes.

'Better order the food. I'm starving,' Jilly said.

They enjoyed their meal and didn't leave the restaurant

until after ten. Afterwards Seb saw Jilly to her car and was taken aback by the huge top-of-the-shop Jaguar, although he didn't say a word.

Jilly leaned forward and kissed Seb's cheek. 'Thank you for a lovely evening. It does me good to talk to you and I think I've decided to take your advice. It'll be hard for someone like me but I believe I could make it.' She unlocked the car, then said ruefully, 'This thing will have to go. Can't turn up at school driving this, can I? Give the wrong impression altogether. See, I am learning. Give me a ring, please.'

Seb waved her off and wondered if she really would take that first step. With a life as comfortable as hers appeared to be, it would be a tremendous hurdle to leap, to say nothing of understanding the lifestyle and ambitions of the children she would teach.

Chapter 6

The new client with the alpaca farm lived a good fifteen miles from the centre of Barleybridge, and Seb had to turn back and retrace his steps twice before he found it. By the time he drove into the entrance he was already twenty minutes late for his appointment. A shining new sign announced that this was the 'Goddard Alpaca Farm'. As he went up the drive he paused to admire the alpacas in the field beside the drive. He immediately took them to his heart. They were utterly beautiful. Their colours ranged from snow-white to a light biscuit colour, with one brown and two black ones. Curiosity got the better of them and some came to the fencing to get a better view of him.

They were sweetly appealing and Seb couldn't wait to examine them. He pressed on and eventually arrived at some buildings; one obviously a private house and the rest apparently indoor stabling for the alpacas.

As he got out of his estate car he patted it. He hadn't expected a new car, only a hand-me-down from someone else in the practice, but Mungo had stretched to a new one for him and he loved it so. He'd never before felt the slightest bit sentimental about a car – so long as it started up without any trouble it was OK by him – but this one ... well, he was drawn to the Prussian blue colour, its style and the fact it was so easy to drive. 'You're just the ticket, you are,' he said to it.

A voice called out, 'Hi! You must be Mr Partridge?'

Seb blushed bright red, feeling a complete idiot, even more so when he turned and saw who was speaking to him. She was a tall, slim, dark-haired girl, pretty in an odd kind of way.

'That's me. I'm from the Barleybridge Veter—'

'Of course you are. We've been expecting you.'

'I got lost. Twice. Sorry.'

'That's fine. Everyone gets lost, no matter how well we explain where we are. Still, next time you won't.'

As she approached him he saw she was a woman not a girl, but her clothes and the way she wore her hair – fluffed out in a great cloud almost as wide as her shoulders – made her look younger than she actually was.

She reached out her hand to shake Seb's and he found his gripped in a strong clasp. 'Maggie Goddard. My parents own this place. I'm resting at the moment.'

'I'm sorry. Have you been ill?'

Maggie laughed brightly. 'No, I've not been ill. I'm an actress. Resting is what we call it when we've no work in hand.'

'Ah! Right. Shall I be meeting your parents today?'

'Of course! Here they are, look.'

Seb turned and saw Mr and Mrs Goddard crossing the yard. They couldn't have looked more unlike their daughter if they'd set themselves out to be so. They were haphazardly dressed with nothing matching: sleeves too long or dramatically too short; jackets too bulky; boots that looked too big for their legs and faces. Even Seb, who didn't really care what

77

people looked like, noticed their faces were heavily lined, as though they'd weathered badly or had an appallingly traumatic life.

'Good morning! Mr Partridge, I assume.' Mr Goddard marched towards him with an outstretched welcoming hand, as though he too were an actor resting from the stage.

Mrs Goddard gave her greeting as if she were about to swoon from the burdens of this life. She clutched his hand and held on to it for support, saying breathily, 'So glad you were able to come. We do need a person we can rely on … completely.'

Poor Seb couldn't extricate his hand and had to follow her to the field at the back of the house at a good rate of knots, with her chattering hysterically as though deprived of human contact for years. Finally they reached a small field and there were the young alpacas, en masse.

Mrs Goddard let go of his hand and propped herself against the fence, seemingly lost in thought.

Maggie came to his rescue. 'These are the babies. Weaned now and ready for sale. Well, almost.'

Seb loved the look of these fluffy junior alpacas. They were comical and full of fun. One suddenly began a crazy gallop around the field, as if trying to entice the others to follow him.

Mrs Goddard muttered, 'It's the males. We're needing them … we need them to be …'

'Castrated is the word, Mother.' Maggie raised her eyebrows at Seb and tutted.

'Maggie, you're indelicate. They're very sensitive.'

'Why do you want them castrating?' Foolishly, Seb

whispered the last word but received a grateful glance of approval from Mrs Goddard.

It was Maggie who explained. 'Some of these are not good enough to be bred from. Nothing massively wrong with them, but they're not quite up to snuff.'

'I see. I'm afraid I haven't brought the necessary with me. I'll make an appointment and come back fully equipped. How many?'

Mr Goddard took charge. 'Four, that's all. Had a spate of boys, you see, and we don't want the bother of them getting frisky. In any case, we need to sell them ... as pets. Not everyone wants to go in for this job like we've done.'

'You've certainly got some beauties here. How long have you been keeping alpacas?'

'Five years. We bought four from a champion herd, then three more and suddenly in five years there was a crowd.'

'Do you get much demand for them? For sale, I mean.'

Mrs Goddard groaned elegantly. 'Please, don't talk about selling them. It breaks my heart.' She dabbed here eyes, tucked her hand into the crook of Seb's arm and drew him away from the fence. 'Come and see.'

She took him into the nearest stable where there were two mothers and their very young babies. 'Aren't they beautiful? This is why I can't bear to part with them. I spend a lot of time in here and get far too attached to them. Some of the people who come here wanting to buy! My dear, they are dreadful. Quite dreadful. We couldn't possibly let our babies go with them. Heaven alone knows ...' She rolled her eyes dramatically and Seb could see where Maggie got her acting ability from.

'Tea. A cup of tea. I've got it all ready. Come!'

The cups and saucers were an odd collection of old leftover tea services. The spoon for the sugar bowl was wiped clean on the corner of a tea towel which had seen better days, and the milk jug given a quick rinse under the tap to avoid disturbing the mountain of dishes piled in the sink.

Even though he was meticulous in his own kitchen somehow it didn't matter to Seb, because the whole amtosphere of the establishment was so kindly and relaxed, and he really rather enjoyed it.

'Call me Ruthie; everyone else does,' Mrs Goddard said as she poured the tea. 'I like being called Ruthie.'

'Ruthie it is, then.'

'And my husband is always known as Sandy. Don't ask me why because his hair couldn't have been more black as a young man.'

'Thanks for this tea. It tastes lovely.'

'You're welcome.' She seated herself at the kitchen table. 'What do you think to my Maggie?'

'I don't know her, obviously, but what I've seen of her is very pleasant.'

Ruthie bent her head closer. 'She's a brilliant actress but never seems to get the parts. Sad, really. She's on the verge of giving up. One can rest for so long and then … money rears its ugly head.'

Maggie came in to have her tea and seated herself at the table, hugging the mug in her elegant hands. 'Are you interested in the theatre, Mr Partridge?'

'I'm afraid I've never had the time. School, university, work to do, you know how it is.'

'No, I don't. I'm producing a show, though, and I'll see you get tickets. Two?'

'I would be delighted.'

'First week in November. Any particular night?'

'It's difficult to know if I shall be on call. I'll let you know nearer the time. But thank you very much.'

They chatted a while longer till Seb remembered he would be needed at the practice. Standing up, he replaced his chair under the table. 'Thank you for your hospitality. I've enjoyed meeting you and your alpacas. Shall we say next Monday? About three?'

Ruthie came over very solemn. 'Excellent, Mr Partridge.'

'Everyone usually calls me Seb, short for Sebastian.'

Immediately Ruthie gushed her delight, thrilled by the familiarity. 'Oh! I've never met anyone called Sebastian before. What a lovely name!' She leapt from her chair and embraced him. 'I can see we're going to get on famously.'

Maggie also got up to embrace him but hers was not the motherly one that Mrs Goddard's had been, more the embrace of someone who fancied him. Seb gently released himself and fled the kitchen. He drove away from the yard in a welter of embarrassment, red-faced and appalled. How could she? They didn't even know each other. Not the slightest little bit. But then he calmed his nerves by remembering she was an actress and of course they were in the habit of over-egging the pudding when emotions were involved.

Before he left, Seb pulled up alongside the fence to take another look at the alpacas. He got out and buried his fingers in the coat of one standing close to him. It was rich, warm and very soft and he tugged at it, thinking how warm an alpaca jumper or scarf would be in a cold winter. They clustered round him and he found himself hugging them each in turn. They were delightful. No wonder the Goddards had decided to breed them.

Yes, he'd definitely enjoy looking after them.

The whirr of bicycle wheels interrupted him and he glanced up to find Maggie racing hell for leather towards him. She braked abruptly and leapt off her bike.

'Glad to have caught you,' she said. 'I don't suppose you fancy a drink? Tonight?'

'Sorry,' Seb stuttered, 'I'm on call tonight so I have to stay in Barleybridge.'

'Well, I'm in Barleybridge tonight for rehearsals. I could see you after.'

Seb's brain was working overtime but he couldn't come up with a credible excuse. 'If we arrange to meet and I don't arrive it's because I've been called out. It's my night, you see.'

Maggie rooted about in her pockets and gave him a business card. 'No probs. There's my mobile number. We try to finish at half past nine. St Andrew's church hall. It's the church next to the precinct. See you!'

She swept away up the drive towards the house, her hair flying out in a great cloud.

What had he done? He wasn't into acting and such, and that kind of exuberance alarmed him. He didn't really want to go.

His night on call began at seven when the practice was closed for the day, so he made sure he ate in good time so that he wouldn't have to go without his meal. He then spent the next part of the evening on tenterhooks waiting for the

82

phone to ring, but it didn't so at 9.15 p.m. he set off to meet Maggie, feeling as though he had no other option.

There was a large car park outside St Andrew's church hall and after he'd squeezed into the very last space, Seb went inside to search out Maggie. The rehearsal was just finishing and that wild cloud of black hair helped him to pick her out.

'Seb! How lovely you've come! Look, everyone, this is Seb.'

He was greeted with loud 'hellos' and a few wolf-whistles and a couple of 'I says!', which embarrassed him to death.

'See you next time. Remember – word perfect by then. No mumbling, or sneaking a look at your script,' Maggie called out cheerfully. 'Goodnight, everyone!' Then she tucked her hand into Seb's elbow and marched him out.

They adjourned to a nearby pub and sat at the smallest table, it being the only one available. It brought them into close proximity.

'What would you like to drink, Maggie?' Seb asked politely. 'I'm having orange juice in case I'm called out.'

'I'll have a whisky and soda, please.'

'Right. Whisky and soda it is, then.'

As he put her glass down for her he said, 'Most unusual to find an English person having soda with their whisky. I mean, it's all right. I'm just a bit surprised, that's all.'

'I got used to it in the States.'

'You've been acting in the States? Wow!'

Maggie laughed loudly. 'It isn't what it seems. I say that sometimes to impress everyone. They all imagine it's Broadway at the very least; in fact, it was a high schools tour. Taking Shakespeare to the masses.'

'Wonderful opportunity, though!'

'I do love your enthusiasm. We were all second-rate, although the venues were marvellous. But the miles we travelled! God! Some days I woke up and couldn't remember which city we were in, still less which play we were doing that afternoon. I came back and needed a month to recover. I lost weight, mind you, that was a good thing. I'm always just that bit too plump. You, on the other hand, look superbly fit.'

Seb humbly agreed he rarely gained any weight at all.

'That's wonderful. Wish I was the same.' She downed the last drop of whisky and said, 'I need to apologise for Mum for being so ridiculous about what she says in front of the alpacas. As if they know what she's talking about.' Maggie smiled at him and Seb's heart thudded. She was perhaps the most extrovert person he'd ever had anything to do with and she was apparently captivated by him. Touchy-feely, too, always patting his hand or nudging him or downright flirting with him. There was no pretence, so he might as well allow himself to enjoy it. After all, it did no harm.

By the end of the evening he had willingly agreed to see her again. Seb did have a touch of conscience about Jilly Askew, but then there was nothing going on between them. They were, as they say in the celebrity columns, 'just good friends'.

For a brief moment they kissed each other. She was responsive, warm and cuddly, and it was a case of mutual attraction. It seemed to be his year for older women. He didn't think she was as old as Jilly, although not far off. But he didn't care.

What with a job so well suited to his capabilities and with

Maggie so exciting and welcoming, Seb went to bed that night full of happiness. And best of all, he managed the whole night without a call-out. Bliss!

Chapter 7

Seb set off for work the next morning eager to begin the day and looking forward to immersing himself in his job. Yesterday evening had been very successful. He'd thoroughly enjoyed Maggie's company and looked forward to seeing her again. She was the kind of woman he needed – jolly, fun, talkative. You'd never be short of things to talk about when you were in her company, and he loved that.

The postman left him two letters in the entrance to the flats and he'd laid them and the rest of his post on the passenger seat, so at the first set of traffic lights he flicked through them. There were three rubbish ones which would go straight in the bin when he got to work, one from his dad and – what was this? – a letter from his mother, too. That was odd.

At the practice Seb took his post inside with him and opened the letters from home immediately. From his father's letter a cheque fluttered to the floor, and another cheque was neatly stapled to his mother's. The cheque from his dad was wages paid to Seb for helping out on a nearby farm while he was waiting to start at Barleybridge, and the cheque in his mother's letter was from the local newspaper for an article he'd written: *They're asking if you'd be willing to write once a month about your experiences in veterinary practice as a series just for six months as an experiment*, she wrote.

Seb punched the air with delight. Rather more for the money than the idea of writing an article every month. His mother didn't include the editor's letter because she'd put it down somewhere and it had disappeared under his dad's pile of accountancy papers. Seb had to smile. That was typical of their house. It had been the same for as long as he could remember. Briefly he felt a longing for home and went to stand at the window. He looked out across to Beulah Bank Top and thought of the Yorkshire Dales.

Taking his eyes away from the hills he studied the car park for a moment. Surely that worn-out car that had just rolled into the car park didn't belong to the practice? It was far too early for it to be a client. Was it being dumped? No, it wasn't – there was someone still sitting in the driving seat, a woman, and she turned so her eyes scanned the building and came to look directly at him. Immediately she jumped out of the car. Carefully closing the car door behind her, she rushed to the back door, opened it and dashed in. Seb went to greet her.

'Good morning. You're too early for the clinic – it doesn't start until eight-thirty. I just happen to be early this morning. How can I help?'

She was a tiny person, lightly built and exceedingly nervous, and for some reason it took her a while to answer. 'I left home at five. It's my dog, Tatty. He's badly hurt. He fell from our cottage window. He jumps up onto the thatched roof of the outside wood store, you see, and then leaps onto the window sill of the bedroom and sits there in the sun. Someone mentioned Mungo Price to me. That he was a miracle-worker. Are you ... Mr Price?'

87

'No, I'm not, but he does work here and he'll be down shortly.'

'A neighbour said … he'd be able to help … if anyone can.'

The frailty of the woman struck at Seb's heart. There was something very strange about her and he felt an overwhelming urge to solve her problems for her. 'I'm Seb Partridge.' He held out his hand.

Hers was the thinnest, boniest hand he'd ever shaken, and it trembled as he grasped it, with no strength in it at all.

'Look, let's bring Tatty inside in the warm. It'll be better for him in here.'

'I can't pick him up. He's in such pain we'll have to bring him in laid in his bed.'

'That's fine. I'll carry him in for you. What breed is he?'

The smallest hint of a smile flickered at the corner of her mouth. 'He's called Tatty because he's an all-sorts breed, but lovely … yes, lovely nature, you know.'

Tatty whimpered as Seb manoeuvred his bed out of the back of the woman's estate car, and whimpered again when he placed him carefully on the table in the intensive-care room. As the woman's gentle, bony hand stroked Tatty's head to soothe him Seb saw she was wearing a wedding ring.

'And you are Mrs …?'

'Mrs Evie Nicholls.'

While Seb carried out a gentle examination of Tatty, Mrs Nicholls nervously chattered on. 'I knew straight away when I heard him yelp that it was very serious. He's done foolish things before, he's so adventurous. Tom wasn't up. I don't sleep, you see. I'm up at five most mornings. Yesterday that was. I took him to the vet in Culworth and he said a couple of days' rest, but if he had a bad night to bring him in today and they'd X-ray him and see what needed to be done. It's his right front leg, I'm certain. They did their best. But I knew. I knew it was very serious. This Mungo Price, he's good?'

'Well, if anyone can help him he can. I've not been here long but I've assisted at a couple of his operations and he's well ... he's brilliant. But he will tell you the truth, you must be prepared for that.' The moment the words were out of his mouth he knew he shouldn't have said it. She went three shades whiter and almost fell to the floor. He caught her and sat her down on the nearest chair.

'Have you eaten this morning?' he asked with concern.

Evie Nicholls shook her head.

As Seb was about to offer her some coffee Joy arrived, bursting in through the back door as she usually did as though she was already an hour late.

'Oh! I wondered whose car it was. My name's Joy. I'm the practice manager.'

But Mrs Nicholls was past speaking so Seb explained everything.

'Well, I think the best thing is for me to ring up to Miriam and get her to give you breakfast. You can freshen up in her bathroom and Mungo will come down and take a look at ... Tatty, is it?'

Mrs Nicholls nodded vaguely, her strength almost gone.

Joy disappeared to ring Miriam from her office telephone and came back within minutes to say that Miriam would gladly give her breakfast. Then she escorted Mrs Nicholls upstairs.

Miriam and Mungo were both in the kitchen where Mungo was finishing his breakfast.

'This is Mrs Nicholls,' she said. 'Her dog Tatty is downstairs

89

in intensive care with Seb. He fell from a bedroom window and Mrs Nicholls knows something is not quite right.' Joy gave Mungo her special look indicating a serious problem which she didn't want to discuss in front of the client.

Mungo and Joy departed, leaving Miriam with Evie Nicholls.

'Let me show you the bathroom,' Miriam said kindly, 'and I'll put the kettle on and tidy up. There's no hurry. Tea or coffee?'

'Tea and some toast, if that's possible.'

'As much toast as you like.'

Miriam swept away the detritus left by her and Mungo's breakfast and set the table again for Mrs Nicholls. Toast in the toaster, kettle filled, teabags in teapot, fresh butter, jam as well as marmalade, and a quick think about this Mrs Nicholls.

Mrs Nicholls returned from the bathroom and surveyed the welcoming table. 'That's so kind, Mrs Price.'

Very gently Miriam said, 'Everyone calls me Miriam – will you?'

Mrs Nicholls nodded and then added, 'I'm Evie.'

A silence fell. Miriam sat down opposite Evie. She thought she'd wait until Evie had eaten something before she encouraged her to talk.

It wasn't until the toast shot out of the toaster and landed in the African violets on the window sill that the atmosphere lightened. Miriam apologised, saying it happened almost every time but that the best place in the whole flat for the violets was the kitchen window sill as it was where they thrived the best. She brushed the slices of toast down with a clean tea towel and placed them on Evie's plate. Evie giggled a little, but then the giggles turned to tears.

Instantly Miriam was sympathetic. 'My dear.'

With Miriam's arm around her shoulders Evie sobbed. Moved by the sympathy of a total stranger, she broke down for the first time since Tatty's accident.

'There's no one better than Mungo for putting things right, you can be sure of that,' Miriam comforted her. 'He'll probably be up in a while to tell you the situation. He always puts the animal first and will tell you straight from the shoulder—'

'He won't say he can't h-help, will he?'

'He will tell you the truth, and he won't allow your dog to go through hell unless he is sure he will be successful. He can't bear for animals to be in pain, you see. How old is Tatty?'

'He's about four. We got him from a dogs' home, you see, so they didn't really know. He's my life-saver, is Tatty. I was going to kill myself and just in time Tom took me to buy a dog, thinking it might do me good, and it did.'

'He's got youth on his side, then.'

Evie decided to wade into the toast so silence fell again, leaving Miriam sipping her tea and desperately wondering what on earth to say next. Kill herself? Dear God. She couldn't decide whether Evie was trembling because of her anxiety about Tatty's fate or whether she always trembled because of the delicate state of her mental health. Suddenly she wondered whether 'Tom' actually knew where his wife was.

'You told Tom where you were going, did you?'

'I didn't think. I just knew I had to get here.'

'When you've finished your breakfast you should ring him to tell him where you are.' Privately Miriam decided that

Tom must be out of his mind, what with no dog and no Evie, and Evie in the state she all too obviously was.

'I came in a rush. It was Sheila Bissett told me about your husband. She brought her dog here some years ago. I never met it because it died before we moved there and she never bought another, but she said how good your husband was, so about half past four this morning I got the map book out and decided I had to come. I never drive a long way but I had no alternative. Tom is the manager at the village store, so he can't not turn up for work.'

At that moment Miriam heard Mungo coming up the stairs. With both hands under the table she crossed her fingers.

Fearing the worst, Evie got out her handkerchief.

Absorbed though he was with the animal more than the client, even Mungo recognised the desperate state of Evie's emotions, and went about his task very delicately. 'Now, Mrs ... er ...'

Miriam stepped in to save embarrassment. 'Mungo, it's Evie.'

'Ah! Right. Now, Evie, you have a very jolly little dog there, he's a sharp little character and I like him very much, but ...'

Evie swallowed hard when he paused. 'He is a poorly dog. You were quite right to come here. Two days taking life easy is most definitely not the answer. Falling from a bedroom window is not a good idea, and the shock of his landing has broken his right elbow really rather badly. Other than that he appears to be sound. I shall have to scan him and see exactly what I'm talking about. He needs some fluids pumping into him as he's dehydrated and then, when the swelling has gone down, an operation. I can do it, but I have to warn you it will be expensive.'

'You mean you can make him walk? Like before?'

When Mungo nodded his head Evie almost collapsed again with relief.

'I don't promise he will be *perfectly* all right, but he will be much much better and certainly not in pain, which he is at the moment. I've given him something to relieve the pain and make him comfortable, and now I'm waiting for your decision.'

'I wouldn't want him to suffer, Mr Price. Not that. But you haven't said anything about putting him ... well ... to sleep so ...' Evie almost tore her handkerchief to shreds as she struggled to keep control of her feelings.

'If I thought I couldn't help him to have a good quality of life then I would seriously recommend putting him to sleep for his sake, not yours. But I'm confident we shall have a successful outcome.'

Evie left her chair on winged feet and flung her arms around Mungo. 'Thank you! Thank you!'

Miriam interrupted. 'Might it be a good idea to ring Tom and tell him where you are and say how expensive the operation is going to be?'

Evie, with dread in her eyes, stared hard at Mungo, who was slow replying.

'Just over a thousand pounds but that includes aftercare, like drugs, drips, supervision, my time, scans and the anaesthetic that Tatty will need. Why don't you go down to intensive care and spend some time with him? He'll be sleepy because we've given him something to ease his pain, but he'll know you're there. I have clients coming this morning and time is pressing. I certainly shan't operate today as it's too swollen, and he'd have to be here a few days after the operation for me to check him. You could ring each day for a progress report.'

After Evie had gone down to sit with Tatty, Miriam said softly, 'A thousand pounds! That's nowhere near enough, is it?'

Mungo looked embarrassed at being caught out. 'It should be nearer two thousand but I can't tell her that because I'm sure that would be beyond their means. Don't say a word, please. The poor woman. Think what it cost her in fear driving from wherever she's come from when she's obviously on the verge of a nervous breakdown. I can't break her heart, too.' He got up, planted a kiss on Miriam's mouth, lingered there for a moment to gather strength from her love, and went back downstairs to begin his day's work.

While she sat beside Tatty, with one finger poked through the bars close to his nose, Evie rang Tom on the mobile he'd bought to help her feel safe. 'Tom?'

'Evie! Thank God! Where are you?'

She told him what was happening while he served customers in the village store

'But Evie, why didn't you wake me? I'd have driven you. Have you had breakfast?'

She explained that Miriam had given her something to eat.

'They sound very nice people.'

She agreed.

'Evie, how much is all this going to cost?'

'About a thousand pounds – well, over a thousand pounds

– but he promises Tatty will be free of pain and have a good quality of life. You are going to say yes, aren't you?'

'Of course. We'll find the money. Now, please keep in touch and tell me when you're coming home.'

They chatted for a few more minutes then she said, 'I promise I'll call as soon as there's any news,' and rang off. She had to do this all by herself, to prove something, although quite what she was proving she didn't know.

Bunty came in. 'How is he?'

'Sleeping. Thank goodness.'

'Good. We've a rabbit and a cat coming in here shortly; they'll be no trouble so stay where you are if you wish. The shops are quite close if you fancy a walk. I'll keep an eye on Tatty for you.'

'I'll do that. You're all so kind. I won't be long.'

'Be as long as you like. He's well doped up with his pain-killer.'

It took Evie three attempts to leave the premises. She remembered she needed to comb her hair, returned to ask to use the facilities, and came back again for her handbag she'd left in the bathroom. She smiled apologetically at Bunty then gently padded out through the reception room, which was already half-filled with clients and their pets.

When Seb went to see Tatty during his morning coffee break, Evie still hadn't returned from the shops. He said, 'Hello! Tatty,' and was greeted with a slow, sleepy wag of the tail before Tatty fell asleep again.

'What's going to happen to him?' he asked Bunty.

'Waiting for the swelling to go down, then Mungo's hoping to operate on his elbow. Difficult and complicated. But you know Mungo, nothing defeats him. What I dreaded was him having to say that putting him down was the kindest thing. She'd have been devastated, then having to drive home ...'

'Where is home?'

'Some obscure place. I can't remember. Don't ask me where it is.'

'Not round here, then.'

'No, definitely not.'

Evie still hadn't returned by three o'clock and Miriam had reached panic stations. She'd promised Evie lunch in the flat and had now placed it in the fridge to keep fresh. Seb and Mungo scanned Tatty and what they found made them very hopeful of success, but still no Evie. Her car remained in the practice car park looking empty and forlorn, and they were on the brink of ringing the police. Miriam wondered if she'd rung Tom and he'd said no. That had happened before, and they'd had ringside seats to witness rows between a wife who adored her dog and her husband who thought the dog meant more to his wife than he did. Which, considering what a brute he appeared to be, was probably true.

Just as they were closing at 7 p.m. Bunty's husband, Constable Dicky Bird, arrived with Evie. They could see without being told that she was exhausted and fearful.

Miriam instinctively put her arms round her and gave her a powerful hug. 'Evie, my dear! How lovely you're back. We've got a meal all ready for you and you're just in time. Have you had a lovely time?'

Evie nodded helplessly and clung to Miriam with relief, whispering in a tiny voice, 'Thank you.'

Dicky Bird winked at Miriam and said cheerfully, 'I met her heading for here so I gave her a lift in the car. Is Bunty ready for off?'

'Yes. She is just putting her coat on.' To Evie she said, 'You go upstairs and freshen up for supper, Evie. I won't be a moment. You know the way.'

Dicky tactfully waited for Evie to get out of earshot and then, speaking softly, he told Miriam how he'd found her fast asleep on a bench in the precinct and finally sorted out that she couldn't find her way back to the practice and had become totally disorientated, hungry and desperately in need of help. 'Nice little woman, but she's too frail to be out on her own. Bunty!' His face glowed with love which he quickly masked.

Bunty had arrived in reception in her coat. 'Aubrey! What a lovely surprise! I was just going to catch the bus. My car'll be ready tomorrow lunchtime, so I'll be OK tomorrow night. Goodnight, everybody.'

She and Dicky went off arm in arm. They made an odd couple, Miriam thought, but at least they appeared to be happy.

Against all the golden rules, Evie Nicholls was invited to stay the night with Miriam and Mungo. Mungo disappeared back to his office as soon as they had eaten, leaving them choosing chocolates from a huge box that lay between them on the sofa. Perkins curled comfortably on Evie's feet.

'Evie, just help yourself. If you don't I shall, and then where will my hips be?'

Miriam laughed but Evie was finding very little to laugh about because her heart and mind were with Tatty downstairs.

'How do you keep so slim, Evie?' Miriam asked.

'Worry keeps me slim. I worry about everything. Without

97

Tom I don't know where I'd be. Well, I do – in a psychiatric hospital for sure.'

'He sounds a lovely man.' Miriam smiled.

Evie pondered hard.

'He is. As a younger man he was in the police, you know. Drug squad and all that. Sometimes I never saw him for days, although the station rang me, from time to time, to say he was all right. I've never got over it.'

'But you said he was a manager of a village store.'

'He is now. He's safe and so happy. The owner is lovely and they get on well. May I?' Evie helped herself to another chocolate.

Miriam paused while she got a hard caramel chocolate under control; she really would have to stop eating chocolate. 'So if he's safe now, why do you worry still?'

The silence was so prolonged that Miriam was convinced she'd asked the one question which was going to tip Evie ever deeper into depression. But eventually Evie answered, 'I really don't know.'

'Let's think about all the things you should be grateful for. Come on, I'll start you off: a loving, helpful husband with a job that he enjoys. That's a plus. Not all women have that.'

'A lovely house in a beautiful village where everyone likes me ...'

And the list went on for a while until Evie admitted to being an embroiderer.

'No! Really? What a gift!' Before Miriam knew where she was, any idea she might have had that Evie embroidered tray cloths for pleasure was squashed flat as her guest talked about the banner in the church, the hanging commissioned for a cathedral, the piece her embroidery group was working on at the moment for the new council office, the tapestry she'd made ... Miriam listened open-mouthed.

The box of chocolates was put on a side table and Miriam moved along the sofa and gave Evie a tremendous hug. 'What a wonderful talent. Just think how much pleasure you give people, how valuable you are to us all. What a fantastic contribution you make to beauty in this world when so much is so very ugly. My dear, I wish I had a talent like that. I really do.'

Evie's heart gave a leap as she acknowledged Miriam's genuine admiration. She swallowed hard.

'I don't expect you have photographs of your work that I could see?'

'Tom's taken photos although I haven't got them with me. But I could send you copies if you really mean it.'

'Of course I mean it. If you lived nearer I'd come round to see them. You must believe in yourself, Evie. Most people with a heaven-sent talent like yours would be shouting it from the rooftops. I know you're not that kind of person, but you should have a quiet confidence right inside yourself, you know. Your village must be so proud of you. Anyway, look at the time! Horlicks and bed?'

As Evie was wandering off to bed in Miriam's small cosy guest room, which was all restful and inviting in soft greens and cream with one of Miriam's nightgowns awaiting her, she took Miriam's hand. 'Tom has told me the same things, but somehow you saying them ...' Timidly she reached up and kissed Miriam's cheek. 'Thank you.'

Evie went to sleep filled with happiness. She couldn't put her finger on what it was about Miriam that had so appealed to her but as her eyes closed Evie felt contentment flooding through her mind. It was just like stepping into a warm bath.

That night Evie slept right through until the sun broke through and she could hear Miriam in the kitchen. There was a tiny shower room for her to use and this she did thankfully because she never had the confidence to share with other people, worrying overmuch about when was the best time to try the bathroom door and scurrying back to her room if she found it already occupied. When she smelt the coffee she emerged to find Mungo at the breakfast table and Miriam making a pot of tea. Mungo rose to his feet as she approached, which embarrassed her to death.

'Good morning, Evie. Do sit down. I've been to see Tatty and he's ready for the operation. He's made great strides. Why not ring Tom and see if he can come to collect you tonight and take you home? He could come on the train and then drive your car back. You'll know by then that Tatty is OK and you can go with your mind at rest. Ring every day about nine if you wish and we'll give you an update. Eh? How about it?'

Full of excitement, Evie clasped her hands together below her chin. 'Oh! That's excellent. You're more than kind.' Miriam was hovering with the teapot in hand. 'Both of you. Yes, tea, please.'

Miriam asked if she'd slept well.

'Yes, I did. Really well. I was so tired after not sleeping the previous night because of Tatty. That's a lovely bedroom.'

The morning appeared to drag but Mungo sacrificed his lunchtime and began operating as soon as his last client had left. He co-opted Seb to give him a hand and together they tackled the problem of Tatty's right elbow. They began at one, and by half past three the operation was finished. Evie had sat all morning in Miriam's sitting room silently staring out of the window at Beulah Bank Top, hoping and hoping. Miriam had gone out with Perkins and then to the shops in Barleybridge, and finally rang her to invite her out to lunch. Evie was so delighted at the idea of lunch with Miriam that she said yes straight away.

Surprised, Miriam suggested that she ask Dodie to take her to the restaurant. 'It's quite tricky to find, you see, and then I'll take you back in the car. OK?'

For Evie it was a glorious lunch. She couldn't quite put her finger on why Miriam was so good for her but she was. With Miriam there she had no doubts about the success of Tatty's operation and could talk to her like a lifelong friend.

Miriam, aware that things were difficult for Evie, still didn't sense quite how deeply demanding Evie found every aspect of her life to be, and chattered on about this and that, hoping it all might do some good. As for Evie, it was the loveliest lunch she'd ever had. Gone were her anxieties about dealing with the waitress and eating in public, which closed up her throat and made swallowing so hard, and she could talk about going into hospital and how she 'lost' the real Evie once she got in there.

'Evie! How terrible for you. It won't do, you know. With the wonderful gift you have for embroidery, what do you have to worry about? Tom is safe now, no longer do you have to fear for his life, and Tatty is going to be well, I'm sure. So?'

Evie finished buttering another cracker and piled some Brie on to it, but before she took a bite she put it down saying, 'There isn't anything, is there?'

'No.'

'I would have loved to have given Tom children but there's no way that can be now, as I'm too old.'

'Does Tom go on about that?'

'No.'

'Then ...'

'I'm going to have to try to be cheerful and confident for Tom's sake, aren't I?'

'Yes, make that your target. Think how wonderful it would be for him to have you well and happy. And for your own sake, too.'

Evie popped the cracker into her mouth, chewed it, and swallowed it down with a gulp of coffee. 'I've been selfish, haven't I?' she said.

Miriam protested. 'No, no.'

'You're not selfish, are you? Not for one minute.'

Miriam studied this question and then had to smile. 'I try not to be.'

'Then I shall try, too. Can we go now? I want to see Tatty. Will they have finished, do you think? I can't believe that life might go right for me, because it never appears to.'

Miriam looked hard at her. 'Maybe from now on it's going to go right for you and for Tom. OK?'

When they eventually got back to the practice the operation was over and Mungo was well satisfied. Tatty would be properly awake in an hour.

Colour flooded Evie's face and she kissed Mungo on the cheek. Then she spotted Seb settling Tatty in a cage in the recovery room, and he received a big kiss too, as well as a hug. He flushed with embarrassment, and so did Evie, astonished at herself for spontaneously kissing total strangers. But then they were no longer strangers but dear friends. Above all, Tatty was to be restored to her. She'd have the pleasure of taking him over the fields behind Hipkin Gardens every day with the wind blowing his rough, gingery fur in every direction and his dear bright eyes checking her whereabouts every two minutes as he ran about. In gratitude, she'd put Tom first from now on and remember each day to count her blessings, just as Miriam had taught her.

Chapter 8

When Seb arrived at the practice the following morning he went first to see Tatty, and found him comparatively perky. His eyes were bright and he was munching his breakfast.

'Good morning, Tatty. You look better than you did last night.'

Sarah came in. 'Morning, Seb. He looks good, doesn't he? Very bright this morning, is our Tatty. Evie Nicholls is such a lovely lady, isn't she? I did like her.'

'Yes, she is a real lady, but so afraid of life. Has he tried standing up?'

Sarah shook her head. 'Not that I've seen, but it's early days. He's had his prescription, after some persuasion, and he's eaten most of his breakfast.'

'Excellent. Mungo never fails to impress, does he?'

'I remember only once when he didn't impress. The dog never recovered, and the owners were devastated and threatened to sue him. However, they changed their minds, thank goodness. It wasn't Mungo's fault. Oh, listen! That sounds like Kate! Must go. Come and meet her!'

So this was the famous Kate. No one had ever said a bad word about her so he wondered just what she would be like. A paragon of all the virtues, perhaps? Arrogant with it?

She was standing in the midst of what appeared to be the whole of the staff. He stood on the fringe, listening to the excited chatter.

Mungo was saying, 'Champagne tonight when we've closed, Miriam says, in the flat. Everyone must stay. Welcome on behalf of us all. We've waited a long time for this day, haven't we, Kate?' He kissed her on both cheeks and then stood back. 'Yes, a long time. Welcome to the Barleybridge Veterinary Hospital.' He was beaming from ear to ear. Seb had never seen him looking so genuinely gleeful.

Then he looked at Kate. She appeared to him to be a clean-cut, no-nonsense sort of person, and the word that sprang to mind as he looked at her was wholesome; clear-skinned, bright blue eyes, long fair hair. Lost in admiration, he didn't notice that Dodie was saying, 'And this is Seb, our newest addition and already beginning to make a name for himself.'

'How do you do,' Seb managed. 'I hope you'll be very happy here. I've heard a lot about you.'

Privately he didn't think he could have found a more trite thing to say. He sounded like something out of a teach-yourself-social-skills manual. He felt a complete fool and wanted to creep away as fast as possible. So he did, muttering, 'First client here any minute.'

In fact, no one was due, but he hid in his consulting room trying to look busy. How could this Kate make him feel such an idiot when she'd not said a word? She was, according to what he'd heard, very bright and Seb felt intimidated by that prospect. He guessed she'd be the first with a diagnosis and a cure, one of those super-vets with that special something which made every dog and cat putty in their hands.

After a long, gruelling day attending to every sort of illness, every single awkward client and a cat whose illness he simply couldn't diagnose, he crawled up the stairs to Miriam and Mungo's flat for the champagne 'do' to celebrate Kate's arrival.

What impressed him most was the enthusiasm they all had for Kate, lay staff and vets alike, and he willingly admitted to himself that Kate was something special, not to mention attractive and outgoing. He imagined she'd have been very popular at college.

He sipped two glasses of champagne, persuaded to the second one by Dodie who was determined he should enjoy himself, but he kept well to the edge of all the chatter, somehow needing time to assess Kate. She might be bright but he'd heard that, like himself, she hadn't passed her finals first time round, and had to do a re-take in November.

A great deal of the time at the get-together was spent remembering incidents which had taken place when Kate spent a year working on accounts before she went to college.

'Remember that time when she had to throw water from the old fire bucket over Perkins and Adolf fighting and most of it landed on Mungo's trousers,' said Joy. 'And that time when Scott fell in Phil Parson's slurry pit right up to his chest and came back to the practice covered in cow dung and she had to hose him down outside the back door?'

'And,' said Rhodri, 'don't forget that time when Phil Parsons came looking for Scott waving that billhook at the clients and frightening us all to death, and Kate calmly took the billhook off him and got him to sit down and wait for Scott? That was her big moment and not half!'

Kate laughed. 'I'd forgotten all about that. Joy wondered if Scott must have been making overtures to Blossom.'

Scott was indignant. 'I most certainly had not.'

Seb had no memories, of course, but he enjoyed the stories and laughed as loud as everyone else. When the party began thinning out Seb went home to cook his evening meal. Afterwards he cleared up and made his kitchen tidy, then he sat down feeling rather lonely after all the fun. So he was glad when his phone rang just as he'd decided to relax and drown his sorrows in mindless TV.

'Hello-o-o! Maggie here, Seb. We've just finished rehearsal. Fancy a drink?'

'That would be lovely. Same pub?'

He listened to the breathy excitement that was Maggie. 'Exactly. Ten minutes?'

'See you then.'

Maggie had chosen to sit at a table all by herself in the bar, leaving the raucous crowd of amateur actors to take care of themselves. Seb marched in and greeted her with a kiss.

'My treat!' he declared, seeing she had waited for him to arrive before ordering a drink. He sensed a lot of nudging and winking going on in that crowd of friends but he didn't care.

'G and T, please.'

As he made his way towards the bar, the theatre crowd whistled at him. He acknowledged them with a nonchalant wave and ordered the drinks.

Returning to Maggie he caught an admiring look on her face which she quickly disguised when she realised he'd noticed. 'Had a good week so far?' she asked him when he'd sat down.

'Yes, thanks. And you?'

'Well, believe it or not, I have exciting news.' She drew in a great big breath and paused just long enough to make him tip-toed with curiosity. 'I've an audition for a new TV soap next week!'

'No! That's wonderful news. You must be so excited.' He grasped her hand and squeezed it.

'I am! But one never knows. You can get taken on and then they change their minds or the pilot doesn't work out or the script-writer can't follow it up with more good episodes. It's all so unpredictable.'

'But still, getting asked puts you in the picture, so to speak. A real plaudit for your ability as an actress.'

'Oh, yes. I've been on cloud nine since I heard. This could be my big break-through. I've always imagined I was destined for the RSC – you know, Stratford and the rest – but since I've got older I've decided to lower my sights. Got more common sense now.' Maggie tapped her glass against his. 'So wish me luck.'

'Of course. All the luck in the world. I'm very pleased for you.' Seb was so delighted with her chance to succeed that he leaned across the table and lightly kissed her cheek, enjoying the fresh floral smell of her. 'I'll be thinking of you. Are you auditioning for a specific part?'

'Well, certainly not the young romantic lead; those days are long gone. I shall be a divorcee determined not to get ensnared again, hiding her dissatisfaction with a quick-fire sense of humour and, on occasion, an acid tongue. I'm a sad librarian. In the soap, I mean.'

Maggie asked him about his day, then, so Seb told her about Tatty and how it looked as though the operation would work out, how sad it was about Evie being so scared of life, and about their new member of staff. Maggie listened so intently to his tale, demonstrating an awareness of how Evie must feel, that Seb warmed to her more than ever before.

'And Tatty? What are his chances of a normal life?'

'With Mungo having done the operation his chances are high. He is so gifted. It's a privilege to watch him at work. I'm very lucky that he lets me assist.'

'You must be good if he lets you assist him. You've only been there a short time.'

Seb smiled. 'I've an awful lot to learn yet. Believe me.'

'Don't under-estimate yourself. I don't mean be overly confident because you're not that kind of person, I know that.'

Seb attempted to change the direction of their conversation. 'How are your alpacas?'

'Fine.' Maggie reached across the table to pat his hand. 'Mum was most impressed with the efficient and kindly way you dealt with them. You're her kind of vet. She thinks you're lovely because you must have a soul.' She giggled helplessly.

Seb threw back his head and laughed. 'That'll do for now. I'm not used to lots of praise. In Yorkshire you're thrilled to bits if someone says, "Tha's done well there, lad," and that's all you get, but when it's well meant ...'

'Exactly.' Maggie downed the last of her gin and tonic. 'Have you seen that new film just out? The one about the mountaineer up Kilimanjaro?'

'No.'

'I know one of the minor actors in it – worked with him in a children's theatre group – and I'd like to see it.'

Seb, without being asked, checked his diary. 'I'm not on call till next Tuesday.'

There was a hint of relief in her voice when she answered him. 'You'd like to go? What about Sunday night?'

'Absolutely.'

'Good.'

'Shall I pick you up?'

'No, thanks. Too far for you to come. I'll meet you outside the cinema. You know Cineworld, the one in the precinct?'

'I don't know the screening times.'

'I thought we'd go to the late one so we'll meet at a quarter to eight outside the cinema and go for a drink first, all depending on times. OK?'

'Great.'

Outside the pub Maggie reached up and gave him a kiss on his cheek, hugging him briefly. 'Goodnight. Thanks for the G and T.'

As Seb drove home he decided that Maggie was a thoroughly pleasant person. A very lovable person, in fact, and he looked forward to seeing her on Sunday.

The next day Seb had a request from the Goddards for an afternoon visit, and a full morning clinic for the very first time. He felt enormously bucked by that because he found the slow building of a regular clientele was becoming irksome. One of his clients was the canary man, with a sickly-looking canary in a box.

'Good morning, Mr Smithson. What can I do for you this morning?'

'It's this little girl of mine. She's drooping all day long and it can't be right because all the others are springing about the aviary, singing and enjoying life, and she sits huddled up doing nothing.'

'Let's have a look. You get her out.'

Mr Smithson gently lifted the canary out. 'She's called Joan, after Joan Sutherland. You know, the singer?'

Seb nodded, wondering when Mr Smithson was going to run out of opera singers. He examined Joan very gently, not wanting to alarm the poor thing. 'Have you got the nest boxes fitted up?'

'Indeed I have. Ever the optimist, I've got six boxes. I'm just waiting, hopefully, for some eggs ...' He smiled.

'Is she eating?'

'No, that's part of my worry. I don't catch her eating.'

'I wonder if ... Joan ... is broody. They can have very funny moods when they are. What she's really wanting is some eggs to sit on. After all, she'd be huddled up if she had eggs.'

'My word, young man, I never thought about that. Am I glad I met up with you! Of course, that could be it.'

'I'm not saying it is, but I can find nothing wrong with her at all. So it is a possibility. They do go off their food sometimes.'

'If I got a couple of pot eggs to give her the idea, like ...'

'It might satisfy her.'

'I'll put the pot eggs in a nesting box and see how she does. OK? That carpenter friend of mine who helped make the aviary has got so interested he's been round nearly every day since I got these, and he's decided to get some for himself. So I've recommended he uses you as his vet. How about that?'

'I'm very flattered.'

The morning wore on with clients involving him in all sorts of problems, but the last one before lunch caused him to ask for a second opinion from Valentine.

Valentine came in between clients.

'Let me see. How old is he?'

Seb explained the situation. 'This is a seventeen-year-old male cat called Hector. Been fit as a flea all his life then developed kidney problems. They're new to this area and recently the tablets he's been having regularly don't appear to be working any more. He's become seriously incontinent.'

'Right.'

Seb realised he hadn't introduced the client to Valentine, so anxious was he to relay the symptoms to him. 'I'm sorry, this is Valentine Dedic. Val, this is Mrs Benton.'

'Mrs Benton.' Valentine inclined his head and clicked his heels, and the client blushed.

'Does he have free access to the outside as he's always had? Cat flap, you know?'

'Yes.'

'Has he changed at all? He is old, you see. Do you think he appears confused?'

'Funny you should say that, but, yes, he does. He gets mixed up with which doorway is which and can't always find his water bowl. He's always slept in his own bed at night, but now he goes to sleep in the silliest of places.'

Valentine examined Hector's eyes. 'Nothing wrong there, no clouding of the eyes at all. So it's not poor sight that's causing confusion. Look, if Seb here agrees, I suggest we change his prescription. His old tablets are obviously not working any more. That should do the trick. If not, he might be getting mixed up because of moving house, and his age is making it difficult for him to adapt. Seventeen is very old. Will you do as I suggest? Come back if there is no improvement. Let's face facts, Mrs Benton, an incontinent male cat is not the best thing in a nice house, is it?' He smiled at her, then clicked his heels and retired to his own consulting room leaving Seb to arrange a new prescription.

Mrs Benton heaved old Hector back into his carrying basket. Breathing heavily, she said, 'He's really saying that ... in view of Hector's age ... if there's no improvement, it would be kinder ... you know ...'

'Yes, I do believe he is.'

'Do you agree?'

'Let's wait and see. Perhaps another few weeks with the new prescription will sort him out. Find his way about your new house, you know. Give it a try.'

Mrs Benton rose to the occasion. 'Look! He's been our best friend all his life. I'm not going to have him put to sleep for my convenience. Nice house indeed! What's that to do with anything? I ask you! My old dad lives with us and I wouldn't put him to sleep just when he needs extra care. I'm not going to put Hector to sleep, either. So there.'

Mrs Benton stormed out of the consulting room in high dudgeon. Seb did consider rushing out after her but decided against it. Val's idea of putting him to sleep might be the best in the end. He rather hoped that time and the new prescription might solve everything.

In the staffroom during lunch Valentine asked Seb what Mrs Benton had decided to do.

'She was furious you implied that Hector should be put to sleep.'

'I said no such thing.'

'No, but you hinted at it and she's determined she's not doing it.' Seb had to laugh at Valentine's angry face.

Dodie Pilgrim, listening in to their conversation, asked Val if he always recommended the final solution when an animal proved difficult.

Now he really did get angry. 'Of course not! But can you imagine what it must be like in their house with a tom cat urinating everywhere? Disgusting. I'm afraid animal-lovers can be soft in the head at times.'

Dodie patted his arm. 'I was only teasing. Where I worked a few years ago we had a vet who put anything on four legs to sleep almost before the owner had understood his intentions. We got very good at treating clients for shock.'

'What happened to him?'

'Well, Val, his client list dwindled to a point where he had to go. Clients refused to have their pets treated by him. They'd ask for an appointment and say,"I don't want to see Killer Kershaw, thank you very much." It all got very embarrassing.'

'Well, rest assured that won't happen to me.' Val wandered off.

Thinking of Maggie, Seb asked, 'Dodie, this dinner we're having at The George, can we bring a friend?'

'So long as it's someone appropriate. I know you've not been here very long to have lots of friends.'

'It's Maggie Goddard, daughter of a new client of ours.'

'Oh! Right. I see. Well, yes, all right, if she's free.'

At the Goddards' that afternoon, Seb was asked to look at two of the alpacas.

'You see, Seb, it's nothing in particular, like walking lame or coughing or something, it's just a feeling I have.' Ruthie put her head to one side beguilingly. 'I have this instinct where animals are concerned, you see, and it's my instinct which made me ring you. This one here by the fence must know you've come to see him! Bless. And the brown female just the other side of him. Off colour is the best thing I can describe it as. Yes, off colour. Mimi! Carlos! Come to Mummy!'

Seb clambered over the fence and began an examination of the pair of them. The other ones in the field came to see what the fuss was about, pushing in with their noses and trying to take part in the examination. The two of them were definitely too thin for comfort, and not so lively as the other young ones. He climbed back over. 'Need my stethoscope. Won't be a moment.'

He came back with it slung around his neck looking every inch the professional man and, what was more, in Ruthie's eyes, very interesting. Despite the age gap between him and Maggie, because Seb couldn't be much more than twenty-six and Maggie was in her late thirties, she felt he would be a suitable match. Yes! This could be the one, she thought.

When she noticed that Seb was looking grave her heart almost stopped. 'What is it?'

'I don't know for sure. I'll have to get a second opinion. Have you ever had TB?'

'Me?'

'No, I mean have the alpacas ever shown up as having TB?'

'Oh! God. No!'

'I could be very wrong in my diagnosis. But they haven't lost weight for no reason at all.'

At that tragic moment Maggie returned home. 'Seb! I thought you'd have gone by now. How lovely I've caught you.'

Ruthie, on the point of swooning, said stoically, 'Seb thinks they've got TB.'

Seb protested. 'I said I didn't know for sure. It might be something quite different.'

Knowing how her mother would be affected by this news, Maggie put an arm round Ruthie's shoulders. 'Which ones, Mum?'

'Mimi and Carlos. My dearest ones.'

'Mum! *All* of them are your dearest ones, let's be honest.'

Ruthie reached out over the fence to catch hold of Seb's arm. 'Will it mean ...?'

'Let's stay positive, shall we?' He climbed back over the fence and stood leaning on it, staring at Carlos and Mimi.

'What now?' asked Maggie.

'I'll be in touch tomorrow. Just to be safe, separate them from the others.'

'Sandy saw a puma a few weeks ago, along the bottom of the hedge in the top field. Could that be to blame?'

'Really? That's interesting. No, that can't be blamed.'

'He fired his gun and it ran off. People have been sighting it for months now, although the police pooh-pooh the whole idea. But Sandy's no fool.' Ruthie said this proudly, as though Sandy were six years old and had been a clever boy at school. 'No, if he saw a puma then he saw a puma and no mistake.'

Seb remembered about the dinner and turned to tell Maggie about it. 'Would you care to go?' he asked, hoping she'd say yes.

Her face lit up. 'If you're sure that's OK. I wouldn't want to intrude where I'm not wanted. Yes, I'd love to. Dinner at The George, you say. I'll need a smart frock, then. When is it?'

'Two weeks today. Seven for seven-thirty.'

Seb said goodbye to Ruthie and he and Maggie walked back to his car.

'Thank you so much for inviting me. I feel privileged,' Maggie said.

'I'll ring in the morning about Carlos and Mimi. Don't let Ruthie worry too much. I could be completely wrong.'

'Or completely right.' She stood in the sun in the yard looking perfectly splendid, waving energetically to him until he disappeared from view. Glancing through his rear-view mirror, Seb saw her skip with delight just before he lost sight of her. He couldn't help but like her. She really was a lovely person, so fresh and attractive.

A phone call interrupted his thoughts. It was Joy asking him to call on the Parsons at Applegate Farm. 'His chickens have all died. They can't understand it. Poor Blossom is having hysterics as usual. Stay calm, Seb. Bye!'

He arrived at the farm and, as he'd been advised the first time he came, put on his wellington boots before he entered the farm yard. Blossom was hovering in the doorway of the house, waving desperately.

'Seb! It's you. Joy said it might be. Oh, Seb, whatever shall we do?'

'Let me look first.'

So he studied the five chickens laid out almost reverently, side by side, in the chicken run. Blossom had covered them with a plastic sheet as though they were human corpses. Seb kept a straight face.

'Well, they've definitely not been attacked.'

'Oh, no. Hamish locks them up every night for certain. Foxes, you know.'

'Phil about?'

'No, he's very upset. This is Lavender. He bought her when he decided to go in for chickens in a big way.'

'How many did you have?'

'Twelve to start with, as an experiment, but it never got any further. These are all old. Most of them are past laying.'

'You didn't wring their necks, then?'

Blossom's reaction to this question was to draw a lace handkerchief from her skirt pocket – did he say skirt? It was more like a pelmet – and blew her nose. 'Of course not. How could we? They're our friends. The first one is Lavender, like I said, then there's Clarissa, Clementine, Goldie, on account of her lovely colour – well, it was lovely, looks a bit worse for wear now – and that's Lolita.'

'Well, I think the best thing is for me to get them to the Veterinary Investigation Centre and they'll do a post-mortem. It must be something in particular for all five to go at once. You need to know what caused it.'

Blossom gripped Seb's arm to steady herself. 'I'll have to ask Phil. Oh, God! Post-mortem. Oh, no.'

'We need to know, as I'm sure you'll want to re-stock, and knowledge is the best weapon against it happening again, you see. Bring in new stock and the same thing could happen all over again. But we will know once the centre has done the post ... investigated them.'

Eventually Seb was allowed to depart with the chickens carefully secured inside a large plastic bag.

He reported what had happened to Joy when he got back to the practice. 'They were devastated. Phil had been hiding in the house but Blossom insisted we ask his permission for the post-mortem and he had to have a brandy to brace himself. Are they always like that?'

'Always. They are sentimentally attached to every animal they own. Not in it for the money, you see.'

'They don't *look* well off.'

Joy leaned forward over the counter. 'Between you and me, no one's supposed to know, they own Applegate Caravan Site further down the lane. Started more as a fluke than anything. Someone stopped one day and asked if they could camp in that field for a few days and it quite simply took off from there. They make a fortune between May and September, I understand, and surprisingly, considering the state of the farm, the caravan site is immaculate and the facilities second to none. Anyway, we'll wait for the result on these chickens, Seb. Thanks for that. Off you go home.'

Seb got the results two days later and made space in his day to call in at Applegate Farm. Blossom was out shopping with Hamish, so it was Phil who received the news. He was standing leaning against a wall keeping his prize bull, Star, company. 'Come in, come in, Seb. Well, tell me the worst.'

'Good thing we had a post-mortem done, because if you'd re-stocked immediately exactly the same thing would have happened again.'

'No! Whatever is it?'

'An attack of red mite.'

'What's them?'

'Tiny little beggars who run along the perches, up the chickens' legs and into their feathers to suck their blood.'

Phil paled. 'But I've never seen little red things. Never. How can it be?'

'They're very crafty. They wait till it's dark and then emerge.' Seb felt he had to be very blunt otherwise he'd never get the message home. 'Eventually the chickens drop off their perches due to lack of blood in their veins.'

'I don't believe it. It can't be true. Tell the chap to do it again.'

'I'm afraid they'll have been incinerated already. So—'

'Stop right there. I'm telling you I've never seen any red things in that chicken house.'

'When they're full of blood they go back to any nook and cranny they call home before it gets light, Phil. That's why you don't see them.'

'We've no red mites in that chicken house. Why, before we bought the farm it was a chicken house and has been all the time we've been here, we've never had a problem, ever.'

'If you re-stock immediately the same thing will happen.'

'Well, I don't believe it. They come out in the dark, you say?'

Seb nodded.

'Well, whatever it was, the end result's still the same – I've lost all my two-legged friends. Thanks, anyway, Seb. Be seeing you. I don't expect you'll forget to send the bill.' Phil took out his handkerchief and wiped his eyes. 'Blow me, they can't be that clever, the little beggars.'

When Blossom and Hamish came home Phil told them the bad news. They couldn't believe it, either. Blossom was incredulous. 'Something that size with a brain? I don't believe it. I honestly don't.'

Hamish, however, remembered a long-forgotten lecture at college. 'I do know there is such a thing, and they can cause havoc, but I've never seen anything red in there.'

Phil agreed. 'Neither have I.'

'What shall we do?' Blossom asked.

'Tonight I'm going in there with a torch to look for the blighters,' Phil said.

'We could all go,' Blossom suggested.

'If we all go there'll be no room to see what's going on. No. I'm going on my tod to prove I'm right.'

Hamish doused the conversation with cold water. 'You might find he's right, this chap from the Investigation Centre. Very right.'

'And then again I might not. About six I'll go, it's well and truly dark then. Get that torch out, Hamish.'

Hamish shuffled off to the goat shed where he sat with the goats of a night before shutting them up for their own safety. He liked sitting there, especially if there were babies, which he adored. That had been the place where he'd first felt able to begin speaking again. Nursing a baby goat was what had healed the harrowing experience of watching his baby half-sister being killed in front of him by that brute his mother had taken up with. That and Blossom and Phil taking him in and not telling the Social about him being there. He stroked all the goats who were trying to get into his pockets for treats and promised them their supper titbits before bedtime. He picked up the torch from a hook specially hammered into the wood at shoulder height so the goats couldn't get it, and wandered back to the farmhouse. The welcoming kitchen lights were on and he could see Blossom doing something at the sink. The realisation came to him that this was his home for ever, that he really and truly belonged here. It was the only place in all his life where he'd found comfort and, best of all, love.

'Here we are, Dad.'

Phil was taken aback. Hamish had never called him Dad before.

'You called me Dad.' Phil shook his hand and then clasped him to his chest. 'I'm proud to be your dad, very proud. And Blossom would be delighted if you called her Mum.'

'Mum it is, then.'

'Good. Call her Mum in front of me, then I can see the pleasure on her face. Right, another hour or so and then I'm off to the chicken house.' He banged his chest with his fist. 'There'll be no damn red mites in my chicken house, you wait and see. Thanks for calling me Dad. I'm right proud. Now I can call you son.'

Phil had his supper before he went out to the chicken house and was there to see Blossom's face when Hamish said, 'Thank you, Mum,' as she passed him his plate.

'Why! Hamish.' She jumped up and flung her arms around him. 'That's lovely. I've been waiting a long time for this day.'

As Phil put on his coat in preparation for his investigation into the red mite situation, Blossom said, 'Hamish, I want you to think about this. I don't want an answer this minute, because it's an important decision. Would you like for Phil ... your dad and me to make your name Hamish Parsons, all legal like. It's up to you but it would give us a lot of pleasure, believe me. Wouldn't it, Phil?'

'Brilliant idea. It would be great, would that, but think about it, son, it's a big step.'

'I've thought about it already and there's nothing I'd like better. Hamish Parsons. Excellent. Thanks.'

Phil set off for the chicken house full of delight at the sudden turn of events. There'd be no more need to explain Hamish to anyone. They could call him their son and no one would question it.

He pushed open the chicken-house door, then closed it behind him and shone the torch round. Red mites, my eye. There wasn't a sign, not one sign. He shone the beam all along the perches, round the edges of the window, along the roof supports, along the walls, back to the perches. Nothing. For all their science and their la-di-da qualifications the people at the Investigation Centre were completely wrong. Phil decided to switch off the torch, wait and then try again. He leaned against a perch for comfort.

There was complete silence, but then there always was once it got dark. There was only ever the occasional car going slowly down the narrow lane that went past the farm. He heard the barn owl that used his old barn hooting as it flew across the valley. His attention went back to Hamish deciding to call him Dad and his chest swelled with pride. What a day, what an important day. He got an urge to scratch his leg, then his back, then ... yes, it was a very important day, a milestone and ... he'd have to scratch his back again but he couldn't reach where it itched the most. God, he itched all over. What the hell was it? His arm now, then his neck. He felt as though he was not just itching but *hurting* all over. What the hell ... Now his hand. He switched on the torch to inspect his hand and he knew at once. It was the blasted red mites! He fled back to the farmhouse faster than he'd run in years.

'Blossom! Blossom, they've got me! They're sucking my blood!'

In the panic Blossom refused to allow him in the house, insisting that he strip outside and leave his clothes out there. It was a perishing winter night and he begged to be allowed in but she wouldn't have it. Hamish sat in the kitchen helpless with laughter.

Blossom shot every bolt on the door and shouted through the keyhole, 'Get your clothes off and leave them outside.' When he continued hammering on the door she shouted, 'I said get them off!'

So he did and flung them as far from the house door as he could. When he was finally stripped bare, she let him in, but made him go straight to the shower. 'Downstairs in the utility room. Don't want any of 'em upstairs. There's hardly any hot water left but you'll have to put up with that. Hamish! Go get your dad a big towel, go on. It's all right you laughing.'

Warmed through with a brandy and sitting by the roaring fire dressed in fresh clothes, Phil made a vow. 'Once I've got my courage back, before I go to sleep, I'm going out with that can of spare petrol from the van and some matches and I'm setting light to the blasted thing.'

Hamish, still laughing, couldn't believe it. 'You mean you're burning the chicken house down?'

'Exactly!'

'I shall watch from the landing window when you do. Can't miss a bonfire – I love 'em.' Then he burst into laughter again and Blossom joined in.

And true to his word Phil went out, pulled the hay from

the nesting boxes and threw petrol on it. It took only one match to set it ablaze then he fled in case the mites came looking for his blood again.

Chapter 9

The night of the dinner at The George Seb took particular care getting ready. Best shower gel, another shave just in case, best suit, newest shirt, and a stunning tie he'd bought specially for the occasion. Then he did what he always did – remembered his shoes needed cleaning after he was completely ready. He slid his shirt-sleeves up his arms to make sure they didn't get polish on them, thought that possibly furniture polish might do just as well and safeguard his shirt into the bargain. So spray polish it was and it worked just as well, thank goodness.

He checked his car keys and money, though he wouldn't need any if it was true what the others had said: that if Mungo organised anything he always went the whole hog and paid for it all. Then he was ready for a whole evening with Maggie Goddard. Dear Maggie. She was so comfortable and cuddly, though he'd never cuddled her. Perhaps tonight he might.

The car park at The George was almost full, but Seb found a space next to Mungo's Range Rover, locked his car and went to wait in the foyer for Maggie. She was already there, looking quietly sensational in a short black dress, understated but obviously classy. Her hair had been slightly tamed but not enough to make her look ordinary. As he greeted her with a kiss on her cheek he smelt that lovely floral perfume of hers and was inordinately pleased at his choice of dinner guest. Maggie was well aware of how to conduct herself at such an event and he had no qualms about her fitting in.

He began introducing Maggie to everyone, and what pleased him most was the fact that they all took to her immediately and she to them. Valentine arrived alone, looking edgy and ill at ease. At the bar Seb asked him if his guest hadn't been able to come.

'That's right,' Valentine said shortly. 'Must say, I like Maggie. She's lovely. Who is she exactly?'

'The daughter of a client. The one with the alpacas. She's an actress.'

Valentine's eyebrows shot up his forehead. 'Is she indeed? I'll get these.'

They all stood around in the bar chatting while they waited for Rose and Dan to arrive. Which they did in a last-minute flurry, explaining that the babysitter's car wouldn't start and Dan had had to go and get her, and the children, small though they were, had become fractious knowing Rose was going out.

Rose caught up with Seb while she waited for Dan to get her drink. 'Hi, Seb. My, I hear you've made a good start, what with canaries and alpacas and the dog called Dai. And this is a friend? Hi! I'm Rose, Dan's wife.'

Maggie took to Rose's open American approach and before long they were chatting about the theatre like two old friends, finally having to be called to attention by Dan, who was hungry and didn't want to miss his dinner.

'They've all gone in, Rose. Come along, darling.'

Joy's seating plan put Seb and Maggie between Valentine on one side and Scott and Zoe on the other. Scott found

Maggie enchanting, and while he had very little knowledge of the theatre he did enjoy talking to her about the kind of people she met and the audition she was about to go to. Seb was delighted to listen to the pair of them.

When Seb had turned to talk to Valentine Scott said, 'We're all very pleased with the way Seb is fitting in. New clients already and doing very well indeed for someone so new to the practice.'

Maggie raised her eyebrows. 'What else can you expect? Seb is a gem. He's already won my mother over and she's very hard to please. I daren't add up the number of vets she's gone through. I haven't enough fingers anyway!' She laughed then said seriously, 'Seb looks quiet and doesn't push himself forward, but he's very deep and very passionate about being a vet. Nothing will stop him doing an excellent job, believe me.'

'Yes, I'm sure you're right. How long have you known him?'

Scott looked her straight in the face, testing her out, but Maggie was equal to his questioning. 'A few weeks, but I feel I've known him for years, and that's a good start to a relationship, isn't it?'

'Oh! Yes.' This unsophisticated, open-hearted Australian was unaccustomed to Maggie's type of conversation and felt at a loss. A relationship? After all, it was obvious to anyone that Maggie was considerably older than Seb.

'Scott, who are the partners?'

'Mungo is the senior partner. Colin is the one with the very thin wife who looks anxious all the time, but not nearly as anxious now they have a little boy. Dan Brown has the dashing American wife with a houseful of babies, though you wouldn't think it, would you? I'm the newest partner. My wife Zoe here used to be one – didn't you, darling? – but when we married she decided to give up practice and have babies instead, and I am the partner in her place.'

'How many children do you have?'

'A son at school and two babies – so far.'

'I see. I didn't say what I said about Seb because I knew I was talking to a partner, you know. I'm not that kind of person. I've very little guile.'

Scott laughed. 'I would have thought in your profession guile would have been very useful.'

Maggie gave one of her uproarious laughs which drew everyone's attention to her. 'Maybe I'd have gone further up the ladder if I had more guile.'

Mungo cut across everyone's conversation. 'The time has come for every second lady to move round to their left, please, starting with Miriam.'

During the ensuing chaos Miriam ended up next to Maggie, Valentine on his own making the even numbers awkward. 'Maggie? I'm so pleased to have a chance to talk. When will I get a chance to see you acting?'

'Well, I'm going for an audition shortly. If I get the part I shall be on TV in a series. I've seen the script and I have free choice which scene I choose to do for the audition.'

'Have you chosen your scene yet?'

The puddings came round and the two of them tasted theirs immediately because it looked so tempting. Miriam, a lover of puddings, said, 'Mmmm! Wonderful. I never know which I like best, strawberries or raspberries, but these raspberries are so sweet and tangy. Do you like puddings?'

'Much prefer them to the main course.' Maggie giggled that charming giggle which so endeared her to people.

'So do I!' Having found common ground Miriam asked, 'Well, have you chosen yet?'

'I've chosen the last scene where she confesses in a round-about way to a murder. Years ago, but she never got found out.'

'You're not a nice character, then? I mean, the part you will play!'

'The murder was almost justified.'

'I see. I can never see that murder can be justified in any way at all. Still, that's me all over. Have you known Seb long?'

'A few weeks.' Maggie smiled. 'You're the second person to ask me that tonight.'

'Sorry. We're a close-knit group, that's why we ask. The first year as a vet in a new job isn't easy. You have to prove yourself every time you see a client and they can be so touchy, so we keep an eye.'

'Seb's very adult for his years, very sympathetic. But ...' Maggie paused. 'But I think something happened to him ... I don't know what, but I sense it's something that almost broke him.'

'Really?' Miriam put down her spoon and fork and gave her whole attention to Maggie.

'He hasn't told me, it's just my over-sensitive emotions – actress and all that. Sometimes you see more than there is.' To divert Miriam from asking more Maggie offered, 'I understand your Mungo is much admired for his orthopaedic work. Seb is full of admiration for him.'

'He specialised in orthopaedic surgery after he'd qualified

and, though I say it myself, he excels at it. But he's lovely as a person, too, and that's important.'

'Of course it is.' Maggie's eyes strayed over to Seb and they smiled at each other.

Miriam noticed the exchange of smiles and, putting two and two together, made up her mind to have a word with Joy. She'd know, would Joy. Maggie must be at least twelve years older than Seb and it simply wouldn't do. Then Miriam almost kicked herself for not remembering that nowadays people often had relationships based on friendship, and that romance never entered the equation. She wondered what had happened to Seb, this thing that Maggie sensed had gone wrong with him. But it was none of her business. After all, everyone was pleased with Seb's work and no one more so than Mungo. And that was all that was of interest to her and the practice. She glanced across at Mungo and he caught her eye. He toasted her with his wine glass and for a single second they were the only two in the dining room.

It was when Mungo stood up to make a speech of welcome to everyone, and Seb and Kate in particular, that the fun began. He was a brilliant raconteur and he had a very willing audience, well primed with drink all evening. It was a good thing that they had a private room because each of them seemed to have a speech to make.

Ginny's Gab volunteered first. 'I have an announcement to make.' He made sure he had everyone's attention before he said the next sentence. 'As the eldest of the six Bridges brothers – even if it is by only twenty minutes – it is only fitting I am the first to enter the state of matrimony and I wish to say that it is the very best thing I have ever done in my life. I asked Ginny to marry me and, believe it or not, the immediate answer, almost before I got the words out, was "*Yes!*" I'm well aware that many people are of the opinion that Ginny and I make an odd sort of couple, but my mother wholeheartedly approves of Ginny. They get on like a house on fire. Both of them are opinionated, bossy and wilfully determined to have their own way, so I haven't a chance. But marriage is the best and I can honestly say that I recommend it.' He grinned all over his face and pointed at Seb. 'Come on then, Seb, get cracking!'

It came to Valentine's turn and he stood up. There was a sparkle about him they hadn't seen for a while, not since his Nina had gone back 'home'.

'I had to leave the table a few minutes ago to take a phone call. It was my wife Nina to say ... to say what I've been waiting for these long long months since she left. She is coming back next week – for good!' A great sigh of pleasure went round the room. Miriam got to her feet and put her arms around him, giving him a kiss. 'That's wonderful!'

No one else quite knew what to say. Was it 'congratulations'? Or 'more fool her'? Or 'perhaps when she's back you'll manage not to look for women outside your marriage'? They were all pleased for him, though, very pleased, but they all had long memories and remembered Nina's almost continuous distress at his extra-marital adventures.

Everyone else's speeches were good fun and lots of clapping ensued but none had quite the impact of Gab's and Valentine's.

That night in bed Maggie, who felt she'd made a good job of being Seb's dinner guest, recollected the conversation she had with Miriam and contemplated how she felt about Seb.

He was a gorgeous, sympathetic man, certainly a man not a boy, even though she was years older than him. How many? Twelve years? There was a strength about him which wasn't immediately apparent to people. She loved his choice of career, his gentleness ... Well, she had to face it ... *she loved him*. She rolled over in bed to gaze out of her open window to the fields beyond. She was besotted. It was ridiculous of her because she scarcely knew him. He'd kissed her on her cheek, held her hand, admired her with his eyes and that was all. But he was unlike any man she'd ever been out with. Though his origins were humble there was a distinction about him – his bearing, his smile, his thoughtfulness. An owl flew across from the wood. Actors, sensitive beings though they were, could be manipulative, scheming and, very often, after one thing and one thing only, and she'd never been a bed-hopper. But Seb wasn't like that. She mustn't rush things with him. She'd play it cool.

Seb, on the other hand, went to bed thinking not only about Maggie but also about Kate. They'd chanced to sit together for a while in the mad moving-about game Mungo apparently always played at these kind of events.

He'd been overcome by Kate. Tongue-tied, inadequate and wishing he was anywhere but where he was. It was stupid really because she treated him with nothing but respect and showed a lot of interest in his work, but it was how she affected him. He tried, really tried, to be interested in her, but it didn't work. It was that superior look she had – not snooty nor arrogant, just superior. It unnerved him. To add to his problems he sensed Miriam was watching their reaction to each other and it embarrassed him. As for Kate, she was completely at ease and for some ridiculous reason this fact annoyed him.

But he fell asleep thinking about her good looks and comparing her to Maggie. Maggie was crystal clear. You knew where you were with her. But they were, to quote a well-used phrase, just good friends.

The next morning everyone made a point of thanking either Miriam or Mungo for the splendid dinner they'd enjoyed the previous evening. When Seb thanked Mungo he replied, 'Pleasure, my boy, a pleasure. Glad you enjoyed yourself. I must say, that Maggie of yours seems a nice person. Someone said she's an actress?'

'Yes, she is.'

'And what did you think to our Kate? Lovely girl, isn't she?'

'She is indeed. She seems to have settled in well.'

'She's known us for a long time, Seb. You could do worse!' He grinned, waved a finger in the air as a goodbye, and went swiftly off to his consulting room.

Miriam couldn't help being concerned that Seb was getting involved with someone so much older than himself. She popped down to Joy's office the afternoon after the celebration party and suggested they had a cup of tea together.

'Something on your mind?'

Miriam laughed. 'You know me better than I do myself. Yes, there is.'

Joy said, 'There's no one in the staffroom; we'll make the tea there while we talk.'

'Good party, wasn't it?' Miriam said once they were ensconced.

'Excellent.' With the spoon poised over the box of sugar Joy asked if Miriam was still dieting.

'Drat it, yes. But today I'll have sugar. Mungo's so good; he never has sugar in his coffee, and I know he loves it.'

Joy gave Miriam a rather sceptical look and instantly Miriam knew. 'He has sugar? He doesn't. Does he?'

Joy nodded. 'I'm afraid so. We're not supposed to tell you but—'

'I shall tell him I know. I asked him not long ago and he swore he didn't.'

'Well, there you are. Black with two sugars.'

'Two! I don't believe it.'

They settled down to drink their tea and Joy's first words were. 'I liked Maggie very much, but she's far too old for Seb.'

Miriam nodded. 'Exactly. I intercepted a look between the two of them. He likes her, that's obvious, but it's more than that on her part and I don't think Seb realises.' She sipped her tea. 'Seb is a lovely young chap. I'd hate him to be wasted on a fool. I don't mean Maggie is a fool, she's a lovely warm person, but rather that it would be *foolish* for them to get together.'

'Too true.'

'Maggie says something has happened to him in the past which he hasn't quite got over. Her instinct tells her, she says.'

'That's interesting. I wonder what.'

Miriam stirred her tea to make sure there wasn't any sugar still lurking in the bottom, then drained the mug. 'Be nice if he found someone worthy of him.'

They looked at each other with the same thought in their

minds, and said together, 'Kate!' Then they burst out laughing.

After Joy had dried her eyes and calmed down she said, 'We really mustn't, you know. This gossiping has to stop. Oh, dear! But I think Seb feels intimidated by her. He scarcely said a word to her.'

'Just give them time!' Miriam put down her mug. 'Got to go. Perkins has not been out this afternoon. At least he doesn't want to go as far as he used to do. At one time he'd have walked to Weymouth and back.' She paused at the door. 'Don't mention a word to Mungo but I do believe Perkins is on his way to doggy heaven.'

'He is old, Miriam.'

Miriam's eyes filled with tears. 'I know. I know. Be seeing you. Nice news about Valentine's Nina, by the way.'

'It is. Unfortunately we haven't a job available here at the moment, except for stepping in when we're short-handed.'

'I can't see it working, can you?'

Joy came out in his defence. 'He's been a very, very good boy since that blasted Eleanor whatever-her-name departed for the bright lights. Now she *was* a pain. I think maybe he's realised how much he loves Nina. He's been a different man since she told him she'd had enough of his affairs. One can be too tolerant and a good boot up the backside is sometimes what's needed, not just forgiveness and understanding.'

Joy's phone rang and Miriam waved a silent goodbye, opened the door and left, bumping into Seb as she turned to go upstairs. 'Good afternoon, Seb. Did you enjoy last night? It was good, wasn't it?'

'Yes, it was and I would like to say thank you on behalf of Maggie and myself. We both thoroughly enjoyed ourselves.'

'Good. I liked Maggie very much.' She looked quizzically at him with raised eyebrows and sparkling eyes. Now was as good a time as any, she thought.

Seb sensed what she was asking and felt uneasy. 'We're only friends, you know, nothing more. She's good fun and good company.'

That's what you think, thought Miriam. But she said nothing.

Chapter 10

Seb had intended to ring Ruthie and Sandy Goddard to tell them the results of the tests on the two alpacas, but Tim, who'd carried out the tests, suggested otherwise.

'It seems to me it's possible that before these two were taken ill the Goddards had another incident and never told anyone. I guess they didn't know it was TB but the animal died and they've quietly buried it, innocently, no doubt. But if they did, that's perhaps where it all started. So go to see them and find out if I'm right. There's probably more than two with it now.'

Seb planned to go that afternoon as he knew that Tatty would be coming in during the morning with Evie and Tom for his check-up. Eleven o'clock was the appointment and on the dot they arrived. Evie was breathless and Tom carried Tatty. In view of their long journey Seb suggested they might like a coffee or a drink of tea. Dodie offered to make it for them and settled them in the reception area, hoping no other clients imagined they qualified for refreshments. She really would have to tell Seb it just wasn't on. Then she saw how apprehensive Evie was and decided he'd done the right thing.

Mungo came to the door of his consulting room to say goodbye to his previous appointment. 'Glad to have been of help. We'll contact you when we've studied the scans and made a decision. In the meantime, don't worry. I think perhaps it's not as bad as you think.'

'Thank you, Mr Price,' said the client. 'I'm so grateful for your help. Tiger is, too, I'm sure. We'll wait for your call.'

Dodie carried the tray of tea into Mungo's consulting room and Bunty ushered the Nicholls in.

Mungo shook hands. 'Evie, Mr Nicholls. Good morning. How are you?'

Tom answered. 'In a much better frame of mind than when we saw you last. He gets better as each day goes by, except he's stopped climbing onto the wood store and then jumping up on to the bedroom window sill.'

Mungo laughed. 'Let's see him walk.'

Tom put Tatty down on the floor and Mungo persuaded him to walk by tempting him with a corner of a biscuit. There was a slight hesitation in his right leg, but it was nothing to worry about at all. And best of all he obviously wasn't in pain.

Evie spoke for the first time. 'We're so delighted. He can walk ever so far now, and he and I have a lovely time in the woods because he loves rabbiting. If I hadn't come to you that day ... I can't begin to imagine ... Thank you so much, so very much.'

Mungo gave them a warning. 'When he begins to get ancient, really ancient, he may have a limp. Arthritis always seems to go for the weakest point. Just a pet theory of mine. It's been a long way for you to come, but I'm delighted to see he's so well. He's such a jolly little chap, isn't he?'

Evie smiled. 'He is.' She bent down to pick up a carrier bag she'd laid down beside her. 'Is Miriam about?'

'She said she'd come down when you arrived. I'll give her a ring.'

'Oh! I don't want to bother her if she's busy.'

Mungo winked at her and picked up the phone. 'I'd get shot at dawn if I didn't tell her. Miriam! Evie's here with Tom. Right, see you in a minute. Here, Tatty!' He opened his arms wide and Tatty took a flying leap, landed on his knee and sat there, his tongue lolling out, enjoying being stroked by Mungo. 'Not an unpleasant bone in him. I wonder what his history was?'

'As a puppy he was bought by a family and the children were allowed to tease him, so then he began snapping and the parents took him to the dogs' home. We saw him and loved him.'

'Then you've done a good job because he's lost all that. Children do have to be taught how to care for a pet, don't they?'

Miriam walked in with Perkins, and Tatty jumped down, as if sensing that Perkins was not at all amused by another dog looking down at him from Mungo's knee. They sniffed each other and began a silly game of chase.

Mungo intervened. 'Perkins! That will do! Sit. Tatty, sit!'

They both did as he said.

Miriam kissed Evie then Tom, and said how pleased she was to see that Tatty had recovered. Secretly she rejoiced at how much happier Evie looked.

'All thanks to your dear husband.' Evie held up the carrier bag she'd brought. 'Now, I've brought you a present. I do hope you like it. You were so interested in my embroidery ... I hope you don't think me too forward.'

'Never!' Miriam opened the bag and took out a framed

embroidered picture. It could have been Beulah Bank Top in the spring with all the hill flowers in bloom on the lower slopes. It brought tears to Miriam's eyes. 'This is beautiful. I love it. I shall treasure it always. Look, Mungo! Oh! There's someone here, look, walking up the path with a dog! Just like I do. Look at the flowers, such vibrant colours! How clever! Thank you so much, Evie!' Miriam hugged her.

Evie said, 'Tom framed it for you. We're so grateful.'

All this time Seb had stood quietly in the background enjoying their gratitude and delight. But Evie hadn't forgotten him. She turned to say, 'And thank you to you, too, Seb, for all you did. You were so kind to me, so very kind.' She stood up and boldly hugged him. 'Time you found yourself a wife. You know, a nice girl who loves the work you do. You'd make a lovely husband.'

Seb blushed.

Miriam said, 'We're doing our best. They're lining up to be Seb's girlfriend. He's spoiled for choice, the lucky man!'

By this time Seb was red-faced, appalled that his private life was a topic of conversation in the practice.

'In time, in time,' he said, trying hard to laugh it all off. But it was difficult.

Tom and Evie, with an excited Tatty in tow, said goodbye to every member of staff they met. Evie told them all the same thing: 'I don't want to have to see you again, because that means we have trouble, but you will all be in our thoughts. Thank you for everything.' Shy, timid Evie that was had suddenly flowered and when she kissed Miriam goodbye for the final time she whispered, 'Thank you, Miriam, for our little talk, it's done me so much good.'

Tom, when he shook hands with Miriam, looked her directly in the face. 'Thank you for your understanding and kindness, it's meant so much to Evie.'

Seb went out into the car park to see them off and Evie was still waving as their car disappeared out onto the main road. He went inside for an early lunch, still hot under the collar about the discussion of his private life. Well, he'd have to get over it; he supposed it was better than no one caring at all.

That afternoon Seb went to see the Goddards. His heart was heavy as he knew they would all be devastated. It would probably mean a culling of their alpacas. They'd be compensated, but in their eyes that would mean nothing; they'd be losing their dear friends.

They were delighted to see him. Both Ruthie and Maggie gave him a kiss and a great big hug. Sandy shook his hand warmly. It made him feel an absolute traitor and he wished more than anything that the story he had to relate was not the truth.

He headed towards the indoor housing where he'd asked them to put the two infected alpacas, but Ruthie called out, 'They're over here.' She was pointing to the nearest field.

'You didn't isolate them?'

'Well,' said Ruthie, 'they were miserable alone in the shed so I gave in and let them have the freedom to roam. I'm very keen on freedom, you see. I feel they don't thrive if they're not free.' She smiled up at him and for one terrible moment he felt like grabbing her and shaking her till her teeth rattled.

But he swallowed hard and kept control of his temper. 'It

looks as though Mimi and Carlos have a serious infection.' He didn't say the dreaded words TB, as he wanted to allow them to come to it gradually, even if he felt like strangling them for their soft-hearted approach.

Ruthie clutched the front of her sweater in horror. 'What kind of infection?'

'I'm afraid the very worst kind.' He looked gravely at the three of them and saw it was Maggie who was the first to realise the fatal situation.

'Not … TB?'

Ruthie fell on Sandy's chest and burst into a storm of hysterical weeping. 'Oh no! Please say Maggie's wrong.'

'Tim, who did the tests, is very experienced in these matters and is one hundred and ten per cent sure he is right.'

'Another test?'

'Of no avail. I'm sorry.'

Sandy, choking with emotion but trying to keep a level head, asked, 'That means …' and drew a finger across his throat, unable to say the word 'cull?'

'Yes. We have to inform the police, too, and Mimi and Carlos have to be … well, taken away, not buried on your land.' When he said this he eyed the three of them carefully and saw, just for a moment, a flicker of shock in Sandy's eyes.

'You see, Tim wonders if you had an instance of an animal dying before these two showed signs of TB. You know, losing weight, then looking poorly, ears down, loss of appetite.' Seb waited for a response, noting the shifty look Ruthie gave Maggie. He decided not to say anything, just wait.

The silence grew longer until eventually Sandy said, 'Yes, you're right. It was Jose. Found him dead one morning. Truthfully we didn't know what he'd died of, but we just buried him. Strapped for cash at the time so ...' He shrugged. 'We just did it. If we'd realised ...'

Ruthie, on the verge of collapse, muttered, 'We didn't know, otherwise we wouldn't have done that. Believe me. Oh, God!'

'Let's have Mimi and Carlos out then and we'll inform the State Veterinary Service and they'll deal with it. This one here by the gate looks like Mimi. Is it?'

Ruthie's eyes grew wide with horror. 'No, that's Loretta, you don't mean ...'

Seb dug his fingers into Loretta's coat and felt for her ribs; they were already too bony for her to be healthy. He looked at Maggie and she saw his thoughts in his bleak, shocked eyes. Great tears began rolling down her cheeks and Seb's heart trembled. In the heat of the moment he opened his arms wide and she went into them and clung on. In the midst of all the sadness he still found pleasure in having Maggie in his arms, then felt ashamed of himself.

'We've got to be practical,' he said eventually, clearing his throat. 'I'll have to examine every one of your alpacas to see if there are any more that might be infected. Then we're in the hands of the State Veterinary Service.'

Ruthie, between her tears, managed to ask, 'What about this Tim? Can he do something for us? Can we cure them if they're not too bad? We do it with people nowadays, so why can't we do it with our alpacas?'

The last desperate plea from Ruthie almost finished Seb. He released himself from Maggie's grasp and tried hard to be impartial. 'Any we find testing positive for TB will have to be put to sleep and taken away for ... disposal. There is no way round it.'

'Well,' Ruthie took a defiant stance against the gate, 'I for one shall resist. I'm not having it. What harm have they done to anyone at all? Totally innocent, they are. Totally. It's not on! I shall stay here all night and all day if necessary. I will not allow any slaughter.' She tossed her head in defiance at Seb and glared at Sandy and Maggie in turn, daring them to disagree.

Maggie, being more of a realist than her mother and wanting quite desperately to be on the same side as Seb, said, 'Mum, you can't.'

Sandy, torn between loyalty to Ruthie and desperate not to have, in all probability, their whole herd slaughtered, hovered between joining Ruthie at the gate and accepting the law. Finally, he said, 'So they could all be infected, and it's our fault for not isolating Mimi and Carlos?'

'Most probably the damage was done before I asked you to isolate them, but worrying about their freedom and letting them mix with the others won't have helped certainly.' Seb took a huge breath and said, 'I cannot let the matter drop. Professionally. I have to report what I find, whether or not you like it. It is entirely out of my hands. Sorry.' He stood, head bowed, desperate to get away, but so very conscious of their predicament.

Maggie took the matter in hand. 'Come in the house, Seb. Bring your phone numbers and such, and we'll deal with it together. We can't bury our heads in the sand. Come along, Mum, you're only delaying the inevitable and well you know it. Dad, bring her in. Go on. *Please*. Seb's right. He doesn't want to do it but he has to. I'll make us all a drink while we try to take it in. Come on.' The last sentence she shouted impatiently, trying to hurry her parents up, anything rather than this stalemate. She walked towards the house with one arm around Seb's waist, for reassurance more than anything, and Seb found it comforting. Slowly Sandy and Ruthie followed, Sandy white-faced and tense, Ruthie still sobbing.

In the kitchen Maggie said, 'Tea, I think. All right, Seb? We have Indian *chai*, green tea, red bush, or ordinary.'

'Ordinary. I'll use my mobile but not here in the kitchen; the reception won't be any too brilliant, will it?' He glanced behind him, aware of Ruthie approaching and having to listen to his conversation.

'Go into the hall and turn first right. You'll be all right in there.'

Being new to the area, Seb didn't have the local Veterinary Service number on his phone and rang Joy. But it was Dodie Pilgrim who answered. 'Joy's day off. How can I help?'

She listened intently to his news. 'I'll attend to this for you. No problem. Very sad. They must be devastated. Don't forget to tell them they mustn't sell any of their stock; no movement off the premises at all. Emphasise that. I've known people sneakily sell some and not let on. Thoroughly irresponsible, but there you are.'

'Right. Yes. I'll be back as soon as I can. Thank you.'

'Good. Mungo's got an op you might like to watch.'

'OK. Thanks, Dodie.'

'Remember, Seb, lots of sympathy but absolutely no soft-hearted nonsense.'

Seb had to smile at her reminder.

As they all sat at the kitchen table drinking tea Seb felt humbled by their stoicism. Ruthie appeared to have accepted the inevitability of their situation, Sandy was trying to put on a brave front and Maggie, well, she was admiring his forthrightness. 'You've been very kind, Seb. We do appreciate that,' she said.

'I don't feel very kind. What I must stress is that you should, under no circumstances, *sell* or move any of your alpacas off the premises for any reason. I feel rather like the Grim Reaper.'

Ruthie couldn't bear his sadness. 'My dear Seb, it's not your fault.' She squeezed his forearm. Then the sadness of their intolerable news overcame her and she wept and couldn't be consoled.

It took Seb well over an hour to look at all the alpacas. He pulled out three who already were showing signs of lost weight, plus Mimi and Carlos and Loretta, and had them all isolated. 'The Veterinary Service will contact you to say when they're coming, but it'll be within the next day or two. Let me know, OK, Maggie?'

'What I really need is to go out for a drink tonight with you.'

It was a plea he couldn't refuse. 'Fine. Same place. Half past nine? OK?'

'Yes. That's lovely.' She reached up to kiss his cheek and smiled in such a lovely way that her whole face was engaged by it. He'd never noticed before what beautiful eyes she had.

'I'll be on my way. Tonight, then.'

'Great. Thanks, Seb, for being lovely. Mum's heartbroken, but I'm glad it was you who came to tell us. It made it a bit easier.'

Seb spent what was left of the afternoon watching Mungo amputate a dog's leg. There was no other answer and the dog was only two years old, so it had every possibility of adapting. Still, it didn't boost Seb's spirits after the episode at the Goddards', and he was glad when his day was finished and he could go home with the thought of meeting Maggie later that night.

Maggie was already sitting in the bar when he arrived. She got to her feet and greeted him with such pleasure he was taken aback. She reached up and kissed him on the lips, gripping his forearms, standing close. Unprepared, Seb didn't respond in the same way.

Maggie shrank with embarrassment. 'I'm so sorry. I just wanted to let you know how I felt ... Obviously I've jumped the starting pistol. Sorry.'

'No, no, it's not you. Not at all. I'll get our drinks and then I'd be glad to tell you.'

So over two gin and tonics they mulled over the situation of the alpacas' pending demise.

'But there's nothing more to be said,' Maggie said. 'It has to be done. Hopefully we've caught it early and shan't lose the lot. Let's be glad you recognised the problem. Please cheer up.' She smiled at him and squeezed his hand. 'Please?'

Maggie knew there was more to this story than Seb was revealing and she had the idea that whatever it was, it was to do with the terrible hurt she felt always surrounded him, so any setback seemed to cause him to feel things more deeply than appeared justified.

Seb suddenly said, 'You're right, but I can't bear distress ... At least tonight we haven't got that mob of extroverts watching our every move.' He slid across to the chair next to her and took hold of her hand. 'I'm off this weekend. Shall we go somewhere interesting? I haven't had the time to visit anywhere since I arrived. Everywhere's new to me round here.'

'I enjoy walking on the coast path. It's all so varied, with no two views the same. Do you walk?'

Seb grinned at her. 'Not often, but it would be lovely with you.'

'When you smile you look like a little boy.' This gave her the opportunity to ask the question she didn't want to ask. 'How old are you, Seb?'

'I'm twenty-seven.' He nearly added, 'And you?' but held back.

'Ah.' Maggie fiddled with her glass, took a sip and then obviously made up her mind. 'I believe in being truthful, especially with someone who matters to me. I'm thirty-nine.'

Slightly fazed by this candour, Seb quickly covered his embarrassment and replied, 'I hadn't realised. You appear much younger.'

'You are a charmer, Seb Partridge. A real charmer.' An awkward silence fell, which lasted too long.

Eventually Seb said, 'What's twelve years between friends?' And he laughed and so did Maggie, who was delighted it didn't appear to be a stumbling block.

When they both finished their gin and tonics at the same moment Seb said, 'It's not far to my flat. Do you have the time to come back with me? The chairs are more comfortable.'

Maggie answered in a very level voice, terrified of appearing too forward with him and spoiling it all, 'That would be nice.'

Her mouth curved into a conspiratorial grin and they both laughed again.

Back in the flat Seb served their drinks and sat beside her on the sofa. For a reason Seb couldn't identify, after his first sip of his drink, he put the glass down on the coffee table and leaned towards Maggie to kiss her. As a tentative experiment really, because he didn't know what her response would be, but it turned out to be no experiment at all. Maggie launched herself into the kiss as though kisses had been forbidden since her adolescence and she was greedy for them. Before they knew it they were kissing frantically, short of breath and longing for more.

There seemed to be nothing to hold them back, and the sheepskin rug, so carefully selected by Miriam, saw the pair of them making love with an urgency and an empathy surpassing anything either of them had experienced before. Finally they lay exhausted in each other's arms and fell into a wonderfully deep, deep sleep.

Seb was the first to wake, a slow waking in which he felt filled to the brim with happiness. He turned to look at Maggie and gently stroked her arm. She was cold so he went to get a duvet from the bedroom to cover her.

The duvet touching her woke her, and she reached out to hold him close. They said nothing, because there was nothing to say.

Eventually she murmured, 'Must go, Seb. What time is it?'

'Oops! It's almost twelve.'

She got to her feet and began dressing as fast as she could. 'Really must go. I've that audition in London tomorrow at four. Oh! I feel fantastic.'

He nodded. 'I do, too.'

'We'll do it again some time.' She smiled joyously at him,

gave him a peck on his cheek, and grabbed her bag. 'You'll ring?' she asked as she raced down the stairs.

'I will. Good luck for tomorrow.'

Maggie rang Seb from a friend's address in London the following night, obviously over-excited. He loved that about her, that almost childlike zest for life she had. It bubbled over onto anyone who was with her and one felt swept along by an irresistible tide of fun.

'It's me.'

'How did it go?'

'Millions of hopefuls there, just millions, but I know I did really well, the best audition I've ever done. I even silenced the technicians and that's going some.'

'I'm so pleased.'

'It's you.'

'What is?'

'It was you, last night, who helped me. It was wonderful and it stayed with me all day today. I'm coming back tomorrow. Shall I see you?'

'I'm working tomorrow and on call tomorrow night, so I can't stray far.'

Maggie's famous giggle came over the phone, 'I shan't lead you astray, Seb, I'm not that kind of a girl.' She giggled again.

'So long as I am in the environs of Barleybridge in case there's a call ...'

'I'll come to your flat about eight. OK?'

'Fine. I'm so glad you've done well.'

'It doesn't mean I've got the part, but ... I know I impressed.'

'That's excellent. I'll do a meal, shall I?'

'That would be fun. Thank you, Seb. Goodnight.'

'Goodnight, Maggie.' He added, 'Come earlier if you can.' But the phone had gone dead and he didn't think she would have heard him.

They'd just finished their meal the next evening and Seb was contemplating repeating the events of their previous date, when his phone rang.

'Good evening. Barleybridge Veterinary Hospital. Seb Partridge speaking. How may I help?'

He'd scarcely finished his opening patter when he was interrupted by an almost hysterical voice. 'Barleybridge Police here. Constable Bird speaking. There's been an accident. A horsebox has overturned; two ponies were inside. One has been badly injured when it tried to escape and the other has completely disappeared. You're on duty? Will you come?'

'Certainly.'

'Thanks. Bye!'

'Hold on! Hold on! Where are you?'

'Sorry! On the by-pass east of the turning for Tesco, near the roundabout. Know where I mean?'

'Yes. I'll be there as quick as I can.' He slapped down the receiver and called out to Maggie. 'Got to go. And I need to call at the practice for a pistol. Sorry.'

'A pistol? Can I come? What is it?'

'A badly injured pony. I need a pistol just in case. I'll ring the practice on the way.'

By the time they arrived at the practice Mungo had taken the pistol and bullets out of security and was waiting at the back door.

'Here we are, Seb. If you need help don't hesitate to ring, and I'll be there. It sounds as though the pony's in a bad way.'

'Yes, I think it is.'

'Do you want me to come anyway?'

'I'll let you know. I'm going to take a lethal dose, too, just in case there's too many people about to use the pistol. OK?'

By the time they arrived, the police, the fire engine and the ambulance were there. A large 4x4 was slewed across the road, a pony laid on the grass verge and a horsebox was standing badly damaged in the nearside lane, with another car into which it had all too obviously crashed.

Seb got out his head-torch and the big torch and went straight to the pony on the verge. It had already lost a lot of blood and was desperately struggling to rise to its feet, but Seb's examination proved that both front legs were badly broken. The worst part was the blood seeping constantly from a huge tear in its chest.

Maggie looked distressed. Seb talked to the pony, desperately trying to reassure it, but to no avail. 'It's no good, Maggie,' he said, 'it'll have to be put to sleep. Can you find out who is the owner?'

Within minutes Maggie was back, accompanied by a tall man in smart country dress.

'You the owner?'

'Yes.'

'Seb Partridge, Barleybridge Veterinary Hospital.'

'Good evening. Things are bad, aren't they? I've been trying to keep my little girl from seeing him. It's her pony, you see, and hit by our own car, damn it. What's the verdict?'

'My honest opinion is that it would be a kindness to put him to sleep. Both his front legs are badly broken, and you don't need me to tell you how much blood he's lost.' Seb held up his bloodied hands to show the owner and displayed his shirt and trousers. 'Can I get on with it?'

A little girl rushed up. 'Daddy! Daddy! Silver! Oh, no. Please, no!'

Seb deliberately shielded her from seeing all the gore issuing from Silver's chest.

'Got a gun with you?'

'I have.'

'Get on with it, then.' The owner carried the little girl away, trying to find words of comfort for her but failing miserably.

Maggie brought the gun from Seb's car and handed it to him. She was crying.

'Maggie, hush. He'll be out of his pain in a moment. Just soothe him, will you? Stroke his head, you know.' But Silver had other ideas and still pursued his intention of escaping, lifting his head and then his neck in his desperate efforts. Immediately before he loaded the pistol Seb came to the conclusion that there was too much happening around the scene of the accident, and that the risk of live bullets flying about was too much to contemplate. So he put the pistol in his bag and instead prepared the syringe with a lethal dose.

As he was doing this the owner's wife emerged from the darkness and introduced herself. 'It's my daughter's pony. I'll try to quieten him from this end. Too busy to use a gun, eh? Injection's the best, then. Anne-Marie won't hear the gun shot. Loveliest pony we've every owned. Anne-Marie's heart-broken. There, there, Silver.' At the sound of a voice he recognised Silver lay more quietly, enabling Seb to inject him with safety. In a moment Silver lay still, out of his pain.

Maggie was still crying, not quite able to reconcile having to kill the pony and Seb doing it without, apparently, any emotion.

He asked the little girl's mother if she saw which way the other pony ran.

'This one, ours, ran straight at us. We were following our friend's horsebox with both the ponies in it but we got left behind at the traffic lights and were catching up. Silver ran straight at us and we couldn't avoid him. So we never did see which way the other one went. Thanks for dealing with him so quickly. Much appreciated. I'll get back to my daughter. We'll make arrangements to move ... the ... body. The Hunt will have it.'

'Thank you.'

Maggie said, 'Oh, Seb, you're so brave.'

'Hush, Maggie. I'm not brave at all. It's only the second time I've needed to do that. I had to remain absolutely unaffected by it all for the pony's sake. Now for the other pony.' He stood up and Maggie saw he was covered in the pony's blood.

'Oh! Seb, you're—'

'I've been covered in a lot worse than this, believe me. Come on. Bring the torch and we'll have a look around. Let's hope the second one isn't badly injured, too.'

She watched him store his bag with the pistol inside it in his car, carefully lock the doors and then shine the torch around, hoping to catch a glimpse of the other pony. They couldn't see it but they could hear it crashing about in the field next to the road.

They soon found the place where it had burst through the wooden fence and stepped over the broken rails. By the light of the big torch they realised he was rushing about, scared out of his wits, in a field of well-kept allotments. Suddenly he changed tack and began running up and down from the top of the field to the bottom on a wide grass verge.

'He's puffing a lot. Almost out of breath. If we keep still at the bottom here, he'll start slowing down soon. Watch.'

Indeed, Seb was right. There was a noticeable slowing-down. The pony was breathing noisily and seemed to have very little strength left.

Maggie whispered, 'I daren't catch him. Can you?'

'I'll give it a damn good try.'

'Here he comes.'

Seb stepped out to snatch his halter, but the pony was too quick for him.

'Damn.'

'Next time, perhaps. You're right – he's really slowed down.'

Seb began talking to him as he approached and this time he was able to catch hold of his halter and, putting all his weight behind him, hung on, eventually bringing to pony to a halt.

'Find Silver's owner. He needs a horsebox to get this one home. I'll wait here on the verge. Mind the traffic.'

While Maggie spoke to the man Seb checked the pony. There were a few bad cuts where he'd obviously been hurt in the crash, and some lighter cuts inflicted by bamboo sticks and panes of glass, which he'd broken in his mad rampage among the allotments, but nothing of a serious nature. 'There we are, boy. Who's a clever chap? Mmm? You've had a real fright. You're OK now, though.'

Eventually Seb and Maggie were free to leave, but first Seb had to call at the practice to return the pistol.

Mungo called from the top of the stairs to the flat. 'Come up, Seb ... Oh! And you too, Maggie. Have a drink with us. You deserve it.'

While Seb and Mungo locked the pistol up Miriam whisked Maggie into the kitchen to decide on a drink. 'Well, for me hot chocolate would be more than welcome, not alcohol as I'm driving home. I don't know about Seb.'

'He likes hot chocolate, too.'

While Miriam bustled about the kitchen she very gently probed into the relationship between Seb and Maggie. Maggie smiled to herself because she realised it was only Miriam caring about Seb.

'He's a lovely chap, isn't he? I've become very fond of him.'

Maggie agreed. 'Yes, he is lovely.'

'He's got a great future, you know, according to Mungo. He needs to stay focused.'

'Right. Shall I take the tray in?'

'Yes, please.'

Seb apologised to Miriam. 'I won't sit down, I'm such a mess. Sorry.'

He told the story of the evening's events and Mungo said, 'Anne-Marie? Tall chap, a bit commanding? Well-spoken?'

'Yes, that's right.'

'Know who that is, don't you, Miriam? One of Lord Askew's sons. Thoroughly nice guy, he is.'

Miriam agreed. 'Oh, yes, of course. I've seen his daughter competing in shows. She's a dear little thing and doesn't look like a rider at all. Frail and very pretty. I'm sorry about her pony. It'll have cost a packet, believe me. Anything to do with horses and the Askews don't worry about the price. They're horse-mad. Have you met any of them, Seb?'

'I've met Lord Askew and his niece, Jilly, but none of the others until tonight. Must go – Maggie still has to drive home. Thanks for the drink.'

'Let's hope you don't get called out again tonight.' Miriam smiled one of her famous smiles and Seb felt warmed by it.

Chapter 11

The following morning Dodie took a call for Mungo and put it through to the flat. 'Good morning. Mungo Price speaking.'

'Morning, Mungo. This is Jolyon Askew speaking. Just a quick call to say thank you to that young vet of yours. He came out to attend a traffic accident which involved Anne Marie's pony having to be put down. He dealt with the whole episode very competently indeed, and very sensitively, too. Hang on to him – he's going to do you a lot of good in the future. Once you get a good man keep him sweet, I say.'

'That's very good of you to ring. Yes, he's shaping up nicely. How's Anne-Marie this morning?'

'Very distressed, of course, but we're taking her out to-morrow to buy another pony. The only way to get over it. Thanks again.'

The line went dead, leaving Mungo staring at his receiver surprised at the abruptness of the call. However, it was a good start to the day to have a fulsome compliment about a member of his staff.

Dodie told Seb when he arrived to begin work. 'The Hon. Jolyon Askew rang to thank you for the way you dealt with the road accident last night. Full of praise, he was. Keep it up,

Seb, you're doing well. In fact, I've never known a new vet collect a patient list at such a speed. You've had a call from Mr Smithson, by the way, the canary man. Two of his birds are looking distinctly seedy and he wants you to call in. Doesn't want to bring them to the clinic in case it's infectious. Such a nice man but so anxious.'

'Can you ring him back and say I'll call about twelve noon? Poor chap.'

'Of course. Your clients are already waiting, Seb, so get cracking.' Dodie smiled at him and gave him a push in the direction of his consulting room.

The waiting room was already filling up and Seb felt a powerful surge of enthusiasm as he walked through the waiting room to a concerted cheer from everyone, all of whom had obviously heard about his adventure last night. He waved his hand to acknowledge their greetings, went into his room and switched on his computer to see who his first client was. It was Miranda Costello.

He called her name from the doorway of his room and watched her dash forward wearing another of her exotic, mismatched outfits, carrying a cat basket.

'Good morning, Seb. It's little me again.' She burst in through the door and placed the basket on the examination table. 'You'll never guess what I've got in here. I found it in the garden last night, looking dazed and ravenously hungry.' She cautiously opened the door of her cat basket and, reaching inside, gently drew out a ferret, not fully grown and looking scared to death. 'Now, isn't he a beauty! Do you have any experience of ferrets?'

'None whatsoever.'

'Oh dear.'

'But I know a man who has. Rhodri Morgan used to keep a ferret called Harry. I'll go and see if he's free to take a look.'

Rhodri's face lit up when Seb explained the situation. 'Brilliant! Bring him in here. I'll be delighted to take a look.'

Miranda and Seb went together into Rhodri's room carrying the ferret.

Rhodri greeted him with such delight that Miranda was thrilled. 'I'd no idea you knew about ferrets, Rhodri. Isn't he lovely?'

Rhodri took the ferret from her. 'Actually, he's a she.'

'Oh! I imagined all ferrets were male. But then they couldn't be, could they? I am silly.'

'Where's she from, A breeder?'

'No, my ramshackle garden. Found her this morning. I wondered about keeping him ... her ... but I don't think so. She's not really my kind of thing. Is she fit and well?'

The ferret bit Rhodri well and truly in the soft part between his thumb and forefinger.

'Oh! I'm so sorry. Oh! Look at the blood. Oh, dear.'

Seb swiftly removed the ferret from Rhodri so he could stem the flow. It was a vicious bite and must have hurt, but Rhodri took the whole incident in his stride.

'She's a sparky little thing, isn't she? Not quite fully grown, I would have said, but lovely colouring. Give her back to me.'

Rhodri held her by her scruff but even so she tried her best to bite him again, wriggling and scrabbling to get a hold on him. 'She's not a domestic ferret, she's certainly wild. Never been handled, you can see that. If you don't want her I'll take her on.'

'Are you sure? I'm not really into being bitten. I'll be glad for you to take her. If I hear someone's lost a ferret maybe she'd have to go back?'

'That's OK. I'll keep her as and when, and I'll be delighted to give her a home.'

'But you can't keep her in the house with babies there, can you?'

'No, but she'll be in a stable. I know the very place and I might buy another one to keep her company. I've missed having a ferret since Harry died. Thank you very much, Miranda. In fact, I'll call her Miranda, shall I?'

Miranda blushed to the roots of her hair. 'Oh, Rhodri! That would be wonderful. I'd be so pleased if you did. What do I owe?'

Rhodri shook his head. 'Nothing, Miranda. All you've done is bring me a ferret. No fee required.'

'Well, I call that decent of you, yes, very kind.'

She meandered out into the waiting room carrying her empty cat basket, recognised a neighbour and related the whole story to her and, incidentally, to all the other clients. 'So, would you believe it, Rhodri's adopted her. Isn't that lovely?'

'Good thing, too, Miranda, what with that menagerie you've got at home already. A smelly ferret would be just too much.'

'She isn't smelly.'

'She is. I can smell it on you now.'

'That's disgusting. You can't.'

'Oh yes I can. Sniff your cardy and see if I'm right.'

Not for the world would Miranda have admitted to smelling of ferret, but she did smell her cardigan and knew the neighbour was right. 'Nonsense. Not a thing does my cardigan smell of,' she said.

'That'll make a change, then, cos it always smells funny. Time you had a sort-out with them animals of yours. I'm sick of 'em coming into my garden to relieve themselves. Sick of it. As for that mess you call a garden! Well, the mind boggles. A dump, that's what it is. *A great big dump.* In fact, worse than the council tip. They do clear up sometimes, but you never do. I shall be reporting it. Definitely.'

'What? Report my garden? What about me reporting that blasted dog of yours for barking?'

'Barking? He doesn't. Do you, our Benjy? Quiet as a mouse, he is.'

Whereupon, Benjy treated Miranda to a savage barking session, and she was thankful he was on a lead.

This so enraged Miranda that she swung the cat basket at her neighbour, forgetting she hadn't fastened the door, which swung open. Her neighbour's head went right inside the basket. Miranda snatched it off but not before the smell from the basket almost choked the client sitting beside her neighbour, as the blanket inside flew out on to her lap.

Dodie dashed out from behind the reception counter in high dudgeon. 'Now, ladies, all our animals are going to be severely distressed by this behaviour. Mrs Costello, go into my office, please and ... Now!'

The day was saved by the neighbour being called into Seb's consulting room. She marched majestically towards Seb shouting, 'Round one to me!' She punched the air with her fist and closed the door behind her.

Miranda had been a client at the High Street practice where Dodie used to work so Dodie knew her well, and the memory of the smell came back to her when she followed Miranda, who was deeply upset, into the office.

'Here! A tissue.' She thrust a tissue into Miranda's hand and sat down to wait, occupying herself with paperwork until the tears stopped.

'Miranda, you should never have let her rile you. I've no doubt your cardy does smell of ferret. It's quite a distinctive odour. They need brushing very regularly to keep the smell at bay. Rhodri's decided to adopt her, has he?'

Miranda briefly stopped weeping and nodded. 'Such a kind man, and that Seb, he's kind, too. Well, I'll be on my way. Sorry to have caused a fuss but I'm fed up of that woman, she's got no sensitivity.'

Dodie answered in her no-nonsense way. 'Frankly, I feel sorry for her.'

'Sorry for *her*? The old cow.'

'I've passed your garden and been glad I don't live next door to you.'

Miranda was horrified. In a very small voice she said, 'Is that true?'

Dodie nodded. 'It had to be said. If she complains to the council then they'll be sending you a massive bill for clearing it up.'

'They couldn't, could they?'

'They could and they will.'

'Hell's bells. But I've got treasures in there! My mother's old mangle, a fridge I took a dislike to, a dog kennel I've never used, you name it.'

'In that case you could clean them up and sell them, and perhaps that'll go some way to paying for a man with a lorry to take all the rubbish away. Think about it, Miranda. At the very least it'll give your dogs space to run about.' A thought occurred to Dodie. 'You don't let them roam, do you?'

A silence ensued while Miranda thought about how often her dogs went missing for days at a time. As a diversionary tactic she replied, 'I'm not without money, you know.'

'Good, I'm glad to hear it.'

'Dad's money. I invested it, hardly spent any of it. So I could, couldn't I?' She cheered up enormously after this thought and got to her feet.

Dodie suggested she left by the back door so as not to encounter her neighbour, and this Miranda did, with a spring in her step and purpose in her voice. 'Thanks for talking to me. You get in the doldrums living by yourself; same thing day in day out, no comfort, just the animals. I love 'em but there's a limit, isn't there? I just needed a push.' Very softly she whispered, 'Do you really think my cardy smells?'

Dodie nodded. 'There's been a definite deterioration in your attention to your personal hygiene since I first knew you.'

'Oh, God! I am sorry.'

Miranda tiptoed down the corridor to the back door. Climbing in her van, she noticed for the first time in years that the van smelt, too, mostly of cat wee and ungroomed dog. There'd have to be a big change. She wasn't having that blasted neighbour telling everyone she smelt. No, sir! Her mother would spin in her grave if she knew. Then she remembered how lovely the garden was when her mother was alive, with lupins and delphiniums and marigolds, and that dear little pond that had now disappeared under all the mess — she spared a thought for the newts that used to be in there. That chap Fred! Fred with his ramshackle lorry, that's who she'd get. Definitely. And just as important, out would go the broken-down washing machine and she'd get a spanking new one. The very latest. Thank you, Dad. Smelly cardy, indeed. Huh!

At noon Seb left for Joe Smithson's to see his sick canaries. Various possibilities raced through his mind on the way but he decided not to pre-judge the matter and arrived at the house with an open mind.

Mr Smithson and his carpenter friend were peering at two very dead canaries laid on a piece of sheeting on the old table outside the conservatory, but Seb was more interested in the living birds. There were two canaries on the floor of the aviary breathing noisily. Their feathers were fluffed out and they looked thoroughly miserable.

'The birds who've died, did they behave like these two?'

'Yes, but not for very long. They seemed to take ill and die in no time at all. Missis thinks they have pneumonia, but I said that was daft.'

'In one way she was right. I think they've got air sac mites ... or a bad cold. But the speed makes me think it might be air sac mites. They invade the nostrils, the throat and the lungs, and eventually choke the bird to death. I can do a tracheal swab. You're more likely to get these kind of diseases with an outside aviary, because there is contact with wild birds. I know they're not in the aviary but they will pause on the aviary from time to time and it could happen then.'

'Oh, God! How can I stop it?'

'I can give you drops to use on the birds themselves and you need special stuff for cleaning the aviary. When I say clean I mean detailed cleaning in every single corner, every joint of wood, every feeding dish, every water container. And I don't just mean a swish under a running tap, because these little beggars are so small we can't see them with the naked eye and they hide *everywhere*.'

'I'd better start straight away.'

'I can't see any water for the birds to bathe.'

'I didn't know they needed any.'

'Well, they do. Every day if possible. Good husbandry is essential. Can you hand me those two that are squatting on the floor, please? I think ... I know ... they're going the same way as the other two.'

Mr Smithson blanched. 'Shall I lose the lot?'

'Not if I can help it. Follow me back to the surgery and I'll get you the stuff you need. Thorough cleansing. Nothing less will do. They'll have invaded every nook and cranny if I'm right. But do a massive clean-up, even if I'm not right and all they've got is a cold.'

Seb took swabs from the throats of the two canaries and recommended that they be isolated. 'Take heart, Mr Smithson. Between us we'll sort it out.'

His carpenter friend spoke for the first time. 'Can I have some of this stuff for mine? You never know.'

'Certainly. I'll give it to Joe here. Right, Joe, we'll be off.'

Back at the practice Joe took charge of the items Seb had suggested. With an almost overwhelming gratitude he said, 'Am I glad I found you! I'd no idea there was an avian vet at this practice. It's just remarkable what life throws up at the right moment, isn't it? They say vets like you are a rare breed. There's a chap down the road from me who has a hawk, a kestrel, I think. Flies it, you know. I shall tell him he's got the very vet he needs right here.'

Seb decided not to destroy Joe's faith in him. 'Thank you. Will you pay at the desk, please, Joe? Take care.'

'I *will* take care, to the very letter.' With his spare hand he clasped Seb's and shook it vigorously.

Seb went in to the staffroom to snatch a bite of lunch, sad that Joe Smithson was having such bad luck with his birds. Dodie was in there reading the paper. She looked up as he walked in.

'What was the problem with the canaries?'

'I've brought some samples back. I think they've got air sac mites. Two have died and another two are on their way. Poor chap, he's so upset.'

'All in a day's work, Seb, all in a day's work.' She smiled encouragingly at him and leapt to her feet to put the kettle on. 'I'll have another mug with you. Coffee or tea?'

'Coffee, please, with two sugars.'

They sat companionably drinking coffee, and Seb ate his sandwich.

'Has Maggie heard about her audition?' Dodie asked.

'Not yet but she feels she did really well. I do hope she gets what she wants. She's been sidelined for so long she's beginning to despair.'

'I hope she does, too. She'll be moving to London, then? You'll miss her.'

'Yes, I expect so but if it's her big break-through she has to go.'

'Of course. She'll want to go, especially if she's spent a long time in the wings, so to speak.'

'She lights up at the mention of it. I just hope it works out for her.'

'So do I. Must go, I've been here too long already. Mungo says you might like to help this afternoon if you've no clients. Take advantage while you can. At the rate you're going you'll soon be too busy to watch anything at all.'

Seb smiled at her, crumpled up his sandwich-wrapper, threw it in the bin and went to find Joy, as he needed to get the canary swabs off to the lab.

'They'll go in the afternoon post, Seb. Wait till we get our own laboratory set up. Won't it be exciting? I overheard Mr Smithson saying about you being an avian vet and how lucky he was.'

'He gives me far more importance than I deserve. It's embarrassing.'

'So long as you keep a step ahead and don't profess to be specially trained or anything ...'

'Right!'

They laughed together and Seb went off to enjoy his afternoon in the operating theatre. That afternoon Tim from the Investigation Centre rang to say he would visit the Goddards the following afternoon and would Seb be free? So they arranged to meet there at 2.30 p.m.

'Tim Hopkinson. Pleased to meet you.'

'Seb Partridge. Glad you could come. They've taken it very badly, because, although they sell them, each of the alpacas is a close friend. It's been hard for them. I'll introduce you.'

Sandy and Ruthie were very restrained and extremely solemn when they met Tim, and it was hard work making conversation. They stood at the gate looking at the healthy part of the herd and then showed him the ones they'd isolated in the barn.

Ruthie burst out, 'We don't like keeping them inside. They're not used to it. It doesn't seem fair. We love them all, you see, and we feel heart-broken about it. It's nothing we've done, is it?'

'Believe me, it can happen to anyone. TB is no respecter of persons. I know top-class pedigree herds of both alpacas and llamas decimated by TB, and not through bad husbandry, so don't blame yourselves. Seb has told you about not selling any of your herd, or moving any of them off your land, I expect.' Ruthie and Sandy nodded. 'That is extremely important. TB in cattle, and in alpacas and llamas, has to be controlled very rigidly. I'll examine these you've isolated.' Ruthie offered Tim a cup of tea. 'Love one.'

'I'll bring it out here, then.' She wandered off, anxious to do whatever she could to help. Sandy, shotgun in hand, watched and waited.

'Tell me, what wild animals do you have on your land?' Tim asked.

'Rabbits, rats, badgers in the farmer's top field, hares occasionally, mink that escaped from a mink farm. I keep the rats down with this.' Sandy patted his gun.

'Dairy farm next door, is it?'

'That's right.'

'Do his cows ever come into a field adjoining yours?'

'Well, yes, occasionally, in rotation.'

'So they have contact over the fence, nose to nose?'

Sandy nodded. 'Could it be from them?'

'All sorts of possibilities, but I'll go and see him just in case. I can't emphasise enough that the matter is out of my hands.

I have to abide by the rules, and being kind has nothing to do with it. The State Veterinary Service must be made aware and they will deal with procedures. You are not able to sell any alpacas or move any off your land until you are given the all-clear.' Tim, in response to a dig from Ruthie's elbow, turned to see what she wanted. 'Tea! Lovely. Just what I need.'

Ruthie gave it to him in one of her best cups and saucers and smiled sweetly. Seb saw she was about to launch into a campaign of charming him to get her own way.

'No one would know if none of us said anything about this?'

'*I* would.'

'Yes, but you could say ... I mean, they're so lovely, so appealing, it's not right. Couldn't you cure them?'

Tim downed his tea in one long drink, put the cup in the saucer and handed it back to Ruthie. 'No.'

She tried again but to no avail.

'Mrs Goddard, lovely, appealing, yes, they are, but my hands are tied. I should be failing in my duty if I ignored this situation. Putting them to sleep and keeping a watchful eye on the others for several months, perhaps for as long as a year, is what is going to happen and no matter how hard you plead, I'm afraid ...' Sadly Tim shook his head at her.

Ruthie slowly nodded her agreement. 'It's so hard, you see. So hard.'

'I know. I know. I'll take my leave when I've done a thorough inspection. We'll be in touch almost immediately.'

Seb and Sandy tried to console her but it was no good; she was going to grieve and that was that. Sandy, with an apologetic smile at Seb, guided her into the house and Seb left. He passed Maggie coming up the drive on her bike, pedalling like mad as always. She slewed to a stop and he wound down his window.

'Maggie!'

'Seb!' She reached her hand inside the car and grabbed his. 'Well?'

'He's here and it's like I said.'

'Ah. Well. I expect Mum tried her best to persuade him?'

'She did, but there was no way he could change his mind.'

'I knew she would. I can never understand why she thinks she can persuade people when they've a job to do. Do we know why they've got it?'

Seb shook his head. 'Maggie?'

'Mmm?'

'Maggie? Are you free right now?'

'Yes.'

'Do you fancy ...?' Seb looked at her, so obviously asking her ...

'Yes!'

She flung her bike into the grass at the side of the road, got into his car and they fled at speed to Seb's flat, raced up the stairs, stripped off and fell into bed.

An hour later Seb opened a bottle of wine and they spent another two hours enjoying themselves in his bed. They woke and Seb saw it was already seven o'clock. 'Shall we go for a meal? I should have shopped tonight but I haven't. We'll treat ourselves, shall we?'

'Why not? I'll shower before I dress. That Italian restaurant?'

Seb nodded. 'We'll shower together. It's a double shower so there's lots of room.'

So they lathered each other with some aromatic shower gel he'd bought in a mad moment, and they laughed and enjoyed themselves like two children, but with adult matters in mind.

'Oh, Sebastian Partridge, I do love you,' Maggie said. 'You are such fun. It's as if some sadness has fallen away from you now and you have permission to enjoy yourself at last.'

Her unexpected insight came as a shock to Seb, and he paused as he reached into the airing cupboard to get her a towel. 'I didn't know you knew.'

'Well, I don't, it was a shot in the dark, but I've thought you had a sadness about you right from the first time we met. I'm right, aren't I?'

He didn't answer.

'I'm sorry. I've spoken when I shouldn't. I'm so sorry.'

'You're right. But making love to you has ... helped me. You see, you give your all without any hidden agenda and that's wonderful for me.'

'Hidden agenda. Of course I haven't. Why would I?'

He wrapped the towel sarong-wise around her and put his own around his waist, and they stood in his tiny bathroom in the lingering steam while he told her what he hadn't told anyone before.

'A year before my finals, I met someone called Carly at a party at college. She was a friend of a friend of a friend, not a student. I was completely dazzled by her, and I wasn't the only one. She dressed outlandishly and expensively, and compared to the women students she looked fantastic. For some reason she took a fancy to me, and got my phone number. Was I flattered when she rang a couple of days later and suggested we met. I believe the expression is swept off my feet. She was every bit as good as I'd first thought. Every bit. We had a whirlwind time and when she suggested she came to share my bedroom in the student house I lived in, well, I most certainly didn't say no. When I look back on it I never told my parents what had happened. I mentioned I had a girlfriend but not the fact that we were living together. Stupid really, but something ... something held me back.

'We lived together all that year and when it came round to my finals I knew I had to work to catch up, never mind just revise. So I had to spend long hours working in the college library, I couldn't settle in the house as it was always so full of people. She was so generous she never once complained. Three days before finals started I knew I couldn't study any more. I had to get some sleep because I'd ground to a halt, reached complete saturation point.'

At this moment Maggie propped herself on the edge of the washbasin and Seb, glad of a reason not to say any more, said, 'I'm sorry, I'm boring you.'

'No, Seb, you're not boring me, not at all. Go on.'

Seb shook his head.

'Please, go on. You need to tell someone and I'm honoured it's me.' She reached up and kissed his lips so sympathetically ...

'Well, I went home on the bus and when I got there two of the other students were watching sport on the TV. I stuck my head round the door and said something about being exhausted and I was going to sleep for a couple of hours. They both leapt to their feet and tried to persuade me to sit down and watch the football, but I'd have none of it and raced upstairs. I thought it odd that they came into the hall and persisted in shouting up the stairs asking me to watch TV. I walked into the bedroom and there was Carly naked in bed with a man I didn't know. In *our* bed where we'd *loved* ... Through the haze she kept saying, "I'm so sorry. I'm so sorry." *Apologising*? For ...'

Seb couldn't go on. Maggie held him close until his voice returned to him. 'No wonder she'd been quite happy for me not to spend much time with her. I just blacked out with exhaustion and shock. I had to leave college and go home I was so ill. The college was very understanding and said something would be sorted out for me once I was better, and I'd be able to take my finals as and when. The upshot of it was I never saw her again. You see, I thought she loved me as I loved her, and I was convinced we'd marry and be together for life. But Carly was conducting, as she saw it, a sexual initiation for this dope.' He tapped his chest. 'I simply had no clue that that was what she was doing. That was why the betrayal was so ... appalling to me. The others told me they knew what she was up to but had to assume I knew because they'd kept telling me in all sorts of ways, which I'd not been willing to recognise, me being so completely in love.'

The steam had cleared now and Seb could see Maggie more clearly than before. He knew how much she meant to him, but perhaps she didn't want him after what she'd heard. He braced himself. 'Sorry, I should never have told you. If you don't want me ... don't want that meal ... I'll drive you home.'

But they did go to the Italian restaurant, and Maggie restored something of Seb's natural happiness for him and told him how much she cared for him. 'After a betrayal like that, no wonder … Anyway, now we've cleared the air, can we still be friends?'

Her mobile rang. It was Ruthie. She listened intently then said, 'I'll be home in an hour. Thanks for telling me. Yes, I'll ring them first thing. Yes, I am.'

Maggie put the phone back in her bag and looked at Seb, positively bubbling with excitement. 'Can you bear to listen to some good news? Very good news?'

Seb nodded.

'I've to go for a second audition!'

'No!'

'It's absolutely excellent news, the best I've ever had. It doesn't mean I've got the part but … Mum was bursting to tell me.'

'I'm so pleased, so very pleased. When it's something you really, really want you've got to go for it.'

'Oh, Seb, have I really done *you* some good? You've done *me* good. That was why I acted my socks off at the first audition because I felt so lit up by you after that first time, and I'm sure that's why they want me back.'

The Goddards were so delighted at Maggie's news that it took a bottle of champagne and a lot of laughing before Seb could leave. He kissed Maggie passionately before he left, and as she waved him off she shouted, 'I'll ring you tomorrow morning after I've spoken to them.'

Of course, the news the next day was that she had to go to London straight away. She'd see him when she got back.

Seb faced the fact that the comfort she gave him was going to be lost to him for ever if she got the part. But he would have to steel himself to let her go without allowing her to feel she was abandoning him. He wanted none of her joy to be spoiled by regret. That was the best of gifts he could give her – his full permission for her to leave him with no strings attached.

Chapter 12

Seb's phone rang at 7 a.m. the following morning and he didn't need to be told who was speaking. He knew instantly that it was Maggie. She was full of excitement.

'I know it's early, but the audition yesterday went excellently well and ... we'll wait and see. But they did ask me when I would be free, which sounds promising. I'm coming straight home. Can I see you for a meal tonight? Our favourite Italian restaurant? Yes?'

'Yes. I'm glad it all went well. Fingers crossed. Seven-thirty? I'll book a table. Shall I see you in the multi-storey? That'll be easier, won't it?'

'Yes, it will. I'll tell you all about it when I see you. Love from me to you, Seb, darling.'

'See you, then. I am looking forward to it, Maggie.'

They'd just met and were taking time to greet each other after being apart for two days when Maggie's phone rang. She rooted in her handbag and eventually found it amongst all the vital debris she carried around with her.

Maggie listened intently. 'But why didn't they ring me? I gave them my mobile number. Anyway, what did they say?' She began to hop up and down, then she ran round in circles, kissed Seb on his cheek, leapt up and down like a child on a trampoline and shrieked.

She switched off her phone and said, 'I've got it. Oh, God! I've got it. They need me on Monday.' The people in the car park stared at her but Maggie continued springing up and down until Seb felt breathless. 'That's marvellous!' he kept saying. Maggie apparently hadn't heard him, because she took hold of his jacket lapels, looked directly into his face and breathed excitedly, 'Do you realise I've got a part in a TV series, and it's the best part of the whole lot. The *lead* part! I can't believe it. I've done it at last, what I've been waiting for all these years. Isn't it wonderful? Kiss me, Seb, kiss me like you've never kissed me before.'

So he did. He felt he had no alternative because her excitement was so catching, and they were still kissing five minutes later. 'Oh, Maggie, I'm so pleased for you. So very pleased.'

'Should we go to your flat? You know, the two of us? What do you think?'

'I don't think I can. I haven't eaten since breakfast and I'm truly starving right now.'

Maggie burst out laughing. 'Honest to God! Well, I never. Right, food it is, and then ... Can't have you under-performing from lack of sustenance, now can we?'

They found their favourite table vacant and their favourite waiter in attendance, and they knew that it was so perfect it couldn't be bettered, especially on a night as important as this one. Seb chose one of the most expensive wines on the list, with the best steak dish, side orders of mushrooms and green salad, and they sat gazing at one another, dreaming of world-wide success for Maggie.

'You never know, Maggie, what it might lead to. The

West End! All sorts of opportunities! Scripts will be landing on your doormat every other day. It's so wonderful, Maggie, just unbelievable.'

'Hey! Just a minute, why is it unbelievable, eh?'

'Well, I didn't mean it was impossible for *you* to get a good part, I meant ... well, I don't know what I meant, it's just so fantastic. I'm sorry, I didn't mean to offend.'

Maggie sobered up and went from being drunk with success to being downcast. 'It's a terrible responsibility, isn't it? I mean, if I don't get it right I could ruin it for everyone. No more series, no more anything. From high profile to zilch.'

'You were wild with excitement not five minutes ago. Come on, now.' He took hold of her hand with both of his. 'Smile?'

But Maggie couldn't. She'd just faced up to what she would lose by becoming totally absorbed in her acting career; and she would need to be totally absorbed to make a success of it. Then she remembered her life-long ambition was about to happen, the one thing she'd worked towards for years. Could she let it slip away for Seb's sake?

Seb recognised in her eyes the dilemma she was facing and did what he knew he must. 'You have got to go for it. You *have* to step out on to the world's stage and see where it leads. If I was selfish and self-seeking I'd beg you not to go, but I'm not going to. I'm going to say, at whatever cost to myself, *go*, Maggie. Go.'

Tears slid slowly down Maggie's cheeks. She nodded very slowly. 'We've only known each other a matter of weeks, but I love you as dearly as if I'd known you ten years, not ten weeks. I could marry you tomorrow and not go to London and—'

'No, you won't, because I shan't propose.'

A broad grin spread across Maggie's face. 'Oh, you heartless man, you. Cruel, that's what you are.'

'No, not cruel to you, only to myself. I should never forgive myself if I persuaded you not to go. My parents expected me to run the farm for them, but I knew I had to disappoint them because I simply could not do it. I would have withered away. Now I'm doing what I love best in all the world. Despite the disapproval and the upset, I stepped out and so can you. That doesn't mean I shan't miss you, because I shall … I … I …'

Their main course arrived and put an end to their conversation and they didn't get back to it until after the waiter had cleared away their plates.

'Maggie, I … I think it would be best if …' Seb said.

'Yes?'

He breathed deeply. 'I think it would be best if we make this our last evening together. It's so beautifully perfect – our favourite table, our favourite restaurant, our very own waiter we '

Maggie was devastated because she had plans for the evening to go on well into the night. 'You do?'

'We know we have to make the break. I've to let you concentrate on the job in hand and be able to give your all to it without me hanging on your coat-tails.'

'But I haven't got any coat-tails!'

'You know what I mean. You need to be free.' He spelt out the word for her, writing it with his finger on the palm of her hand as he spoke. 'F.R.E.E. So I'm suggesting that's what we do, free you to … devote yourself to what it is you have to do.' Seb's eyes filled with tears and for one terrible moment he thought he would break down. Maggie clutched his hand.

Then the dessert arrived and it looked so tempting they couldn't sit looking at it.

They each picked up their long-handled spoons. He scooped some cream onto his spoon and fed it to Maggie, and she did the same for him until the dish was empty; the bananas, the raspberries, the cream, the meringues, the honey sauce, the toasted almonds ... a beautiful memory. They laid their spoons together side by side and looked long and lovingly at each other. Seb tenderly ran the back of his forefinger up and down her cheek, enjoying the incredible softness of her skin.

Maggie whispered, 'You're right. We must finish tonight before we get too ...'

Seb drove her to the multi-storey car park. He got out of his car and watched her searching in her bag for her car keys. It took a while, but he didn't mind, he loved watching her expressive hands as they found one thing after another that proved not to be her keys, realising she couldn't see properly for the tears flooding her eyes.

'Oh! Here we are.' She held up her keys triumphantly. 'It doesn't mean we shan't see each other again, does it?'

'No.'

'When I come home for a break.'

'Of course.'

'Thank you, Seb, for a wonderful summer. Carlos, Mimi and Loretta went yesterday. Mum wore black all day. Three more tomorrow. Hopefully that'll be the end. Look after Mum and Dad for me. Mum's very down about me leaving home. Anyone would think I was going to be put down, too, not leaving because of a fantastic career move.' Maggie paused for a moment, then forced herself to look up at him. 'I'm sure you're right, Seb, to say goodnight now, but it's very hard to c-cope.' With her voice barely audible she whispered, 'I've fallen for you in a big way. What a lovely man you are.'

'You're lovelier. Goodnight, Maggie, and thanks ... for ... you know ...'

Maggie reached up and kissed Seb's mouth sweetly, bravely, almost tremblingly. She waved briefly and drove erratically away.

Chapter 13

The devastation and loneliness Seb suffered after Maggie left for London was far worse than he'd ever imagined it would be. He'd been so sure and so brave the night he'd suggested they said goodbye, he'd had no idea how badly he would be affected by not seeing her.

She'd phoned him a few times and sent him a silly postcard; he'd phoned her and sent her a beautiful art deco card. But still, for Seb, the pain dragged on. Maggie had a whole new world to contend with and she was so thoroughly absorbed in it he could feel the bonds which had held them loosening and he didn't quite know what he could do about it. Even though they'd agreed to part, Seb contemplated a weekend in London and rang her to suggest it, but she was so full of her first week's rehearsals that he knew he mustn't. After all, it was he who'd suggested she needed to be free so it was he who had to keep his word.

So he decided to go to Sarah Cockroft's engagement party and make himself enjoy it. She was celebrating her engagement to a soldier from the local military barracks and she'd invited absolutely everyone at the practice to a night at the Fox and Grapes with a meal, dancing and free drinks.

Seb didn't feel the slightest bit interested in someone else's happiness and almost said he couldn't go, but couldn't come up with a single genuine reason why not. He'd tried offering to be on call but Mungo had said absolutely not. He, Mungo, would be on call so long as Seb brought Miriam home when she was ready.

'Seems to me you need cheering up, Seb,' said Mungo. 'I don't know why, but you do.'

'But I'd much rather—'

'*You're going.* She'd much prefer you to be there than an old has-been like me, so there's an end to it. Party and drinks and dancing and laughing are just the right recipe for a chap in the doldrums. That's an order!'

Seb arrived late, had to park outside in the road and then felt anxious most of the evening about his car and the possibility of damage being done to it until Kate asked him to dance.

They danced well together, chatting, laughing and perfectly in time with each other. He could have danced with her all night, but she was in demand so he had to relinquish her to Rhodri and then Scott and then all the other male members of staff.

The little band Sarah had booked to provide the music played the hottest tunes possible and Seb found it grated on his nerves after a while. He escaped into the bar to find a quiet corner, but that was denied him as the bar was packed and everyone knew him so he had a constant supply of colleagues willing to talk, or rather shout at him. His phone rang and because it was impossible to hear what was said he went outside into the garden so he could hear better, desperately hoping, he had to confess, that it would be Mungo needing help. But it wasn't. It was Jilly Askew.

Seb sat down at one of the tables and greeted her with enthusiasm, glad to have someone to talk to who wasn't full to the brim with alcohol.

'Seb, long time no see. Drink tomorrow night? I'm still at Uncle Fergal's so shall we meet at the Fox? How about it?'

'I'd like that. Yes. How are you? Made any plans?'

'That's what the drink is about. Tell you then. Eight-thirty? No, I'm eating with my cousins and Aunt Cecilia and Uncle tomorrow night, so better make it nine-thirty. They always drag it out. See you then. Bye.'

As Seb switched off his phone he heard a voice say, 'Can't hack it, then?'

Seb looked up and found Kate standing at the end of the table he was sitting at.

She happened to be standing under an arc light which the pub used to illuminate the garden on summer nights with an eye to keeping everyone buying drinks long after dark. He didn't reply for one long minute. Instead he gazed up at her, collecting his thoughts. She looked at him, thought he didn't want company and began to move away.

'No! Don't go. Sit down and finish your drink. Please.'

He patted his end of the long bench he was sitting on and she sat.

Seb offered his excuses. 'I can't stand the noise. That's why I'm out here just for a while.' The light still shone on her hair and lit her face, that face he'd thought was arrogant but tonight looked ... vulnerable. 'Not enjoying life?'

Kate nodded. 'Exhausted. Had a long night on call and I'm not used to it.'

'On call already? They gave me a fortnight's grace before I

started and then I was lucky. One call and I was back in bed by midnight.'

'Mmm. I got up at two and didn't get back to bed till seven, by which time I had to be up for a day's work, and this party. Couldn't not come. I've known Sarah a long while, seven years, and she has always had time for me. But all I want is to go to bed.' Kate smiled at him.

'Have a quick kip here if you like.' He studied her face and decided that perhaps she wasn't arrogant. She looked it only because she had classic good looks. With her fine-boned straight nose, large blue eyes, discreet make-up, elegant forehead and lovely smile, she was exceptional.

'If I fell asleep here, right now, I'd still be here tomorrow morning.'

Seb laughed. 'I recognise the feeling. Why do we do it? We must be mad.'

'On the other hand we could be dedicated and devoted. I've fought every fight to get myself to veterinary college and stay there, and then at the end failed one of my finals and had to take it again last month.'

'I did wonder why you started so late.'

'Now you know. My stepmother almost died of disappointment for me. But at last here I am.' Kate finished her drink.

'Would you like another? I'll get it for you.'

'Thanks. Orange juice this time or I really will be fast asleep. I've no head for alcohol.'

Seb disentangled his legs from the bench, picked up her glass and disappeared into the bar. It took a while for him to get served and when he came back she was fast asleep, her head resting on her forearms on the table, dead to the world.

She'd put her coat beside her on the bench so he picked it up and carefully placed it over her shoulders and tucked it around her to help keep her warm. He sat down with her to enjoy his drink. Miriam came by so he put a forefinger to his lips and nodded his head towards Kate.

Miriam sat down opposite him, saying softly, 'I've come to escape the noise.'

'So have we.'

Miriam was delighted by this situation. It was just what she and Joy wanted, the two of them making contact. Well, not contact exactly, because Kate was fast asleep, but it was progress.

'Kate was on call last night and didn't get much sleep. Not used to it, you see.'

'Of course. Wonderful party. The food's coming soon. We shall lose Sarah, you know, because Steven's going out to Germany and of course Sarah will go with him. I'm glad she's found someone so worthwhile. She's a lovely girl. How's Maggie doing? I suppose you've heard from her?'

'Maggie's doing well. We've agreed not to see each other.'

'You have?' Inside Miriam almost rejoiced.

'This chance is what she's been wanting for years and years, right from being at school, and I knew we had to let go. So she could be free.' Seb swallowed hard, taking a mouthful of his drink to cover his distress.

'Maggie was ... I mean ... is a lovely person. She thought the world of you. Did you realise?'

Seb nodded.

'It's too cold out here. I'm going in. I'm sorry Kate is so weary. All part of a vet's life, though, isn't it? She's a lovely person, just like Maggie was … is …' Miriam wandered off to find Joy and tell her what she'd seen in the garden.

Shortly after Miriam returned inside it was announced that food was to be served, so Seb gently shook Kate's shoulder, because he didn't want her to wake up and find she'd been abandoned.

She struggled to sit up and rubbed her eyes. 'Oh, God! I didn't fall asleep, did I? I'm so sorry. Food? Well, I am hungry. I'll collect a plate of food and come back out here to eat it, then I'm going home.'

Kate disappeared, embarrassed by being so tired and wondering if ever she would get used to being on call. At college there'd been a member of staff with her on night calls. Maybe she'd chosen the wrong profession. Still, Seb appeared to survive OK. Maybe she would.

Seb dragged himself into his consulting room the next day. He grunted his good mornings, checked his appointment list with bleary eyes and wished himself anywhere but where he was. His first appointment was Mrs Bookbinder with her Chang.

'Do you mind? I usually see Valentine, I know, but it's his day off and it's urgent. Chang here has been poorly all night. I rang first thing and they said I could see you.'

'What's the problem?'

'Well, that's why I've come. There's something wrong but I don't know what it is. He had no dinner last night and this morning, when I thought he'd be starving, he didn't even have his breakfast.'

'What would he normally have for his breakfast?'

'Something hard to chew on, like a Bonio or something

to clean his teeth. That's all. I don't want him to have rotten teeth in his old age, you see. But he's behaving most oddly.'

'Let's put him up on the table and I'll have a feel.'

Mrs Bookbinder was trembling with anxiety and Seb sensed something was very wrong because she'd intimidated him when he'd had dealings with her before and here she was almost a total wreck.

Seb felt all over Chang's body and found it swollen and obviously painful. Chang jerked away from him and was close to snapping at him. He felt his undercarriage again from the end of his ribs right down to between his back legs, very, very gently. 'It seems to me that he needs an X-ray because there's something causing him great pain in his abdomen. Has he passed a motion this morning or yesterday?'

So as not to mention such intimate matters in Chang's hearing Mrs Bookbinder whispered, 'Friday first thing but not since.'

'I see. Mmm. That's four days. An X-ray it is, then.'

'Oh, dear. It's serious?'

'Does he play with stones when he's out? Pick up sticks?'

'No, not usually.'

'Will you leave him with us? I'll get him X-rayed and give you a ring when I've had a look.'

Mrs Bookbinder was horrified. 'Leave him? Leave him here on his own?'

'Mrs Bookbinder, he couldn't be in better hands, now could he? There's definitely a blockage of some sort. You must face the fact that he may need an operation ...'

'An operation?' She sank down on a chair, suddenly white and faint.

'Put your head between your knees, please.' Seb rang his emergency bell and Dodie came rushing in.

'Yes?'

'Mrs Bookbinder feels faint. Could she have a glass of water, please? I'm admitting Chang here for an X-ray, you see.'

Dodie got the silent message from Seb and set about quietly removing Mrs Bookbinder in a very sympathetic manner from the consulting room. 'I'll send Sarah in for Chang.' She nodded to him and left with Mrs Bookbinder.

'I'm so sorry. It's the shock, you see. He has a blockage and we all know what that means.'

Whereupon Dodie had to call for help, as she couldn't support Mrs Bookbinder in total collapse all by herself, as she weighed twice what Dodie weighed, so Joy had to lend a hand to get her seated.

The clients waiting their turns secretly enjoyed this happening to Mrs Bookbinder as they all knew her as a very domineering woman, and several of them had personal experience of her sharp tongue. Poor Chang, though. He was a sparky little dog.

The word went round the waiting room and back again, softly so Mrs B. didn't hear what they were saying. The glass of water did wonders for her, and gradually the rapid breathing and trembling slowed and she looked more like herself.

Dodie relieved her of the empty glass and said soothingly, 'Seb knows what he's doing. So sit quietly and when you feel better let me know and one of us will drive you home.'

'I thought I'd stay here and take him home with me.'

'Not today. If he needs an operation the very earliest he can go will be tomorrow.'

'I see. But my car's here.'

191

'Well, we'll see how you feel, shall we? Tea?' Dodie got a nod. 'Sugar, for shock?' Another nod but no words. After half an hour Mrs Bookbinder got to her feet and said she felt well enough to drive home and she'd ring in a while. 'Tell Mr Partridge I am relying on him *completely*.'

'Of course. Now take care, Mrs Bookbinder, as you drive. I'm sure it won't be as bad as you think.'

In a gap between clients Dodie went in to see Seb. 'What is it?'

'What?'

'Chang, what's wrong with him?'

'I think he's swallowed something and it's got lodged in his stomach.'

'She says you used the word blockage.'

Seb agreed he had.

'You see, "blockage" to a lay person implies cancer, and that's what's made her almost faint.'

'Ah! Right. Sorry.'

'Choose your words carefully.' She smiled so sweetly that Seb knew it wasn't a reprimand, simply good advice, and he accepted that.

'Thanks, I didn't think about that.'

'Don't worry, you'll learn. She's gone now, so let's have the X-ray done a.s.a.p. and then we can let her know. She's a good client of ours. We don't want her upset, OK?'

'OK.'

The X-ray showed that in fact Chang had swallowed a child's toy of some sort, which was too big to pass into his intestine, and would have to be removed surgically. So Seb rang Mrs Bookbinder and reassured her that he would be operated on that very afternoon. 'He'll never be able to pass it through. I'm amazed he managed to swallow it in the first place, but there we are.'

'I know exactly what it is. Two of my grandchildren stayed the night on Friday and brought toys with them, and when they went home on Saturday they couldn't find a nasty metal alien from outer space. That must be where it went. It made a vile whirring noise when they wound it up and Chang didn't like it. He must have decided to chew it up to get rid of it. The naughty boy! I'm so relieved.' She burst into tears.

Seb managed to make himself heard above her sobbing and told her to ring about five, but no, Chang wouldn't be able to go home tonight. Post-operative care, you see.

'Of course, of course. Thank you so much, you're so clever. Five o'clock it is.'

Having handed Chang over to Bunty, Seb called for his next client. 'Tyrone Foster, please.'

There was a message from reception on the screen warning him that they were concerned about the dog and that this was a new client. Tyrone was a cross pitbull terrier and big with it. He walked awkwardly into the consulting room, looking mortally afraid.

'Good morning, Mr Foster. This is Tyrone, then?'

'Yes. He's been in a road accident and he seems to be in pain.'

'Did you see the accident?'

'Well, no, I didn't. Why?'

'Because if you saw it you could tell me if he went under the wheels, or merely got bumped by it, or trapped underneath. You weren't with him, then?'

'Well, no, he slipped out and I didn't realise.'

'I see. So how do we know it was a road accident?'

'Well, I guessed as much, the way he is.'

'Seeing as we don't know where he got hit I'll examine him standing on the floor. Lifting him up could only make it worse for him. Is he accustomed to being examined by a vet?'

'No, he isn't.'

'How old is he?'

'Two years old.'

'Good with children?'

'Well, yes, if he ever meets 'em.'

'You haven't got any, then?'

'No. Can we get on with it? I can't waste time like this.'

Seb began by trying to reassure the dog. It was difficult because he shrank away when he tried to stroke him, shivered when he did get touched and tried to growl but didn't quite succeed, presumably because of the pain he was in.

'He's very nervous.'

'Well, so would you be if you'd been hit ... by a car.'

'I expect I would. If you don't mind, I'm going to put a muzzle on him. He's far too unhappy to be examined without one.'

Mr Foster didn't answer, so Seb left him in the consulting room for a moment while he went to get one. 'Joy, I need a muzzle for this dog. He won't let me near him.'

'I'll be hard put to find one. It's ages since one was needed. This is the pitbull cross?'

'He's certainly unsafe to touch never mind examine.'

'Hold on.' Joy disappeared into the back and came out with an almost new muzzle. 'I'll give Rhodri a shout. Two opinions are better than one. Just as a safeguard, you know.'

Seb took the muzzle back in and told Mr Foster that if he wanted to use a muzzle, legally he needed another vet in attendance and someone was coming. Seb didn't know if it was a legal requirement but felt safer saying that.

'Well, that'll cost me.'

'Let's wait and see.' Seb offered Tyrone a couple of chocolate drops but he wasn't having any of it, which was very unusual. Many a difficult situation had been resolved by the consumption of chocolate drops, but not this time.

Rhodri came in. Between them they fixed the muzzle and fastened a leash on Tyrone so Rhodri could keep hold of him while Seb did the examination. By this time Mr Foster was becoming agitated. 'Well, all this fuss about a few bruises. What a carry on, I think I'll just go and let you get on with it. I'm doing my best for him, and here you are making a song and dance about it.'

'He could have cracked ribs if he's been in a car accident.'

'Well, I expect he could, but what's a cracked rib? They don't even do anything for humans nowadays. Not even strapped up, they aren't.'

Seb began examining Tyrone. It was taking all Rhodri's strength to hold on because Tyrone was absolutely frantic to escape. Seb managed to feel along his ribs, gently squeezed his flanks, tested his legs in view of the difficulty he had walking when he first came in, felt his jaw, but it was the ribs where Tyrone hurt the most.

'I think we shall have to X-ray him. He's in such pain a broken rib may have punctured a lung. Can you leave him with us? We'll sedate him and X-ray the vital bits.'

'Well, not Pygmalion likely. I'm not leaving 'im 'ere. 'eaven alone knows what you might do. Charge me the earth, I've no doubt. Take that blasted muzzle off and I'll be off. Then you can't charge me a penny 'cos you've done nothing.' Mr

Foster grabbed at the leash but Rhodri was too quick for him.

'I agree with my colleague that this dog needs veterinary attention and we would be lacking in our duty of care if we allowed you to go. The dog is the important one in this situation. So leave him with us, give us your telephone number and we'll be in touch later today.' Rhodri's lilting Welsh voice must have reassured Mr Foster because he eventually nodded his head and gave him a number.

'Is this a landline number? It doesn't look like it.'

'Well ... no, it's my mobile number.'

'And your address in Barleybridge?'

'I'm just passing through. Been helping on the new road they're building. We've been using Tyrone as a guard dog, but he ain't no use as he is now. I'll be off.'

Rhodri grew suspicious and with it very firm indeed. 'I think you're going to do a runner. To abandon a dog is an offence and I'm not going to allow you to do it. Tell me the truth: who was it who injured this dog?'

'*Who* was it? I said it was a car accident.' Mr Foster began eyeing the door out of the corner of his eye.

'*No.*' Rhodri roared this word and Mr Foster jumped. 'I asked for the truth. It can't be that hard.'

Seb asked why the dog was so nervous. 'Someone's been maltreating this dog, haven't they? Who is it? You?'

Mr Foster stripped off his sweater and showed them his bare arms. Both of them had several deep teeth marks made by a big dog. The one on his right arm was already going septic with inflammation circling it, almost visibly spreading. Seb was appalled and saw that his first instinct to muzzle the dog had been all too right.

'It's me what's been maltreated, not 'im.'

'Well?'

Rhodri blanched when he saw the wounds. 'Have you had a tetanus injection?'

'Never.'

Seb, angrier than he had ever been, said, 'Sit down, Mr Foster, will you. I'm taking Tyrone and tying him up in one of our isolation rooms, out of harm's way. Then I'm coming back to you to ask you some questions. So you'd better have some answers ready. The truth this time.'

Rhodri stayed with Mr Foster. Seb took the dog and locked him up as he said he would and then went to find Joy. 'We've got a problem. I've locked the dog in the isolation room, fastened him tightly to the hook that's there for the purpose. I'm keeping the key. No one is to go in there, no matter what. He's too dangerous. Apologies to my next client.'

'Don't worry. I'll get Kate to see them.'

By the time Seb returned to his consulting room Rhodri had got the truth from Mr Foster. 'All right. All right. I use him for fighting. Betting and that, you know. He's a killer. Best dog I've ever had. Never a mark on 'im. Then he turned on me two days ago. He was asleep and I caught him unawares and startled him. I spoke to him like I always do, so he knows it's me what feeds him, but he went for me, something he'd never done before. Could always rely on 'im, I could, but I must admit to being a bit nervous of him just lately. Different, he's been. Gave me a right shock, he did, the daft beggar. Couldn't get him off and my mate had to kick him hard as he could, in his ribs, to get me free. If my mate hadn't been there ... I just don't know what to do.'

'So you're not just passing through while you work on the road?'

'Well, no.'

'It's my opinion that this is a pitbull terrier.'

'Well, it ain't. On his papers it says he's a cross.'

'Where do you meet for the fights?' Rhodri could tell that Mr Foster was getting a lot of pain from his arms so he knew this was the moment to get the truth.

'I ... this doesn't half hurt.'

'Tell us. Now is your moment and then we'll have a word with the police and say how much you helped us.'

'The police! My God! They'll make me have him put down.'

'Exactly. The poor thing, when it's not his fault. Life isn't fair, is it?' Seb was so angry now he had difficulty speaking without venom in his voice. 'So we're still waiting for the answer. Where do the fights take place?'

Mr Foster delayed answering while he examined yet again the great gashes Tyrone's teeth had made on his arms, some of them fifteen centimetres long and jagged, too.

'Imagine the damage he could do to a small child if he'd startled him? Mmm? He'd have been killed.' Seb left that to sink in for a moment and then said in a persuasive tone of voice, 'Come on, then, tell us. You know it's for the best.'

'Well, I love Tyrone. He's always been my best friend.'

'Best friend? I don't think so. He's lived in fear of you, hasn't he? I'm afraid that my experience tells me that Tyrone is a dangerous dog and that he must, I repeat, *must* be put down.'

Rhodri said, 'If you tell all, and you sign a paper to say you gave your permission for us to put your dog to sleep,

198

then the police will be impressed, believe me. I know from experience. I'm not saying you'll be let off but it will certainly improve your chances. Is Tyrone your only dog?'

Mr Foster nodded. 'Well, at the moment, yes, he is.' He winced again, then his words tumbled out in a rush. 'A farm over Beulah Bank Top, in that giant barn they have there. That's all I can say. We only go at dark. Don't know its name even.'

Seb wrote a declaration on his computer and printed it out for Mr Foster to sign. They had to read it out to him as he said he couldn't read. The signature was written painfully slowly in an almost child-like script. Then Seb asked him for his address and wrote it below Mr Foster's signature: 'The Dark Blue Bus, Station Car Park, (back of) Barleybridge, Dorset.'

As sympathetically as he could Seb said, 'You live in a bus?'

The man nodded.

'Now, Mr Foster, we'll attend to Tyrone. He won't know a thing, he'll simply fall asleep and that will be that, he'll be beyond pain. What you must do is get yourself straight to hospital before those wounds get any worse. You don't want septicaemia to set in. I've never seen such a serious dog bite.'

'Well, you haven't lived. I've seen a lot worse. Do it gently to him, the blasted daft beggar. What did he have to turn on me for, eh? I ask yer? Me what feeds him.'

Rhodri, in a very controlled tone, said, 'Out of fear, Mr Foster, out of fear. Good afternoon. Pay at the desk on your way out.'

Seb prepared to put Tyrone to sleep. 'I wouldn't mind if Tyrone was to blame, but he isn't. It feels so cruel.'

'It isn't, Seb. He's had one hell of a life, the poor thing, and we're putting him out of his misery. I've recorded our conversation, OK? Didn't get a chance to tell you. We'll get it transcribed and then fasten the letter he signed and the tape and the printout in a big envelope and put them in the safe for security. I don't trust that chap further than I can throw him. Come on, let's get the job done.'

So they both went to the isolation room, unlocked the door and found that Tyrone had spent his time attempting to drag the strong steel hook the leash had been tied to, out of the wall. Another five minutes and he would have been loose. In his eyes was the same frantic fear he'd shown when he first arrived.

'Get that needle in quicko, Seb,' Rhodri said. 'No conscience about it, if you please.'

Tyrone collapsed immediately. Seb stroked his head, knowing it was all too late, but not liking the poor dog to go without what was perhaps the first compassionate touch he'd had since he was born.

That night Maggie rang. She was full of excitement, thrilled to bits at being with her theatrical soul mates, and wondering how her darling Seb was getting on. She'd known the moment he answered her call that things were not right with him. 'What's the matter, Seb?'

'I'm being ridiculous really. It's nothing.'

'It is, I can tell. Tell me, please. I wish I were there to hug you.'

'I had to put a dog to sleep today and it wasn't his fault.'

'He was too ill, you mean?'

'No, he was dangerous through no fault of his own. You

200

see, he'd been used for dog-fighting, betting and that. There's big money in it apparently. When they're going to use them for fighting they don't get loved and cared for like they should. Don't want to make them soft, you see, but he turned on his owner and they had to kick his ribs in to make him let go. I know we couldn't let him live, obviously, because he was dangerous, but I rather felt it would have been a good idea to stick the syringe in the owner not the dog.'

'You sound so angry about it.'

'I am.'

'In Barleybridge, though? Sleepy old Barleybridge. Where-abouts?'

'The other side of Beulah Bank Top. We've informed the police.'

'Good. They deserve all they get. Don't worry about the dog any more. It wasn't his fault but it would have been yours if, knowing what you knew, you'd not put him down and he'd then killed someone. At least you've nothing on your conscience.'

'No, you're right.' Seb felt consoled by Maggie's sound common sense.

'Change of subject. Seb, I'm having a wonderful time here, it's all going so well, but I do miss you.' Maggie hesitated, and had to clear her throat.

'I miss you, Maggie, very much. You know we're all root-ing for you, willing you to come out tops. Do you feel happy with what you're doing?'

'So happy, Seb. Got to go, there's someone at the door. Goodnight. Miss you.' She sent a kiss down the line and Seb returned it. 'Soon be Christmas. See you.'

The receiver went down before Seb could tell her he had

all of Christmas off and was going home. He'd tell her next time.

Tyrone's death never left Seb's mind. Joy's Duncan, who for years had walked on Beulah Bank Top, guessed exactly which farm it was.

'That's Beulah Heights Farm,' he said. 'They built a huge barn for some reason or another years ago and the idea for it fell through so it's never been used since. The farmer's not a bad chap; let me shelter there one day for an hour when it was tippling down. Not making much of a living, though, I shouldn't think.'

Bunty's Dicky was celebrated at the police station for being hot on animal cruelty and the news stirred him like nothing else could. 'Right! That's me sorted for a few days,' he said. 'Foster? Foster? I'm sure that name rings a bell. Little chap, like a weasel, nasty little face.'

So Seb knew that something would be done, but the whole episode had left a nasty taste in his mouth.

Chapter 14

While his head was still full of the dog-fighting problem there came a knock at his consulting-room door. Kate put her head round. 'It's only me. Are you free?'

Seb smiled. 'Of course!'

She came in and closed the door behind her. 'Feeling better after the party?'

'Yes, thanks. And you?'

'I went home, fell into bed and slept the sleep of the innocent until half past seven. Mia, my stepmother, knocked on the door to wake me up. God, I was tired. She'd like to invite you to a meal one night, by the way. Thinks you won't be feeding yourself properly.'

'That sounds lovely. Yes, I'd like that. It gets boring eating all on your own. When would she like me to come?'

'Tonight?'

'Sorry, I'm seeing someone tonight.'

'Friday night, then?'

'That'd be great.'

'Best explain. I call Mia my stepmother but she looked after me from when I was two weeks old, because my mother walked out on me. Thoughtful, wasn't she? Then Mia married my dad while I was still a baby, but he died of a heart attack six years ago so we've stayed together in a new flat ever since. She's now married again to a very nice man she met through the art gallery where she works. His name's Gordon Buchanan. Scottish obviously. We get on very well indeed. He's kindness itself to me. So now you know. Best for me to tell you, then you won't drop a clanger.'

'Thanks for putting me in the picture. I'll look forward to that. What time?'

'About seven?'

'Right, seven it is.'

'I've been in to see Chang. He's looking good, isn't he?'

'Yes, he is.'

Seb went to check on Chang Bookbinder for himself. He stood in front of his cage in the intensive-care room as Bunty called it. He felt in a daze. Automatically he checked the notes tucked into the front of it where Chang couldn't chew them, read them, opened the cage door to be greeted by Chang struggling to wake. He stretched and yawned and wagged his tail.

Seb rolled him over onto his back and examined the site of his operation and felt satisfied with it. He was so absorbed he didn't notice Bunty come in.

'He's doing fine. I reckon he could go home tonight, don't you?' she suggested.

But she got no answer. All that happened was Seb scratched Chang behind his ear. The dog loved it and braced himself to get the maximum enjoyment.

'Are you all right?' Bunty asked loudly.

Seb, his eyes glazed, said, 'Yes, of course. I think he could go home tonight, don't you?'

'That's what I thought. I'll give Mrs Bookbinder a ring, shall I?'

He still wasn't hearing what she said. 'I'll ring Mrs Bookbinder and let her know, shall I?'

'Good idea.'

Bunty reported back to the staffroom that she wondered if Seb was losing his marbles.

'Really?' replied Joy. 'Well, I never.'

Bunty saw the grin on her face. 'Is there something I don't know?'

'Nothing at all. Just a joke between Miriam and myself. Right, Bunty, get your lunch. Mungo's wanting to make an early start this afternoon. That grey cat that he's operating on isn't looking any too clever. His owners will be distraught if it doesn't work out. Mungo's told them it's risky and that he's not sure about it, but they're willing to take the risk, so I'm keeping my fingers crossed all afternoon. They're the sort who won't find it at all funny to have to pay for the operation and no cat to take home. Have you noticed the decorations? I wonder, shall we have a Christmas mince pies and drinks event to show them off? Mulled wine, that kind of thing. I'll ask Mungo, see what he thinks.'

Christmas events were not uppermost in Bunty's mind. 'Why not? Are you *sure* Seb's all right? He was very upset about that dog he had to put down yesterday. But he'll have to learn, won't he?'

'Exactly. Don't worry. Off you go.' But she still had that unfathomable smile on her face.

Seb could not concentrate on the job in hand the rest of the afternoon. From the operating theatre he couldn't hear

Miriam and Kate's voices but in his mind he could see Kate's face, hear her voice, see her smile. She was so good-looking, so very good-looking. Not pretty, more distinguished. Classical almost. He couldn't understand why he hadn't noticed her at college ... he knew Mungo had spoken to him, but he hadn't the faintest idea what he'd said.

'Seb! Did you hear me?'

'I'm sorry, no.'

'I said, ask Bunty to come and take ... what's this cat called?'

Seb referred to its notes. 'Sweetie.'

'That's right, what a godawful name. No dignity. No wonder the poor thing hasn't any interest in staying alive.'

'But she has. Stayed alive, that is.'

'Yes, thank goodness. The owners would have gone berserk if she hadn't. But I did say she might not. However, we're not out of the woods yet.'

Seb didn't make a move at all, but stood staring at Sweetie. Neatly stitched up and off the anaesthetic and waiting ... waiting ...

'Seb! Bunty, please. You do realise that Bunty's nose is out of joint with you assisting me. All we need is you arriving in intensive care with dear little Sweetie then the balloon really will go up. I can't afford to have her storming out in a temper, she's too valuable. Now, shift yourself.'

Mungo confided in Miriam that evening when he got up to the flat. 'It's no good. Seb's going off the boil. He was useless this afternoon. Absolutely useless. Didn't hear a word I said. I'm having serious doubts about him. Dazed he was, absolutely dazed, and it won't do.'

Miriam kissed him and handed him a whisky. 'You deserve that.'

'Why?'

'For ... for operating on that poor cat's hips when you weren't at all sure you should, but you did and it worked well. Just be thankful.'

'I'm not talking about the cat. Didn't you hear what I said?'

Miriam smiled. 'Perfectly.'

'What's the secrecy?'

'There isn't any.'

'Miriam! It's not that scheme of yours and Joy's, is it?'

'She gets lovelier, you know. Just ... lovelier.' Miriam stared out of the window for a minute, lost in thought. 'Joy says how about mince pies and mulled wine for the clients one afternoon before Christmas? Then they can see the decorations. They are especially lovely this year. Kate has quite an artistic bent, you know.' Miriam paused, then said softly, 'In a way she's the daughter we lost. We get on so well.'

'She's the daughter Joy never had, too.'

'That's perceptive of you.'

'Well, she is. I wonder. Is that what's the matter with Seb? Has he gone all gooey-eyed over her? You know, I may be right.'

'Oh! Surely not.' She was still looking out of the window so she could afford to smile because Mungo couldn't see her face. 'Must check the supper. You sit down, darling. After such a strenuous, perceptive day, you must be tired.'

In the kitchen Miriam smiled. He was the dearest man. Then she chuckled as she lifted the casserole from the oven. Seb being absent-minded was a very good sign. Had she and

Joy been successful with their match-making? Only time would tell.

Seb used his mouthwash before he left the flat, changed his shirt, put on his smart jacket, went back to the bathroom to use his electric razor and his aftershave, and rushed to meet Jilly. He was curious to know what decision she'd taken about her career. It was all very well him telling her to go for it, just as he had done, and as he'd advised Maggie to do, but Jilly had a far greater problem with a big family all entrenched in money, estates, horses and the Hunt. Jilly was stepping right out of the mould and that took courage.

Dressed impeccably, she was waiting for him to arrive, without a drink in front of her and deep in thought.

'Jilly! Good evening. How are you? No drink? What can I get for you?'

'A double whisky and soda.'

Seb made no comment on the word 'double'.

She tossed half of it down in one gulp before she added any soda. Then she said, 'The dinner tonight was a disaster.'

'I'm so sorry.'

'Even Aunt Cecilia joined in the fray. No one but Uncle was on my side.'

'What about your parents? How do they feel about you being a teacher?'

'I haven't got any. That's why I spend a lot of time at Uncle's. My father was his younger brother. I don't know what to do. I told them I'd got the offer of an interview and how thrilled I was about it, and they all fell about laughing except for Uncle.'

'You've got an interview? That's brilliant, I'm so pleased.'

'Pleased? That makes only two who approve.'

'Does it matter? You're not wanting to train as a pole-dancer, or a variety artist, are you? It's completely sane and very worthwhile. You'll be magnificent at it – stylish, charismatic, fabulous.'

'Seb! You are good for me.'

'When's the interview?'

'Ten days away.'

'Another drink?'

'I'll get these. My turn.'

'You'll be a sensation in a secondary school,' Seb said when she returned.

'Shall I be able to cope, though? Behaviour problems, disinterest, scorn.'

'I can remember waiting for a new teacher to enter the classroom and knowing in an instant whether or not they had a grip on discipline. That's the secret, going in meaning business. You knew exactly which teachers could control a class and which ones couldn't. It's a technique, I suppose, and it has to be there. Don't you remember that?'

'My dear Seb, I always went to schools with very small classes that were very much under control. No one got away with anything at all.'

'I see. Whatever I say, it is *your* decision to make. And as for your family, it's still your decision. They might think it ridiculous for an Askew to teach, but if that's what you want ...'

'I'm more lost than ever. But you are right. I'm not asking *them* to go to university again, am I? Only me. Come to think of it, I'll do it. Yes, I definitely will. I'll do it. I'm going back to tell them all that and to hell with it.' Jilly rose to her feet, with the light of battle in her eyes. Seb stood up to find himself being kissed by Jilly. 'That's my thank-you for making me brave. You're very good for me, did you know that? You put fire in my belly. I'm going. Don't think this is the last of me, I shall be ringing you up when things get too difficult and asking for advice. OK?'

She left Seb with his drink still to finish. Jilly had smelt wealthy, he thought. Even her handbag had smelt of money, gloriously soft and smooth, as he'd handed it to her. He admired her determination but sincerely wondered if she had any idea what she was in for.

Mungo burst into the staffroom at lunchtime with an announcement. 'I'm sorry to have to tell you this but I've just heard on the veterinary grapevine that Harvey Johnson-Munt has died this morning. Only thirty-nine. Can't believe it. Right out of the blue. Out riding with some friends and he came off. He was dead the minute he hit the ground. Terrible. Leaves a wife and four little girls. The eldest is eight. Tragic. I'm very upset. Very upset. Thought you ought to know ... just in case.' He paused in the doorway as though about to say something else, then apparently changed his mind and left.

Kate, who couldn't for the life of her recollect who the man was, opened her mouth to ask, but was stopped by Ginny. 'If anyone here dares to suggest that we take on being Hunt vet instead of that man, I for one will—'

'Good for the practice, though, if we were. I mean, I'm sorry he's dead, of course,' Kate said innocently.

Colin, being anti-Hunt, stood quietly to one side, allowing the explosion to occur without his assistance. Rhodri muttered under his breath. Seb prayed Kate wouldn't put her foot in it any more than she already had done. Dan, who'd walked in just in time to catch Mungo's announcement, said, 'Now is not the time to discuss the matter. The poor fellow's scarcely cold. Let's show some respect.' Though he knew he was only postponing the argument, what he said sufficed for the moment and cooled things down.

Ginny stormed out.

Kate caught up with Seb before his first client. 'I said something terribly wrong in there, didn't I?'

'Mmm. 'Fraid so. Someone saw me having a drink with Jilly Askew after I'd examined a hound that her horse had struck when it reared. You know, Lord Askew's niece? They mentioned it in the stallroom and it all blew up from there. There's only Dan and myself and Mungo who have no strong anti-Hunt views; the rest are dead against it. So this Harvey man dying has opened up a whole can of worms.'

'I see. Thanks. Well, I can honestly say that I don't mind either way. After all, they'll have to find another vet, won't they?'

'Mungo would be very pleased if they came to us. Nowadays a veterinary practice can't afford to turn away business. Unfortunately, Ginny's threatened to resign if we take the Hunt on.'

'Whoops! I shall watch out in future, then. I like Ginny, even though she's so forthright, but she can be stroppy and sometimes very wrong.'

Mungo attended Harvey's funeral, seeing as they had met on several occasions in the course of their work, and Harvey had been a prominent member of the county veterinary profession for the last ten years. When Ginny heard he was going she sniffed derisively and turned her back on him. The other anti-Hunt staff just quietly allowed him to get on with it, because they were generous enough to recognise that his reasons for attending were right.

The whole matter blew up a week later when Lord Askew arrived without an appointment to see Mungo. Seb happened to be in reception by the 'knick–knack' shelf, talking to a client about suitable toys for her new puppy.

'I want to get it right, Seb. I'm determined this puppy is going to be intelligent, you see. Oh!' The client covered her mouth with her hand and muttered, 'I say, look who's here!'

Seb turned and saw Lord Askew waiting. 'Good afternoon, Lord Askew. Can I help?'

'You're the new vet who's been seeing my niece, Jilly, aren't you?'

Seb agreed he was.

'Thank you for the support you've given her. My brood can't believe it of her, but I think one should do what one feels is right for one to do. My life was mapped out for me the second I was born, you see, so I approve of freedom of choice. She went yesterday for her interview and it appears to have gone well. Now, my business is with Mungo Price. Is he about?'

'He's operating, I believe. If you'll take a seat, I'll find out.'

Mungo was doing exactly that, but guessing what Lord Askew's business would be he decided Seb had better get a gown on and continue with the operation for him.

'Bunty knows what we're doing. The X-rays are up. It's a fractured femur job, very simple, good experience. Where is

212

he?' Mungo dragged off his gloves, Bunty untied his gown, and Mungo marched into reception, hand outstretched in welcome.

'Lord Askew, good afternoon. My office is this way. Pot of tea, Dodie, please.' Just in time, he remembered to ask his lordship if tea would be satisfactory.

'Absolutely right, with a drop of whisky in it if that's possible.' So Dodie unearthed the medicinal whisky from the back of Joy's cupboard and took the tray in for the two of them, best cups and saucers without question.

Reception echoed with the gossiping of the clients all trying to second-guess why on earth his lordship wanted to speak to Mungo. Various theories were aired but nobody really knew. Some were lucky enough still to be waiting when he departed but they learned nothing, because Mungo saw him out and rushed straight back to oversee the operation he'd left with Seb. In fact, he said nothing to anyone, except to Miriam, and that was up in the flat at the end of his working day.

'I had to leave Seb with the operation and he did magnificently. Most impressed I was. He went as white as a sheet when I said he'd to take over, but he excelled himself.'

'No time for preparation, either.'

'Exactly.'

'So what *did* his lordship want?'

'You know full well.'

'The Hunt?'

'Naturally. Who else is there to turn to? He wants us all right, but I've got our staff to deal with. So far, Dan and Seb appear to be on my side. Ginny will resign; she's already said so and I shan't cry in my soup over that! Rhodri won't know what to do, Colin will simply keep quiet and hope it'll go away, and Scott will say no because he can't do any other owing to Zoe's strong objection. So that leaves me.'

'And Kate.'

'Ah! Yes, Kate. If Ginny leaves, Kate'll be very necessary. Anyway, she's got her head screwed on OK so I've no doubts she'll agree with me. You see, we can't afford not to go for it. What with the extra consulting room over and above the first extension, and now the lab, which still needs fitting out, we need the brass, as they would say in Yorkshire. If we're offered it I shall definitely say yes. After all, the hounds are kept in spanking good health, far better than any dogs we have coming in here, so we shan't be running backwards and forwards caring for a host of overweight, sick dogs, shall we? There'll be only a handful of horses, and the added bonus is the prestige of the appointment.'

'My word, Mungo, you will have to travel slowly and very carefully. You may even lose clients if they're anti-Hunt. It's a very delicate subject, and I can't possibly imagine any new government daring to rescind the legislation.'

'They should never have voted for it in the first place. Face it, it's an impossible task, policing all the hunts. Is my food ready? I'm starving. Can I smell beef and ale casserole? Excellent!'

That evening Kate put her head round Seb's door when she heard the last of his clients leaving and asked Seb if he had any plans.

'No, I haven't. Have you?'

'Well, Mia and Gordon are both out tonight and I don't fancy cooking just for one.'

'Neither do I.'

'Do you like the idea of a meal out with me? I'll pay my share.'

'I fancy the idea very much indeed but it's my treat.'

'I didn't mean for it to be your treat, I can pay my way.'

'Well ... mind if I pay this once? It would give me much pleasure.' He gave her a very charming smile as he said this and she could do nothing but agree.

'With a smile like that, how can a girl refuse? What about the Italian? It's my favourite.'

Seb felt embarrassed by her choice, more so when they were shown to the same table he and Maggie had preferred and got the same waiter.

'Good evening to you, sir,' he said with a wink at Seb. 'Good evening, madam. What can I get for you?' With notebook poised he waited but received no reply. 'I'll come back later, shall I?'

'Yes, please.'

'So-o-o, how did the op go?'

Seb had to confess it went fine. 'I was almost shaking with the horror of it, but Mungo disappeared so quickly I just had to get on with it. The X-ray was excellent and of course Bunty could do it herself, I swear, she's so experienced. My hands trembled a bit but once I got involved and Bunty had pointed out one or two things suddenly my confidence was there and Bunty and I coped very well. We were just closing when Mungo came back.'

'Did he say anything about what Lord Askew wanted?'

'Nothing at all. Bunty was really disappointed. Come to that, so was I.'

'So it was a triumph?'

'Come on, not a triumph. All right, though.'

'Did Mungo criticise it in any way?'

'No, he just said, "Excellent, I knew you could do it."'

'Praise indeed from Mungo. What was the problem?'

'A fractured femur that had pierced through the skin.'

He looked at her eager face and completely lost himself in his admiration of it. Even to the shape of her eyebrows. She was wearing a softly tinted pink lipstick that flattered her skin tones so perfectly and he wished ... then he noticed she was blushing.

'Sorry, shall we order?'

Kate nodded, embarrassed to death. She sneaked a quick glance at Seb's face and thought how handsome he looked, not conventionally but in an unusual, well-proportioned kind of way, and greatly in need of mothering. 'Have you chosen?'

Once they'd got food inside them and the greater part of a bottle of wine, the two of them relaxed and as suddenly as switching on a light they became tuned in to the same wavelength and everything felt right between them.

They kissed goodnight in the multi-storey when they went to collect their cars. Just once, but it seemed to seal a bond.

'So it's Friday for the meal at the flat. I'm looking forward to meeting your stepmother and Gordon.'

'Good. Gordon's a lovely man. You'll like him, I know. Goodnight, Seb, thanks for the meal. Next time I'll pay.'

'Not till you get your second month's salary. I know what it's like.'

They stood close, admiring each other, silent, simply absorbing and liking. Then they said goodnight again and parted reluctantly.

*

Seb was still awake a whole hour after he'd got to bed, going over and over what they'd talked about, what she'd said, what he'd said, how she'd laughed at a joke he told her about one of the tutors at college, which had led them on to talking about college life and their prospects in the veterinary world and ... then she'd jumped up and said, 'Must go. Look at the time. I promised I'd be home well before bedtime because Mia worries about me being so tired all the time. Which I am but it's par for the course in our job, isn't it?'

He went over again in his mind how they'd said goodbye in the car park. He'd wanted to kiss Kate more than once, but it occurred to him just in time that the pair of them had to go so slowly, so very slowly, because this relationship was suddenly precious to him and, he was almost sure, precious to her, too. He didn't want to ruin everything by rushing in. As he fell asleep Kate's face filled his mind.

Chapter 15

The shock news they received from Dicky Bird the following afternoon was that Mr Foster had died in hospital during the night. Dicky laid his uniform hat on the reception desk and told Dodie the whole story. 'I need to see Seb really but he's got clients, I expect, so I'll tell you. This Fred Foster went to the hospital with his dog bites yesterday morning. Very, very ill, he was, and they diagnosed possible septicaemia. They began treatment immediately, hoping for the best, but he had a heart attack and died, a direct result of the bites, of course. They took pictures of them for their records so I've seen them. They were ... horrific.' Dicky looked as though he might fetch up all over the desk.

Dodie moved back a bit, just in case. 'Poor chap.'

'Poor chap! My sympathies are with the dog. Foster was a brute of the first order. I could almost say he deserved to die.'

'Dicky!'

'Dicky nothing! The high-ups want to interview Seb. He said he had some evidence so they want to see it. If they come later today – say four o'clock – would that be all right?'

Dodie wrote it down. 'I'll tell him. Rhodri was there, too. Shall they want to speak to him?'

'Of course.' He turned to look at the new decorations. 'I always know Christmas is coming when I see these. Looks like Kate's been to do it?'

'Well, she's just started work here now she's qualified and so she helped Miriam as she does every year. They are beautiful, aren't they?'

'It's them silvery bits cascading down between the windows that make it special, and them baubles, stunning they are. Why, the walls are almost covered with 'em.'

'Her stepmother bought them at a Christmas market in France or Belgium somewhere.'

Dicky leaned closer. 'That Kate is a stunner, isn't she? I keep wondering who I could find to marry her. Me and my Bunty are so happy I want everyone to be married.'

Dodie tapped the side of her nose. 'The matter is in hand. I can say no more.'

He was too short to get really close but try he did and whispered, 'Who is it?'

'Ah-ha! Mum's the word. Now I'll pass the message on about the police. Oh, look, Seb's here. You can tell him yourself.'

One of the waiting clients, whose son had had far more to do with the police than she liked, shouted out, 'Dicky! What're you whispering about? Can't we all have a listen?'

'Constable Bird to you, madam.'

She positively crackled with amusement. 'Ooo! Listen to 'im. Constable Bird indeed. You're Dicky to me and to everyone else. Come on then, tell all.'

Dicky wasn't nearly the self-confident constable he purported to be, and brash women like this client almost always got the better of him, him being small and she being tall and big with it.

'I'll be off. Seb, a word outside?' He nodded his head pointedly at the main door and set off, expecting Seb to follow. But Seb had other things on his mind, in particular the client he was currently dealing with, and couldn't go. Constable Bird, disappointed he wouldn't be able to tell Seb the whole story, got into his car and texted Seb on his mobile to tell him about the dog fight that had been arranged. He just hoped Seb might manage to get there. Constable Aubrey Bird would be there – in disguise, of course. What do you wear when going to a dog fight? He couldn't ask Bunty's advice because she would forbid him to go. He'd learned in the past not to disobey Bunty when she got a protective note in her voice. Gardening clothes. Yes! Just scruffy enough without being too obvious.

Quite by coincidence Mungo took Perkins out for his evening walk that night as Miriam had a cold coming on and was feeling pretty grotty. 'Look, it'll do me good, I spend far too much time inside and you certainly can't go at this time of night in weather like this with that awful cold. Perkins!' But he was already at the door waiting for the off. 'Oh! There you are. We're going for a long walk tonight, Perkins, so brace yourself. I need the exercise even if you don't. Whisky and hot lemon, Miriam, and in bed when I get back.'

'OK. Thanks.'

'You're doing me a good turn, believe me.'

He dug out his old anorak he used for fishing, his thickest scarf, and a pair of holey gloves, and in the pocket of his anorak he discovered a woolly hat. Just right for the night.

He glanced in the hall mirror and said, 'God! I look like a burglar. A real rogue.'

He began by striding out vigorously, but as the slope up Beulah Bank Top became steeper he slowed and so did Perkins, and by the time they reached the top they were plodding along, heads down against the wind. Perkins made up his mind that Mungo had taken leave of his senses, and quietly and unobtrusively turned round and set off for home. By the time Mungo lifted his head to check for Perkins he was already out of sight, steadily marching home to Miriam and his warm bed. Mungo paused to survey the side of Beulah Bank he hardly ever saw. Below him there were lights on in a big barn towards his right and men with dogs walking up the farm track towards it. The barn door opened briefly, and he saw in the light three men and a dog entering the barn. His hackles rose. What was this? Something illegal? Then he remembered how Seb, only a day or two ago, had been upset at having to put that dangerous fighting dog to sleep. His scalp tingled with trepidation. Had he stumbled on a dog fight?

He turned to go home, then saw a van coming from the opposite direction, its headlights turned off, its shape outlined by the lights in the barn windows. Two men got out from the back of the van with a dog, which looked muzzled. Curiosity drowned out any caution he might have felt. He remembered the camera he always had with him when he went fishing so he could convince Miriam without any doubt about the size of the fish he'd caught, and patted his pockets. It was still there, long-forgotten.

This was a golden opportunity. He checked to see if he had any money with him, because he would need to look genuine by betting on a fight. His wallet was in his back pocket. Good.

He walked steadily downhill towards the barn, conscious of keeping out of sight as much as possible as he didn't imagine that men involved in betting on dog fighting would be choosy about who they clobbered in order to keep the event from the police.

For a few moments he paused behind some rocks and peered over them into the gloom to estimate how much open ground he had to cover before he reached the barn, and if he should go in or find a window he could look through without anyone knowing he was there. Feeling that was the safer option, Mungo decided to creep away to his right, approaching the barn from the back rather than the front.

Just as he'd decided to move off, someone joined him behind the rocks. The hair on the back of his neck stood on end and his heart pumped hard. A hand grabbed his collar and a voice muttered in a fierce whisper, 'Got yer!'

Two men had hold of him. His woolly hat was snatched off, his arms grabbed, and a small torch shone into his face. Mungo couldn't see who'd got him, and he braced himself for a thumping. Instead, a shocked voice whispered, 'My God! It's Mr Price!'

Constable Bird was stunned, and so was Seb.

'What are you doing here?' Dicky whispered.

'I could ask the same of you,' said Mungo.

'We're on police business.'

'You gave me a terrible fright.'

Dicky was amazed that Mungo had got through the police cordon without being spotted. 'Don't know how you got so far. The place is surrounded.'

'Really? I didn't know. I was out with Perkins and saw the lights.'

Seb asked where was Perkins now.

'Gone home, I suspect. He likes his bed at this time of night. What are we going to do?'

Dicky declared firmly, 'Wait, that's what. Just wait. We're moving in in ten minutes. Got to give them time to begin otherwise it's their word against ours. We need to catch 'em at it in full swing.'

Mungo was disappointed, having hyped himself up to pretend he was attending the dog fight as a spectator. 'I'll go in and pretend to be one of them. Got all my old gear on. They'll never know the difference.'

'What? They'd spot you a mile off, believe me. You're staying where you are. Don't want the whole plan ruined before we get 'em.'

But Mungo wanted to get in on the action and suggested to Seb that they both went in as punters, flashing their money. 'What do you say?'

'I think we should keep out of the way,' Seb said. 'The place is swarming with police, and I've no intention of getting a beating just for the fun of it. Sorry, Mr Price.'

The whole of their conversation had been conducted in stage whispers, but Dicky put his fingers to his lips and tapped his ear, indicating they should listen and not talk. It became all too obvious that the dog fighting had begun, judging by the fearsome snarling they could hear. The sounds coming across the desolate hill in the darkness were horrible and both Seb and Mungo shuddered. They waited another five minutes, in which absolutely nothing happened except for the bone-shattering snarling of the fighting dogs. Then torches were switched on all over the hill and what seemed to be a score of men running silently towards the barn and all hell was let loose.

The three of them heard the barn door being slid back as the first of the police went in. Some men escaped, dragging their dogs with them; some leapt into their vans and tried to drive away; others simply headed away on foot down the hill and out of sight. Dicky raced forward to help. From nowhere police vans were there and men and dogs were bundled in. In minutes it was all over, and the vans were driving away.

Seb said, 'Let's go down and see if any dogs need help.'

By using the headlights of the vans driving away and Dicky's torch they went down to the barn and walked in. In a fenced-off ring lay two dogs, panting heavily, way beyond struggling to escape. Dicky was searching every nook and cranny for punters who'd tried to hide. Fortunately for him, there was no one left.

Seb cautiously approached the dogs but the smell of him was wrong and they were immediately on their guard and on their feet. Both of them were covered in blood. One in particular had a huge tear down the front of its throat and had obviously been losing the fight.

Mungo roared, 'Leave 'em, Seb.'

Dicky shouted, 'Get away, you fool!'

Seb sprang back, recollecting the wounds Fred Foster had received.

Mungo, not fancying the idea of being sympathetic to two dogs in fighting mood, said, 'Those dogs are pitbulls, without a doubt. They'll need putting down. They're illegal. You'll have to get your police vet out, Dicky. Can't leave them all night. There's a bucket of water here; I'll put it in the ring for them. Now out!'

The three of them trudged up to the top of Beulah Bank, then walked down the other side towards the practice.

'Come in for a swift whisky to warm you up, Dicky, Seb?'

Dicky refrained. 'I ought to get back to the station. Sorry, lots to do. Thanks, both of you.'

But Seb accepted. 'I'm glad I went. At least we've got them. Put a stop to it for a while.'

Sitting propped against the back door was Perkins, waiting for someone to let him in. He was shivering with the cold and looking thoroughly miserable.

'Perkins! Serves you right for running back home. Come on, in you go.' Mungo unlocked the back door and the two of them went up to the flat with Perkins trailing behind them, looking weary.

'Miriam's in bed with a bad cold, Seb. Help yourself to some whisky, or a brandy if you prefer. Give Perkins a splash in his bowl; he's getting a bit old for midnight shenanigans. I'll just check on Miriam.'

Perkins had had whisky before, it was obvious, because he lapped up what Seb had put in his bowl and then looked up, hoping for more. 'You'll be rolling drunk, you will, Perkins, but go on, then – one more splash and that's it.'

Mungo came back, gave Perkins a good pat, took off his collar and sent him off to his basket. 'In your bed! Goodnight!' he said, then sat down companionably with Seb to drink his own whisky.

'Miriam's going to have a really bad cold tomorrow. Just hope it isn't going to be 'flu.'

'Let's hope not.'

'You did that dog a good turn when you put it to sleep. I hope you're not letting it upset you too much. It's a cruel, devilish sport is dog fighting. Those dogs never know what kindness is. When I think how much love and care our Perkins gets ...' he shook his head, 'and how a fighting dog gets none, we'd be doing them a good turn to put them all to sleep, pitbull or not. Enjoying working here, Seb?'

'I do, very much indeed. I'm learning so much, and I should thank you for taking me on and letting me help with the operations.'

'They're a good bunch, aren't they, the staff?'

'Absolutely, and always so helpful to me.'

Mungo cleared his throat, wagged a forefinger at Seb and launched into his advice mode. 'What you need is a good wife. Makes such a difference when you've been out on a night call and you get back and the bed's warm and there's a pair of welcoming arms. Anyway, there's time for that, you're still young, but when you choose, choose wisely. A vet's life isn't easy. Right, I'm off to bed.'

Seb finished the last of his whisky and got to his feet. 'I gave Perkins some whisky as you said and he asked for more. He really enjoys it, doesn't he?'

'Bad habits, but there we are. I shall miss him when he goes. Goodnight, Seb.'

Dicky Bird screeched to a halt in the practice car park at eight-fifteen the next day, bubbling over with the news about last night's raid.

'Seb in? Or Mr Price?'

Joy loved Dicky's enthusiasm and always played up to it with verve. 'They both are. Which would you prefer?'

'I'll speak to Seb, then, seeing as he was my co-conspirator last night.'

'Come on, Dicky, I can't imagine Seb or Mungo conspiring to anything.'

Dicky leaned on the desk, placed his hat beside his elbow and confided in Joy. 'They were both with me up Beulah last night in a raid on an organised dog fight. I nearly arrested Mr Price by mistake. You should have seen his face. Scared to death, he was.'

Joy found this piece of information more than a little surprising, as no one believed that Dicky could put the fear of God in anyone, still less someone as self-possessed as Mungo.

'Arrested him? I think you were going above and beyond your call of duty, Dicky.'

'Hiding behind some rocks he was, dressed in a woolly hat and an old anorak, having threaded his way between a host of armed policemen.'

'This I don't believe.'

Indignantly, Dicky drew himself up to his full height and was about to explain in full about last night when Seb appeared.

'Hello, Dicky. How many did you arrest, then?'

'We got twelve of the bas— beggars. A good haul, eh? Just telling Joy about me nearly arresting Mungo.'

'To use common parlance, Mungo got his collar felt.'

Joy burst out laughing. 'No! Wait till I see him.'

'Seb. About those two dogs. The duty vet put 'em down. They were both in a bad way, poor things.'

'Well, I must say last night proved very interesting. Thanks for letting me in on it, Dicky. My first appointment, Joy?'

227

'Not till nine so you can relax for a bit. New client. Don't know where she's been going before. Male dog can hardly walk, but he's only three. Sounds like bad news. A Jack Russell, it is.'

Dicky clapped his hat back on and made his departure, delighted with his success in the dog fight matter. He just wished he worked in a place where everyone was so happy and helpful. A police station wasn't exactly a happy place; you were more likely to be harassed and threatened.

Mrs Prior, Seb's nine o'clock appointment, carried her dog into his consulting room. 'This is Patch, Mr Partridge. Shall I lay him on your examination table?'

'Yes, please. Hello, Patch!' The dog was white except for a black patch over his left eye. 'Will you explain to me as clearly as possible what the matter is?' Seb looked carefully at Patch, who looked back with a baleful eye, and for a moment Seb felt as though Patch was telling him something but he didn't know what.

'He can barely walk. I can't take him out for a run. I have to carry him outside when I see the signs he needs to go ... you know. He manages to stand long enough to relieve himself. Other than that he just lies around all day long. I can't understand it. We've had him since he was a puppy and loved him and taken care of him, fed him properly—'

'He isn't overweight, so you must have done well on that score.'

'No, I know he isn't. For a Jack Russell cross he's got just the right amount of flesh on his bones, hasn't he?'

'Does he eat well now he can't walk?'

'Average. Not like he did when he was growing, of course.'

'How long has he not been walking?'

'It started about a year ago, just a bit, but then it got worse and worse, and now it's like I said – a slow stagger in the garden to find his favourite spot, and then I carry him back in and he collapses. I tell you, it's his legs, it must be. Or his hips.'

Seb began examining Patch. He listened to his heart and his lungs and felt his legs, pumping them up and down. There was nothing wrong there, no obstruction to movement, no wincing, no resistance. His hips too were perfectly flexible. He stood Patch up but Patch wasn't having it and crumpled down again, and once more there was that baleful look which Seb found unnerving.

Mrs Prior gasped when Seb tried to stand him up, and immediately went to Patch's aid. She stroked him, kissed his head and sympathised with him, and Patch wallowed in it.

Seb had to admit that he honestly couldn't find anything wrong with him.

'Look! We'll give him a vitamin boost, shall we?' he said. 'See if that helps at all. Come back if there's no improvement.'

'I'll give it a try, but I don't hold out much hope.' Mrs Prior stroked Patch's head. 'I've left my purse in the car. Will you take care of him while I go? I'll just get it and pay, and then I'll pick up Patch and the medicine and we'll be off. My poor darling Patch. Who's a poorly boy, then? I'm just sorry you can't sort him out.'

Seb turned away to put some notes on the computer. What the heck was he missing? He turned round again to find Patch standing up on the table wagging his tail, the baleful look replaced by a pair of sparkling eyes. Seb couldn't believe what he was seeing.

Then he heard Mrs Prior calling out to someone on her way back to his consulting room and Patch immediately collapsed back onto the table.

Seb was speechless.

Mrs Prior came back, purse in hand. 'My poor pet, Mummy's back. The medicine, Mr Partridge?'

'Oh! Yes. Now, Mrs Prior, you will not believe what I am going to tell you.'

Mrs Prior's face lit up. 'Have you found out what's wrong with him?'

'Well, no. I mean, yes, in a way. You see, when you went out Patch here stood up immediately.'

Horrified, Mrs Prior clutched her chest. 'Oh, no! He might have fallen off.' She stroked his head more vigorously.

'No, not at all. His tail was wagging and he was ... well, he was almost laughing.'

'Laughing?' Mrs Prior was shocked. 'Laughing?'

Seb nodded. 'Then he heard your voice in reception and flopped down again. Look at him now, laid out. I can't believe it. You know what it is, don't you?'

Mystified, Mrs Prior shook her head.

'I guess when he lies down you sympathise with him, kiss him, love him, stroke him, give him treats, and he likes that. So he's learned to do it to get your attention. You see, he doesn't get all the patting and sympathy when he's running about, does he? He's got you right where he wants you – under his thumb, so to speak.'

Mrs Prior had to sit down on the chair rather heavily. She was aghast. 'It can't be true. How can a dog work that out?'

Seb tapped his temple. 'Your Patch is extra-clever for a dog and *he's* worked it out, no doubt about that.'

'What shall I do? I can't not love him.'

'Of course not! Look, let's try something. Give him a wave, tell him you're leaving and go out, stand outside my door, but don't make a *sound*, then he'll think you've gone away. Count silently to twenty-five slowly and come back in, quickly. Go on, let's try it.'

Mrs Prior gave Patch a kiss then waved bye and left, closing the door behind her. After twenty-five seconds she came quietly back in and caught Patch standing up wagging his tail. He quickly dropped down when he saw her but he was too late. She'd seen him.

'I can't believe it. What have I done to him? How can it have happened? Have I got it all wrong? For his sake should I give him to someone else? Should I? But I couldn't, I love him too much.'

Seb had to laugh. 'There's no need for that. He's a clever dog, but you and I will put a stop to his antics. It will take a while. Be patient and from now on, when he's lying down, ignore him. Not even eye contact. If he does move about give him lots of attention, even to the extent of rewarding him with a chocolate drop, or something you know he likes. Got the picture? Walking about must be the one thing that brings him rewards. Come back in two weeks and tell me the result.'

Seb picked Patch up and laid him on the floor and then dipped his hand into his plastic box full of doggy chocolate drops. He placed four in a line towards the door, then opened the door and made another line across the waiting-room floor towards the main exit, then went back to put one in Patch's mouth and stood by to watch. Patch ate the drop in a trice, hovered and then slowly got to his feet.

'Quick! Tell him what a good boy he is. Go on. Quick!'

Mrs Prior said the magic words with real enthusiasm. 'Good boy. Patch is a good boy. Who's a clever boy! What a good dog!'

In no time at all Patch was walking, whisking up the drops with an eager pink tongue, with Mrs Prior walking alongside him. The clients watching this procedure shouted encouragement.

'My God! Look at that, Seb's got 'im to walk!'

'Why, it's a miracle and not half! Good on yer, Seb!'

'He hasn't walked for months!'

'Well, did you ever!'

Mrs Prior, half embarrassed at having made the dog ill and half triumphant to find him cured, punched the air with both hands as she reached the door and called out, 'See you in two weeks! Thank you, Mr Partridge.' Out of habit she bent down to pick up Patch, reminded herself she mustn't, picked up the last two drops instead and placed them outside the main door and got him out.

The clients clapped and cheered Seb's expertise.

Seb, grinning from ear to ear, bowed ostentatiously and called for his next client. It was Mrs Benton about her old cat Hector.

'I've come not to say how ill Hector is but to let you know how well he is. Remember he was weeing all over our new house and he didn't know where he was?'

Seb nodded. 'Of course I remember.'

'Well, those new tablets you prescribed have done the trick. He's as good as new, and what's more, now that's sorted he's settled into the new house. Knows exactly where to sleep, where the door is, so I thought I'd come and ask

232

for a further prescription of the magic tablets and tell you the good news. Truth is, it made me wonder about my dad and his tablets, so I took him to the doctor's instead of collecting a repeat prescription for him and he's had his tablets changed and he's like a new man, too. So you see, Mr Partridge, what you've done. You've changed the Benton household in one fell swoop. In fact, I could kiss you for what you've done for us, and I will.'

Mrs Benton leaned across the examination table and planted a great big sloppy kiss on Seb's cheek, squeezed hold of his hand, and said, 'You're the best vet anywhere at all Good morning to you.'

'A pleasure. Don't forget Hector's prescription!'

'Oh! Yes. Thanks.'

It was Joe Smithson next, on his own without a cardboard box.

On a high after his successful morning Seb greeted him with enthusiasm. 'And you're more than welcome, Mr Smithson. What can I do for you this morning?'

'I've joined a canary society. Well, the Barleybridge Cage Bird Society. Thought I'd mingle with them who's as keen as me. Believe it or not, they didn't know they had an avian vet here in Barleybridge, no idea at all. So I've suggested that we make you our official vet for the society. They said I should come along and talk to you about it, so here I am. What do you think?'

'I'm very flattered, Joe. Very. But I don't know if I'm qualified enough to be your official avian vet. I'd hate to let anyone down.'

Joe Smithson puffed out his chest. 'Not qualified enough?

That's ridiculous. Of course you are. Look what you've done for me. Taught me all I know.'

'Yes, but—'

'All right then, think about it. It'd mean all the members would use you when they had a problem, and if we had an annual show, which I intend to start up, you could be vet in residence on the day. Just think, eh!' Inspired, he came up with another idea. 'I know, you could come and give us a talk. How's that for an idea?'

Seb swallowed hard. 'I'd have to consult Mr Price. He's the senior vet and it's his practice, but I've no official avian qualification, you see. It's just what I've ... learned, kind of.'

'So? You've learned it, that's what counts. Anyway, talk to Mr Price and if you need a letter of recommendation or anything, let me know. You saved my canaries that day when they had them thingumabobs. I'd have lost the lot if you hadn't told me what to do.'

Seb smiled. 'Can I let you know? I can't just say yes as I'm not a partner, you see.'

'No, but one day you will be with talent like yours. They're all right impressed in the waiting room. Got that dog to walk when he couldn't. How's that for a miracle? I saw her carry him in. I shan't forget this morning in a hurry, believe me. You, Mr Partridge,' Joe pointed at Seb, 'made the paralysed walk. My word! What a story.' He turned to go. 'Right. Let me know. You've got my number, haven't you?'

'But Mr Smithson, I didn't—'

'Hush yourself and take credit where it's due. Good morning.'

By the end of the morning there didn't appear to be a

single client who hadn't heard of Seb's miracle. Even Mungo came in to have a word. 'God, what have you been up to, making the lame walk? They're all full of it.'

Seb protested. 'He could walk, but he simply wouldn't because he'd worked out that if he didn't walk he got all sorts of loving care, and titbits and sympathy and cuddles, and it served his purpose to lie down.'

'Never mind, it'll have done the practice a lot of good. They'll be queuing up for an appointment with you and the ones you can't solve with your magic chocolate drops, *I will* with an operation! Good work!'

Seb had to laugh. 'The other thing is, Mr Smithson, of canary fame, wants me to be the official vet for the Barleybridge Cage Bird Society. I said I'd have to ask you.'

'Is there no end to his talents?' He clapped Seb on the shoulder in his delight.

'Yes, but I'm not qualified. All I've done is learn about birds.'

'Does that matter?'

'Well, I think it does.'

'Swot up on it in your spare time. We shall have 'em coming from far and wide – owls, hawks, budgies, eagles, you name it. Have we got room for another extension, I ask myself? I'll think about that. Must dash, I need my lunch.'

'How's Miriam today?'

'Bit low, but we don't think it's 'flu. Thanks for asking. Keep up the good work! After lunch I have a very interesting operation – are you free?'

'Yes, I am.'

'Then come. Bunty's day off, so I need your help. See you.'

The next person to call in his consulting room was Kate, brimming with *joie de vivre*, and, in Seb's eyes, looking ravishing.

'Thought I'd call to say how pleased I am that the wonder vet works in the same practice as me! A miracle-worker no less!'

'OK, OK. All I did—'

'You made the lame walk! What more can a man do?'

To divert the attention away from himself Seb asked her how she felt this morning. 'Not so tired?'

'I seem to have caught up on my sleep debt, thanks. See you tonight?'

'Of course. Looking forward to it.'

At lunchtime he went to the precinct and bought flowers and a box of chocolates for Mia. He got back for his lunch to find Jilly Askew waiting for him.

They stood in reception to talk as there were no waiting clients. 'I hope you don't mind but I had to come.'

'That's fine. How are you?'

'Excited! I couldn't wait to tell you. I got the letter this morning, I'm going to college next September to do my post-grad! Isn't it wonderful?'

Delighted for Jilly's sake Seb kissed her there and then on both cheeks. 'I am so pleased. So very pleased.'

'Also, I've got a temporary student place at a secondary school near home so I can get some practice in! At least I shan't be completely wet behind the ears when I start.'

'That is excellent. Really brill.'

'So I'm saying *au revoir* for now as I'm leaving Uncle's tomorrow and going home to begin at the school on Monday.'

'I shan't see you, then.'

'No, but I can always give you a ring when I come to Barleybridge to see my Uncle, can't I? I did wonder—'

They were interrupted by Ginny marching in to reception. 'You must be Jilly Askew!' she said. 'You've got the Askew nose.' She shook Jilly's hand very vigorously in an 'I'm taking charge here' manner.

'That's right. Just called in to see Seb.'

'Didn't know you two were an item.'

'We're not, just friends.' Jilly knew instinctively that Ginny was on the war path. 'Just called in to give Seb some good news, that's all.'

'You ride to hounds with the Barleybridge Hunt?'

'Occasionally.'

'You do know that as a practice we're opposed to hunting?'

'So am I.'

This statement completely took the wind out of Ginny's sails. 'But you ride to hounds.'

'That's right. But I'm still opposed to it.'

'So why do it?'

'Because I don't want to give offence.'

'To whom?'

'My uncle.'

'What about the offence you give to a poor helpless fox who's never done you any harm?'

'My uncle frequently gives me bed and board without question and is the best uncle anyone could hope to have. I'm not prepared to hurt his feelings. Horses and riding are his life and very important to him.' Jilly's accent had become more and more upper-class with each word she spoke, and

Seb could see the superiority of her accent was becoming exceedingly aggravating to Ginny.

So he interrupted their dialogue, saying mildly, 'You have butted in on a private conversation, actually, Ginny.'

Ginny's hackles rose. 'I don't know who the hell you think you are, Seb Partridge. It's a free country and if I wish to make a point I shall.'

Seb said between gritted teeth, 'In fact, you're being rude. Jilly is a friend of mine and should be treated with respect by you and anyone else on these premises.'

'Seb,' Jilly laid a soothing hand on his arm, 'don't worry, I am well able to take care of myself.' To Ginny she said very softly and without rancour, 'I shall hunt or not hunt exactly as I like, and neither you nor anyone else is going to dictate to me whether I do or not. So go away and leave us alone.' She turned away so Ginny couldn't see her face and winked at Seb. 'Are you free tonight to celebrate? Thought you could come to Uncle's place and have a meal. Just tête-à-tête, not all the family.'

'I'm so sorry but I'm busy tonight.'

'That's fine. I don't own you.' Jilly kissed his cheek. 'Bye, Seb. I'll be in touch and let you know how I get on.' She turned to Ginny and smiled graciously at her, and knowing she would annoy Ginny by being excessively polite she said as sweetly as possible, 'A pleasure to have met you.'

Seb escorted Jilly to the main door to say goodbye.

Ginny was waiting for him when he returned. 'How dare she treat me like that? Who does she think she is? You should choose your friends more carefully, Seb.'

'My friends are nothing whatsoever to do with you. Are you expecting me to ask you to vet them?'

'Of course not, but you know my views about hunting.'

'Only too well. I have mine. You have yours. So be it.' He walked away from her before he said more than he should. He couldn't remember when he'd been so steaming with temper.

Joy met him in the staffroom. 'My word, Seb, I didn't know you had it in you. I wondered if I should wade in on your behalf but you managed very nicely on your own. The consultative paper's going out on Monday, then the balloon will go up and no mistake.' Joy noted the flowers and chocolates. 'My, my. What's the celebration?'

'They're for Mia Buchanan, Kate's stepmother. She's invited me for a meal tonight as she's convinced I'm not eating properly living on my own.'

'Ah! You'll enjoy that. She's a lovely person, is Mia. Get your lunch — Mungo's starting operating soon. You know, he's very pleased with your surgery skills. Thinks you're very impressive. Perhaps that might be the way for you to go. Think about it.'

Chapter 16

Kate got home early that evening and began preparing the meal. She'd had friends home for a meal more times than she could remember but tonight felt especially important to her. Mia arrived home only half an hour after Kate.

'I've skipped off early. Business has been so slow today. I can't think what to do to buck things up. Running a gallery, as "she" calls it, is a dodgy way of earning a living at best, and I have a feeling she's concentrating on all the wrong things for the area in which we live. After all, how many hippies do you know in Barleybridge?'

'None. Shall I cut the carrots into wheels or strips?'

'Strips. No, and neither do I. But it's not my business so ... when she retires in the New Year – because it will carry on in the same vein, seeing as the new owner thinks along the same lines as she does – I might even give in my notice. It's so maddening when you know what needs doing but you can't have any influence.'

'Just a pity you can't buy it yourself.'

'That's not likely. Selling that old house of your dad's and buying this modern flat took all the money from the house and then some, so that's out of the question. Anyway, I'm so looking forward to meeting Seb. He sounds lovely.'

Mia got no reply to this statement and when she looked at Kate's face she saw that inscrutable look she knew so well. It occurred to her that maybe this Seb was rather more important than she'd realised.

Kate filled the carrots' pan with water. 'Can I leave the rest to you? I need a shower.'

'Of course. Do I have to be on my best behaviour tonight?'

'Certainly not. He's the most comfortable person to be with, believe me.'

'Gordon said he's looking forward to meeting him.'

'Good. Are you?'

'Am I what?'

'Looking forward to meeting him.'

'If he's important to you then yes I am.'

Kate turned away and looked out of the window. 'I think maybe he is.'

'In that case he's appeared on the scene at just the right time, hasn't he?' Mia couldn't resist smiling when she said this.

Kate looked at her and smiled, too. 'Maybe. I've just seen Gordon's car pull up. I'll go and have a shower.'

When the doorbell rang, and the three of them knew it must be Seb at the door, Kate became incredibly embarrassed and hid in the kitchen, doubting everything she'd ever felt about Seb and wishing she hadn't invited him as Mia had asked her to do.

Gordon opened the door, shaking hands and introducing himself. 'Come in, Seb, come in, very pleased to meet you.

Go through. Kate and Mia are in the kitchen. Still raining, I see.'

Seb, who'd been looking forward to the evening, suddenly found himself shy, something he hadn't experienced since leaving home to go to college. He was convinced he'd gone bright red and was so nervous the flowers in the bouquet were trembling. He handed them over to Mia as quickly as he decently could and found her so delighted with her flowers and the chocolates and her greeting so very warm that the nerves began to subside. But then he had to greet Kate for the first time in front of her parents. Well, not parents but he knew what he meant.

'Hi, Kate.'

As soon as he looked at her he knew that she was embarrassed, too, and concern about her nervousness filled his kind heart with confidence and he walked across the kitchen floor and kissed her on both cheeks. 'OK?'

'Yes, thanks. Gordon, have you got the drinks ready?'

'Indeed I have, Kate. Come along, Seb, we'll leave the kitchen to the ladies.'

'It's almost ready, Gordon, we shan't be long.' But of course the white sauce had gone too thick, the carrots hadn't cooked yet, they'd forgotten to put out the napkins, and Kate and Mia felt themselves to be in the middle of a huge disaster.

Mia sighed heavily in desperation. 'This is ridiculous. Since when did I last make such a mess of a simple white sauce? I'll start it all over again. Wash the pan out for me, there's a love.'

With the second lot of white sauce a complete success and the napkins found and the carrots cooked to a T, Mia muttered, 'He is lovely, I'm so impressed. He's nervous too, don't forget. I like him already.' She gave Kate a kiss. 'Right, give them a shout. Gordon likes him, and that's a good sign. He's a good judge of character, is Gordon.'

Mia went to bed that night bursting to hear Gordon's verdict. She found Seb lovely, kind and warm-hearted. Yet at the same time he was a man who knew his own mind and was principled to boot.

Mia settled herself under the duvet and asked the inevitable. 'Well?'

'Well?'

'Don't tease, Gordon, you know what I mean.'

He too got under the duvet, turned out the light and then gave her his verdict. Hands behind his head he stared up at the ceiling. 'It is my opinion that with a bit of care and a following wind those two could be just right for one another.'

'Bit of care? What does that mean?'

'I mean, we need to leave them alone and they'll find their own way together. They're both lovely people and I'm sure—'

'So am I sure! Oh, if they're half as happy as I am they'll do fine.'

'Think so? Is that Kate coming to bed?' They stayed quiet and listened but no.

Mia grew anxious. 'They're taking a long time to say goodnight.'

'Of course they are. One does at their age. He's a very nice young man, but we must wait and see.'

'Yes, you're quite right. Do you have any regrets?'

In the dark Gordon grinned. 'About what?'

Mia nudged him. 'You know what I mean – about marrying me.'

'Absolutely none. In fact, the longer we're married the better it gets.' He kissed her. 'Goodnight, Mia. Love you.'

Oddly enough that was just what Seb was saying downstairs in the sitting room. 'Goodnight, Kate. Love you. Do you mind me saying that?'

Kate hesitated before she replied. 'No, I don't. But I can't say it back just yet. I've always been slow with decisions about people. It's not that I don't like you because I do very much, but saying "I love you" is something very different. I'm enjoying your company and feel we are compatible, absolutely on the same wavelength, but I can't say those three words, not just yet. You see, all my life I've been aware of the fact that my mother walked out on me when I was two weeks old and somehow it's made me cautious. I can't trust people till I know them better ... Sorry.'

'Don't be sorry. We've only known each other a matter of weeks, and I like the idea that you're taking your time.'

'And there's someone else, isn't there?'

Seb looked puzzled.

'Jilly Askew. I saw her in reception having that row with Ginny.'

'Jilly is simply a friend. We met by chance and she needed someone to keep her feet on the ground. All I've done is advise her to follow her star, that's all.'

'Which is?'

'Taking a post-grad teaching diploma.'

Kate was stunned. 'An Askew? Teaching? Really?'

'Yes, honestly. Everyone in the family disapproves and finds it amusing. Only Lord Askew backs her, but then his life was mapped out for him from the second he was born, obviously, so he sympathises with her. And I back her because I followed my star instead of doing what everyone expected.'

'I can see her show-jumping or running an art gallery or being a researcher for an MP with an eye on the bigger picture, but teaching! Well, I must say, I admire her for sticking to her guns.'

'Exactly.'

Kate found her hands of particular interest at this moment and examined them closely. Seb saw that something was obviously still worrying her. Finally she came out with, 'And Maggie?'

Seb laughed. 'What's this, an inquisition? It's supposed to be the father who asks questions like these.'

'Sorry, just needed to know. Someone mentioned her ... and I wondered.'

So the whole story of Maggie came to light, but Seb avoided telling her about how she'd healed him after his disastrous affair at college. That could be left to another time. One thing he did know for certain was he wouldn't be thinking in love-making terms with Kate, not for a long time. She needed more space in this relationship than he'd dreamt, and space she would have because she had become so important to him.

'Must go. Early start.'

'And me, too. Thanks for coming, and being so frank with me, it's cleared the air. Goodnight, Seb.' Kate stood up. 'I can see why you have all these women after you. You're lovely and sympathetic.'

She kissed his cheek and in return he tenderly kissed her lips. 'Goodnight. I love you, Kate, and I'm more than willing to wait. Please thank Mia for that lovely meal. I've really enjoyed myself. I'll let myself out.'

Monday morning arrived and there was a copy of the consultative document in everyone's pigeon hole along with their post. At the bottom in larger print was the notice of a meeting on Friday morning at eight-thirty in reception. In brackets it said consultations would not begin until 10 a.m. that day. Seb didn't have a chance to talk to anyone about it because his first client was there waiting so he had to begin work immediately.

This first client brought Seb back down to earth with a bump. As she strode in, his consulting room was flooded with a sensuous eastern perfume that almost clogged Seb's lungs it was so overwhelming. She was well dressed in a smart indigo top coat with matching trousers, a sensational scarf peeping out from her coat collar, her hair was shining and beautifully braided, and her face glowed. No garish lipstick emphasising the usual surprising pallor of her make-up, no strangely misplaced eye shadow, no rouge lavishly applied. Was it her?

Seb checked the screen. Yes, it was Miranda Costello. It definitely was because he recognised Goliath, the smallest adult Yorkshire terrier he'd ever seen.

'Good morning, Mrs Costello, very nice to see you. You're looking stunning this morning. How's things?'

'Miranda! Miranda, if you please. Extremely good, thank you, and how charming of you to comment on my appearance. It's Goliath's time for his booster, that's all. I got your card.'

'Right. Booster it is, then.' He managed to keep a straight

face but it was very difficult, because she'd even changed her behaviour, too.

Miranda lifted Goliath onto the examination table and closed her eyes to avoid watching the needle going in.

'I'll give him a quick examination while he's here. He must be getting quite old.'

'Well, I reckon he could be at least ten. I took him over from neighbours, you see, and they couldn't remember how old he was. He's very energetic still. I've got rid of my other dogs.'

'You have?'

'Yes, it all got too much for me. So difficult to keep everywhere clean and tidy. Someone had wanted the lurcher, Jack, ever since I took him in, so he's gone, and the two Jack Russells, Bill and Ben, they've gone — couldn't be separated 'cos they're brothers. My cousin's got them and they're real happy with him. He's got hours in the day to walk 'em in the woods, and they love that. The little Heinz 57 terrier, well, he disappeared one day and I've not seen him since. Been run over p'rhaps. And the two King Charles, well, believe it or not I sold them. I was given their pedigree papers when I took them on from that old lady so they went for a good price. Embarrassing, really. As for the cats, they're coming in to be neutered next week. Can't stand no more kittens, though it's easier to get rid of 'em nowadays now everyone has their cats done. But all the same, you can't go away, you know, it's hopeless.'

'So what about the mice and the rabbits?'

'Had the vermin people in, and though it broke my heart to see, they got rid of the mice and I've cleared out the shed so there's nowhere for any to hide and the last rabbit I gave

247

to a boy what's disabled and it's giving him a lot of pleasure. Hutch and the lot gone with it. I never felt the same after poor Lettice. Remember you put her to sleep, the one I thought was pregnant except she wasn't.'

'Ah! Yes. So there's been a real clear-out at your place?'

'Yes, even the rubbish in the garden. I've started planting things out and I've rescued the pond. And best of all, I've got a job. Gets me out of the house three days a week.'

'Where at?'

'Pet shop in the High Street. I love it.'

'Wonderful. You'll be good at that. Well, Goliath appears to be in robust health.'

'Good. Ta-ta for now. Be seeing you. You're a great vet, you know. Stick at it. Bye!'

Somehow, the aggravating pleasure that had been Miranda Costello was all gone, and it was quite disappointing because there was nothing to be amazed about any more, though he expected the neighbours must be glad. He'd tell Kate at coffee-time, because she would remember Miranda.

But when he went to get his coffee he found the staffroom heaving with argument and Miranda Costello's transformation was the last thing on anyone's mind.

Ginny had engineered her morning rounds to make sure she was in the staffroom at the appropriate time and it was she who raised the temperature.

'If any of you decide to back Mungo on this and it goes through then I for one will resign. It is an abomination. I've read every word of this ... paper and I disagree with everything in it. Colin, how about you? It's no good behaving like an ostrich. It won't go away, believe me, so stand up and be counted. Well?'

Colin appeared to shrink. 'It is my opinion ...'

'Yes?'

'It is my opinion that I shall have as little to do with the Hunt as I can because my clients – and I have a longer list than most of the large animal vets – keep me fully occupied.'

Ginny exploded. 'Hell's bells, Colin! Have you been in touch with your solicitor? That sounds like a typical statement from a lawyer. A great yes and no statement all at the same time. Come out with it, man. Don't hide behind Letty.'

Colin took exception to this and drawing himself up to his full height, which was only 5ft 8in at best, he said, 'If I have listened to Letty it's no business of yours. She does have some very sound opinions.' He put his mug, still three-quarters full, down in the sink and quietly took his leave.

Ginny attacked her next victim. 'Seb, how about you? How do you stand?'

'I stand where I stood before. If the practice needs the income then we should go ahead, and I am willing to take my turn.'

'How dare you? I'm astounded.'

'You can be astounded as much as you like. That's my stance and I'm sticking to it.'

Ginny swung round to tackle Kate, who'd been hoping to melt away before she was challenged. Some of the old animosity which had flared between Ginny and Kate when Kate had been seeing practice as a student came between them and Kate, hating the way she'd been put on the front line, said, 'I shall react as I see fit.'

'That's called sitting on the fence and there's no place for that in this situation. Declare yourself.' Ginny glared at her and Kate shrivelled.

Seb, anxious on Kate's behalf, interrupted Ginny's attack. 'We don't have to answer to you, Ginny. In fact, we don't have to tell anyone at all besides Mungo how we feel, so just drop it, please. Did anyone see Miranda in reception this morning? She's a changed woman. I got a shock.'

Dodie, who'd been on the fringe of the argument, quickly picked up on Seb's change of subject.

'I saw her. Amazing improvement. Couldn't believe my eyes. Just goes to show what some outspoken words can do. I told her in no uncertain terms that she wasn't hygienic and she'd to smarten up her act, and she has done. Got a job, too.'

Ginny, furious that the heat had been taken out of her coffee-break opportunity to get everyone on her side, flung her mug in the sink with such anger that it smashed. She paused for a moment and then marched out.

The row rolled on in varying degrees all week and most of the staff were glad when it was Friday so that they could get the whole matter thrashed out. Frankly some of them wished Ginny would resign because they were sick of going over the subject again and again, and they'd taken to avoiding her if they could.

Miriam provided croissants with their tea and coffee for the meeting and by eight-thirty all the chairs in reception were occupied. Dodie and Joy stayed behind the reception desk so they could hear but were available to answer the phones if they rang.

Mungo, a sheaf of papers in his hands, walked masterfully in to stand behind the table provided for him and said in quiet tones, 'Hands up everyone who is willing to support me in this new venture.'

Ginny stood up before anyone could raise their hands. 'We have yet to decide whether we take the Hunt on or not. You speak as though it has already been decided, and I object to that. It has not.' She sat down and in her anger almost missed her chair. Only a quick reaction from Scott saved her from falling on the floor. Quiet sniggers could be heard but Mungo glared so angrily at them all that the sniggers quickly faded.

'I beg your pardon. Yes, I phrased that rather awkwardly. Of course we haven't agreed, so I'll begin again. Hands up everyone who would be willing to support us in this new proposition offered to us by the Barleybridge Hunt.'

Seb's hand went up first, followed by Dan's, Kate's, Valentine's, Rhodri's and, surprisingly, Scott's.

'With the addition of my name that makes seven of us willing to take it on, five of whom are partners, so their decision carries more weight. Well, that settles it.'

Scott stood up. 'Could I add something to this?' At a nod from Mungo he continued, 'I know Zoe, my wife, is totally opposed to this idea and I had to take her opposition into account. However, I have decided that with money getting tighter and costs going up, the practice cannot afford to ignore this offer. So I agree to assist whenever. Also, it will, one would imagine, bring in more business because of the prestige of being the Hunt vet. Zoe accepts my decision, albeit reluctantly.'

Ginny sprang to her feet trembling with anger. 'Money! What's money got to do with it? It's principles and morals that count, not money. I am resigning here and now, this minute. No notice. Sorry. But seeing as we've set on two qualified vets in the space of a few weeks I'm sure *my* absence won't be even noticed.' She glanced piercingly at both Seb and Kate. 'And as for you, Colin, you can add some of my clients to your list to make sure you're far too busy to help. Then you truly will be hiding your head in the sand – as usual.'

Ginny fled, and Miriam rapidly got to her feet and followed her into the staffroom.

A sigh of relief passed round reception. In some ways none of them regretted Ginny leaving. Was she actually going this minute? She must be very passionate in her opposition. In particular, Mungo, who'd found her a thorn in the flesh since the first week he'd employed her, felt bucked by her decision.

In the staffroom Miriam found Ginny in tears. 'Here, my dear, a tissue. Sit yourself down.'

Miriam waited for a few moments but still the tears flowed. 'Now see here, who made this decision? You or Gab?'

'I did.' The tears flowed even faster.

'If you're so upset about it tell me why you decided on this course of action when apparently you didn't really want to.'

'Because I'm too good at being cussed.'

Miriam had to laugh, but she smothered her mirth when Ginny looked like opening the floodgates again. 'I'm sure that's not the case. Now pull yourself together and tell me the truth.'

'Gab's told me I'm being foolish and I do believe he's right. I get a bee in my bonnet and ... No, that's not it, I'll be frank. There's something about Mungo that gets my back up. Always has done since the first day. I've felt an element of superiority in him and I'm sure he's not aware of it, but there is and it angers me, and I don't know why. It's a question of a conflict of personalities. We just don't get on. I know I'm difficult—'

'No more than everyone else. Now stop this self-pity. You've made a decision so stand by it. You're a well-experienced vet with plenty of good qualities and you should get a job in no time at all. Is what I'm saying the truth? Are you? Have you?'

The real Ginny came to the fore. 'Of course I am. There's no reason why not, is there? Except ... no, I'm being ridiculous. No, I won't say it.'

'Go on, there's no one here but me, and I won't tell anyone – you can rely on that.'

'Of course I can. Yes, you of all people I can rely on. When I lost my first fiancé in that car crash along with my parents, I decided that never as long as I lived would I have children, not if they couldn't be Simon's. Now, right out of the blue, I've found myself pregnant. With Gab, of course.'

Miriam's face lit up with pleasure at her news.

But she didn't get a chance to say how delighted she was because Ginny rushed on. 'Totally unexpectedly, as you might say. You see, I've kind of primed myself not to think about children. The shock, you know, of Simon's death did that. So I think being pregnant is what's made this Hunt business even more important to me, or else it's skewed my thinking and I've gone nuts. So it's not due for six months but I shall leave now, like I said, give myself time to adapt to this whole new path my life is taking.'

'I'm very pleased for you both. I'm sure, though I haven't spoken to him about it obviously, that Gab would be delighted to have children, coming from a large family as he does, and

I'm also certain that they would be beautiful children with you both as parents.'

There was a long silence in the staffroom and Miriam prayed that no one would come in to interrupt them. No one did, and eventually Ginny said, 'Would I be any good as a mother?'

'It's something you grow into, believe me. After all, we're not born as mothers, are we? The miracle of loving a baby will happen in a flash, you know. It happens as we mature, and when the baby is the child of someone you love, well, that makes all the difference, believe me. That's a bit jumbled but I expect you get my drift.'

'I'm a complete fool, aren't I?'

'No, just a loving person who will keep being bossy, and it's got to *stop*.'

'You're right there. Gab would like it better if I stopped it. I don't know why I'm like it.'

'It's never too late to change, Ginny, especially now you've *acknowledged* you're bossy. Now, I have Perkins to attend to. He hasn't been out yet due to the meeting. Are you going home this very minute?'

'Yes, the sooner the better. I shan't miss the clients, honestly I shan't, although I should. But I am going to try not to be so bossy, especially to Gab.'

'Good idea. There's more ways of getting your own way than being bossy all the time.' Miriam reached across and kissed Ginny. 'Take care, my dear. There's lots of compassion in you; it just needs unwrapping. Love to you both.'

'Thanks.' For a brief moment Ginny hugged Miriam and then left.

*

Back in reception Mungo continued the meeting.

'Right, so that's that,' he said firmly. 'So we can get on with organising and discussing how best to deal with the Hunt as and when. We've found someone to work afternoons in charge of the laboratory so that will be set up as soon as possible. Then we certainly will be a fully kitted-out practice with nothing, absolutely nothing – and no one – to stand in our way.' Mungo didn't mention Ginny by name but they all knew what he was thinking.

Kate felt quite sad that Ginny was leaving, because, although she was a pain in the whatsit, Kate never forgot that terrible tragedy she suffered just before her wedding when her parents and her fiancé had been killed in that road accident. There was no wonder she was bitter sometimes. Kate thought about Seb and how she would feel if anything happened to him. She felt sick at the thought.

Suddenly the first of the clients with appointments began arriving and the meeting had to close. They all went their various ways.

Mungo, hugely satisfied by the outcome of the meeting, didn't get a chance to speak to Miriam until he went upstairs for his lunch.

'Not got much time. I've two operations this afternoon. What is there for lunch?'

'Plenty – it's almost organised. The meeting went well. You must be pleased.'

Mungo sat down at the kitchen table, flicked the newspaper open and began reading. 'Yes.' He put the paper down and added, 'Ginny was a bit of a surprise, wasn't she? Thought she might at least work her notice, but oh no! Blasted awkward, right to the end.'

'Well, Mungo, she never has quite fitted in, has she?'

'Did you calm her down?'

'Here's your lunch. Mustard on the ham?'

'Yes, please.'

'Of course I did. She wept bitter tears.'

Mungo looked up in surprise. 'Bitter tears? Ginny?'

'Yes, she's not made of stone, you know.'

Disbelievingly Mungo answered, 'No?'

'No. If I tell you something it's strictly between ourselves.'

'Yes?'

'She's expecting a baby.'

Mungo choked on his sandwich, and needed a drink of water to sort him out.

'Is she, honestly? I can't believe it. Ginny with a baby? That's a laugh.'

'You've never got on with her, and I think you're being unkind.'

Mungo sobered up. 'You're right, I am unkind. But she is damned difficult. At least all the others are absolutely fine. Seb and Kate are brand-new, but they've slipped into their slots so easily. I spotted them gazing at one another during the meeting. Anything in it, do you think?'

Miriam poured more tea. 'Could be, could be.'

'I'm off. Got some X-rays to study before I begin. Complicated. Lovely lunch, thanks. Where is Perkins?'

'Asleep in his bed. He's been there ever since we got back from our walk, but not for much longer, I'm taking him out for his lunchtime walk shortly.'

'OK, see you soon. Kiss?'

Miriam cleared up then called Perkins. Walkies!' She'd go

her warm jacket out and the woolly hat she wore on cold windy days and still he hadn't emerged. 'Come on, you silly old thing!'

His bed was by the radiator in the utility room so she went to find him. He was laid as he so often was, his head hanging over the edge of his bed with his chin resting on the floor. But his head when she touched it, was floppy and lifeless. Miriam's heart felt to burst with the horror of it. He'd passed away. Perkins had quietly died in his sleep. All alone.

If only she'd known she would have sat with him, but she hadn't and that brought her the greatest grief. Perkins, whom she'd deeply loved for all of his life, was alone when he died. Only that morning she'd sat out of the wind in a hollow behind some rocks up Beulah Bank Top and he'd come to sit beside her, leaning on her so companionably, so relaxed, and she'd stroked his head and said, 'You're a love, did you know that, Perkins? An absolute love.'

And he had been, right from the age of eight weeks old when they first brought him home. She'd chosen his name, and where it came from she didn't know, but it suited him, rather as though he were a superior butler. Now she had no companion upstairs in their flat, when Mungo was busy saving lives. How could she tell him what had happened?

She kissed the top of Perkins' head and slowly went downstairs to find someone who would understand. She knew Joy wasn't on duty but perhaps Dodie would listen.

She was in Joy's office doing paperwork and looked up at Miriam as she walked in.

'Why, Miriam! Whatever's the matter?'

'It's Perkins.'

'Oh, no!' She came round the end of the desk and put her arms around Miriam. 'Let me get someone, perhaps ...'

'No, it's all too late. Much too late. I've got to tell Mungo, and I don't know how.' Miriam burst into tears and sat down in the spare chair, sobbing as if her heart would break.

Dodie had never seen Miriam like this before, she was usually so composed and contented, and she was at a loss to know what to do. 'Look, I'll see if anyone is free.' Kate was between clients and when Dodie explained what had apparently happened, Kate raced upstairs to the flat to see for herself.

But Miriam was only too right.

Kate fled downstairs to find Seb. 'It's Perkins. He's died, and Mungo doesn't know yet.'

'Oh! Poor old Perkins. Mungo's operating, isn't he?'

'Could you take over?'

'I don't know.'

'Go and see. Go on.'

So Seb went in to find Mungo and stood anxiously hovering.

Mungo looked up. 'Yes?'

Seb didn't reply.

'Come to watch?'

'No, just wondered if I could take over.'

'Help the old man out, is that it?' Mungo looked up and laughed.

'No-o-o. There's a crisis, you see.'

'Crisis?' Mungo straightened his back and, scalpel in hand stared hard at Seb.

'Upstairs in the flat.'

'*Miriam?*'

258

'No, no. We think ... it's ... Perkins. Can I take over?'

'I've almost finished. Bunty will tell you ...' Mungo left the operating theatre at a run.

A minute later he walked out of the utility room at a snail's pace and found Miriam waiting, for she'd come upstairs when she heard him rushing past the office. Mungo opened his arms wide and hugged her. She clung to him, and neither of them could find the right words to say.

Chapter 17

But whatever happened in their personal lives the work of
the practice had to go on as usual and the open Saturday
simply couldn't be cancelled. Since Perkins had died Mungo
had been intolerable to work with, and everyone had avoided
him as much as possible, sympathetic though they were to his
sadness. It was Miriam who'd faced the fact that Perkins had
gone and Mungo who could not.

Dodie and Joy had taken on the brunt of the organisation
and were both becoming more and more harassed the closer
Saturday came.

'It's the catering, Dodie. Do I ask Miriam or not? Are we
being fair expecting her to organise the mince pies and all the
usual stuff?'

'Let's face it, it is only a dog that's died ...'

'Dodie! Honestly!'

'Well, it is. He's not a child that's had no chance of a
life ...'

'Well, that's it, you see. They lost both their children to a
genetic disease when they were quite young. So perhaps thi
death has affected them more than it would have normally.
Perkins used to go out walking with the children and Miriam
you see, so in a way it's brought it all back.'

'Ah! I didn't know that. So they haven't tried for any more then?'

'Too late now, anyway, but I don't think they dared. What if it happened all over again? They couldn't, could they?'

Dodie apologised for being brusque. 'But the trouble is we still have to deal with this open day. We can't not have mince pies and mulled wine, can we? And we need napkins and tea for everyone, in case, and extra cups and saucers and wine glasses. Joy, you'll have to face up to it and *ask*.'

Joy opened her mouth to retort, 'All very well for you to say.' But she didn't. Instead, she marched upstairs to see Miriam and get everything sorted out. The whole idea was abhorrent to her but she chose to blurt it out rather than Miriam feel they were shutting her out.

'Miriam? Oh! There you are! Only me. Are you free?'

'Of course. Come in. Cup of tea?'

'Yes, please. Only if you're having one, that is. I don't want to be any trouble.'

Miriam smiled rather sadly at Joy. 'Glad of something to do and someone to talk to. Sit down. I have to say this ... I'm sorry Mungo is being so difficult. No, no, don't pretend he isn't because I know he is. I've heard the shouting. I've tried but he won't be consoled.'

'Well, it'll pass, eventually.'

'Thank you for being so understanding. I'll pour the tea. I'm glad you came I was just about to sit down and have a cup myself. The days feel so empty. No walking to do, you know. I'd never realised how my days were punctuated by taking him out. I suppose if we lived in a house with a garden it wouldn't be so important to go out, would it?'

While Joy stirred her tea she had an idea. 'I've had a thought!

261

We urgently need more office space, with the practice getting so big. If you don't like the idea, ignore me, but it would be wonderful if we had this flat for administration and you and Mungo went to live in a house. After all, that was what you always did until we had these premises built.'

'Joy! What a wonderful idea! Of course we could!'

'See! I do have bright ideas sometimes.'

'Then Mungo could have another dog. You see, we couldn't possibly have a young Airedale in a flat − it would go mad up here. Come to think of it, so would I!'

'I shan't say a word, I'll leave it all to you.'

'It's inspired. Truly inspired.'

Miriam sipped her tea with ideas spinning around in her head. Joy decided that now was her moment to mention the mince pies.

'I hope you don't mind me mentioning this but ... have you thought, this Saturday is ... well, it's the open day and I ...'

'Oh! That's all in hand. It's what's saved my sanity this week, organising it all. I've made a list, bought everything, dug out the big pan I use for the mulled wine, collecting the fresh mince pies at nine a.m. Saturday ...'

Joy leapt to her feet and flung her arms around Miriam. 'You absolute angel. I told Dodie I didn't know what on earth to do about it all.'

'Worry no more. I wouldn't let you down no matter what had taken place. It'll do Mungo good to have to pull himself together, too.'

Joy put down her cup and stood up. 'Must go. Time for Dodie's tea break. She's been on duty since eight. Thank you, thank you. You're a brick. It's all been so upsetting for

us. Remember how Perkins always knew when Mr Featherstonehough and Adolf, that thumping great Rottweiler he
used to have, were due, and the fights they had? The old fire
bucket with the water was always ready. Happy memories!'
She leaned over and kissed Miriam's cheek. 'Looking forward
to Saturday, eh?'

Miriam nodded but didn't answer.

Saturday dawned bright and sunny but icy cold, so Joy turned
up the heating and the clients arriving for their morning appointments roasted in reception but were glad they did.

Every member of staff had their own designated duties
and Kate, Seb and Dan were delighted to find themselves
completely in charge of guiding people around the practice,
explaining the use of the different areas and the equipment
that had become more high tech as the years went by. Ginny,
of course, having left in such an abrupt manner, was not
involved. In some ways Kate quite missed her busy presence,
then decided she didn't because she'd only have been dictat-
ing to the three of them what to say.

The door to the drugs store was the stable-door type so
the visitors could see all the drugs but had no access to them
apart from standing at the door and looking through the top
half. Colin had decided he'd stand in the drugs store and talk
about drugs, old and new, to anyone who hesitated even for
a moment. He'd done a great deal of thinking about what he
should say and with Letty's help had planned a short talk to
highlight the most important drugs. He'd even found some
old packaging buried away in his memorabilia cupboard at
home and dug them out to illustrate the huge changes there
had been in prescriptions, along with some appallingly antique

tubing and whatnots that had been in use some fifty years ago when his own father was a vet.

Scott was organising the parking, but by three o'clock he'd almost abandoned the whole idea because the car park was packed and he had begun refusing drivers entrance to the premises and asking them to park out in the road. The number of children arriving caused him anxiety, too, as they would wander off from their parents and get lost amongst the cars.

What fascinated everyone was the window in the rear corridor which gave people a view of the main operating room where Mungo, completely unaware of the people peering through the window, was working on Declan Tattersall's huge Irish wolf hound that had wandered away from the farm while Declan's back was turned and been accidentally shot by someone shooting rabbbits. It was his left hip that had been hit and the Tattersall family had gone into a state of mass grief over the incident. Consequently, all seven children and Declan were camping out in the car park in their minibus awaiting news. One or two visitors went green at the sight of Mungo's protective gloves covered in blood and had to be revived with cups of tea. The two Sarahs were in charge of serving wine, mince pies and tea.

The 'knick-knack' area, which Dan had introduced against such strong opposition, did a brisk trade, partly due to Miriam having inspired ideas by continually sourcing new toys on the internet and any large pet shops. She always kept in mind the strong opposition to the 'knick-knack' shelves and was determined to keep them popular just to prove how right the decision had been.

By the time Kate had seen three groups of visitors round

the building she was gasping for a mince pie and a glass of mulled wine. To her surprise she found Seb already wolfing mince pies.

'What's this? You're supposed to be working, Seb!'

'Needed a break. Here, look, a mince pie for you and I've saved a glass of the wine in case they ran out before you got here.'

'Seb?'

'Mmm?' he answered, spraying mince pie crumbs into the air. 'Sorry!'

'Mia's right, you don't feed yourself properly!'

'I do, but I love home baking. I just never get round to it myself. Tell you what, Kate, I wish my family lived nearer, then I could take you to see them.'

'So do I. I'd like to meet your mum, dad and brother.'

'They're all supposed to be coming down for a few days in the New Year. Would you like to meet them then?'

Kate studied his face and saw how important it was to him. 'OK. But for now I'm just a friend as far as they are concerned.'

Slightly disappointed by her response he answered, 'Of course.' He paused. 'Are you free tonight?'

Kate nodded.

'Meal first?'

Kate nodded. 'Yes, although you won't want much feeding after three mince pies.'

'Actually it's four, but don't let on.'

'Seb, that is disgusting. I say, shall we skip a restaurant meal and have fish and ships out of a bag sitting in the car? I'd like that.'

Seb studied her face, preferring to treat her to a good meal but not at the Italian restaurant again in case they ever said something about Maggie. 'That's fine. We could park partway up Beulah Bank Top and watch the stars while we eat. I don't fancy those ghastly fizzy drinks they sell in the fish and chip shop. How about if I get a bottle of wine and borrow two glasses from the staffroom?'

'Wonderful! There's Dan waving. Got to go. That's a lovely idea, Seb.'

She'd no sooner disappeared than in walked Maggie.

He knew she might be home this weekend but it had gone completely out of his mind. She looked different, smarter and more sophisticated, with her hair shorter and not sticking out in a cloud. London had obviously changed her.

She weaved her way towards him between the visitors and kissed him without further ado. The two Sarahs, heads together behind the mulled wine pan, had been listening to Seb and Kate's plans for the evening and could be heard tut-tutting.

'Seb! How lovely to see you! It seems ages. Are you free?'

'Just for a few minutes, I've got to relieve Dan in a little while as I'm supposed to be doing guided tours.'

The two Sarahs decided to join in the fun. 'Wine, Maggie? A mince pie?'

'That would be lovely. I missed lunch.'

'How's the TV series going? It must be exciting!'

'We've three more weeks of rehearsals and filming, then there's a break for Christmas and New Year. It's going really well. The producer is thrilled with it, which is a blessing, believe me.' She turned to look at the crowd. 'I must say, it's much busier than I thought it would be. The decorations are beautiful. Did the two of you do them? They're very artistic.'

'No, we don't do them. A bit of holly behind the pictures, mistletoe over the door, and a few balloons, that's more us. No, it's Miriam and Kate who do it each year. Kate does the design and buys some new baubles or whatever, and Miriam follows her directions. She's very talented, is our Kate, isn't she, Seb?'

'She is.' Seb began to feel very awkward as he sensed the way the conversation was leading, and he was going to be in a fix tonight because Maggie would expect ... 'Kate is our newest vet,' he went on. 'She worked here for a while before she went to veterinary college, before my time.'

He'd under-estimated Maggie if he thought he was going to get away with this subterfuge, inferring that Kate had no place in his life. She was too astute for that and one look at the two Sarahs was enough to make her realise that this weekend things were not to be as she'd visualised.

Sarah Cockroft said, 'Dan's signalling to you, Seb.'

'So he is. Sorry, Maggie, got to go. Do you want a tour? You can come with me now, if you like?'

'I'll finish my wine and have another mince pie, then I'll catch you up. You go on.'

Maggie turned her back on Seb so he wouldn't see the disappointment she felt. The two Sarahs were busy again which gave Maggie a chance to take another mince pie without them thinking she was greedy. Which she did and then stood with her back to them, apparently watching the crowd. At this very moment she had to face the fact that the twelve years there was between her and Seb had suddenly become an issue.

She remembered seeing Kate at the dinner at The George but they hadn't really spoken so she'd wait her chance and see for herself. The wonderful evening with Seb she'd promised herself was not to be, she could see that. Never the less, she'd see Kate first and feel the vibes between them before she finally gave up hope. Perhaps Kate only needed brushing aside and Seb would be hers all over again. Her heart thumped as she saw Kate shepherding a group of visitors straight towards her. There was something rather stunning about her, a grace and a charm not many girls her age possessed. She could see now the possibility of she and Seb being fascinated by each other.

Despite the flood of visitors needing serving, one of the Sarah's, fancying spicing up the afternoon with a bit of gossip, said, 'Maggie, this is Kate who's done the decorations.'

The other Sarah said between ladling mulled wine, 'Maggie's been admiring the decorations. We told her they were your brain child.'

Kate blushed slightly. 'Thank you. I'm afraid I don't know your name, sorry. I know we were both at Mungo's dinner.'

Maggie was about to say 'I'm a friend of Seb's', but she rapidly changed that to, 'Seb's been dealing with some alpacas belonging to my parents so I thought I'd come and see the hub of his empire.'

Sarah Cockroft reported that Maggie was an actress.

Kate, being the well-mannered person she was, genuinely showed interest, turning to Maggie to ask what she was working on right now.

They chatted together for a few minutes and while they were doing so Maggie knew at the very bottom of her heart she'd never be anything other than a client's daughter to Seb, not now he'd met Kate; they were made for each other.

Maggie put down her half-empty glass of mulled wine, and her paper plate with its half-eaten mince pie in the bin provided, and said hastily, 'Must go. Busy, busy. You know how it is.'

Kate was disappointed. 'Oh! But I haven't shown you round. There's an operation in progress to watch—'

'Very kind, Kate, but I must go. Things to do. Tell Seb I'll be in touch when I get back to London.'

'Of course I will. Nice to have met you.' Kate reached out to shake hands and, as Maggie took hold of Kate's hand, she knew she was right about her. The girl was just the one for Seb. Something in her forthrightness, in the good heartedness that shone from her communicated itself to Maggie, and she felt her own heart throb with a sharp pain.

She left Kate and dashed out into the car park, head down, wishing she'd never come and then she wouldn't have known for certain.

Seb remembered a bottle of wine he had in the fridge back at the flat so when the crowds began thinning out, he drove home and picked up the wine, a kitchen roll to do duty as napkins, and two glasses. He paused for a moment to look at himself in the mirror to gauge if he needed to rinse his face before going back to pick up Kate, but the image he saw in the mirror was Maggie's. The new Maggie, with the smart clothes and the restrained hair. The new Maggie whom he knew had sensed things were not as they had been. And they weren't. There was still a corner of his heart holding Maggie very dear, but for him it was Kate now. Had Maggie realised this? After all, the two Sarahs told him they'd met, so she may well have done. She was very astute where emotions were concerned.

Seb washed his face, brushed his hair, checked his wallet for money for the fish and chip shop, and headed back to pick up Kate.

She was waiting for him in reception, well wrapped up and looking fabulous. Her cheery red beret, matching scarf and tweed coat with a small red fleck in it enhanced her good looks, and he could have taken her in his arms and kissed her then and there. But he didn't because Dan, Mungo and Scott were there with Colin hovering on the fringe of the group.

'It's been a good afternoon, hasn't it?' he said. 'Everyone seems to have enjoyed themselves.'

Mungo agreed. 'Never been better, I couldn't believe the crowds. All good for business.' He rubbed his hands together and they all laughed. 'We're going from strength to strength. I'm delighted and thank you all for the hard work you've put in. Bit of a log jam outside the drugs store with Colin and his ghastly old instruments, but they loved it, didn't they?'

Dan asked him how his operation had gone. 'Very well indeed. He's sleeping it off as we speak, though we couldn't put him in a cage to recover. He's just too blinking big. We should have drawn the curtains over that window but when I saw how pleased people were to be witnessing an operation I decided to leave them open. Bunty was delighted we were so popular.'

'You'll have to plan to do an operation next time, seeing it was such a success!'

'Good thinking, Scott! Yes. Thanks, anyway, all of you.'

Seb and Kate bought their fish and chips in the shop Seb

had patronised that first week he came to Barleybridge, and drove quickly up to Beulah Bank Top to park.

'I asked for salt and vinegar – is that OK for you?'

'Shows how little we know about each other.'

'We've got all the time in the world to learn.'

Kate turned to look at him 'Yes, we have. Plenty of time.'

They ate in silence. The only words they exchanged were when Seb asked her if she wanted more wine.

'Yes, please, although I shan't be able to drive home for at least an hour. I'm hopeless with alcohol. One glass and I'm away; two glasses and I don't know what I'm doing.'

'Well, we can sit here as long as you like, or I could drive you home.'

'Do you mind sitting here?'

'With you? No, I don't mind.'

'I can't see any stars, can you?'

They both peered through the windscreen.

Seb faked the sight of a star. 'There's just one I can see. Look, over my side.'

Kate bent across Seb to see and found the back of her neck being kissed.

'There wasn't one actually, but I did fancy a kiss,' he said.

She gave him a polite peck. 'That's all you're going to get, for now.'

'That's fine by me.'

'Seb?'

'Yes.'

'Seb, in the future ... if you and I have one ... you remember little Mrs Nicholls with Tatty? Well, when she was sitting with Tatty while he waited for his operation, she showed me some photos of where she lives, place called Turnham something or other, odd sort of word, and I thought it absolutely perfect. If I didn't live here I'd live there for sure. There's a village green with white thatched cottages all round it, a pond and, believe it or not, *stocks*. They don't even have street lighting. It's amazing, isn't it? Would you like living in such a countryfied sort of place? I know I would.'

'I think perhaps I would. With you, that is. It sounds idyllic.' He took hold of her hand and kissed it, grateful she was for the moment seeing the future as something they would be sharing.

'Good. I'll bear that in mind then.'

Kate paused for a minute, looking out of the window as though she were thinking about them together in Turnham whatever. Then she turned back to him. 'I met Maggie again this afternoon. Tell me about her.'

Seb sat for a moment contemplating her question, worrying about his answer. Eventually he said, 'We were very close and very happy for a time, but she's twelve years older than me, although she didn't seem like it. She's a very generous person, very loving, and at the time I needed her. Then she got this fabulous offer to play the lead in a TV series, and it was what she'd wanted all her life. But for two pins she'd have turned it down and stayed in Barleybridge. With me.'

Kate couldn't help but show her surprise. 'As serious as that!'

'I wanted her to stay, but not at the price she would have to pay, knowing for the rest of her life that she'd turned down the chance of a lifetime.'

'So you *persuaded* her to go?'

'She didn't need much persuading. I saw there was no

alternative. It hurt me to say it, but I said she had to go before we got too serious about each other, and us breaking up had become too painful to bear.'

'Oh, Seb. I guessed there was something there between the two of you. She just left as though ... she'd no alternative but to go.'

'But from today ... seeing her ... it's all very different. She's still a generous person for whom I have the greatest respect, but I've met this other girl, you see, who's stolen me away and I can't escape. I'm positively chained to her, but I don't mind. She fills my heart and my mind and I want her for ever. So there it is.'

He switched on the light over the windscreen. 'But you know that, don't you?'

Kate nodded. 'Yes, I do. But not yet. I'm not ready, you see. I can't commit until I'm absolutely sure. Damn my blasted mother for doing what she did to me. You think you don't care, that it doesn't affect you, then it comes out of the woodwork and ruins everything. What does it make me? Shall I be just as careless of someone I love? That's the worry.'

'Perhaps the difference is she wasn't capable of loving anyone but herself so leaving you didn't break her heart. But it doesn't mean *you* won't ever love someone completely, so when you do, you wouldn't do what she did.'

'I'll think about that.' Then Kate began to laugh, peal after peal of laughter, and simply couldn't stop. Finally she did have to stop because she got a stitch.

'Kate! Kate! What's so funny?'

'You sound just like an agony aunt!'

For a moment Seb felt cross because he'd tried so hard to make sure she didn't feel too badly about herself and here she was ... then he began to laugh, too, and the two of them laughed together, uproariously, absolutely unable to control themselves.

Then Seb took her in his arms and stopped her laughing with a kiss, and she kissed him back.